ALSO BY KURT A. MEYER

Salvage Man

Noblesville

Noblesville

BY KURT A. MEYER

Little Rock, Arkansas
2014

Edited by Jim Wilson
Cover design by Paula Guajardo

www.RiversEdgeMedia.com
Published by River's Edge Media, LLC
100 Morgan Keegan Drive, Ste. 305
Little Rock, AR 72202

Manufactured in the United States of America.

ISBN-13: 978-1-940595-07-8

For my son, Jack

CHAPTER ONE

Love is now the stardust of yesterday
The music of the years gone by.
From the song "Stardust"
Hoagy Carmichael and Mitchell Parish, 1929.

It was an accident, really, that dazzling splash of crimson light that appeared in David's front room. If he were religious he might have called it a blessing. If he were superstitious he might have called it an omen. But as he was, a man firmly settled in the empirical world, he treasured it and regarded the mysterious effect as a glorious stroke of luck.

He remembered that three prisms placed together make a lens. It must have had something to do with the focusing of light in some chance circumstance: optic serendipity.

At the front of the house was a large multipaned window with a matching transom window above. In the outer corners of the transom window were deep crimson panes of stained glass, two inches square. Sunlight coming through the reddish pane on the lower right reflected through an antique medicine bottle, its glass pale blue, that David had set on the sill. The bottle's wavy glass bent the light up and out and projected its rich color against the right half of the double doors separating the front and back parlors.

The red light began to appear in late March for short periods around noon, coming earlier and remaining longer each day. While the days of spring grew longer and the sun brighter, it increased in intensity. As the sun moved across the sky, the reflected red light spread across the floor, starting at the base of the right-hand door, reaching up nearly six feet and nearly spanning the door.

The velvety, blood-red light bathed the raised panels of the door and shimmered faintly in the heat. Intrigued by the effect, David was careful not to move the bottle for fear of disturbing the warm, glowing light.

One unseasonably hot May afternoon, David stood by the front door holding a cold beer in a Ball mason jar, watching the beam for a moment. He went outside and sat down on the porch steps, sipping the BarFly IPA he'd poured from a growler brought home from Barley Island the night before. He wiped sweat from his forehead with the back of his wrist

Paint chips smeared through his dark hair. He'd been on the ladder, stripping paint from the clapboard siding with a heavy, cast iron heat gun. The assortment of paint chips encrusting the hair on his head and arms told the story of more than a hundred years of paint jobs.

As a My Morning Jacket playlist cycled from his phone, plugged into an old, tattered boombox, he sat resting and surveying the neighborhood, deserted but for the endless sweep of anonymous cars passing down Cherry Street. He had bought the house a year ago that month and still knew little about his neighbors beyond their names.

Across from him were the Williamses, a retired couple who only came out to mow the lawn and sweep the sidewalk. They had a porch with a swing that always sat empty. Diagonally across the street was Jim, an overweight widower in his mid-fifties. He came and went from the driveway behind his house. His blinds were always drawn.

East beyond Jim lived a young couple named Wilkinson, whom David saw outside only when they were walking from the front door to their cars. He'd greeted them one day as they left. They initially seemed shocked, as if he had disturbed their personal space, but eventually made polite small talk. After that meeting they occasionally said "hello," but always seemed in too big a hurry to talk. At night, he could see the flickering blue light of a TV against a white window shade that was never opened.

His neighbor to the west, Shelley Campbell, was a single mother with a teenage son. He rarely saw them, but he was intrigued by the house, which appeared to be a twin of his own, perhaps built at the same time.

Beside his house to the east was a little bungalow. The week he moved in, he was disgusted to see white vinyl siding being put on over a layer of asbestos siding that had buried the original wood clapboard. The window trim that once stood in prominent relief from the outer walls to capture the sun was now recessed behind the layers of siding that mummified the once charming house. The elderly couple who lived inside this cocoon left only in a small car, operating the garage door with a remote control. At night a halogen light burned on the gable of the attached garage, casting a harsh glare across the garage door and tiny, paved backyard.

He took another swallow and leaned back against the upper step, resting the jar on his belly. He mused about his very public seclusion in fast-growing Hamilton County, about all those nameless people in the malls, quickie-marts and grocery stores. After four years of hyperactive socializing in high school and another four in college, he found the isolation antiseptic. To take the edge off, he kept his TV on almost constantly, with the volume down while he played music. He spent endless late-night hours at his laptop computer or the iPad the school system had issued.

David sighed, set down the empty jar, and got back to work. Sweating already in his *Noblesville Millers* football T-shirt, torn blue jeans and work boots, he climbed the wooden ladder with the heat gun in one hand. Balancing at the top, he pulled out a putty knife, flipped on the heat gun, and held it close to the faded paint. It bubbled and blistered; he scraped it away and exposed the greenish poplar wood nobody had seen since the house was built in 1891.

As he worked, his neighbor Jim stood looking out the tiny window of his front door, watching him. He took David's efforts as an insult. In the past twenty years he'd done the opposite of restoration, gladly torn the bric-a-brac off the front porch and removed the turned posts, proud to replace them with wrought iron. He put aluminum siding on and just this past year installed replacement windows. Everything was new and maintenance free.

When Jim had vinyl replacement windows installed, David crawled into the dumpster where the old windows had been thrown and unscrewed the hundred-year-old locks from the sashes. During the winter, Jim peeked out his window and saw David stripping the paint from inside the multi-paned front window on his home, replacing the cords and reattaching them to the weights so that the sash would move up and down for the first time in forty years. The crowning insult was when he put those locks, the ones Jim had thrown away, on the window. David had stripped the paint on the locks down to the cast, floral pattern and repainted the bases in their original glossy black, polishing and lacquering the brass thumb latches on top. To Jim they were crusty old hunks of metal. To David they were archaeological finds. The intricate floral patterns he found—the vines and leaves standing in bold relief—were to him like runes from an ancient people, the imprint of their long dead, hieroglyphic language.

He went on scraping. The sweat ran down his face and dripped off his long, narrow nose. A text message chirped on his phone, briefly dimming the music volume. He looked down at the phone and replayed the odd events of the previous day.

He'd gone inside to check his e-mail, using his phone as a Wifi hotspot. The sun was bright and the red beam was warming the right-hand double door. He plugged his phone into the charger, and when he activated the hotspot app, rainbow-colored shards of light pierced the crimson beam, flowing up and disappearing like bubbles in a glass of champagne. He quickly unlatched the door and walked through the newly colorful beam in wonder. An effervescent lightness rose through his body as he disturbed the flow of color and warmth. A second pass through, then a third, and on the fourth he was startled at the apparent distant sound of a woman's voice.

Had he imagined it, the way wind or machine noise can confuse the mind into constructing sounds that aren't there? Perhaps, but the house was silent. He was sure he'd imagined the voice. Plunging his head into he beam, he cocked it side to side and got the faint hint of static electricity, but no voice. And then! A finger grazed his face as he withdrew.

Did it? He jerked back and examined the beam of light with wide eyes. Then a cloud passed overhead and the beam evaporated.

After graduating from college David took a job teaching American history at Noblesville High School. He saved graduation money from his grandmother and any other cash he could get his hands on and tracked repos and short sales that looked like good restoration candidates. The previous spring, he had found the house on Cherry Street.

It was one and a half stories. The upstairs rooms had sloping ceilings that followed the roofline. His favorite feature was the double-hung front window, which, like many from the 1880s and 1890s, consisted of a large, clear pane surrounded by small stained-glass panels, divided by mullions. The two front doors looked to be original, but the porch had been enclosed with cinder block, windows, and aluminum siding.

David intended to turn back the clock, to resuscitate the house and reveal its hidden beauty. He took so much pleasure in working on the house that little else could hold his attention.

The front door David used opened up into what he called the "front parlor," a square room graced by the multicolored window on the south wall. A plastered chimney protruded into the room in the center of the north wall. To its left was a large pair of double doors that could be opened to connect the front parlor to a matching room that David called the "back parlor" but intended to use as a dining room. When he moved in, the walls in both rooms were covered with horrible wood-printed paneling, dark and dreary.

Upstairs were two modest-sized bedrooms, one facing north toward the backyard, and the other south, with a window onto Cherry Street. On the stairway landing was a small leaded-glass window, a flower-like medallion of blue and sea-green glass. It was buckled and warped from a century of weathering. David promised himself to repair it soon.

After closing the purchase, he rented a dumpster and filled it with junk from the basement and garage, and the brown shag carpet that had covered the worn but beautiful oak floors. With school out and all summer to work, he began by jacking up the porch roof, temporarily suspending it with four-by-four posts.

Next, David spent a week removing the aluminum siding. With a pry bar and hammer and his old wooden extension ladder extended to the top of the front gable, he pulled the siding from the top and found what he had hoped to find: fishscale shingles. The shingles ended near the bottom of the upper window; the remainder of the face of the house was covered with common wooden clapboards.

When he had removed all of the siding from the front, he walked across the street and stood on the sidewalk in front of the Williamses' house. He couldn't suppress a convulsive smile as he looked at what he'd done. This was no piece of invaluable architecture; David knew that. But it was pretty, it was old, and it was his. He felt like an archaeologist uncovering some long-forgotten temple.

He found an abandoned house that was about to be torn down near the town of Fishers and salvaged the porch posts and ornate brackets. He spent the better part of that first summer re-creating his 1890s porch. He stripped the paint from the posts, brackets, and front doors, and built handrails and balusters. At a yard sale on Logan Street he stumbled across two old screen doors with scrollwork brackets; he spent a week stripping and repainting them and stretching new screen. By the time school started at the end of August, he had transformed the porch from a 1950s mess to a vision he had gleaned from old architectural plan books.

After reading a book about Victorian paint colors he chose a creamy tan for the clapboards, with deep green and rich burgundy for trim and decoration. Window trim and porch posts were green, and the exterior window sashes and some segments of the turned posts were painted red.

The porch was the place where David and his friends drank beer and listened to music. On many evenings, late that summer and through the fall, he pulled himself away from the TV and computer to listen to the birds or the rain and observe, with a jaundiced eye, his sterile neighborhood and rapidly growing hometown.

Whenever he had a date, they would usually end up there, on the porch swing, talking. Since college, dates had been few and far between. Heather was his most recent girlfriend. That had ended painfully in early March.

His friends from college, Jeremy Wren in particular, would go to downtown Indianapolis bars and craft brewery tasting rooms almost nightly. Sometimes David went along, but he found bar small talk and the singles game tedious.

He spent the autumn weekends of his first year in the house priming the newly bare wood. He decided he'd tackle the rest of the exterior next summer. For the winter, he turned his attention to the interior. He'd neglected it to pursue his relationship with Heather, but now he was back on track.

He stripped the wallpaper and paint from the lath-and-plaster walls in the front two rooms and repaired the cracks. When the front rooms were finished, he decorated them with bits of one hundred and fifty years of American history: an antique bookshelf and dining-room table, an angularly ornate Eastlake end table, and an oak rocking chair—all pieces from his grandmother's attic. The 1920s upholstered couch and some chairs were housewarming gifts from David's father and stepmother. Other odds and ends came from David's mother and her husband. Latent divorce guilt, even after fifteen years, kept the gifts coming, but they helped furnish the rooms in a way that a teacher's salary couldn't. The only concession he made to modern design was a small TV that he set on a small marble-topped table.

David began working outside again in late March. Through April and early May he stripped paint with the heat gun, and on this sweltering Sunday afternoon he was nearing completion on the front facade.

He pulled up Count Basie on the Spotify app on his phone and climbed the ladder for another hour of scraping. His yellow tabby cat, Sophie, slept on the front windowsill. As he scraped his way across a row of clapboards, he replayed the strange change in the beam of light.

After dark, David sat on the floor of the front parlor unboxing a cable modem and Wifi transmitter. After he had spent a maddening hour on the phone with Comcast, connecting and disconnecting the cable and repeatedly restarting the modem, finally the lights on the front of the black box awoke and blinked in the prescribed sequence. Once connected, the Airport transmitter blinked to life and his iPad connected to the Wifi signal. David opened Google in a flash. No more tethering with his phone.

He arranged the clunky black modem and the sleek white Airport on the walnut marbletop table, finding he liked the contrast between cutting edge and vintage. When he turned out the lights to head to bed, both devices flickered in the darkness.

CHAPTER TWO

*Primeval nature left upon rock and mountain and earth a
trail so broad that it may be easily followed by the scientists of
this day ... looking out over the broad acres we may readily
know where the walnut, the poplar, the burr oak and the beech
grew and flourished. But in the rising time of civilization the
trail of the pioneer is obliterated ... the plow has gone over his
farmyard grave. While the deeds of these ancestors were great,
their trials sore and their achievements many, yet necessarily
they were recorded mainly in the hearts of those who now
slumber in the tomb.*
A.F. Shirts, Noblesville, Indiana, 1901.

Cheered by a forecast of afternoon clearing, David finished his breakfast. Knowing he would need a project for rainy days, he took a few
minutes to pull out the stained-glass window on the stairway landing
and laid it on the table saw, temporarily fitting a piece of plywood into
the window's opening. He then went outside to start putting a primer
coat on the front of the house. He got out the old boombox, plugged in
his phone, and listened to NPR while he worked. He propped his heavy
wooden ladder at the peak of the gable, tugged the bill of his Pacers
cap around to the back, and climbed up. All through the morning he

painted the gable's fishscale shingles.

By noon the clouds were gone, the sun was out and David was sweating. He took a break to have a slice of cold pizza and another glass of beer from the growler.

Sun streamed in through the front window, painting its colors across the floor. The beam of light blazed through the deep-red corner pane of the transom, and passed through the cobalt medicine bottle, projecting its blended crimson onto the right-hand door of the dining room. Deciding to switch to music, David set his pizza and beer on the top step and knelt down and stared into his phone to change apps, discovering that he had no Wifi signal. His phone had been running off the cell signal all morning.

Exasperated, he went inside to check the modem, munching on a slice of pizza. As expected, the lights weren't blinking in sequence. He knelt behind the small table and disconnected the modem's plug and coaxial cable, waited 60 seconds, then reconnected both.

As the modem lights resumed their proper sequence, David noticed from the corner of his eye that the beam was changing, flickering from solid red to flashes of aqua blue. As the full signal recharged and the Wifi transmitter rebooted, he saw the beam of light change dramatically. No longer red, it was entirely greenish blue. Even stranger, it didn't end at the door; it seemed to be projected onto a vertical semi-transparent plane about six inches in front of the door. It hovered there like a fluid, colored pane of glass, like smoke caught in a narrow ray of light.

David rose and took a few steps toward it. On a whim, he stepped back and unplugged only the Wifi transmitter. In a single flash, the beam returned to its usual form and color, bathing the door panel in its familiar red. David plugged the Airport back in, and as the Wifi signal rebooted, the beam reassembled half a foot forward, turning greenish blue again.

Still holding half a slice of pizza, he waved his hand in the middle of the room. Wherever his shadow fell, the light rays were disrupted, as the red beam had been. He envisioned a line extending from modem and Airport to the ray of light from the window. The strange projection was at the right angle point of intersection. David walked right up to the door and peered around the projection and saw that its color and texture looked different from the other side. He unlatched the right-hand door, swung it back into the dining room, and stood directly behind the projection.

This side of the beam was different. It looked like millions of yellow snowflakes swirling against a black background just inches from his face. The hair stood up on the back of his neck. He reached out to touch the beam with his index finger. As his finger passed into the beam, it disappeared. He felt the faint static charge he'd experienced the day before, and even though he couldn't see his finger, he could discern the faint image of the front parlor beyond the swirling colors.

Holding his breath, David moved his entire hand into the beam, and it disappeared. He ran his hand in and out of the sparkling yellow flakes, watching it disappear and reappear. Then he put his whole arm in ... and touched something. He couldn't see his arm or hand, but he could see the dimmed shapes of the furniture beyond the beam—none of it close enough to touch. Yet he'd felt cloth ... and hair!

He groped after the invisible object and heard a distant, muffled scream. He froze. Then something unseen but hard struck the back of his outstretched hand, knocking his arm out of the beam and against his chest.

Stunned, David stared into the shaft of twinkling lights, massaging his aching hand. Curiosity and fear warred momentarily within him, and then he gathered his nerve and stepped through the beam.

That step took him out of his house and into a room he didn't recognize. Staring at him were a dark-haired young woman in a long, yellow dress and a frightened-looking young man. The man's right fist was tightly clenched.

"What the hell?" stammered David.

Both of them stepped back, the woman wide-eyed, one hand over her mouth, a look of terror on her face. She spoke in a near whisper: "Oh, my God! Who are you?"

David looked over his shoulder with a momentary impulse to step back through the beam and into his own home. "Where am I?" he asked, eyes searching and mind racing. Beyond the woman was a window with panes of colored glass, and outside in the street, a horse and carriage.

The woman spoke again, her voice still shaking with shock but more demanding this time. "Who are you?"

As David hesitated, the young man stepped forward. "Tell us who you are, sir, or we'll call for the police."

David took two steps backward through the beam. The blinking and swirling lights were just inches from his nose. He could see the two people in front of him as if through a veil, just as faintly as he had seen his parlor moments before. He stepped forward, extending his hand. "I'm David Henry." As he took that one step through the beam, he was back in his own front parlor, alone. His knees gave out and he dropped to the floor.

He moaned, forehead on the rug. His heart beat so hard he thought he might vomit.

After a moment to catch his breath, David lifted his head and looked around the room, trying to confirm that it was, in fact, his room. It was

He hoisted himself off the floor and sat on the couch. Thoughts rushed through his head, none of them clear. Was he crazy? Was he hallucinating? He was seized by the fear that he might have imagined it. Then, that he did know the room that he had stepped into. It was his own front parlor.

The woodwork and the placement of windows were the same. He'd seen the carriage in the street through a window exactly like his stained-glass window. The proportions of the room were the same—the chimney was in the same place. But there had been a small stove in front of the chimney and a hanging light fixture in the middle of the room. The room was decorated differently than his. Running around the wall about eighteen inches down from the ceiling was a picture rail with patterned wallpaper between rail and ceiling. Heavy draperies flanked the window.

As he pondered this, from the corner of his eye David saw something move in the beam. A finger and then a hand appeared and disappeared … then two hands.

David stood up and backed toward the front window. Slowly, a face emerged from the beam. It was the young man he had seen, sticking his head through the beam. Their eyes met. He glared at David for a moment, then quickly jerked his head back.

David rushed to the Wifi transmitter and pulled the power cord. The beam of light returned to red. David grabbed the phone, deciding to call somebody who might have some answers.

Eric Bennet, David's friend from Ball State, taught earth science. The two of them occasionally spent an hour over beers at a bar on the courthouse square, griping about their teaching jobs. His hands trembled as he dialed.

"Eric?"

"Hey, hi, David. How ya doin'?"

"Fine. Got a quick science question for you."

"Shoot."

"Well, I installed a new modem and Wifi transmitter, and they're making things go wacky in my house." David wasn't quite ready to tell Eric about stepping into a strange room and seeing a face come through a beam of light.

"Like what?"

"First off, if the Airport unit is on, it messes up the picture on the TV. And I've got this stained-glass window on the front of my house, right?"

"Yeah, what about it?"

"I've got some old antique bottles on the windowsill of the transom, and when it's sunny, the light from one of the red panes of glass passes through a bottle and shines a really deep red on the dining room door. But when the Wifi unit is on, the color of the light changes to greenish blue. My question is, what could make it do that?"

"That sounds really weird. But actually, all the light we see is just waves emitted by the sun or a light bulb or a candle or whatever. There's lots of other waves out there—like radio waves. All these different waves are part of the spectrum of radiation wavelengths. The only ones our eyes can detect are the visible light waves and they make up a really small part of the spectrum."

"But why is it screwing up things in my house?"

"The disturbed TV picture is easy to understand. When I was a kid we didn't have cable for a while; whenever my mom ran the electric mixer or the sweeper, it messed up the picture on the TV.

"Now, a Wifi transmitter like your Airport emits waves of energy in the 2.4 gigahertz frequency range, same as a microwave oven. Each wave carries a tiny volt of energy."

"Then why doesn't the Wifi signal cook things?"

"Well, the Wifi waves' total energy output is in orders of magnitude less than a microwave oven. But it's interesting to consider that a microwave oven creates heat by exciting molecules. That motion, like friction, causes heat. And the color of light coming through the window is another question. Are the microwaves from the Wifi unit exciting the waves of light into motion?"

"What do you mean?"

"Light can be bent or filtered. It would seem to me that you've got both of those things happening. The medicine bottle bends and focuses the light on the door like a lens in a camera or projector. All of that is pretty straightforward. But the Wifi waves somehow canceling out some of the colors in that beam of light, leaving you with just the green and blue. I've never heard of a Wifi transmitter doing that."

"Well, it's happening," David said emphatically.

"I'd like to see it sometime."

"Could it affect … like … my brain?"

"No, I don't think it's a health hazard," Eric said, laughing.

"I'll give you a call later in the week and we'll have a beer. Thanks for the info."

David set down his phone and tried to decide what to do next. He could move the bottle and stop it from happening again, but he didn't want to do that. Maybe he had been hallucinating, but maybe—just maybe—he had traveled in time.

Deep inside, David knew what he was going to do. He wanted to go back through the beam, but he wasn't sure he had the nerve. He wanted to talk to the two people and find out who and where they were. He went to the refrigerator and poured the last glass of IPA from the growler. He went back outside to his painting, trying not to think of the beam.

An hour later he mustered his nerve and returned to the living room. He plugged in the Airport. The beam changed just as before. He sat in the rocking chair, watching its bluish-green face projected out in midair, trying to summon the courage to step through again. It was clouding up a little outside, and as clouds intermittently blocked the sun the beam disappeared and reappeared. David walked around the beam and sat down in a chair in the dining room, watching the colors of the back side sparkle and spin within the veil of blackness. Sophie's cloth ball was on the floor in front of him. He grabbed it, turned it in his hand, then tossed it through the beam. It didn't land across the room, but instead disappeared. Sophie came charging out from behind the chair and jumped in after it. She, too, disappeared.

David leaned forward, rubbing his forehead with a trembling hand, trying to decide what to do. Suddenly, a folded piece of paper dropped into the living room from the forward side of the beam. He opened and read a message written in fluid cursive: "Who are you? What do you want?"

The tingling urge to simply jump on faith seized him. He stood, put the note in his pocket, and stepped through.

As if rising up out of still water, he emerged on the other side. The very atmosphere shocked his senses. The temperature was cooler, the humidity lower, the room darker. There was an aroma of food cooking. He struggled to orient himself, but immediately a thick arm was thrown around his neck and clamoring hands pulled him to the floorboards.

He struggled under the weight of at least one man sitting on his back. He strained to lift his head but had it pushed back to the floor. Hands pinned his arms flat to his sides. Something hard—a stick or a rod—was being pressed into the top of his head. David stared into the hem of a carpet laid upon a hardwood floor, noted the faint smell of moth balls. Eyes closed and breathing hard, he fought to stay calm and focus his mind.

"Hold it right there!" a deep, chalky voice commanded. The hard object against his head quivered as the man spoke.

"Whatta we do?" a youthful voice asked from behind.

"Okay," the first voice barked, "we're going to let him raise his head so he can look at me. He needs to see we mean business."

The hand at the back of his head let go and pressed hard, palm flat between his shoulder blades. The hard object lifted. David craned his head up, chin dragging the carpet. Upon the richly colored carpet ahead, a well-worn but polished black boot came into view, connected to the kneeling figure of a bearded, balding man pointing a pistol in his face.

The weight forcing his chest upon the floor robbed him of full breath, but David managed to grunt, "Don't shoot. I don't mean any harm to anybody."

"Check his pockets. See if he's armed," the man said. Two hands held him fast while two others searched his pockets. "You gotta gun or a knife?" the man prodded, pointing with the gun.

"No. Why would I have a weapon?' David strained through clenched teeth.

The bearded man's narrowed eyes softened and he laid the gun on his kneeling leg. He nodded and asked, "Why, indeed?"

He stood, leaving only pant legs and boots in David's view. "Let him up."

The two men behind David released him and stood, stepping back to give him room. David stumbled to his feet, rubbed the ache from his neck, and looked about the room.

He again was in the same strange room he'd seen in the beam. Of the two men behind him, one was the young man he had seen before, who leapt up from a couch. Another man, perhaps in his late twenties, was standing behind a chair. He stiffened at David's examination, sharpening his gaze in return. Each man wore a drab, dark suit. The balding, bearded man, most likely in his fifties, stood in the middle of the room again pointing the small revolver. "Hold it right there."

He scrutinized David. "How did you do that?" he demanded.

"Um ... I just walked through."

"Are you a ghost?"

What an odd question. David shook his head.

"Are you an angel?"

"No," he answered, dumbfounded and trying to take it all in.

"Are you some sort of magician?"

"No. I'm a school teacher."

The bearded man walked toward David, his gun gripped tightly. "You move, and I'll shoot ya," he warned.

"I'm not moving."

Keeping the gun carefully trained on David, the man slowly reached out with one finger and jabbed David's chest to make sure he was real. He circled around him, inspecting the cap turned backwards, the shorts, and the work boots. "You're dressed funny," the man said, squinting at David.

"So are you," David replied without thinking.

"Why are you in my house?" the man asked.

"I don't really know. I thought I was in my house. Then this beam of light appeared and I stepped through it. That's when I saw a woman ... and him over there," David said, pointing.

"I heard about that. My son came downtown to get me. He was out of breath and all excited about some man who reached out and touched my daughter's shoulder and then appeared out of nowhere. I assume that was you?"

"I assume so, yes," David answered.

"That's him all right, Dad!" the young man exclaimed.

There was another moment of silence that seemed to last an eternity. David scanned the room. Beside the couch where the young man sat was a marble-topped Eastlake end table. In the middle of a large oriental rug lay Sophie's cloth ball. From the middle of the ceiling hung a gaslight fixture with four brass arms and etched glass globes.

The room was filled with furniture and decorative objects. On the brown and beige floral wallpaper hung paintings: two galloping horses to the right of the chimney, and a mill on a river on the west wall. David had seen all these things in antique stores and collectors' houses, but now he had no doubt that he was seeing them in a real Victorian parlor.

All three men wore suits with vests and ties.

"Who are you?" the oldest man asked, still pointing the gun at David.

"My name is David Henry. And your name is?"

"I'm Dr. Albert Harrison," he stated emphatically, looking directly at him. "Fred," he said, indicating the young man, "is my youngest son and the one who struck your hand to protect my daughter, Mary. This is my other son, Harry." He nodded toward the man standing behind the chair.

"I didn't mean to touch her," David said, trying to be as polite as possible. "I didn't even know she was there. I couldn't see anything through the beam and was just reaching through to see where my arm would go."

Dr. Harrison studied David's bewildered expression for a moment. "It's apparent that you're as scared to be here as we are to have someone appear out of thin air."

"Where am I?" David asked.

"You're in my father's house in Noblesville, Indiana," Harry said.

"What day is this?" David asked, almost afraid to have his suspicions confirmed.

"It's Tuesday, the twenty-ninth of May." Dr. Harrison snorted, as if David were crazy.

"Okay, and what year is it?" David asked.

"Why, it's 1893," Dr. Harrison replied incredulously. "What year were you expecting?"

David explained about his house and said that he had apparently traveled through time but had no idea how. Utter disbelief gave way to skepticism, and the doctor put the gun away and invited the intruder to sit down.

David opened his wallet and took out a one-dollar and a five-dollar bill. He handed the five to the doctor and gave Harry the one. The two men examined the bank notes carefully.

"This one reads 2004," Harry said in amazement. "George Washington?"

"This five says 2009," Dr. Harrison added.

"Here," David said as he pulled two nickels out of his pocket.

"1978," Fred said, smiling. "Who is that?"

"Thomas Jefferson," David said.

"Sure, that's right."

Despite the difficulty of believing him, the doctor and his sons found David's enthusiasm and sincerity compelling. They all went into the back parlor, where the Harrison men took turns putting their hands into the beam and marveling at the vanishing act the sparkling projection performed. Dr. Harrison put his head through the beam and looked around David's front parlor. When he saw the TV, computer, and automobiles passing by the east window he was ready to believe that David did in fact come from the future. He pulled his head out of the beam and said he was convinced.

David went to the front parlor window and looked out. He saw the shapes of the houses in his neighborhood, each of them familiar, yet different. All had wood-shingle roofs, ornate porches, and wood siding painted in colors different from those of his day. The street was graveled and the sidewalks were made of wood planks nailed onto supporting joists. In front of the house stood a black horse harnessed to a small carriage tied to an iron post.

"I can't believe this," David mumbled. He looked around at the Harrisons. "I've dreamed so much about what this neighborhood looked like when my house was built—I can't believe I'm seeing it now. I can't believe I'm here."

"You didn't mean to come then, this was truly an accident?" Harry asked.

"A wonderfully unbelievable accident."

"Do people do this often in your time?"

"No! This is a miracle. Nobody's ever done this before, except in books and movies. I must be the first person ever to travel in time."

Dr. Harrison stood, inspecting the beam. He wadded up little bits of paper and tossed them through. They didn't land in his front parlor, but if he put his head into the beam he could see them lying on the floor in David's front parlor. But suddenly the beam faded and disappeared. "It's gone," he said.

"Maybe the clouds blocked the sun," David said. "It was happening before I came through. Whenever a cloud passed in front of the sun, the beam disappeared."

"There's no clouds up there," Fred said, looking out the window and then back at David as if he were crazy.

"On the other side, I mean—in my house, in my time."

They sat in the back parlor for at least thirty minutes, waiting for the beam to reappear. It didn't.

"What are we going to do with him if he can't get back?" Harry asked his father.

"I don't know," the doctor said, snorting. "Who would believe?"

More silence. More waiting.

Dr. Harrison pulled a gold watch on a chain from his vest pocket. "Four forty-five," he said. "What time would that be on the other side?"

"About the same, I guess," David answered.

The doctor studied his watch for a moment, deep in thought. "Tell me about yourself, Mr. Henry," he finally asked.

"Well … I guess I come from a time well over a hundred years into the future. I'm a school teacher and I live," he chuckled nervously, "in this house. I'm twenty-five years old—" he paused, trying to decide what was important about himself. "And I spend most of my spare time restoring this house."

"Married?" Dr. Harrison asked.

"No."

"You speak well. Although you don't look it, are you a college man?"

"Yes. I've been to college."

"What do you mean, you're restoring this house?"

"Well, it was in really bad shape when I bought it. It didn't look anything like it does now." David stopped, thinking how odd it was to say "now" and mean 1893. "People have done things to this house over the years that … weren't very smart or attractive."

"Why?" Dr. Harrison asked, confused.

"Well, times change and styles change. Technology, too. Some of the changes took place because people's ideas about what's attractive changed. Also, the value of a house like this has changed. It's not very important. It becomes a cheap rental, and then the landlord begins doing the fastest and cheapest repairs possible—or none at all. Eventually it's a mess."

"Where would people prefer to live?"

"In a new house."

"This is a new house," the doctor said emphatically.

"Not where I come from, it's not. When I bought this house the porch posts were gone, the outside had been covered with metal siding, the insides had been changed all around—it was a mess, and still is, for the most part, except the places I've restored."

Dr. Harrison and his sons looked upset at this.

David had often imagined how the past would look, but he had never considered what modern Noblesville would look like to someone from the past. "I guess a lot has changed."

"I suppose you're right," Dr. Harrison said, appearing to be lost in thought. After pondering for a few moments, he said, "If the beam doesn't come back today, you'll need someplace to stay. Mr. Henry, would you stay here for the night and tell us about the future?" Dr. Harrison asked.

David grinned. "I will if you'll promise to show me Noblesville as it is now."

"It's a bargain then," the doctor said with a smile, extending his hand to shake David's. "Tomorrow is Decoration Day, as I'm sure you know, and you may join my family."

Decoration Day, David knew from teaching history, was the old name for Memorial Day.

"First off, we'll need some proper clothes for you," the doctor said.

Harry said, "He's about my size. I'll go home and get my spare suit for him."

"I'll tell Mother that Mr. Henry will be staying for dinner," Fred offered.

David sat down in the front parlor. Beyond the door that led to what David called his work room, he could hear the doctor speaking with a woman in hushed, urgent tones. The aroma from the kitchen had changed from baking to roasting.

David was looking at the titles in the bookcase, and the photos and trinkets arrayed on top of it, when a voice surprised him.

"Mr. Henry?"

He turned to see the lovely young woman he had touched when he first reached into the beam. She held Sophie tucked under one arm. In her other hand was a glass of lemonade. There, too, was a short, plump woman with graying hair. Behind the women, who were both smiling apprehensively, stood the doctor.

"This is my wife, Anna," the doctor said, "and my daughter, Mary."

"I'm sorry about what happened before," David said nervously. "I didn't know you were there."

"Well, we're all a bit shocked and surprised," she said. "All is forgiven."

Mrs. Harrison said, "We'll be honored to have such an amazing guest staying with us. But I'm afraid we also need to apologize. We're a little bit crowded in this small house."

"Thank you, ma'am. I'm just thrilled to be here. I appreciate you taking me in."

Mary handed David the glass of lemonade and set Sophie on the rug.

"Thank you." David smiled into her eyes, and her blush suddenly made him realize that his stare was embarrassing her.

She certainly wasn't hard to look at. Her long, full, black hair was swept up into a loose knot. Her pale-yellow dress, tied tightly with a black sash at her narrow waist, both concealed and accentuated her figure. Around her neck was a chain with a pendant in the form of a silver turtle. She had deep-green eyes and high cheek bones, and a dusting of freckles across her finely chiseled nose.

They all sat down. The Harrisons stared at him for a while, half-afraid and half-amazed: a traveler from the future.

"I would like to ask you about your clothing," Dr. Harrison said. "I hope I won't offend you."

"No, not at all." David laughed, lifting his arms and examining himself. "I'm sure I must look pretty silly to all of you."

"It's not what we would expect a grown man to wear," Mary put in.

"I'm a history teacher, so I know that people dress far more formally in your time than in mine. But this isn't what I wear to school. I was painting the house this morning. I wear the hat to keep paint drips out of my hair and—"

"What kind of hat is that?" Mrs. Harrison interrupted.

"It's a baseball cap."

"So you play baseball?" Mary asked.

"Not really."

They all looked puzzled.

"Then the Pacers are a baseball team?" Mary asked.

"No," David said, feeling foolish. "It's a fashion, I guess," he explained, sensing their confusion.

Giving up on that one, Dr. Harrison asked about the shorts.

"Well, it was warm today, and shorts are cooler and more comfortable when you're working hard and climbing up and down a ladder."

"You're not embarrassed to be seen by your neighbors dressed like that?" Mary asked.

"No. Men, women, boys and girls—they all wear shorts. It's no big deal."

"You mean to say, women wear short pants like yours and show their legs in public?" Mary asked, incredulous.

"Surely only women of very questionable virtue," Dr. Harrison said, looking to David for confirmation.

Harry came through the front door carrying a suit on a hanger, sparing David the need to answer.

"We must make some rules to follow," Dr. Harrison said to them all. "First off, we mustn't tell anyone that Mr. Henry is from the future. And you mustn't ever be seen in your own clothes, Mr. Henry. People would think you were a tramp." He laughed shortly. "I apologize for any offense, but we couldn't possibly have our neighbors thinking that we have a tramp staying with us. And besides, the police would direct you to the city limits."

"I'm not offended; I'm sure you're right."

"Second, we must explain where he's come from and why he's here. Mr. Henry, if you would like to go change into these clothes, the rest of us will formulate a few white lies."

David took the clothes from Harry with an awkward smile.

"Mr. Henry, you may change in the upstairs bedchamber on the left at the top of the stairs," Mrs. Harrison told him.

David went up and changed. He pulled on a thin pair of socks that wouldn't stay up, and a starched white shirt with a terribly stiff detachable collar. The black jacket and trousers were too loose, but about the right length. And the shiny black shoes were too long and narrow.

Back downstairs, the Harrisons filled him in on their plan.

"We will say you are a good friend of my brother's family," said Dr. Harrison. "He lives in Michigan and does a lot of business in Canada, so that's where you're from. You're traveling and have decided to stay in Noblesville for a while. When my brother visited here last year he didn't meet anyone who had ever been to Canada, so you should be safe from overly specific questions. No one in this room is to tell anyone under any circumstances how Mr. Henry came to us. Harry, Clara will be coming to dinner here tonight with you, so you must tell her, and she must be held to the same secrecy as everyone else."

For the next hour they interrogated David about details of the future. At the same time, David learned about them. Dr. and Mrs. Harrison, Mary, and Fred were living in this house temporarily, while building a new home. The doctor also owned two other houses on the block, and Harry and his pregnant wife, Clara, lived in one of them.

Dr. Harrison was a Civil War veteran; recently elected auditor, he had given up working full time in medicine to pursue politics. Harry, twenty-eight, was a dentist with an office downtown on the courthouse square. Twenty-one-year-old Mary had graduated from Bryn Mawr. Fred, nineteen, had graduated from high school the previous year and was working with his father in the auditor's office.

Finally, the doors between the back parlor and the dining room were opened by a slender, middle-aged black woman. She turned up the gaslights in the dining room, and she set the table with Wedgewood china and silver place settings, which she took from a mahogany side cabinet.

Anna and Mary went upstairs. David asked, "May I see the rest of the downstairs? Since I live here, I'm really curious about it." Dr. Harrison led David into the kitchen. The black cook was taken aback when David extended his hand and introduced himself. She hesitantly took his hand and introduced herself as Nella.

The gas range against the west wall was crowded with pots and pans bubbling and sizzling. On the center griddle a loaf of bread was warming. To its right was a pot of peas and carrots, and to the left a pot of boiling potatoes and a frying pan with an inch of hot grease. On a table in the middle of the room lay pieces of chicken coated with flour and a baking sheet with a batch of biscuits. The room was hot and filled with wonderful smells. On a side cabinet sat a large bowl of strawberries. Nella set them in an oak icebox.

"It looks like you're cooking two meals at once," David said.

"You folks'll have your picnic in the cemetery tomorrow," Nella replied.

"Tomorrow you'll get to see the town and meet its finest people," Dr. Harrison said.

Within a half hour they were joined by Harry's wife, Clara, a small blond woman, heavily pregnant. Clara coughed repeatedly. Her face was pallid and there were small sores on her lips. David's appearance had created an air of excitement and expectation in the house, but Clara's arrival dampened everyone's spirits. They gazed at her with concern, and Mary took her hands.

"You're not feeling better?" Mary asked.

"I spent the day in bed with a fever," Clara said, "but I feel better now."

"Why didn't you call for me?" Dr. Harrison asked.

"What could you do that you haven't already done?" she said feebly. She took her seat at the table with help from Harry. The rest of the family exchanged worried glances. Nella brought in a procession of dishes, including a magnificent baked ham. The doctor offered a brief prayer and the food was passed.

Mary turned to David. "I'm really relieved to meet someone from the future."

"Relieved, why?"

"I've been reading a story called 'Omega: The Last Days of the World,' published in *Cosmopolitan* this year in serial. I was beginning to wonder if the world was going to be around much longer."

The others laughed.

"The world's still chugging along," David answered, passing mashed potatoes.

"What's the future like, Mr. Henry?" Fred asked. "What kind of great inventions are there?"

"Well, for one thing, you wouldn't see any horses and buggies tied up outside. People get around in cars—in automobiles—in my time."

All through dinner, the history teacher was gloriously in his element. Everything he said was a revelation to students who were hanging on every word. He would describe an invention, and the Harrisons, dumbfounded, would ask more questions. And the credit for the miracles of the twenty-first century fell to him, the representative of the time.

David suspected that to them, he was the most interesting person alive. They treated him with such respect that he felt like a conquering hero. The gaslight burning above the table felt like a hanging hearth that nurtured their conversation. The warmth and animation of their conversation combined with the deep vibrant colors of the wallpaper and draperies, the amber glow of the oak and mahogany furniture and the aromas of the food, making him feel at peace and at home.

While David was reveling in the atmosphere of the past, Mary was observing him closely, but asked far fewer questions than she wanted. She found him exciting and somehow attractive, despite the rough guise in which he had first appeared to her. His features were handsome, but his tanned skin seemed to her the mark of a common laborer. He was flamboyant and animated in a way that was compelling to her, especially in an era that prized reserve. Yet, she had never met a socially acceptable man with those qualities.

For more than an hour David dominated the conversation. The talk turned to medicine, and he reeled off a list of the things twenty-first-century science had identified as bad for the body: the lead-based paint that covered all the houses in the Harrisons' town, smoking tobacco, eating fattening foods. The doctor questioned him on each point.

When everyone rose after dinner, David startled them by picking up his plate and heading for the kitchen with it.

"The women will get that, Mr. Henry," Dr. Harrison urged, nodding to Mary, who quickly took the plate from David. The doctor went to the sideboard and opened a box, took out a handful of cigars, and filled one coat pocket with them. Mary came back from the kitchen and slipped several carrots into her father's other coat pocket.

"Thank you, dear," he said. "Let's go out for a smoke, gents."

David followed the doctor, Fred, and Harry across the backyard and into the shed. A handsome quarter horse stuck its head out.

CHAPTER THREE

Passenger stop as you pass by
As you now stand, so once did I
As I now lay, you too shall be
Prepare for death and follow me
From the gravestone of Pleasant Evans, died 1866,
Noblesville's Riverside Cemetery.

David woke several times during the night. In those moments of disorientation, as he sensed a strange bed, a silent house, unfamiliar scents, the strangest thing was that he was not asking himself, "Where am I?" He was asking, "When am I?"

The household was stirring early, and they had breakfasted by eight. David joined them at the curb in front of the house while Fred went around to the shed, harnessed Butch to the carriage, and brought it around through the alley to the street. David mounted the driver's seat beside Dr. Harrison, and the rest of the family squeezed into the covered seats. The doctor set his whip into the socket, gathered the long reins with a practiced gesture, and clucked to set the horse in motion.

As they headed west down Cherry Street, David saw landmarks he recognized. Remnants of the old-growth forest trees lined the street, creating a lush, enclosed canopy. On the curb in the grass strip, between either wood plank or brick sidewalks, nearly every house had a carriage stone. Most were limestone slabs about eighteen inches tall and two feet square, while larger, more elaborate homes had carefully cut stones with two steps. In front of every house the limestone curb had an iron ring embedded for tying horses. A few houses had a three-foot-tall hitching post of wood or decorative cast iron.

Surprisingly, most of the houses in his neighborhood were still standing, yet they were very different. Gone were the vinyl, aluminum, and asbestos siding. Instead, wood clapboards and gingerbread trim was the rule. Where he expected to see a Foursquare or Bungalow from the early twentieth century, David saw small, modest Victorian homes. A house two blocks down from his, which David knew as a white stucco, could be seen in its original Queen Anne glory. It had a small round tower on the front corner, a large chimney that bulged at the top, and an ornate front porch adorned with fretwork. In David's time all of this was gone or encased with white meringue-like stucco. "Who would have guessed," he whispered to himself, shaking his head in disbelief.

Mary asked, "Who would have guessed what?" David didn't answer, lost in thought.

The entire physical atmosphere was different. There was a dampness in the air, more than just the usual Indiana humidity David knew. The smell of nature was all around. It reminded him of walking in a forest. There were just so many more trees and foliage. David imagined that less of the land was cleared around the town than in his time. And the sounds of birds filled the air, much more so than in the 2000s. Mixed with the fragrance of blossoming catalpa trees and flowers was the occasional odor of livestock manure that lay in haphazard piles in the gravel street.

Half a block from Tenth Street, David looked south. Down the alley he saw the huge high school resting where a small park and pre-fab gazebo sit in his time. Deep-green shutters flanked the arched four-over-four windows, which stood out on a field of red brick. On top was an octagon-shaped bell tower with louvered vents and a copper dome. Just to see it took David's breath away. He'd seen an old photograph of the building and its lawn in a glass case in the historical society museum. A postcard photo showed the large lawn, covered with lush, mature trees, remnants of the forest that once covered the area. The yard was ringed with an ornate iron fence, encircled by brick sidewalks. In his time, not only is the entire building gone, but so too are the large trees and the iron fence. The sidewalk is concrete and there's an eyesore of a school bus shelter, a place where teenagers hang out at night to smoke cigarettes and talk.

When they came to what David knew as Tenth Street, the street sign read Anderson Street. The road bed here changed to brick. He recognized the houses on three of the four corners of the intersection. On the southeast corner was a two-story Italianate. Without thinking, David had expected to see the familiar gas station. Between this house and the high school should have been the Village Pantry. Instead, there was the Second Empire house looking like the Bates Motel from "Psycho." On the southwest corner was the Locke House, another huge Italianate.

Besides a few newer Queen Annes north of the intersection, this was an 1860s-'70s neighborhood, architecturally speaking. No large grouping such as this survives to the twenty-first century. Most older, intact neighborhoods in Noblesville were made up of 1880s-'90s structures. This neighborhood was too close to downtown to survive a new world designed to accommodate cars. A muffler shop, a fast food restaurant, another gas station and several lawyers' offices had destroyed the residential and historic content of the street.

From this intersection, almost immediately the town was busier. Carriages passed by, nearly everyone saying hello. William Locke, a rotund, older man, stood on the porch of his house with a newspaper in one hand. "Good morning, Harrison clan. Albert, I trust you'll put on a good show today," he shouted.

Dr. Harrison smiled and waved. Two large workhorses clopped by, pulling a wagon filled with members of a family. They progressed another block. Again the street signs confused David. This was the intersection of Emmous and Catherine streets.

"The street names are different in my time," David said.

Dr. Harrison scratched his beard, intrigued. "Really, what should this intersection be?"

"Ninth and Cherry."

David was intoxicated by what he was seeing. It reminded him of how he felt when he passed through the gates of Disney World with his grandfather many years ago—so much anticipation and amazement. He hadn't dreamed and fantasized about anything so much since then. This was a Hoosier preservationist's Disney World.

Dr. Harrison loosened the reins and motioned to the south. "Here's where we're building our new house."

Where the yellow brick of the ugly, nearly windowless Ameritech office should have stood was instead a huge Queen Anne under construction. This was one of the things David longed to see more than anything else—a house of this era being built. The skin was nearly complete on the two-story, balloon-frame structure. It had a large gable facing Catherine Street. Nestled to the right on the second floor was what would no doubt be a balcony or sleeping porch. A front porch, still under construction, extended the entire length of the front and ran down the right side.

David noticed that the people who passed all knew one another, a great contrast to the Noblesville he lived in, where people zipped by in cars, barely noticing anyone, and only occasionally seeing a familiar face.

They headed north on Catherine, just two blocks from the center of town. Above the two- and three-story buildings before them rose what would remain the dominant piece of architecture in the city even in David's time, the Hamilton County courthouse. It was an eight-story structure, four making up the body and another four on the central tower. Seven stories up, four clock faces looking out at each point on the compass were capped by an arched mansard dome with four porthole windows.

In the next block came another sight that stopped him in his tracks: the Wild Opera House. Few buildings were more conspicuous in their absence at the turn of the millennium than this one, with its imposing red-brick facade, limestone lintels and the arched entryway that reached out over the sidewalk. Local residents still occasionally talked about the opera house, though few had ever seen shows there. It was the kind of building that people referred to and said, "They don't make 'em like that anymore." Yet, a parking lot would take its place.

Few businesses were opened on the square. As the Harrisons' horse approached Conner Street, people were converging on the square in carriages, wagons, carts, buggies, and on foot and horseback from all directions. Once the square was in view, David could see the bobbing heads of horses coming across an iron bridge spanning White River some two blocks west of the square on Conner. A cloud of dust rose up west of the bridge but didn't penetrate beyond the river. Even though it had not rained, the brick streets were wet, having been hosed down by the sprinkler wagon.

Dr. Harrison had been voted "Officer of the Day" by the local Grand Army of the Republic, Lookout Post; therefore, a special place had been set aside for his vehicle, and several men dressed in their G.A.R. uniforms greeted him and assisted the ladies in stepping down from the rig. David was introduced to veterans, wives and friends.

The half hour between arrival and the beginning of the ceremonies was a blur to him. He shook hands with strangers who asked questions like, "What brings you to the Hoosier state?" All the while he was examining their clothes, smiles, mannerisms and children, plus buildings in the background that he wanted to see.

There was an eager anticipation in the eyes of the young men who made a special effort to approach and greet Mary. When she would introduce them to David, he thought he noticed a glimmer of envy in their eyes, envy that he imagined was due to the fact that he stood with her and was staying in her house. She was apparently a very sought-after young lady.

As the bells on the clock tower began to ring, middle-aged men, either G.A.R. members or the uniformed rank of the Knights of Pythius, filtered through the crowd and asked people to take their seats.

Two uniformed men approached Mary and Anna and offered their arms.

"Oh, don't you look fine today, Jim," Anna said to Jim Bush as he escorted her to her seat.

Mary took the arm of the other man, introduced as Thomas Swain, and exchanged polite conversation with him, tapping her parasol on the sandstone sidewalk to the beat of her gait. They were led to seats in the front reserved for the family of the day's speakers. David and Fred followed close behind. Sitting in the front row of the "civilian" section, they faced the uniformed men, some on a platform that had been erected at the south entrance to the brick and stone courthouse, and others in folding chairs set in a semicircle. Everywhere on the square, American flags fluttered in the warm morning breeze. Red, white and blue banners hung out of upper-floor windows in the courthouse and surrounding buildings. In the crowd, nearly every man wore a hat and stiff collar. Women, too, wore hats. Some wore small silk ones, with flowers pinned to their hair; others wore bonnets tied under their chins.

As David sat surveying the crowd, it occurred to him that Mary was the most beautiful woman there. She had a look of sophistication beyond her surroundings. She was one of the few who wore no a hat but simply a flower in her hair.

She saw him gazing about like a man who had been locked up a very long time.

"So what do you think, Mr. Henry?" she said, looking past him, waving to a young lady in the crowd. "Is this your Noblesville, the little town you know?"

"Yes and no," he said, his eyes fixed on the medals pinned to the chests of the war vets. "It's really wonderful. It's so magnificent to see it as it is now, and there's so much I want to see, so many questions I want to ask."

Reverend Overmeyer approached the podium, and Mary gave David a gently condescending, knowing smile; the kind of smile a parent gives a child who expresses a desire for something petty.

The minister offered a short prayer: "Dear God, thank you for this beautiful day, a day we have set aside to pay tribute to those whom you have called home to your realm. Let not the day pass that we don't stop to reflect on all they created in the days that they walked the earth. Let us not forget that we travel the roads they built and live in the homes they fashioned and follow a faith that served them well. Let us remember that the end awaits us all and that we must do well in the time that you have given us here on earth. Let us remember that we shall travel the roads they traveled to the same place were they rest now, with you. Let us remember them in our time as we would have future generations remember us in times to come. In thy Son's name we pray, Amen."

A group of a dozen schoolgirls, no more than ten years old, climbed the stairs of the platform and sang a hymn that David did not recognize.

Mary knew that many eyes were upon her today, and she liked the fact that it wasn't a local man sitting beside her. She liked that he was a mystery to them, a handsome stranger.

Without really wanting to, she looked down on the people of Noblesville, but not because she thought herself superior. Three years ago she wanted to see the world, and had, to a certain extent, in Philadelphia.

She lived for three years just outside a city that was big and exciting. She lived and studied with girls from around the country, the East mostly, and some from abroad. On trips to Philadelphia she learned and socialized in beautiful restaurants, theaters, museums and galleries. The intellectual atmosphere was "electric," as she often said of exciting things. Coming home to Noblesville after all that was crushing. She felt trapped in the middle of nowhere. The things that local people found important were meaningless to her. It made her feel guilty, but she couldn't help it. It also bothered her that such an attractive and intelligent man could get excited about a place that she wanted so desperately to leave.

When the singing and applause ended, Reverend Overmeyer again took the podium and introduced Dr. Harrison.

David was intrigued by the speech. It was rather trite in its glorification of war, dying for one's country and being patriotic beyond all else. Still, it presented a view of small-town Northern life in the 1890s that he hadn't considered until now. This town was essentially controlled by Civil War veterans. He had heard of the G.A.R. but hadn't realized how much power it wielded. During the speech he looked across the grouping of war vets, many he'd just met. They were the power in town. One, named Wainwright, had been introduced as the owner of a local bank. There was William Locke, also a banker; Mr. Tescher, a business owner; Thomas Swain, a lawyer and politician; James Bush, a schoolteacher; and many others—all veterans. Having fought in the war carried with it a certain social status.

By the time the doctor's speech ended, the crowd had grown so large it overflowed into Catherine and Conner streets. Those close enough to hear clapped politely. Several vets stood, shouting "hear, hear." Dr. Harrison had already descended the platform and was halfway to the street before Reverend Overmeyer asked the crowd to follow the procession to the old Riverside Cemetery. The vets lined Conner in formation, followed by the military band and the uniformed Knights of Pythius. Behind the Pythians were one hundred young girls dressed in white, each carrying a basket of flowers. Dr. Harrison led the entire procession. It was an impressive display, at once festive and solemn.

David followed the other Harrisons as the procession filled the streets and followed the decorated men, the throng making the turn at

Eighth Street, which he noted was marked "Polk Street." Ladies and children carried baskets of freshly cut flowers and garlands. Several boys carried a handful of tiny American flags. These several hundred people walked the four blocks to the cemetery passing through the oldest part of Noblesville. Homes dating from the 1830s to 1850s filled the blocks along the river, its banks falling away to the southwest. David noticed a small house that must have been a log cabin, covered now with wood clapboards painted white.

Those who hadn't come down for the speech stood in their front yards, some saluting the flag as it passed, some with hat in hand, bowing their heads; still others waved at friends once the flag passed.

At the cemetery the vets and Pythians gathered around the east end and the crowd filed around, filling the paths, which were two-wheel wagon ruts at best. Someone had gone ahead of the crowd and parked a carriage inside the gates on the highest piece of ground, just behind the little church resting at the edge of the cemetery. A middle-aged man in an old, ill-fitting uniform climbed into the carriage, stood on the seat, and offered a brief prayer. Taps was played. Rifles were fired into the air.

The work of decorating graves was not a man's job, though many walked among the stones, admiring the ornaments. Children, mostly, led by mothers or grandmothers, scattered among the stones, kneeling to place flowers on graves. Soldiers' graves got a small flag, its stick pressed into the ground beneath the stone. At the base of some were placed small store-bought cardboard plaques attached to a stick, printed with messages such as, "Gone but not forgotten" or "Will remember you always." Many people paid special attention to the graves of family members. Some brought live flowers and planted them on the graves. A few of the children ran to the far end of the cemetery to the river and began skipping rocks and daring one another to cross on the stones. Occasionally a mother would approach the bank and urge a well-dressed child away. The atmosphere was now more festive than solemn.

Most of the men stayed up near the gates, standing in large circles, talking and smoking cigars. Fred led David away from the women to join the men.

The conversations of the night before in the Harrison house had left him feeling like a conquering hero, the lone representative of the technological triumphs of the twenty-first century. But now, standing among a circle of common men of the nineteenth century, he felt insignificant. The conversation moved so rapidly on a course of unexpected twists and turns that he felt as if he'd been dropped into rushing whitewater, tossed among boulders at a speed that disoriented the mind, in an environment that overwhelmed the senses.

The men spoke of free silver and populists, of wheat prices and the World's Fair, economic hard times and gas well drilling, of house building and electric railways. Mixed among it all came lighthearted, rapid-fire one-liners, tossed off at the expense of the speaker of the moment, inside jokes that referenced their personal traits and past mistakes. There were showboats like Thomas Swain, who dominated center stage with their stories and opinions, and others like James Bush, who waited patiently for the perfect moment to counter a point or land a zinger guaranteed to send the circle into uproarious laughter. It was conversation among people who knew each other well and practiced the art of conversation regularly. David was unprepared to swim in those waters. He had no idea how to take part, or what to say if he tried. So he stood silent, hands in his pockets, taking it all in, enjoying the choreography of good discourse.

David saw a young man who had been introduced as Robert Wainwright leave the group and walk over to Mary, where she stood with her mother and several other ladies. He watched this courtship pantomime with interest. From body language he could see that it was small talk. Mary was polite, but cool. From the expression on Robert's face it seemed she was not as friendly as he would have preferred. Still he stayed and talked with the women, and when Mary stepped away to look at a stone, he followed and continued talking to her. She would look up, smile and nod occasionally, but she was aloof—polite, but not warm. When she walked back to the other women, he followed, holding his hat in hand, nervously fidgeting with the brim.

Distracted, watching this awkward silent moment between Mary and Robert, David didn't hear Jim Bush asking a question. "So, what business are you in, Mr. Henry?"

"Oh, I'm sorry," David said, "what was that?"

Bush repeated his question.

"Um," David thought for a moment, and noticed that Dr. Harrison had broken off his own conversation and was listening nervously for David's answer. "I'm in the construction business," he blurted, almost an afterthought. "Took over the family business a few years back, actually."

"What kind of construction?" Jim asked.

"Um … houses mostly. We've never done much in bridges or commercial, really." David was flying by the seat of his pants. He knew a lot about houses of this era and figured he could bluff his way along.

"Seems since this is the start of the construction season, this should be your busiest time of the year," Bush said. "Surprised a fellow in your line of work could get away like this."

"Well," David went on, "an economic downturn has hit Toronto. Business was real good until late last year, but when things fell off I turned operations over to my brother. I made good money and was ready to get away and see America."

"How long do you think you'll stay here?" Thomas Swain asked.

"Well, I'm not sure. Noblesville's a nice place. Think I may stay for a while."

Dr. Harrison pulled a watch out of his pocket. "Time to strike camp, gentlemen," he said. The group lined up near the Whiltshire Street gate and marched back the way they had come.

David and the Harrisons walked back as far as the courthouse and then rode in the carriage to Crownland Cemetery. In David's time, Crownland was on the edge of Old Town, increasingly surrounded by apartment complexes, housing developments, the new Methodist Church and the ever-enlarging school system buildings. But now, as their carriage passed down Monument Street, they were moving outside of town. The cemetery was surrounded on two sides by woods and on the other two by the black, rich soil of Indiana farm fields, dotted in ragged rows with little green sprouts of corn. Though isolated from the central community, a few houses could be seen along Cooper Street, marking the outer limits of town.

The grounds of Crownland were park-like with an abundance of large oak, willow, ash and catalpa trees shading what counts as hilly topography for the unforgivingly flat Hoosier landscape. The whole was surrounded by a simple five-foot-tall iron fence. Many of the gravestones were in fact monuments, far larger and more grand than anything at the old riverside sight.

Upon arrival, the procession repeated the prayers, gunfire and bugle playing. This time it took place at the base of the monument for which the nearby street was named, built in memory of those who had served in the Civil War.

Again David watched Mary deal with the young men who came to greet her and beg her attention. Robert Wainwright tried again. Again, Mary's ambivalence. David thought of other beautiful women he'd known and recognized the physical cues of her disinterest.

Slowly the decorating gave way to picnicking. Anna and Mary spread a blanket on the grass and brought a basket from the carriage, filled with the food Nella had prepared the night before. Fried chicken, potato salad, biscuits, strawberry shortcake, and lemonade seemed to be almost the universal picnic lunch.

The sun had driven off the last of the dew and morning chill and warmed the ground around them. Even with the chattering of voices all around, David was struck by the stillness in the air. No cars passing endlessly on a nearby street, no factory humming in the distance, no lawn mowers—just the distant clang of the bell in the courthouse clock tower chiming high noon.

"Is this how Decoration Day is celebrated in your time?" Anna asked.

"No. In my time it's just a day off work arranged in such a way that the date always falls on a Monday, so people get three days off in a row. Oh, and we call it Memorial Day."

"Well, it's a day off work for most people now," she said.

"But it's also something more," David went on. "Nothing like these ceremonies takes place in the small towns I know. It's simply a day off and nothing more to most people. Sure, a few veterans show up on the courthouse lawn holding flags while someone plays 'Taps,' and maybe the mayor reads a proclamation to the ten or twenty old people who've come from some retirement home, but that's about it."

"That's awful," Anna said.

"Well, then, how does the average Hoosier observe this day?" Dr. Harrison asked.

David chuckled. "With the Indianapolis 500. Most people are at parties, barbecuing burgers, and drinking beer. The Indy 500 is an automobile race. People celebrate automobiles, I guess."

"Why?" the doctor asked, angered at the thought of such disrespect.

David thought for a moment. "I guess the race is a celebration of the automobile … and speed, two of the great addictions of the next century." The Harrisons didn't really understand what he was talking about.

"Getting back to these ignored courthouse lawn events. You said veterans show up," Mary said. "Veterans of what? Another war?"

"Did you expect that there wouldn't be any more wars?"

"I suppose I just never thought to wonder."

"What kind of wars, and with who?" Fred asked.

For the first time, David felt uncomfortable about discussing the future and revealing things that might involve the Harrisons or their children. "None of them were fought here, in America, if that's what you're wondering about," he said, trying to avoid specifics. "Dr. Harrison, tell me about your war service," he went on, turning the conversation away from the future.

That night, dinner at the Harrison home was a bit more elaborate than the evening before. Due to Clara's illness, neither she nor Harry attended. Nella took dinner to them.

After dinner, instead of going to the shed for a smoke, the men sat in the back parlor and listened to Mary play the piano.

"Play a war song for me, dear," Dr. Harrison said.

She sat at the mahogany upright piano, tapping at several keys as if looking for a chord. She began to play the mournful tune "Johnny Has Gone for a Soldier." David recognized the melody but didn't know the name. Dr. Harrison nodded his head slightly to the rhythm.

When the song was nearly finished, Mary stopped abruptly and turned to David. "Music," she said. "What is music like in the next century?" She went on playing.

He thought for a minute, not quite sure how to answer. "Most of the interesting music has come from black culture."

"From colored people?"

He nodded. "Would you like to hear some?"

"I'd love to," Mary said, getting up from the piano to give him the bench.

"Oh, no, I don't play," he laughed, embarrassed.

"Then how can I possibly hear it?" she laughed.

"I told you about recorded music. I'll go home through the beam tomorrow and bring back some for you to hear."

"You have one of those Edison machines that plays a wax cylinder?"

"No, I'll bring a small ... machine that plays music. Some of what I listen to might upset you, so I'll bring something you can relate to, some more relaxed examples of what is yet to come."

"I can't wait," she said with a broad smile. Then, as if drawing back from her sudden warmth, she bent the smile into an impassive thin line. Slowly, deliberately, she began playing the introductory phrases of Beethoven's Piano Sonata No. 8, the "Pathetique."

CHAPTER FOUR

Whereas the city blocks of 1890 usually contained eight lots, the same blocks now contain ten, twelve, and even fourteen. A common practice today is to saw off the back of a lot and insert an additional house fronting on the side street. The implications of this shift for play room for children, leisure-time activities for the entire family, ... (and) pride in the appearance of one's "place" are obvious. The housewife with leisure does not sit so much on the front porch ... sewing and "visiting" and comparing her yard with her neighbor's, nor do the family and neighbors spend long summer evenings and Sunday afternoons on the porch or in the side yard since the advent of the automobile and the movies. These factors tend to make a decorative yard less urgent; the make of one's car is rivaling the looks of one's place as an evidence of one's "belonging."
Middletown, a Study of American Culture,
Robert and Helen Lynd, 1929

When David stepped back through the beam the next morning, his house was just as he left it, even though the front door had been open for two nights. His tools lay in the front yard, and a half-finished beer sat on the dining room table. He showered then set about putting things in order. Lying awake last night, unable to sleep from excitement, he'd made a plan.

David put all his tools away. He cleared the front yard of everything but the ladder. A skin had formed over the surface of the gallon of primer he'd left out, and a paint brush, its bristles hardened, rested on the rim of the can. He spent an hour or more cleaning out the garage and drove his pickup inside, locking the overhead door. Going through all his bills, he paid everything in advance, leaving little in his checking account, then walked downtown to the bank.

On the square the courthouse was encased in scaffolding. Some of its carved sandstone blocks were marked with red spray paint. They were too far gone to save and would need to be replaced. On the west side the outer layer of brick had been removed, to be replaced with new brick. The west lawn had become a staging area for the restoration crew, with chain-link fencing, mortar mixers, stacks of lumber, and several dumpsters.

A crane was parked on the north lawn, its arm and cable stretched seven stories up. Workers in the tower and on the surrounding scaffolding were loading it with the glass clock faces and the mechanical workings that had kept the bell ringing out the hours for one hundred and twenty years or more. For two days now it had been silent.

Some people in Noblesville missed the sound of the bell since it had fallen silent a few days before, but others were relieved. For the past few years the aging mechanism had often rung almost at random. Only a few people noticed. But David was one of them—usually on warm summer nights when he woke up after a dream and lay in the blackness, listening to the stillness of the house and the lonely bell sounding the wrong time. In the winter when the trees were bare, if he looked out the north upstairs window he could see the tower and two of the clock faces rising up above the rooftops.

He stood on the sidewalk for a few moments, watching the last of the huge glass discs being lowered to the ground. Workers in the tower covered the openings with sheets of plywood. He turned and walked across the street to the Trust Bank and spread his three credit cards on the counter before the teller. He bought the maximum number of gold investment coins his credit limit would permit. He almost ran from the bank, anxious to get back and through the beam before it disappeared for the day. Hurrying around a corner, he ran right into Jane Harding, one of his preservationist allies.

"Oh, David, I'm so glad to bump into you," she said. "I've tried calling you the last couple of days but didn't get an answer."

"Cell phone was broken. Just got it fixed. Sorry."

"Well, I was hoping you could help me with something. We just found out the bank is going to tear down the old Diana Theater building, and we want to try to stop them."

"Why are they tearing it down? I thought they were trying to lease the place."

"Well, when I called the branch manager, he said they found asbestos, and lots of it, and that it would be too expensive to remove. But I think they're lying."

"Why would they lie?" David asked.

"I've heard that Noblesville Savings and Loan asked to lease the building from them, and only then did the asbestos suddenly appear. Ever since NSL opened up a couple years ago, it's been taking business away from these out-of-town corporate banks. NSL has grown so much that they need to move out of their little offices, and the Diana building would be perfect for them. I think the corporate boys in Cleveland are trying to ruin NSL's chances of expanding their business downtown."

"You'd have to be pretty rich to tear down a perfectly good building just to keep it away from somebody else," David said. "Last time I was in there it looked fine. It's ugly now, but still a good building. Quite an asset to just destroy."

"I didn't say it made sense, but why else would they suddenly stop trying to lease it two days after NSL asks for a long-term lease?"

"I wish I could help you, Jane," he said, starting to step away, "but I'm on my way out of town for a week or so."

"I know it doesn't look like a great piece of architecture," she went on, following him. "Most of that part of it has been destroyed, but it is in good shape and would just leave this huge blank space downtown. I don't care what the average person says, we don't need any more parking lots downtown. We've torn down enough buildings. I already hardly recognize my hometown. I'm trying to look at this as an economic resource that's being wasted."

"I agree with you, but I can't help now. Maybe when I get back."

"Well, I'm going to get some of the people together and see what we can do. Call me when you get home, will you?"

David went back in the house. The beam was still in place. He sat down at the computer and opened an e-mail from his mother.

"Hi. Called but couldn't reach you the last couple of days. Just hoping that you might like to come out West this summer and see us. I'd love to meet this Heather girl I was hearing so much about last winter—but I'm sure that's too much to wish for with us being so far away. Let me know how you are. Bye."

He typed a quick response about being busy with the house

In the workroom, he pushed the still-unrepaired leaded-glass window aside and set to work on the gold coins. One at a time he held them with a pair of pliers in front of a flame from the little propane tank used to sweat the joints on copper water pipes. When the gold was hot, he held it on edge on the steel saw table and beat it gently with a hammer, turning as he went. He did this until the $5,000 in gold coins were reduced to rounded lumps with no visible imprint or evidence of minting.

David stashed the gold in a green canvas Banana Republic shoulder bag, along with razors, a toothbrush, underwear, his iPhone and earbuds and a miniature pair of battery-powered speakers.

The phone's calendar showed he would miss a preservation meeting next week. No big deal. He locked all the doors, closed all but the front shade, and turned on the porch light. After dressing again in Harry's clothes, he slung the bag over his shoulder and stepped through the beam.

He banged his nose against the back of a folding oriental screen that Anna had positioned to hide the beam. He had to fold the screen back to step out into the room.

"Hello," David called out. "Anybody home?"

Nella appeared in the kitchen door, drying her hands on her apron. "Where'd you come from, Mr. Henry?"

"I just walked in."

"Didn't hear a thing—like you come out of nowhere. Anyways, none of them are here. Dr. Harrison and Fred are at the office in the courthouse and Mrs. Harrison is doing some shopping downtown. Miss Harrison is around here someplace. Her mamma told her to wait for you."

She turned to go back to the kitchen, then stopped. "You a mysterious man, Mr. Henry. You come outta nowhere like a ghost, and you the only white man ever shook my hand."

Mary was puzzled by David's desire to visit a jeweler but agreed to accompany him downtown. After a pleasant walk, they entered the long narrow room of Purcell's Jewelry. The maple floors were scuffed in a U-shaped pattern in front of the glass display cases; the narrow planks creaked under their footsteps. Light spilled in through the broad plate-glass windows and the patterned, leaded-glass panels overhead. At the far end of the room a balding man wearing eyeglasses fitted with a loupe bent over a pocket watch he was cleaning.

He glanced up. "Mary Harrison, how are you, young lady?"

After brief introductions, David produced the gold lumps from his pocket. Mr. Purcell mumbled to himself as he scraped a pocketknife blade across a couple to see that they were solid. He went to the back of his shop, broke one in half with a small wedge and a hammer, and dumped all of the pieces into the cup of a scale.

"You have some very fine gold here, Mr. Henry," he said without looking up.

The old man went back to his desk and scribbled notes on a piece of paper, stopping from time to time to scratch his chin and grumble. He returned to the counter and slid the piece of paper across the glass to David. "This is what I'd give you."

David looked at the figure and was horrified by how little it was. "Is this good?" he said, holding the note up for Mary.

"I suppose," she nodded. "Mr. Purcell wouldn't cheat you."

"I should think not," Purcell snorted.

David took the payment. As they moved down the sidewalk, Mary surreptitiously watched him as he examined the money. "So, do they have gold-making machines in your time as well?" she joked soberly.

"Well, of course, it's America. The streets are paved with gold."

"Well, these streets," she waved her hand about, "are paved with a little brick, a little gravel and a lot of dirt. You wanted a tour, so we might as well get started."

From the southeast corner of the courthouse square where they stood looking east, the street seemed to disappear into forest a few blocks beyond downtown. Majestic elms arched over the street, meeting in the middle. Between the courthouse and the bridge there were several livery stables and, on the southwest corner of the square, the Wainwright Hotel. Along the west side of the courthouse, where the monolithic brick and smoked glass Judicial Center loomed in David's day, he saw a row of gabled, pre-Civil War commercial buildings facing the street. "None of those buildings survive to my time," he said.

As Mary gave him a tour of 1893 Noblesville, he complemented it with a description of the same places in his time.

"That area west beyond the river is total strip mall—individual business buildings surrounded by paved parking with halogen ... well, with harsh electric lighting that burns all night long. It hadn't occurred to me how damn ugly it all was until now."

The finest houses were clustered around the downtown in a crescent hugging the river. David stopped to take it in. "Only one of these grand homes in the first block still stands in my time," he grieved. "It's all parking lots and gas stations."

Mary stopped and narrowed her eyes, shaking her head a little, uncertain how that could be.

"This is the Heinzmans' new house," she said, pointing at a dramatic Queen Anne with a slate-covered tower reflecting the sunshine, "and next door is Thomas Swain and his family." She nodded at a two-story wood-frame house with storybook gingerbread trim and lush vines growing up the chimney. "Both gone?" she asked.

"Don't know when, but gone before I was born."

In the middle of the next block they came across a huge, nearly finished granite foundation.

"This house being built right here," David pointed excitedly, "it gets moved across the street. I was there, I saw it. Somebody wanted to tear it down, so it was bought and moved."

Mary shook her head in disbelief. "This will be William Craig's house. He's very wealthy, so it should be magnificent."

"It is."

Even though the town's well-off citizens were clustered here, near downtown, it wasn't unusual to find little houses wedged in here and there, the wealthiest, the middle class, and the lower middle class living side by side. Occasionally an expensive house cropped up in a neighborhood of workers' cottages. Carriage houses faced alleys in the finer neighborhoods, where David caught glimpses of a few men, mostly African American, grooming horses, moving bales of hay or shoveling manure. The brick pavement ended more or less where the fine houses did.

"Most of the street names are different," David said, looking up at a street sign.

Mary thought this through for a minute. "I suppose the names help us remember who was here first. Josiah Polk and William Conner laid out the town and claimed what would be the two main streets with their names. Then there were the land speculators—streets like Voss, Evans, Wild, and Leonard, for the men who cleared the land and platted the streets. Oh, and Civil War heroes like Grant, Sherman, Lincoln, and Logan. Some of the streets were named after the Indians who used to live around here, like Miami Street. You wouldn't expect it, but Anderson Street was named after a Delaware chief—William Anderson.

"It's rather nice, I suppose," she went on, tapping her parasol on the sidewalk with every second step. "These names have meaning—they connect the people here with important events and people. But what are the names in your time?"

"Well," David said, "somewhere in the years ahead most of the names get changed. The north-south streets are numbered, and the east-west streets are an odd assortment of old and new names. Names like Cherry and Harrison are apparently moved from one place to another."

He stopped at a corner and looked down a street that ended abruptly a block ahead, making a T at a cross street. "The numbering of streets would have made more sense if the city's plat better respected the old grid system, but it doesn't. Some streets like this one dead end into other streets, or jog fifty feet in one direction or another. Y'know, visually it's wonderful; the focal point of the end of a street is a lovely house—always a sense of destination. But because of it, the numbered streets of my time are confusing. When a newcomer searches for a logical pattern to the numbers, they're frustrated when a numbered street ends, only to be picked up elsewhere in town, or continues on half a block east or west."

Standing with his hands in his pockets, he shook his head, looking up at a lovely house that is gone in his time. "Historic identity traded in a foolish attempt at functionality," he said. "It's a pervasive metaphor."

Mary studied him carefully, admiring, if not the meaning, at least the sensitivity of his observation.

Unwittingly, he rudely walked on, leaving her standing there alone, no nod of the head to continue forward, no offer of his arm to help her down the curb—he just went on figuring she'd do the same. She shook her head and followed, relenting to his behavior, though gently exasperated. "You are a puzzle, Mr. Henry," she said, shaking her head.

He turned to her. "What do you mean by that? And anyway, please stop calling me Mr. Henry. That's my father. I'm David."

She tried to understand how a man so obviously intelligent could know so little about etiquette. "As I said, you are a puzzle."

They walked on.

Simple houses filled the outer areas of the town. David found it ironic that the vast majority of these had fared better in the twenty-first century than the handsome structures of the core. He saw a scattering of little one-story houses, obviously quite recent, on the west side of the Lake Erie & Western tracks.

Mary eyed them with disdain. "These shoddy little homes are going up to be rented to the workers coming to town to take jobs in the new factories."

"Still, they're not bad looking," David said, "especially when you consider that the twenty-first-century equivalent is a trailer park. That's little boxes … literally, little boxes like train cars with wheels, and with furniture and kitchens and bedrooms inside."

Mary wrinkled her nose, producing the first undisciplined expression he'd seen on her face. He was rude again, staring too long at her. Drawn out of his obsession with the buildings, he forgot time for a moment, taking in her astonishing beauty.

She finally turned and moved on, leaving him this time.

Nearly every neighborhood had a tiny grocery or general store located in long, narrow one-story buildings. Most neighborhoods also had a livery and a blacksmith's shop.

They were coming upon pockets of farmland here and there among the houses and stables. Corn and wheat grew in patches along the eastern ends of Morton and Monument streets, and there was a pasture with a herd of dairy cows just east of the Harrisons' houses on Emmous. Chickens, pigs, and the occasional cow were penned in backyards, mostly on the edges of town. But these patches of urban country were clearly disappearing. Mary told David that more than one hundred houses were under construction that spring and that the town's population was expanding rapidly.

Women in long dresses, their waists constricted by corsets, walked on the brick and plank sidewalks, passing men in overalls and manure-caked boots. Horses, mules, carriages, and bicycles moved along the streets. People climbed off and on trains that passed on the two lines. Children fished in the river, chased hoops down the street, or played marbles in a circle scratched in the dust.

As they approached the Harrison home, Mary asked, "So what do you think of this little town?"

David had picked up a stick and was tapping it along fences and swinging its end to slice off the feathered heads of dandelions in the lawns they passed. "This town looks like an old-fashioned, stereotypical American small town. I see them in TV commercials at Christmastime, and in old movies like 'It's a Wonderful Life' and 'The Music Man.' They've got one at Disney World: Main Street USA. They make little plastic models of them to sell in gift shops."

He stopped, realizing she couldn't understand his sarcastic references. He sighed heavily. "I guess I mean it's a kind of place that became a real visual stereotype in the century ahead."

"You say stereotype. What does that mean?"

"Trite?" he tried.

"Shopworn?"

"Yeah, but in a way that doesn't really express what it's all about. Superficial, you know?"

"I understand what you mean," she said. "It's just a picture people have in their minds."

They walked up the steps of the house and sat down wearily in a pair of wicker chairs.

David was still thinking about her question. "In an opening page of one of the textbooks I teach from is the line 'The past is a foreign country.' I guess that's what I think. This place is a foreign country. I've read about it and seen pictures of it, but never seen it in three dimensions until now. It's a beautiful place."

"I suppose it's not bad for a small town," Mary said, unconvinced.

"More than how it looks—also how it works. What are there, five thousand people living in one square mile or so? And they do everything here—work, church, entertainment, social life, all within walking distance."

"You find that rare?" she said, eyebrows raised.

"It is where I come from."

Later, David found himself back downtown, standing before the mirror in Tescher's clothing store. Mr. Tescher himself measured David from head to toe. The women tried out hats on his head and discussed fabrics.

"So they're actually going to make these clothes to fit me?" David said at one point.

"Of course," Anna replied. "What did you expect?"

"Well, I thought I might pick something off the rack."

"I can see our customs are somewhat different from yours in Canada," Mr. Tescher broke in gently. "You see, Mr. Henry, trousers off the rack will have a crease in them. This would give you away as a man without means; hardly an image I think you would want to project. You're obviously well educated, you're a business man—you really should look the part."

By the time the store closed at 5:30, David had ordered three suits, two hats, and an array of trousers and shirts. One suit came off the rack so he would have an immediate change of clothes. The other items were to be done in a week and delivered to the Harrisons' home.

The cellar was the only place where neighbors wouldn't hear the music. It had a damp, hard-packed dirt floor. The legs of the dining room chairs, carried downstairs for the occasion, scuffed the clay surface as the Harrisons took their seats around a wooden lemon crate set in the center. Here David unfolded the clamshell halves of the battery-powered speakers. Anna had said they were no bigger than two slices of bread. David pulled the phone from his pocket and handed it to Fred.

"That can't make music," Fred said, smiling and shaking his head, pinching the glass surfaces of the sleek device between two fingers. He was giddy, believing full well he would be proven wrong.

Fred bounced it in his hand, measuring its weight, than handed it to Mary. She handled it like fine bone china. "Don't be afraid of breaking it," David said, taking it and rapping it on his knee. "It's pretty damn strong."

"Let's start with Mozart," David said. He found the speaker cord and plugged it into the phone, woke it and launched the music app. Two coal-oil lamps cast their shadows softly against the brick foundation walls and wooden beams.

In a few seconds the soft, birdlike call of a clarinet lifted out of the silence and built to a melody. Mozart's Clarinet Concerto in A Major slowly filled the little earth-scented space. David smiled to see their wonder. The doctor stared intently at the glowing screen of the tiny machine. No one said a word. Even Clara's cough was stilled for the moment.

Fred couldn't actually appreciate the music; he was too amazed at the machine, smaller than any orchestral instrument but playing all the parts.

"You promised music from your time," Mary said when the piece had ended.

David pulled up a Nat King Cole playlist. "Stardust" began. The shimmering and melancholy, almost foreboding opening flourish of strings again brought smiles to the Harrisons' faces. When the smooth, deep voice rose out of a moment of stillness, *"And now the purple dusk of twilight time steals across the meadows of my heart,"* Mary put an elbow on her knee and bent forward, listening intently, staring at the little machine, as if by looking closely, she might understand it. *"High up in the sky, the little stars climb, always reminding me that we're apart."*

"I've never heard a voice quite like this," she whispered.

"You wander down the lane and far away, leaving me a song that will not die. Love is now the stardust of yesterday, the music of the years gone by."

"Strange, if you ask me," Fred said.

"Sometimes I wonder how I spend the lonely nights dreaming of a song. The melody haunts my reverie, and I am once again with you ..."

"I think it's the most beautiful voice I've ever heard," Mary whispered.

"... when our love was new, and each kiss an inspiration, but that was long ago, now my consolation is in the stardust of a song."

"What kind of music is this?" Harry asked.

"Beside a garden wall, when stars are bright, you are in my arms."

"Oh, I don't know, just a ballad, I guess," David said.

"The nightingale tells his fairytale, a paradise where roses grew. Though I dream in vain, in my heart it will remain, my stardust melody, the memory of love's refrain."

David turned it off. "Well, what do you think?"

"Unusual, but lovely somehow," Dr. Harrison said. "So this is what music in the next century is like."

"Some of it, but there's a lot more—and some of it, I'm afraid, you wouldn't like very much."

"Tell me about this song and the man who's singing it," Mary asked.

"It was written by a man from Indiana—in thirty or forty years. The singer was dead by the time I was born. He was popular in the 1940s and '50s. He was a black man."

"He's colored?" she asked. "His voice is so captivating. I've never heard any voice so naturally human and beautiful."

"My grandfather used to say that Nat King Cole had a voice like melted butter."

"Is there more in there by him?"

"About fourteen more, I think."

David restarted the app, flipping ahead to "Mona Lisa." They listened to several other songs until they were jolted into taking a break by one of Clara's coughing fits. Harry took her home and put her to bed. Dr. Harrison went along to take a closer look at her.

"I'm going to step out for some fresh air," Mary said.

David followed her out into the backyard. She stopped and leaned against the oak near the alley. Butch shuffled and snorted in the shed.

Loud young voices came up the alley: two barefoot boys with fishing poles and a basket full of fish. They passed by without seeing Mary beneath the tree in the darkness, or David standing a few feet away with his hands in his pockets.

Sophie emerged from behind the shed with a dead mouse in her mouth. She walked easily through the grass and stopped before David, dropping the mouse at his feet and staring at its lifeless body, then up at him. "That cat had never been allowed outside until she came here."

"Why?" Mary puzzled, kneeling down and scratching Sophie's head. "Good hunter," she cooed. "You kill those mice."

"I was always afraid she'd get hit by a car."

Mary looked up at him. "A carriage with an engine, right? But did she want out?"

"Yes, a carriage with an engine," David grimaced, realizing that simple description missed reality by a long shot. "And she did want out, very badly. She'd bolt out the door if she got a chance and immediately start rolling in the grass. I'd have to go find her and bring her back in."

"Well, she's a fish in water now." Mary picked up the mouse by the tip of the tail and flung it into the alley. Sophie darted after it.

David smiled and nodded.

Mary stood and returned to lean against the tree, looking out into the evening, where a few neighbors were still stirring, bringing in water from the pump or rocking slowly in a porch swing. "You've said some rather unpleasant things about life in your time," Mary began, without looking at David. "Yet, it's hard to imagine that a future with music so beautiful could be so bad."

"Did I say it was bad?"

"You didn't have to. I've gathered from the things you've said that you don't care much for the time in which you live. I mean, goodness, a cat isn't even safe outdoors."

"Oh, I don't know," he smiled. "It sure is prettier now. But I've gotten the same impression about you—that you don't much care for the time you come from."

Mary laughed self-consciously. "Yes, I suppose you're right. But it's really not the time so much that bothers me, it's the place. I'm having a difficult time adjusting to being home."

"Why?"

"Oh, don't be offended, but I don't really want to talk about it."

They both stood silent for a moment. "That song, 'Mona Lisa,' that's you—isn't it?" David said wistfully.

"I'm not sure I know what you mean," she replied.

" 'Are you warm, are you real, Mona Lisa, or just a cold and lonely, lovely work of art?' That's what the song says. After watching you yesterday and seeing so many young men come to talk to you and so many disappointed, it does make me wonder."

"Wonder what?" she said, irritation in her voice.

"What makes you tick, that's what I wonder. You're just like the Mona Lisa in the song. You're very lovely, but also somehow a mystery."

"Music apparently isn't the only thing that's changed in a hundred years," she said, crossing her arms. "If you're going to get on in 1893, you've got a lot to learn about manners."

David's eyes widened. "I'm sorry if I offended you."

"When you consider we just met," she said, turning sharply toward him and seeing her father step off the summer kitchen steps, "you're just a bit too forward. Just because you wonder something doesn't mean you need to say it."

She gathered up her skirt and headed back to the house.

"I'm really sorry," David called softly.

Dr. Harrison patted him on the shoulder and led him to the shed. "Did you make Mary mad?"

"I guess so."

"Don't feel too special," he said, laughing. "It's not hard to do."

The cigars were a bit much for David, but he didn't mind the nips of whiskey. They talked for a while. David shifted the conversation from talk of the future to talk of the past, pumping Dr. Harrison for Civil War stories.

"I was born in 1844 in Indianapolis and enlisted in the army after Fort Sumter, joining Company B in the Seventeenth Regiment of the Indiana Volunteer Infantry. I got shot in the leg, recovered, then reenlisted and took part in the Atlanta campaign in the summer of 1864. Later, I was at the battles: Chickamauga, Lookout Mountain, and Missionary Ridge. I was even there at the capture of Andersonville prison."

The doctor's stories seemed unreal to David, as if they'd been run through a romantic filter. There was no blood and guts, none of the awful misery of the Civil War. Instead it was all valor and patriotism, unity and fraternity. This drinking ritual, married with war stories, made him think of his grandfather. He felt almost as comfortable with the doctor as he had with Grandpa Henry.

Dr. Harrison finally tired of talking, and they sat in silence for several minutes.

"What's wrong with Clara?" David asked gingerly, breaking the stillness.

The doctor drummed his fingers on a nail barrel. "She's got pneumonia," he said quietly.

"Can you give her any medicine for it?"

"There isn't any medicine for pneumonia."

"Will she live?"

The doctor stared blankly ahead. "I'm afraid she won't live through the delivery of the baby. She's already having trouble breathing, and there's fluid in her lungs. In another month she'll be completely bedridden … or gone."

"There's nothing you can do?"

"No," he admitted, dropping his gaze ashamedly.

"Do the others know how bad it is?"

"They know. They've all seen it enough times—they've seen enough people die from it."

"I don't know anyone who's died from it," David said. "There must be a cure."

"Not in this time, there isn't."

David thought for a moment. "Maybe I can do something."

"What could you do? You're not a doctor."

"I'll go back through the beam tomorrow and do some checking. I have a friend who works for a drug company. It's possible I might be able to bring back something that could help her."

Dr. Harrison was incredulous. "If you could, it would be a miracle!"

He stood, stroking his beard, pacing back and forth in front of Butch. "Do what you can, David. If Harry loses his wife and baby, well …"

David and the doctor went back to the house and sat in the back parlor with the ladies. Anna was knitting and Mary sat reading an issue of *Cosmopolitan*. Dr. Harrison sat down in an armchair next to Anna's rocker.

David crossed to the couch and sat on the far end from Mary. "I'm sorry I offended you earlier," he said.

"It's all right," she said, putting down the magazine. "I'm sorry I snapped at you." Motioning to the magazine, she said, "I'm reading a story in here called 'A Traveler from Altruria.' It's about a man from a faraway land, where people live by different morals and ideas. He comes to America and is rather confused by the way people act. With that in mind, I should have been more patient."

David looked at the magazine. Its cover, red and black print on a white background, wasn't much like the *Cosmo* he knew. He flipped through the pages, eventually laughing to himself. "This is a literary magazine, right?"

"Yes," she said, "what's so funny?"

"It's a fashion magazine in my time. Every month there's a picture of a woman on the front with her … well, it's a fashion magazine."

The doctor had been talking softly to his wife. Suddenly, Anna spoke sharply to David. "You think you can cure Clara?"

"Well, I'm not sure," David said nervously. "I'll go back tomorrow and see what I can find out about pneumonia. I have a friend who works for a drug company. He can help me."

"That's wonderful," Mary said.

"Let's not get our hopes up," David said, picking up his bag and arranging his phone and speakers. "I'm afraid you'll put all your faith in me and I won't be able to find the solution."

"Why should it be so hard?" Anna asked. "If there's a cure, you get it and come back."

"It's not that simple. Drugs are controlled by the government. If they're very powerful, you have to have a doctor's permission to get them. My friend is a salesman for a drug company, and he gives samples to doctors. He can get them for me if I can figure out what I need. It's illegal, but I think I can do it."

"We'll be grateful for anything you can do," Anna said hopefully.

"I'll do my best."

He finished packing his carrying case, suddenly feeling an enormous sense of responsibility.

"I loved the music," Mary said. "I'm dying to hear more."

"Go ahead," David said, setting the phone on the couch in front of her.

"Oh, no," she said. "I wouldn't know what to do."

"It's easy. Take it upstairs with you tonight and listen if you like."

He laid the phone and earbuds on the cushion.

"What are these?" she asked.

"Put these in your ears." He helped her put the first one in and she managed the other one. "Now, put this little plug into this hole."

She did it without hesitation. He showed her how to activate the phone, which small tile launched the music app, and how to scroll among and choose songs. It opened where it had been left; the Nat King Cole playlist. She pressed "Stardust."

There it was again, that flourish of notes, the strings, that voice, that song—inside her head. She couldn't help smiling.

CHAPTER FIVE

The Hoosiers with whom we shall have to do are not those set forth by Eggleston, but the breed visible today in urban marketplaces, who submit themselves meekly to tailors and schoolmasters. There is always corn in their Egypt, and no village is so small but it lifts a smokestack toward a sky that yields nothing to Italy's. At the crossroads store, philosophers, perched upon barrel and soap-box, clinch in endless argument. In olden times the French voyageur, paddling his canoe from Montreal to New Orleans, sang cheerily through the Hoosier wilderness, little knowing that one day men should stand all night before bulletin boards in New York and Boston awaiting the judgement of citizens of the Wabash country upon the issues of national campaigns. The Hoosier, pondering all things himself, cares little what Ohio or Illinois may think or do. He ventures eastward to Broadway only to deepen his satisfaction in the lights of . . . Main Street at home.
A Hoosier Chronicle, Meredith Nicholson, 1912.

Early the next morning, David went along with Dr. Harrison to see Clara. They made no mention of a possible cure, saying only that David might be able to figure out something to help her. David waited in the parlor while the doctor examined her.

"She's breathing easily in the right lung," Dr. Harrison told David, "but I can hear a very labored breathing in the left." She told them that it hurt to lie on the good side; she felt better lying on the infected side. In the night she had begun coughing up mucus and had a fever that rose and fell. David returned to the doctor's house and passed through the beam.

David opened his laptop and Googled "pneumonia."

He quickly decided that the safest drug would be Amoxil. He had to find a drug made by Lilly, the company that his friend Jeremy worked for.

He noticed that the antibiotic was prescribed for ear infections. That would be his lie. He called Jeremy's mobile number from his cell phone.

"Hey, dude," Jeremy said in his best mock surfer-boy accent. "What's happenin'?"

"I was getting ready to go out of town for a while, but I found out this morning I've got an ear infection. The doctor prescribed Amoxil. Can you get me that?"

"We don't make that one, but I got something even better, a real ass-kicking antibiotic called Keflex."

"Will that cure all the same stuff that Amoxil will?"

"Yeah."

"Like pneumonia and stuff?"

"Well, it's not officially approved for pneumonia, but it'll do it, no problem."

"Can you get me some today?"

"I'm in town now. I'll drop it by your house in an hour."

"Thanks a lot, man, you've saved me a few bucks. Just stick it in my mailbox."

"You can't tell anybody I gave them to you, okay?" Jeremy cautioned. "I'd lose my job."

"I won't tell anybody. Give me a lot, okay? Sometimes I forget to keep taking antibiotics after I feel better, and then it comes back and I have to start all over again. And, hey, I've got another question, since I'm taking something I don't know anything about—does it have any side effects?"

"You're not gonna have any problems."

"So it's even safe for pregnant women?"

"I'm not allowed to tell any doctor that it's safe during pregnancy, because of liability issues, but it's safe. Why, you pregnant?"

"Yeah, right. Thanks, man!"

David Googled "Keflex" on his phone, took a screen shot of the side effects list, then plugged in his phone to charge.

He paced the room for a moment, realizing he had to wait for Jeremy, when a thought seized him. He pulled his car out of the garage and drove to the library. He had to travel down congested East Conner Street, lined with fast food restaurants, grocery stores, gas stations, car washes and liquor stores, each with its own sprawling parking lot. With no sidewalks in the area, he couldn't have walked there, and he mused that children couldn't, either.

He entered the building and looked up the atrium stairway. The Indiana Room. Something told him he shouldn't, but he did.

He went to the gray obituary index cabinet and quickly found Albert R. Harrison. Died November 5, 1913. He went to the microfilm files for the *Noblesville Ledger* of that year.

An uneasy feeling crept over him as he fast-forwarded the reel on the reader, watching the blur of dates and headlines. It felt like reading someone's diary, as if knowing his new friends' future was an invasion of privacy. But here he was, opening the pages.

Dr. Harrison's obituary offered few surprises: prominent physician, community leader, good Christian, former county auditor, Civil War veteran, member of the G.A.R. and Knights of Pythias. But in the list of survivors, Harry was missing. And Mary was listed as "Mary Wainwright."

So Robert Wainwright succeeds, David thought.

Back at the file cabinet he made notes. Anna Harrison, May 12, 1917. Harold Harrison, January 7, 1911. Fred Harrison, June, 23, 1921. Mary Wainwright, August 12, 1939.

Back at the microfilm machine, he read that Harry died of consumption—tuberculosis—in 1911. Anna died of "old age." Dr. Fred Harrison fell victim to appendicitis two years after returning from France, where he had headed a field hospital during the Great War. He was survived by his wife, Katie Conwell Harrison, and their daughter, Elizabeth. Mary died from heart failure at the age of sixty-seven. She was survived by three children and many grandchildren. David read: "She was preceded in death by her husband, Robert Wainwright, whom she married in 1898, and her eldest son, Robert Jr., who was killed in France during the Great War."

Still interested, and with a curious pang of jealousy, he switched to an older reel and searched through 1898 newspapers for a notice of Mary's wedding. He found it in June: a pleasant ceremony in the home of Dr. Albert and Anna Harrison on South Catherine Street.

An elderly woman passed behind him and set a stack of notebooks down on the table. She peered over his shoulder as he read.

"Mary Wainwright? She was a lovely woman."

"You knew her?" David asked, turning around.

"Yes, many years ago when I was a young girl and she was an elderly lady. My best friend, Edith, was her granddaughter. Edith's family lived in the big old Harrison place that used to be on Ninth Street. Grandma Mary lived with them. I used to see her often when I was a girl. She had a wonderful sense of humor. I always thought of her as this wise old bird. Of course, I'm older now than she was then! Are you a Harrison or a Cottingham?"

"Neither," David replied. "I'm restoring a house on Cherry Street that Mary Harrison lived in for a short time in 1893 with her parents and brother Fred. I was just trying to find out a thing or two about them."

"You really should go to see Edith—she could tell you a lot."

"Where does she live?"

"Well, she lives on South Tenth Street and is doing real well. I visit her every week."

"What did you say her last name was?" David asked.

"Edith Cottingham. Go see her, she'd love to have a visitor."

"Thanks, I'll do that," David said, jotting down the name and address.

On the way home, as if still being driven against his will, David turned left at the government-subsidized housing project at the corner of Monument Street and pulled into the cemetery, near the Civil War monument. The graveyard appeared packed with stones, compared with what he had seen a few days before. There had been more than a hundred and twenty years of dying since then.

Up and down the lanes he crept in the truck, past the Wild plot, the Teschers, Boyds, Bushes and Craigs. Finally, a large, bulbous gray stone inscribed "Harrison" came into view.

In the foreground were smaller stones: Anna and Dr. Albert R., Harry and Clara, Dr. Fred and Katherine. He imagined the 1913 scene of Dr. Harrison's funeral. Harry was already dead. Anna, Clara, Mary and her husband, Fred and his wife, each weeping and knowing that places were reserved there for them, and that someday others would stand and weep as they were lowered in and the dirt was thrown on top.

The cemetery made him uneasy. Nothing, in fact, made him more uneasy than death and dying. The only person close to him who had died was his grandfather. He had never seen a dead body before that. Seeing all the stereotyped images of death played out around the corpse of the man he loved most in his life was as foreign as a walk on the moon. He had to view the body in the coffin, had to ride to the cemetery, had to hear "Yea, though I walk through the valley of the shadow of death." He had to see the coffin being lowered into the ground. But he threw no handful of dirt on the casket. Nobody does that anymore, he thought to himself.

He stood with his hands in his pockets, trembling, wanting to be anywhere else.

But where was Mary's grave?

David finally went across town to the Riverside Cemetery and drove slowly around until he spotted a huge stone marker inscribed "Wainwright." Beside it was a six-foot-tall gray stone carved in the shape of a tree with its branches cut off. A smooth, shield-shaped panel on the trunk bore the inscription "Mary Wainwright." David shivered as he remembered her lovely form, her slender waist and the sensual billow of her skirts as she walked. And now she was dead, rotted away in a box underground.

He sped away. At home he found two Lilly display boxes stuck between the screen and the front door, with a note from Jeremy saying "Have a good time."

David decided he shouldn't take the labeled boxes back. Each display box held many small packets. He opened each one and popped the pills into a small brown paper bag.

Back through the beam.

There Mary sat, alone on the couch in the front parlor, Harper's Bazaar in her lap. She wasn't dead and buried. Colored light washing through the front window bathed her simple beige skirt and pale blue shirtwaist.

With a bright smile she laid the magazine on the side table and stood up. "Have you done it?"

David held up the bag.

In less than a half hour they had retrieved Dr. Harrison and Harry from downtown. Both of them read the side effects captured on David's phone. They found an empty medicine bottle for the pills, and the four of them went to see Clara.

"I don't want to take any medicine," she said. She was lying on a couch in the gloomy front parlor, propped up on a pillow, her body convulsed with each deep, rattling cough. Her skin was sickly pale, and her eyes red from the tearing brought on by coughing fits.

"I believe these pills will cure you," David said.

"Pills don't cure people," Clara moaned. "They hurt more than they help. They're sold by charlatans."

"Dear," Harry said, kneeling down beside her and taking her hand, "there isn't much choice right now. If you don't take the pills, there's only one way for this to end. I don't want to lose you."

"These won't hurt you," David said. "I promise. If you feel worse in a week, stop taking them."

"You're sure they won't make me feel worse?"

"The odds are against it," he said.

"If you don't take them," Dr. Harrison added, "the odds are very strong that you'll die. Without a quick cure, even if by some miracle you live, your baby may not."

She sat silent for a moment, staring out the window and then up at Mary. "I'd thought of that, actually," she whispered, tears welling up in her eyes.

"What do I do?" she asked with a sigh, turning toward David.

"Take one of these four times a day," David said, holding the bottle up. "You mustn't forget. When you start to feel better, you mustn't stop taking them. You have to take them until they're all gone."

"Why? If I feel better, doesn't that mean I'm cured?"

"Almost. You see, there's a microscopic, infectious organism in your lungs. It's called bacteria and it's the thing that's making you so sick. Your body's natural defenses are trying to fight it off but aren't strong enough. This drug will help, it will slowly destroy the bacteria. Yet, once you start to feel better, some of the bacteria may still be present. If you stop taking the drug before all the bacteria are gone, they may come back again. What's worse, at that point the bacteria may come back stronger than ever, with some resistance to the drug. So you have to keep taking it even after you feel better."

Within a week of beginning the medicine, Clara was feeling much better, though she still had congestion in her lungs. As her condition improved, the Harrisons began to treat David as a miracle worker.

On a sunny June afternoon, he took up Harry on his offer to see how his dentistry office was run.

Harry's office was in the tall, narrow Joseph Building on the square. David paused to admire the sandstone facade and ornate carved ornament, including a balustrade across the top. Harry's office looked out on the square from a large second-story window with arched corners. The floors were narrow oak planks. The fourteen-foot ceiling was clad in pressed tin in a basket-weave pattern.

During a lull between patients, David and Harry sat at the front window and watched the crowds move on the sidewalks and the trains pass along Polk Street. The enormous front sash was open, letting the breeze and street sounds in.

"Will you get involved in politics like your dad?" David asked.

"Oh, no," Harry grimaced. "Not for me, thanks."

"Why not? Fred seems interested and enthusiastic, and your dad is successful."

"Fred's young and naive. He doesn't know yet what it's all about. He hears the patriotic speeches and thinks it's all about making the world a better place."

"And it's not?"

"I don't know what politics in your time is like, but now it's corrupt as hell and there's no way to be involved unless you're willing to do certain things that, well, I'd rather not do."

"I know from my studies that national politics is pretty corrupt right now," David said, "but I always assumed that at the local level, since the people are more involved, it's cleaner—especially in a small town like this."

"It stinks from top to bottom, Mr. Henry. It's not about being a patriot, it's about who's in charge and who benefits from it, even here in our little town."

"Do you mean your father, too?" David asked, shocked.

"Well … Dad's not a crook, but I expect from time to time he does things that aren't exactly right. He does it to help the Republican Party, or to hurt the Democrats."

Harry sat back and surveyed the street below. "When I was growing up, I saw my dad as this great character. He fought in the war. As a doctor he saved people's lives, he was very patriotic and instilled beliefs in me that I always felt were right: moral virtues, republican principles. It all made sense to me, and I was proud of it. But when I got older I started to see how easily adults cheat on the lessons they teach children."

"It seems like a lot of good and bad can exist side by side in a person," David said.

"Ain't that the truth," Harry said with a sigh.

Saturday mornings, Noblesville was crowded with people. Farm families came to town for shopping and socializing. The streets were full of horses pulling every manner of four-wheeled vehicle. People had come to call at the Harrisons' often during the week, but on Saturday afternoon, they appeared in a constant stream. They sat in the front parlor or on the front porch, sipping lemonade and talking. Sometimes Dr. Harrison harnessed Butch to the carriage and Anna and Mary would go visit other ladies.

Saturday night was the peak of socializing downtown. The drugstore soda fountain overflowed with people. Others relaxed on sidewalk benches in front of stores or on the courthouse lawn. Street vendors hawked roasted peanuts and taffy. Children played at the river, fishing and wading in the water.

David loved it. He tagged along with Fred now, meeting people and talking. There were several saloons downtown where the men played pool and cards. A curious pastime was sitting at the depot to watch people and trains come and go, a kind of vicarious travel.

On Sundays, David went with the Harrisons to the Methodist Episcopal Church. It had the only pipe organ in town, played by a pretty young woman named Katherine Conwell. Katie captivated Fred. Knowing they would one day marry, David watched the early stages of their romance with delight. Others joked and speculated about them, but David knew.

On the second Sunday, while the organ played and the choir sang, David looked around at the congregation and thought how familiar the faces already were to him. In just over two weeks he had seen most of these faces regularly. Already, he felt more a part of this community than he had ever felt anywhere. In his own time he had many friends, but he had to make an effort to maintain friendships. These people, though, worked, played, and worshipped with one another, every day. You couldn't really get away from your neighbors, and they couldn't get away from you. It seemed to him that this created an enormous sense of community, and required constant civility.

David felt right; he felt at home and at peace. Of course, he knew it wasn't all springtime and lemonade. In this time, life was harder and more inconvenient. Disaster could hit harder. The people weren't insulated from hardship any more than they were from the central Indiana weather—one hundred steamy degrees on a summer day, and twenty below on a dry, snow-blown winter night in the same year. Joy and sadness seemed less like distant poles at the turn of the millennium. Like the weather on an island, David's people were insulated by a surrounding ocean of amusement, physical comfort, and quick fixes.

On David's first Sunday in Noblesville, Anna invited Robert Wainwright to sit between her and Mary at church. On the second Sunday, Robert came to the house to call in the afternoon. Politeness required that Mary sit with him the entire afternoon, whether she wanted to or not. She was polite, but, as always, distant. David stayed scarce when Robert was around, but at least once Robert sought him out to talk.

David began to notice the tug-of-war that simmered between Mary and her parents. They expected her to marry and to stay in Noblesville. This required that she behave with propriety and show interest in the people and community in which she would raise her family. She defied them regularly, unswayed by Robert Wainwright, his family money, and the power his grandfather wielded in the community. She made it clear who would decide for Mary. She made it clear without saying so, but with aloof independence.

That Sunday evening after Robert Wainwright left, Mary went out on the porch with a book by Emerson. David was there unlatching a shutter and swinging it back and forth on the hinges. She sat in a wicker chair and watched him raising the louvers up and down. He latched and unlatched the sill hook, lifted the shutter off its hinges and then settled it back. He ran his hand along the dark green louvers.

"What's so interesting about a shutter?" Mary asked.

"In little more than a hundred years there's probably only two or three houses left in town that have any real shutters like this," he said, swinging it open and latching it back in place. "People have shutters on houses, but mostly they're made out of plastic and don't really work. Kind of silly when you think about it—I mean, why put 'em up?"

"I don't really understand why you're so fascinated with things like that, with the houses and the town."

"You take this town for granted," he said, sitting down in the porch swing opposite her. "You haven't seen the alternatives; they haven't happened yet."

"I don't know if I take it for granted, and I have seen alternatives. Perhaps I see this little town for what it is."

"And what is that?" he asked.

"Oh, well, it's about the same as any other town its size in this part of the country. More important, from my perspective, it's a place where everything is set out for you—what's expected, what you'll become ..."

"And Bryn Mawr was different?"

He half-expected she'd say again that she didn't want to talk about it. Finally she spoke.

"I could be what I wanted to be there. There weren't such narrow expectations. Here, everybody knows who you are and what they expect you should do. When I was young, that made me feel comfortable, like I belonged. My house wasn't just my home, the whole town felt like home. Now, I just feel trapped.

"I think of what Emerson writes," she said, patting the back of the open book. "I don't want to be defined simply by the fact that I was born and raised in this town. The definition of me becomes the doing of someone else. I want to define myself based upon how I see the world, how I feel inside. In our society people are defined by their economic contribution, so a woman is judged by her father or husband. If I stay here, I have no chance to learn or to define myself beyond the daughter of Dr. Albert R. Harrison and the eventual wife of someone. It's not that those two things are so bad; it's just that those definitions are out of my hands, and the other choices that remain are so narrow.

"A larger city provides anonymity—and therefore the chance to be myself."

"Anonymity comes at a price," David said.

"I'd be willing to pay it."

"You and I are funny. You want what I have and I want what you have, yet it's not within our power to trade."

She tilted her head and looked at him with a curious warmth. "Are you so anonymous in your time? You have friends, don't you?"

"Sure I do. But in my time it seems like every person's house is an island. People travel from island to island in their cars. We live out much of our lives in our cars or in our houses and don't really socialize with one another the way you folks do. We don't really live out our lives in public spaces.

"People don't come and go from my house on visits, and I don't bump into my friends on the street very often. Most people don't walk down the street anymore; they walk through malls and parking lots. I hardly know who my neighbors are, and if I want to get together with a friend we call each other on the phone and plan it. We don't just drop in when we're passing our friend's houses.

"Sometimes I think the best friend any of us has is the television, or our cell phones. What families do together for the most part is watch television. They don't spend hours talking and reading and playing parlor games the way you people do."

"A sense of community—is that what this town represents to you?" she asked.

"Yes!"

"Perhaps because it's so much a part of small-town life that I didn't see it as special," she said. "But, on the other hand, everybody knows your business, and they don't mind talking about it and there's an enormous pressure to conform. I imagine that the people of Noblesville thought it pretentious of me to attend Bryn Mawr at all. I didn't just wait here to get married.

"But I didn't want to be pretentious, I just wanted to get away. Perhaps my father thought sending me to college would raise the family in people's esteem. That's his style—look at the way he wired this little house up for a telephone! My point is, everything you do in a small town is done under a microscope.

"You see," she raised an eyebrow, "a sense of community comes with a price."

"I'd be willing to pay it," David said firmly.

Her smile broadened, and she looked off across Emmous Street. "Touché," she whispered. They sat in silence for a minute or two, listening to the evening riot of birds gathering in the trees.

"You make the future sound awful," she said, turning back toward him, "yet I can't wait for it."

"If I were you I'd try a little harder to appreciate what's all around you," David said.

"And I'll offer that advice right back to you," Mary said, turning the book over. "Think of it the next time you go through the beam. If it wasn't for the miracles of the future, Clara would be dying right now instead of getting better."

"Touché," he said. "That's the catch. I never said what I wanted was reasonable; I want the best of my time and this time."

"As you said, it's not within our power."

"I think I have some vague notion of what you want," David said, "but I'd be interested to hear you say it. What is it exactly that you want out of life?"

She closed her book again and stared down at the back cover for a moment, wrinkling her brow in thought. Finally she took a deep breath and said, "I have a friend from school named Helen Garrison. She lives in a very nice suburb of Chicago. I suppose I want what she has. The world is at her fingertips; the arts, education, culture, society. I want Helen's life. I want a grand house in a grand city. I want the opera and symphony and theater and museums to be a part of my life. I want a life filled with the richness of cultural beauty and passion. I want excitement." She paused and turned away from him. "I suppose that makes me shallow."

"No," he said simply, "that's not shallow at all."

On a day when he had passed through the beam to make sure his other life was in order, David drove through Noblesville. He stopped outside the Corner Drug Store and looked up at the scaffolding surrounding the courthouse. The restoration progressed. There was no time to be read at the top of the tower—the clock faces were still out for repair. On the courthouse lawn, the dormers were being rebuilt. Piles of brick, cast concrete and slate were stacked among heavy machinery.

He looked over his shoulder at the drugstore. It had been in business now for over a hundred years, and you could still get prescriptions filled there. Where the Saturday night crowds had once laughed around the soda fountain, workers from downtown offices now gathered for coffee and conversation around two vending machines and a couple of tables.

Out of curiosity he drove down past the People's Trust to see what the bank was doing with the old Diana Theater building. Jane Harding's e-mails and phone messages said they were proceeding with plans to tear it down.

Why would the People's Trust, the new out-of-state owners, want to demolish it? Did they just want to block the locally owned, up-and-coming Noblesville Bank and Trust from doing business in it?

Just a month earlier, David would have stayed awake at night, fuming about the loss of the solid old theater and constructing conspiracy scenarios. But today, all his energy was firmly focused on the past.

CHAPTER SIX

"What can labor do for itself? Labor can organize, it can unify, it can consolidate its forces. This done, it can demand and command."
Eugene V. Debs at the Chicago World's Fair,
August 30, 1893.

"The people of every land, whether industrialized or not, admire the aspirations and accomplishments of American labor, which they have heard about, and which they long to emulate."
Wendell Willkie

"The intergenerational poverty that troubles us so much today is predominantly a poverty of values."
Dan Quayle

David's medicine saved Clara's life in a grand flourish—something that Dr. Harrison had never managed in his professional life. As a young doctor in rural Marion County in the late 1860s, he'd dreamed of miraculous cures, but he soon discovered that medicine did not work that way. Success was measured in small comforts given, and rarely lives saved.

He had received public credit for saving Clara's life, but when someone complimented him in David's presence, he merely said, "I take no credit for the mercy of God."

But he came to treat David as a peer. The effect of his respect on David was enormous. Like many young men in their twenties, David hadn't really stopped seeing himself as a carefree student. He knew he was a grown man, but he lacked confidence. Respect was something his family and students rarely seemed to accord him with any sincerity.

That this respected pillar of the community respected him filled his heart with that missing confidence. For the first time in his life, David felt like an adult.

Dr. Harrison started asking David along on his house calls. David helped deliver a baby and set a broken arm. When Dr. Harrison advised a man that he had high blood pressure, David took the doctor aside and told him to have the man stop using salt and to reduce the fat in his diet.

In his third week in the past, David was invited to join Fred and the doctor at the Knights of Pythias meeting at their lodge hall downtown.

They reached the lodge by climbing a long staircase from a door in the center of the hardware store building on the north side of the square. At the top was a large, inviting vestibule, furnished with comfortable leather chairs. At each end of the space double pocket doors stood open, revealing the rooms beyond. Behind a third set of double doors was a cloakroom, lined with hooks and wooden lockers; there many of the men David had already met were donning ceremonial robes.

David stepped away into the darkened room that faced the street and gazed at the magnificent space, one of the largest single rooms in the city. Over the entrance, the words "Bernice Lodge—Castle Hall" were painted in cursive script with a stenciled border. Once he stepped inside, his eyes were immediately drawn to the ornate tin ceiling, painted gold. In the center was a diamond-shaped medallion in deep relief; near each corner, smaller diamonds broke the stippled background. The ceiling met the wall in a wide arching cornice, extending down to the chair rail; the wall was covered with more modestly embossed tin. There was a piano in one corner near a podium and several massive ceremonial chairs. Brass wall-mounted gas fixtures dotted the perimeter at eye level.

On the far wall hung three immense horizontal oak frames, each one with a word in gilt: Friendship, Charity, Benevolence—the cardinal virtues of the Pythians. As in all rooms finely outfitted for the best occasions in this time, the curtains were drawn and the space kept dark when not in use.

"Pretty impressive, huh?" Fred's voice came from the doorway.

"Yeah."

"It's not customary to let nonmembers attend meetings or witness ceremonies. You'll have to wait out here while the grand pooh-bah puts us through our paces. Since you're a guest from another country, they've agreed to let you socialize when we're done."

"That's fine," David said.

The men in their robes disappeared into the large ceremonial room in the rear of the building. David walked about the cavernous room, examining the furniture and decor. Finally he found a box of wooden matches in the sideboard and lit a wall sconce.

A moment later, a well-dressed man appeared in the vestibule. He spotted David against the soft gaslight and approached him. "Still doing the old pomp and circumstance, are they?" he quipped.

"Yes, I suppose so."

"E.J. Pennington," said the lanky, dark-haired stranger, extending his hand.

His accent was clipped and crisp, yet David thought it sounded a bit artificial, like a Midwesterner trying to sound East Coast. He had an air of refinement that made David feel inferior. He pulled a pair of glasses from a vest pocket and wrapped the wire stems behind his ears.

"You're the Canadian I've heard about," Pennington said.

"Yes, I suppose so," David said, feeling foolish.

"Well then, we are both strangers to these parts."

"You're from where?"

"Back East," Pennington said, fastidiously taking his watch from a vest pocket and checking the time. "I'm here on business. I'm an inventor of sorts. I and some other investors are getting ready to establish an electric railway through the gas belt."

"Fascinating," David said. "What a project!"

"Oh, yes, it will be quite fantastic. We'll start here in Noblesville, go south to Indianapolis, and then northeast to Anderson and Muncie.

Once we have the gas belt connected, we'll head up to Chicago."

David recalled old pictures of Ninth Street he'd seen hanging behind the prescription counter in the Corner Drug Store. In them, two lines of track ran down the street, and passengers were boarding a car.

Pennington went on for forty-five minutes, describing an electric heater he had invented that would be placed in each rail car. He listed other patents he had applied for that would make this new technology profitable and forever transform central Indiana.

As the meeting adjourned in the other room, Pennington finished his promotional conversation with an offer. "A well-educated man such as yourself would be a welcome investor. We'd love to have you aboard. We've just set up an office two blocks over on South Catherine." He pulled a card from his vest pocket and slid it across the table to David. "If you'd like to get in on the ground floor of the biggest thing ever to hit Indiana, stop by and we'll set you up."

"Thanks," David said, taking the card and rubbing his thumb along the raised print.

The pocket doors opened at the other end of the vestibule and the Pythians filed out, hanging their robes back up in the cloakroom. The two outsiders were motioned into the ceremonial room. David was amused to see a whiskey barrel brought out from behind a serving counter and a big glass jar of cigars opened. Men split into various groups. Some sat down to a game of cards, while others sat chatting.

Fred told a story about a tramp who wandered into town that day. A policeman had asked him his business and when he said he had none, the officer escorted him to the city limits and suggested he not return.

The men in the circle laughed.

"What do you make of the tramp question, Mr. Henry?" Robert Wainwright asked, before gently placing a cigar in his mouth and taking a long drag.

"Well, it seems to me they're pretty convenient scapegoats. I guess they deserve pity more than anything else."

"You must be kidding," scoffed Major Wainwright, Robert's father. "Pity indeed! Lazy rabble rousers, if you ask me."

The major was nearly seventy years old, a big man with a barrel chest and an oval face. He spat the words out as if David were too big a fool to bother with. His white hair was receding, and a bushy white mustache hung over his lip and spread wide past his cheeks, drooping to a point at the ends. His perpetual costume: black coat and trousers, black vest, bow tie, and crisp white shirt. He was often seen around the courthouse square with his work pen wedged atop his ear. He was Noblesville's favorite and most powerful old-timer, a Civil War hero, founder of his own bank and owner of a great farm. His house, a large Gothic Revival built after his return from the war, sat in the country at the north end of Anderson Street, just before it turns and crosses Potter's covered bridge.

"Most of these tramps," David began, reciting a lecture he'd given his students two years straight about labor unrest in the 1880s and 1890s, "as you call them, were workers not long ago. When the economy went bad, their wages were slashed and their hours increased. When a worker could no longer feed his family, he demanded higher wages. For that, he got fired, and all because he asked for what he deserves. I think a little pity would go a long way."

Pennington, who just moments earlier had seemed uninterested, leaned forward.

"We've been hearing this soft-hearted moralizing from the Populists," the major sneered. "But a philosophy like that goes against the laws of nature."

"That's right," William Locke agreed matter-of-factly.

"You see," continued Major Wainwright, "that Darwin fella, as confused as he was about men being monkeys ..." The group laughed. "... was on to something: survival of the fittest." He shook his finger in the air. "In every avenue of human activity, men compete for success. The wise and righteous succeed, the incompetent and the fools lose. The winners naturally make up the upper class. To the winner goes the spoils, as they say. What would you have us do, bankrupt the U.S.A. to pay the poor some sort of unemployment pension, or bankrupt the company by paying them higher wages?"

"I'd do one or the other, but I'm not sure it would mean bankruptcy," David said.

"Consider this, Mr. Henry," the major said, pulling a silver dollar from his pocket. "If I drop this coin, it falls, right?" He dropped the coin on the table.

"Yes, I've heard of gravity," David said sarcastically.

"It's a simple law of nature," the major continued, "and so is the tramp's condition. The government and the company can't fix the tramp's problems any more than I can reverse gravity."

"So you're saying that even if the government has a surplus of funds it shouldn't try to relieve the misery of unemployed people, and that the company owner and stockholders shouldn't give up a penny of their riches to give the workers a little more money?"

"Oh, they could relieve some misery for a while, but where would it end? Bankruptcy! And I'm not so sure these men work so hard. If they did, they wouldn't be out of work."

Several in the group nodded in agreement.

"The situation," Mr. Locke put in, "while regrettable, is somewhat based on divine law. Why would God make some rich and some poor? Those who have been blessed with the best faculties—cleverness, a desire to work hard, and moral rectitude—these men prosper. Those who are lazy and like to cause trouble end up poor. Isn't it really just as God ordains?"

Heads nodded in agreement. Only Robert Wainwright scowled at Locke's words before giving David a sympathetic smile.

David was incredulous. "You mean to say you believe it's ordained by God that the rich are rich and the poor are poor?"

"Well … yes!" Locke said, taken aback.

David took a deep breath and looked down at the floor, wondering if there was any point in arguing. He searched his mental teaching notes about the Gilded Age.

"Do you know," he began, "that your state and national politicians, Republicans and Democrats alike, are crooked as hell? Votes are bought and sold. Senators buy stock in the railroads and then pass laws that help make the railroads rich. Is their wealth ordained by God? They're no better than thieves, and you say that wealth, by definition, is righteous?

"And the industrialists you love so much? Many, no doubt, are good men—but many of them are parasites. Look at how the average company town works! A man is hired and given a house to rent. The only place to buy food or clothes is at the company store, where they give the worker a line of credit. Then there's a downturn like we're having now, and wages are lowered. The company doesn't lower the price of food at the store, or the rent. Now the worker, who before could just barely afford to live, can't. He gets behind on his rent, is in debt to the company store, while he's working longer hours for less money. He becomes a virtual slave to the company. He can't leave, he's in debt, he's living in misery.

"And what is the owner of the company doing at the same time? Building another lavish country mansion, buying a yacht, and throwing parties! No wonder the worker, the one who's creating all that wealth with his hands, gets angry and protests. He's fired, and then the company owners blacklist him. He ends up wandering from town to town looking for work, and because he ends up in Noblesville looking less than desirable, the police escort him to the city limits.

"This is ordained by God!? In church I was always taught 'Do unto others as you would have them do unto you,' not, 'Take every poor sucker for all you can.' I think the tramp's condition has a lot more to do with greed than it does with the Bible." He looked around the group. Few seemed moved.

"And what about the mills and factories men like you own stock in? Lots of these businesses employ children and work them ten to fourteen hours a day for pennies. They're the children of those tramps and immigrants who you think are poor because they're lazy. Are you telling me that you wouldn't give up the price of a few expensive cigars from your dividends," David gestured with his cigar, "to give a childhood back to those kids? Child labor in this country is a disgrace, and regular people who go to church profit from it."

"There's a lot of misery in this world," Major Wainwright boomed, thrusting his cigar at David, "and there always will be! You have to accept that, sad as it may be. We can't destroy what's good in this world in some soft-hearted though well-intentioned attempt to fix what's wrong."

"I'm not saying we should destroy anything," David said, exasperated. "But isn't charity one of the things you men here claim to believe in?" He pointed up to the sign on the wall. "At the very least, wouldn't showing compassion for these people instead of contempt be the most honorable way to behave?"

"Listen, Mr. Henry," the major replied, "that may be how you Canadians see things. But our country has been far more successful than yours when it comes to putting a dollar in a man's pocket. That's what feeds a family. We Americans have made things happen and have prospered because of it. Isn't that good for families? Doesn't that feed people? I can't feed every poor fool that comes along or I'd end up poor myself. I've worked hard and earned my way, and I didn't go out on strike every time things didn't fall into my lap. I earned it, I'm proud of it, and I'm not sorry that I live comfortably.

"And you mentioned immigrants. A foreigner like you who can pay his way is welcome in America, as far as I'm concerned. But some of these pope-lovers and garlic-eaters come here and expect everything to just be handed to 'em. Turn 'em away, is what I say."

The major shoved the cigar back in his mouth and crossed his arms on his chest. Dr. Harrison shot David a speaking look, as if to say, "Let it drop. The major rules the roost, and that's the way folks like it."

"If I might be allowed to say so," E.J. Pennington broke in meekly, clearing his throat, "there is truth in what both of you say. The poor are given a very difficult lot in life, and we must admit that we often are not as charitable as we might be. But on the other hand, weren't most of us here poor once, or at least our parents were? And wasn't that poverty overcome by hard work?" Men in the group nodded in agreement. "That's the ticket—hard work. I say clear the way for the capitalist to do his work, and he will make things happen and give work to the poor. Making the way for the poor man to help himself is perhaps the most successful kind of charity I know of."

David was not moved. "We'll have to agree to disagree," he said. "Your theory would work if the capitalist is …"—he picked the word up off the wall—"benevolent. But in practice that's seldom the case. The argument you made is often used by capitalists as a smokescreen. Many capitalists will argue for free trade and competition while they destroy both for their own gain, and many others will claim to be helping the poor by creating wealth, when in fact the opposite is true—they create wealth by exploiting the poor."

Pennington seemed wounded for a moment, but then smiled knowingly. "I will prove you wrong, Mr. Henry. I am going to hire a lot of those tramps and give them jobs building my electric railway. I won't give handouts," he said, his eyes wide, a finger raised high, "but if they work hard they'll earn their way and be tramps no more."

"As long as you pay them a fair wage for their hard work, I'll have no complaint," David said.

Pennington puffed complacently on his cigar, and the conversation turned to the proposed railway.

"Fred told me that you had a bit of an argument with Major Wainwright last night," Mary said the next morning, with uncharacteristic approval. David was slouched in a parlor chair, reading her Cosmopolitan magazine.

"Yes, I guess I did."

"Good," she said, "the old pompous fool could stand to be knocked down a few pegs."

"I'm not sure anyone else there would agree he got knocked down at all," David said, running a hand through his hair. "I expect most of them think I got the worst of it."

"Yes, but according to what Fred told me, you were right."

"You think I was right?"

"I certainly do! But I'm surprised to hear that you feel that way. So few people around here do."

"And where did your enlightened point of view come from?" David asked, not recognizing how belittling the question sounded to her.

"At college, I guess," she said almost apologetically, then with more enthusiasm added, "and from a wonderful book that you really should read. It's called 'Looking Backwards.' I have a copy you could read."

"Sure."

He went on reading the magazine, only half-noticing that she was looking at him. The way he was slouching in the chair, ankle on his knee, was the kind of thing that offended Anna. "He's not respectful when a lady enters the room," she had remarked to Mary. But Mary was beginning to like his casual posture and gestures. They suggested independence and confidence.

Mary was finding David increasingly attractive as the days wore on. She didn't pretend to understand his obsession with houses and their construction, or his interest in the habits of small-town America, but she liked his views about other things. His lack of self-importance and disarmingly straightforward talk made her want to express things that propriety and convention usually required be kept silent.

She thought David was attracted to her as well, but there were too many mysteries about him to be certain. The music he brought and the little machine that played it, the medicine that was saving Clara's life, the amazing things he knew about the future—it was all suggestive of things about which Mary could only guess.

She dreamed of the future: inventions that would let you fly, machines that would bring the theater into your home. In the future, she thought, the dust and grime of small-town life would be washed away, replaced by smooth roads that would take you rapidly to the world beyond Noblesville. Women would have more freedom to be themselves and not be confined by the male world. David had tarnished that bright image with his dark opinions of his own time, but still it had to be amazing, and it was where he was from.

"Did you say something?" he asked, looking over the magazine.

"No … no! I'm sorry to disturb your reading," she said, standing up and leaving the room.

Later in her bedchamber, Mary went through the nightly ritual that meant physical freedom to her. She undressed.

After turning up the gas light, she unlaced the hard, uncomfortable black shoes that bound her ankles and feet. As the air reached them, the blood seemed to return for the first time since she had dressed in the morning. She slipped down the heavy dark stockings and rubbed the ache out of her feet. She took off her dress and hung it near the window to air out and stood before the porcelain wash basin that sat on the dresser, washing her face and arms and the back of her neck. She placed the basin on the floor in front of the bed and sat down, putting her feet in to soak. She wore the tiny white ear buds. At the end of the wire the black, glass-covered cell phone lay on the linen coverlet, the screen glowing with an array of multicolored boxes.

Reaching back with the practiced flexibility of a contortionist, she untied her corset and worked her fingers into the laces and pulled, loosening the confining undergarment. For the first time since morning she took a deep breath, shoving her chest out. The seams, eyelets, hems and laces left deep pink lines in her back, breasts and stomach. Mary slid her hand into the loose corset, rubbing life back to her skin, massaging the pink lines on her stomach and the freckles that peppered her breasts. She unfastened her smooth black hair and let it fall down her back.

Falling back across the bed, her feet dangled in the cool water. Nat King Cole breathed into her ears his sensual, soothing tones of comfort. She fanned her slip to cool her legs.

The corset, the shoes, the dress from neck to heel—they were the stone covering of a statue, tightened and pulled into position each day for display. That's how she felt about it

He probably thinks I'm a snob. She didn't want him to see her now, like this, it would be a scandal, but if he could he'd see that she was "warm and real" and not "just a cold and lonely, lovely work of art."

Around her neck, Mary always wore a silver chain. From it hung a sterling silver turtle, perhaps an inch long from nose to tail and three-quarters of an inch wide. Her grandmother had given it to her when she went off to Bryn Mawr. Inscribed on its undershell were the words: "So you won't lose your way." Its top shell was hinged at the shoulders. Mary sat there toying with it as she often did, lifting the shell to expose the tiny compass within.

Between songs she heard voices out in the yard and went to the window. She pulled back the curtains, the ones Anna had brought from the old house, from the room that had been Mary's as a little girl. She opened the slats of the shutter and saw David's shadow in the backyard. Her father's form crossed the yard from the outhouse and disappeared under the eaves. The back door bumped closed. In the dark, it looked as though David was staring up at the sky as he often did on a clear night. She wondered what he thought about when he watched the sky for so long. Suddenly she realized that he was looking up at her. He saw her behind the dark stripes of the louvers, the gas light cast across her face, and saw that she had been watching him. For a moment she didn't care that he knew and just stared back, but then pulled down on the center stick and closed the louvers.

She looked back to the small silver turtle hanging from the chain around her neck. The compass within pointed north toward the window and the yard beyond.

Two days after the Knights of Pythias meeting, David rode out to Fox Prairie to see a patient with Dr. Harrison. As they passed along the west bank of White River, down the bumpy Cicero Road shaded by mammoth trees, they came to a spot that David knew well in his time.

In the twenty-first century, five, crumpling, trackless pylons rise out of the White River there. They once supported the tracks of the Interurban, the electric railway. But today the pylons didn't exist, and deep forest grew down to the waterline.

David was silent, watching the unspoiled area pass by as the grade rose. Almost as if he had been reading David's mind, Dr. Harrison confided that he planned to invest heavily in Pennington's electric railway scheme.

"Just can't resist being a part of it all, huh?" David said.

"I don't plan to be just a part of it, I plan to get rich," the doctor said. "I've got enough money to build that house, but I'm going to put everything else I have behind the railway."

"You sound confident."

"I am. When we went out East to visit Mary at school last year, I rode one of the early electric lines in Philadelphia. It's cheaper and more efficient than steam. As soon as they break ground, that'll be proof enough for me and I'll buy my shares. I just feel it: We're going to make big money."

After church on Sunday, Robert Wainwright approached David and pulled him aside. "I was wondering, are you planning to stay in Noblesville for a while?" he asked.

"Yes, I'd like to," David answered.

"Something tells me you didn't much care for the K of P meeting the other night. Am I right?"

"It was all very nice," David smirked.

Robert grinned mischievously. "I thought so."

He gave a nod, indicating that they should move away from the crowd. David followed him a few steps down Clinton Street.

"These old men's clubs are so stuffy. Wouldn't it be great to have a club that was a little more fun?"

"What do you mean?"

"Some fellows I know here in town, all guys you've met, have been thinking that we might start a little club ourselves … something a little more light-hearted! Something in the conversation the other night told me that you might like the idea. We wondered if you might like to come in with us."

David was relieved. "What kind of club?"

"Well, it's to be called the Bachelors' Club." Robert paused for effect. "We'll dedicate ourselves—not too seriously, mind you—to preserving the free status of our members. This will be a good occasion for the members to get together for mutual support, not to mention a game of cards and a nip or two," Robert winked.

David laughed. "Sounds like fun! Who's in so far?"

"Fellas from town mostly, Hare, Jones, Denning, Ben Craig, John Davies, Will Christian and some others. Will you join us?"

"Sure. What's the plan?"

"Everyone's pitching in with some money. We'll need a meeting room and some furniture."

During the next week the Bachelors' Club secured some space above Sowerwine's Dry Goods and equipped the room. It was more elaborate than David would have expected. They bought card tables, wool rugs for the two rooms, comfortable chairs, and a pair of sideboards to stash the "nip or two."

At their first meeting they elected officers in a travesty of parliamentary procedure. Robert was elected Exalted Grand Chief and David, much to his surprise, was railroaded into being Vice Exalted Grand Chief, with an emphasis on "vice." His duty was to use the group's funds to keep the meeting rooms well stocked with tobacco and liquor.

Dressed in tattered graduation robes salvaged from the high school, the charter members composed their bylaws, writing them on a brown paper sack and tacking them on the wall:

1.   *The purpose of the Bachelors' Club is to promote a marriage-free life*

for its members.

2. *The members of the Club and their activities are to be widely advertised to all eligible young women of the City.*

3. *Members caught fraternizing romantically with single women are to be punished by providing the membership with "consumables."*

4. *Sticklers for proper procedure in the conduct of this Club shall be expelled.*

5. *Any other rules necessary for the operation of this Club shall be made up as required.*

They agreed to gather each Thursday evening to pursue their noble purposes.

CHAPTER SEVEN

"I'm not sure he's wrong about automobiles," he said. "With all their speed forward they may be a step backward in civilization—that is, in spiritual civilization. It may be that they will not add to the beauty of the world, nor to the life of men's souls. I am not sure. But automobiles have come, and they bring a greater change in our life than most of us suspect. They are here, and almost all outward things are going to be different because of what they bring. They are going to alter war, and they are going to alter peace. I think men's minds are going to be changed in subtle ways because of automobiles; just how, though, I could hardly guess. But you can't have the immense outward changes that they cause without some inward ones, and it may be that George is right, and the spiritual alteration will be bad for us."
The Magnificent Ambersons, Booth Tarkington, 1918.

Friday, the twenty-third of June, the Knights of Pythias had invited their wives for dinner and entertainment to celebrate the Bernice Lodge's ninth anniversary. During breakfast the Harrisons and David discussed the evening. It was Nella's day off, and the younger folk would have to get dinner themselves. Fred said he was going to play pool downtown with some other fellows.

"Pool, my eye. You're going downtown with hopes of seeing Katie," Mary said.

"Maybe I will, and what does it matter if I do?" Fred snapped.

"Then what will you and Mr. Henry do for dinner?" Anna asked Mary.

"Well, I think I know my way around a kitchen," Mary said, now a bit defensive herself.

"I was thinking it would be best if you went over to Harry's."

"How about we go out for dinner?" David said. "I'll buy."

"I don't know, Mr. Henry," Anna said quickly, with a disapproving glance. "People would talk."

David saw the irritation in Mary's face.

"Mother, I'm twenty-one years old. I can decide for myself what I do," Mary insisted. "And so what if the foolish tongue-waggers in this town care to talk. People should be able to go out to dine without other people making it their business.

"Thank you very much," she said turning to David with a smile. "I'd love to dine with you this evening."

Anna stared into her coffee cup, but Dr. Harrison never looked up from the newspaper folded in half on his lap. David looked over at Fred, who nodded toward the women, bared his teeth playfully, and raised his hands a little, fingers curled like the claws of an angry cat.

That evening, David sat in the front parlor reading the Noblesville Democrat, waiting for Mary. She finally came down, wearing the same yellow dress she had worn the day he first came through the beam. She had pinned a small hat with ruffles and a silk flower to her hair. She nervously clutched a small, half-moon-shaped purse that hung from a cord around her wrist. They stared at each other for a moment. "Shall we go?" she finally chirped.

"You look beautiful, Mary," he said, as embarrassed as a schoolboy on his first date. But he was glad he'd said it, because for the first time, she blushed. Gone was the detached, self-assured, sometimes defensive Mary; here instead was a soft, vulnerable woman.

"Thank you," she said. "Do I still look like the cold Mona Lisa?"

"I never meant that. You're far more beautiful than Mona Lisa."

When they walked down the street, people did talk. A young un-married couple out together, both obviously taking great care with their appearance, was a subject of intense discussion. Were they or were they not an item? When they passed in front of Craycraft Dry Goods, Mary stopped to look in the window. David never saw past the glass. Their reflection caught his eye; a beautiful woman and a handsome man. Was this him? Were they here, together? He stared for a moment into his own reflected eyes, and then to the reflection of Mary looking at him, and then to the images of courthouse, carriages, horses and buildings. She took his arm.

When the two entered the H.D. Hull European Hotel, Mr. Hull himself conducted them to a table. Will Christian stopped at their table and chatted for a minute. Being here in public with her, seeing people they knew, felt good to David.

Throughout dinner, they talked continually. He loved hearing about her life and her interpretation of it. She was just as intrigued by his stories of the future. David had never imagined that conversation could flow so easily with a woman who had seemed so unapproachable just a week before.

"You haven't really spoken much about your family." Mary said. "Does your parents' divorce make it awkward?"

"Well, I'm not embarrassed, although I do avoid the subject. But it was painful for me because I was just ten, and my parents didn't handle it very well. I just got into the habit of not talking about it then … because it hurt so much."

"I'm sorry I asked."

"No, it's a perfectly normal thing to ask about. In my time about half of all marriages end in divorce."

"How awful! How do the children survive?"

"Miserably."

He paused, trying to think of the right place to start. "When I was little, I remember my dad being away at work all the time. Looking back now, I suppose he felt trapped in the marriage. I think that as he preferred to be home less and less, he became a workaholic more and more. The funny thing is that society pats a man on the back for working so hard and supposedly providing for his family. But he was doing just the opposite—trying to get away from us. There was money, but not a lot of love between my parents, at least by the time I was old enough to be aware. My mother would beg him to spend more time at home, and he would tell her to stop nagging, that he was trying to make his earnings catch up with her spending—and it would degenerate into a screaming match.

"From my perspective as a little kid, that's what the trouble looked like, but there was more going on that I wasn't aware of. When I was ten, my mother woke me and my brother in the middle of the night and put us in the car with our pajamas on. She drove to an apartment complex across town. She got out and told us to keep the doors locked, that she'd be back in a minute. She walked to the end building and disappeared into a hallway, and was gone maybe five minutes. Then she came out and went on to the next building. As she went, lights would come on in the windows of each apartment. It finally dawned on me that she was knocking on every door, waking people up.

"When she'd made her way about halfway down the row of buildings, she disappeared into a hallway and didn't come right back out. Pretty soon I heard her scream, 'You bastard, come to this door, right now!' " Realizing he was talking too loud, David lowered his voice and leaned forward. "Finally I heard my father yelling, too. I couldn't imagine what he was doing there. Pretty naive, huh?

"Well, my mother came back to the car crying hysterically. When we got home she made us go to our rooms. Of course we couldn't sleep. We could hear her tearing through things in the house all night long and crying. When we got up in the morning, the driveway was filled with cardboard boxes. It was all my father's stuff—his clothes and things. Mom was asleep on the couch, right where she'd stopped, exhausted. Mike and I didn't wake her up. We got ourselves ready for school and left."

Mary drew back uncomfortably.

"When we got home from school that day, the boxes were gone and my mom sat us down and told us that she and my father had separated and she was going to file for divorce. I begged and begged her not to do it. It wasn't until years later that I realized what my father was doing at that apartment. He was with the woman he's married to now.

"Anyway, when I was ten I couldn't understand any of it. I blamed her, and my dad encouraged me and my brother by blaming her for everything. We were so stupid! My dad even went months and months without paying child support. He had money for vacations and nice cars and a nice house for himself and his new wife, but not for his children.

Mom had to go to court to get him to pay. She never told us any of this. She refused to put us in the middle by attacking him.

"She went through hell for us, but we couldn't see it … too young, I guess," David said, looking away and leaning back. "My dad was the one who deserved to be hated. We only saw him on weekends, and he would buy us expensive stuff and take us to ballgames and cool places. We spent more time with him after the divorce than we did when he lived at home. Life with my mom was completely different. When she and my dad were in college, she had quit school and got a job to help pay his way. So when they divorced, she didn't have many qualifications. We hated her for the divorce and the way we had to live, and we loved our dad for all the things he gave us.

"My mother remarried after a few years and things got a little better, because her new husband had a good job, but we hated him and treated him like dirt. I feel really guilty about it now."

Mary was surprised and touched by his honesty "Have you told your mother that you're sorry … that you understand what she went through?"

David shook his head.

"Why," Mary pleaded, "she must be so deeply hurt!"

"I don't know. I remember loving her so much when I was little, and I still do. But there's so much distance between us, built up over the last fifteen years, I don't know if I could do it. Even though I know she's tried to give me opportunities."

"Does she live in Noblesville?"

"No. She and her husband moved to Denver when I was a sophomore in college." David gave a bitter laugh. "Enough of my awful life! Tell me about your awful life."

"Mine isn't as dramatic as yours. I don't remember being anything but happy. Fred and I have been good friends to one another growing up. I was a bit of a tomboy when I was young, and I taught Fred how to play all sorts of games when he was small. But there comes a time when a girl can't play ball anymore and has to wear a dress and be proper. I get the impression that women have more options in your time than we do in ours. A woman's choices are few, and so life can get boring, especially in a small town like this."

"Hard to forget the bright lights of the big city?"

"Yes, maybe I just got a bit jaded there; well, not jaded—spoiled."

"Is there a difference?"

"No, I suppose not," Mary said, laughing self-consciously. "It's been hard to come back to this little town. There was so much to do there, so much excitement; art galleries, museums, lots of year-round theater. What has this town got? I know you find it wonderful, but I can't imagine why."

They went on eating in silence for a few minutes. David could see the gears working behind Mary's eyes. Finally she spoke. "Despite a charmed upbringing, I don't think you appreciate how trapped I am. And that's not just complaints from a spoiled girl who wants to go to the theater."

"Trapped? How?"

"Growing up with my father, an old soldier of the G.A.R., the whole household has always been very patriotic. You talk about America in such a detached way, and you criticize it, too. We could never do that in our house. Having a veteran for a father is like having your own badge of honor. With him being a doctor too, we've had a bit higher place in the social standing of town than we would if he did something else for a living. With that comes expectations, too, that I'll marry well and that I'll act with a certain reserve. As I said once before, I suppose it's the expectations that bother me the most. I could just be me with the other girls at Bryn Mawr—no expectations."

"So why didn't you stay there?"

"A single woman, in a big city, alone?" she said, incredulous. "That's social suicide, unless you're a widow or something. I suppose I could have gotten a room in a boarding house and taken on a factory job, but women who do that—well that's an act of desperation. And my college education doesn't qualify me for a career. That's for men, not women. My education qualifies me to be a refined wife," she snorted. "And once school was out, I had no acceptable proposal for marriage."

"I can't believe nobody asked."

"I didn't say nobody asked, I'm saying I didn't say 'yes.'"

They left Hull's and strolled down the block. They could hear a glee club singing from the K of P Castle Hall above. When they neared the end of

Emmous Street, where a small, white clapboard church and its parsonage stood by the cemetery entrance, a drop-front phaeton passed by and the driver and his companion called "Good evening!" David and Mary stepped off the gravel onto the rutted lane that led down the hill and into the cemetery. Rose bushes were in bud, and the parklike grounds were green and still. The smell of flowering clover and young wheat drifted on the breeze. Twilight was coming.

David stopped and watched the phaeton disappear down Brock Street. "You know, I'd bet that in my time there are hardly any horses living in Noblesville Township, even though the city itself is nearly ten times the size it is now."

"None?" she asked, surprised.

"There are a few, I guess, on the farms farther out in the country, and some rich people have stables, but they're all used for sport, not work."

Mary sat down on a large rectangular slab of limestone beside the wagon path. On its face was chiseled the date 1824. David recognized it: It was still there in his time. He asked Mary about it, and she said, "Nobody knows quite why it's here. It's not the right size and shape for a gravestone. Some of these markers date back to 1813 or '14, so it doesn't commemorate the opening of the cemetery."

"In 1824 there was only one brick or stone building in the county," David told her. "And that was William Conner's house a few miles up the river, so this probably isn't an old cornerstone."

"I suppose you really don't need horses in your time." Mary returned to the previous topic, adjusting her hat and smoothing the edges of her dress against the stone.

"No, it's a shame. We have way too many cars."

"Cars sound wonderful to me," Mary said. "Maybe you haven't taken enough long rides in carriages and wagons to understand what it's like— hours bumping along muddy, rocky roads until your body aches. In the summer, there are flies and mosquitoes circling your head, and in the winter you freeze. If only I could travel in a comfortable, dry seat, have cool air in the summer and warm air in the winter, listen to music, and get where I'm going in a fraction of the time a carriage takes!"

"It may sound wonderful to you, but what if having that car destroyed the social fabric of your town? What if it meant tearing down buildings, destroying miles of countryside, and polluting the air? Would it still seem like a fair trade?

"I'm only just realizing how completely the car has changed us as people. When you ride in your carriage, you pass people you know, sometimes you stop and talk. And cars didn't just eliminate horses, they killed off the trains, too. When you ride the train you talk to people, you meet people. But if you're in a car, you're in your own little world. It doesn't improve people's manners, either—you're so anonymous, you can cut people off, charge in front of another car, blast your horn. We even have a new crime called road rage. Somebody gets so mad on the highway that they pull out a gun and pump bullets into the offending car."

"I suppose people can be quite rude in any time. I've certainly had to jump out of the way of a silly young buck driving his buggy too fast!"

David went on, pacing up and down the wagon wheel rut. "Cars have destroyed most small-town central shopping districts. An entire interstate road system has been built that moved traffic away from these areas. Eventually your town becomes a place to get through, not a place to go to. The cars speed by, not knowing you or your town, and worst of all, not giving a damn.

"And people don't eat very often in friendly little restaurants like Hull's. Most of the time they eat in fast food restaurants on the highway, because it's easy to get in and out with their car. Never mind that you don't see anybody you know; sometimes you sit in your car and order through a window, and you don't see anybody at all, just some kid's arm handing out the bag of food."

He went on. "We've destroyed most small towns and their social fabric. We've destroyed our countryside, and we're destroying the atmosphere. Have I told you that there are some big cities in my time where the air is so polluted by car exhaust that on certain days people are advised not to go outside because it's too dangerous to their health? It's nuts."

The approach of an elderly couple interrupted David's harangue. They exchanged greetings, and the couple walked on twenty yards before stopping to gaze at a headstone. David sat down beside Mary. Stars twinkled. He found the Big Dipper in the vast darkness overhead.

"I'd settle for the train," Mary eventually said meekly, adjusting her hat. "Why won't people in your time take the train?"

"I don't know. Our love of cars has destroyed that, too. Mass transit's a dirty word. I wouldn't have taken a train four weeks ago myself, but I would now." His voice trailed off.

"You know, Mary, I'm sorry. I've been going on like an idiot. Here I am out for the evening with the loveliest girl in town, and I'm whining about things that haven't even happened yet."

"No, really, it's fascinating," she said, patting him on the back and then self-consciously putting her hand back in her lap. "When will the cars arrive?" she asked with resignation.

"Soon. You'll start to see them at the end of this decade. There's a man named Elwood Haynes who's working on one in Kokomo now. They'll look silly and be awfully inconvenient at first, but as you grow older, they'll start to change everything. By the time you're an old lady, the automobile business will be the most powerful economic force in America."

"When I'm an old lady," Mary said, looking out across the gravestones. "My parents think I'm an old lady already—an old maid."

"Twenty-one is an old maid?"

"Many of my friends from high school are married. Mother and father wanted me to marry instead of going to Bryn Mawr. Really I should say mother; father's afraid to say much about me and marriage."

"Well, a lady nowadays doesn't usually talk about such things with a gentleman, does she?"

"Don't tease me, please," she said, looking away. "You shared some stories of your life with me, and I'm sharing some of mine with you. Besides, what do a young man and woman talk about when they're together, one hundred years into the future?"

"Oh, a lot of things—most of it more explicit than you can imagine. And a lot more than just talk goes on in my time, too."

"Even you?" she exclaimed.

"Oh, no, you're not going to get me to reveal my secrets! My grandmother always told me that a true gentleman never talks about private affairs between himself and a lady."

"I should say not," Mary laughed. "At least your grandmother had morals."

"What did you mean, your mother wanted you to get married instead of going to Bryn Mawr? It's not that simple; you can't just make the perfect man appear out of thin air."

His unintentional irony riveted her gaze for a moment. Then she admitted, "There is a man," she said, "at least in my mother's mind, and his, too, perhaps."

"Who?"

"Robert Wainwright."

"Major Wainwright's grandson? That's the top of the heap," David said, feeling a little jealous.

"I suppose that's what my mother thought, too."

"But not you?"

"I suppose I should be flattered … and I am. He's been calling on me since I was eighteen. He probably figured that his family name would make me jump at the chance to marry him, and so did everyone else. Every summer when I came home, he came calling again."

"But you keep giving him the cold shoulder."

"I just don't love him, and when I tell mother that, she says that I could learn to love him. I always thought that the beauty of love was that it was something you didn't have to learn! Worst of all, now I'm not looking forward to just a summer of mother playing matchmaker. I'm stuck here now. If I don't marry, there's nowhere for me to go. I've met every man in this town, and I don't want to marry any of them."

"What do you want in a man?"

She fixed her gaze on him for a moment, then looked away. "Well, to begin with, a man who doesn't expect me to be a cook and a brood mare! And with one blow," she gestured and laughed, "I just knocked out every man in this town. I want a man who cares about more than the weather and how much hogs and wheat bring at market—a man who loves life and the world beyond here, a man who cares about what I think and not just whether I have child-bearing hips. Is that selfish?"

"No, not at all! But it could be hard to find such a creature around here."

"Maybe not," she said softly, looking him in the eye.

This is it, David thought. You either kiss her now or you've blown your big chance.

He moved closer and she didn't move away. So he kissed her, softly and simply. This gentle kiss was more stirring than any he could remember. They lingered, and she put her hand on the back of his neck, holding his lips against hers.

"Oh my goodness!" she whispered.

"I—I'm sorry if that was the wrong thing to do," he stuttered.

"No," she said softly, with her breath on his neck, "it's just what I wanted you to do." She put her head on his shoulder, and he wrapped his arm around her.

Crickets, cicadas and frogs hummed their songs of riverside darkness. The sound of a piano drifted from the parsonage's open window, and hooves crunched on the gravel road. The graveyard was nearly black except for stray light from the rising moon. The shadowy outlines of gravestones stood out among thousands of lightning bugs, swirling and spinning in the air.

"Oh, fireflies! They remind me of the beam between our time and yours," Mary said. "When I was a girl I used to sit on this stone at night in the summer and imagine that each firefly was the soul of someone who was buried here, alive and free and glowing. Off and on their lights flicker, as if to say, 'Don't forget me.' "

They sat in the darkness listening to the river and the night sounds.

"I've seen you from my window at night in the backyard," Mary said. "Why do you stare up at the sky so much?"

"When I was a little boy, my grandmother taught me a lot about stars. So I like to look at them. There's something comforting about them always being there. They never change."

"Show me something then," she said, sitting up straight.

"Okay, let's start at the start. You know the Little Dipper—Ursa Minor? Well then, Polaris is right at the end of the handle. Beside it is Cepheus, kind of a gabled house-front shape turned on its side. Below Ursa Minor is Draco, which loops underneath it and continues on to the side, ending with a bit of a dipper itself. We can't see Orion now," he said, pointing to the horizon, "because it's behind the sun, but it'll be back in July."

Mary opened the shell of her silver turtle pendant and found true north, comparing it with David's celestial navigation. For more than an hour he walked her through the sky, from Cepheus to Cassiopeia, down to Leo and over to Crater. Mary followed his pointing finger and felt for the first time that she had some understanding of what had always hovered above her. As the dew fell, invisible and silent, they walked home, hand in hand, in the cool, damp air.

Crossing the intersection of Grant and Emmous, they were too absorbed in each other to notice the red glow of Dr. Harrison's cigar on the front porch. But he saw their silhouettes, holding hands. He couldn't hear what they were saying, but he heard Mary's laughter. He noticed what the darkness couldn't hide: the carefree sound of her voice and the way she walked, not stiff and ladylike, but bouncing and gliding, the way she had looked when she was a child, unrestrained by convention.

Mary's laughter stopped abruptly when she saw the glowing red dot, moving back and forth in the spot where her father's rocking chair sat on the porch. Dr. Harrison drummed his fingers on the arm of the chair.

"Good evening," David said as they came up the steps.

"Hello," the doctor said, emotionless.

"Been home long?" Mary asked.

"No, just got here about ten minutes ago."

"Thank you for dinner, David. Good night," she said, and then turned and disappeared into the house.

"May I join you?" David asked the doctor.

"Fine with me."

The two men sat for twenty minutes or more without talking. David felt as though he had done something wrong but knew the doctor wouldn't say a thing. The silent treatment was his way. David assumed that to invite Mary to dinner was a bit presumptuous, and coming home holding hands was a step farther afield.

The next evening, just before dinner, David overheard Anna and Fred talking in the kitchen. Anna was telling Fred that she didn't want him at the dinner table that night. She wasn't angry with him, but he wasn't to ask why. "Go play pool with your friends again. You can buy a sandwich downtown."

At dinner that night it was just Mary and David, the doctor, and Anna around the table. Nella had been sent home early. David could see that Mary was anxious. Halfway through the meal, Anna finally spoke.

"David, Albert and I would like you to tell us how courting takes place in your time." She said this without looking at him, as if she had rehearsed the line.

"Do you mean teenagers or adults?"

"Someone as old as you and Mary," she said pointedly.

"Well, first off, we don't call it courting, it's called dating. Courting to me sounds like it means marriage is the intended outcome. When a man and a woman go out on a date, marriage isn't usually on their minds. It's more for companionship; maybe they're hoping for romance. If a relationship develops and they eventually get married, then okay, but it's not a foregone conclusion that that's why they go out."

"Go out," Anna repeated. "Do they 'go out' alone?"

"Usually, or they might go out with a group of people. Or they might meet in a bar. They might go to dinner or just out for a beer. Sometimes I invite a date to my house and cook dinner for her."

"You have met women in bars—where you both drink liquor?" Anna asked, shocked. "Women go to bars alone?"

"Most often they go with a girlfriend or in a group."

"This isn't supervised by parents?"

"If she has a job, she probably lives away from her parents."

"Despicable!" Dr. Harrison grumbled under his breath.

"Men and women both are much freer in my time," David explained. "It doesn't mean they're bad people; times have just changed."

"But how does your society ensure that unmarried men and women are not engaging in immoral behavior?" the doctor asked, frowning fiercely.

"We don't ensure it. What's immoral is a matter of opinion. We're not talking about murder here, we're talking about what a woman and a man do in privacy."

"But men can be beasts! What if this woman, completely unprotected, doesn't consent and the man refuses to take 'no' for an answer?"

"Then it's called rape, and the man should go to jail."

"But if a woman has gone to the man's house to dine with him alone, hasn't she asked for it?"

"Absolutely not. If a woman says 'no,' then that should be it."

"But what if the woman cannot resist the encouragement of the man?

David was incredulous. "Come on," he said flatly, "they're not as weak as you think. If she can't resist, then she's consented. Women are just as smart as men, and they have just as much responsibility for the things they do."

Anna was beside herself. This was the most sexually explicit conversation that had ever taken place in her house, and she couldn't believe what she was hearing.

"I'm sorry this conversation has gone so far," she said. "You've told me more than I ever cared to know. I hope I die before such changes take place! But our point is this: Last night Albert saw you and Mary coming up the sidewalk holding hands and behaving like sweethearts. I don't know what went on last night …"

"Nothing improper went on last night," David told her. He looked at Mary, wondering why she wasn't speaking up. From the look on her face, he realized that she was where she belonged in this era, passively silent. This wasn't the time for a power struggle, and she knew it.

"It's clear to me that what you believe to be proper and what we believe to be proper are two very different things!"

"Look, I'm in a difficult position here," David said, pleading for understanding. "I don't want to be disrespectful to you. You've welcomed me into you home and been kind and generous. The last thing I want to do is offend you, but I can't believe what I'm hearing.

"In the time that I've known your daughter I've found her to be an intelligent, kind, decent person. Why is it that at the age of twenty-one she has to sit here and listen to three other people argue about whether or not she can control herself enough to be trusted to take a walk with a man? Why do you immediately assume the worst? It really doesn't bother me so much that you might not trust me, but your own daughter?"

"David, please," Dr. Harrison said, holding up his hand to urge calm.

"No, please, let me ask you a question. Did either of you simply ask Mary what went on between us last night?"

"No," the doctor conceded.

"Why not? You could have asked and gotten a simple answer. You don't have to build it up into some horrifying moral lapse. All I'm saying is, please, have some respect for her intelligence and maturity."

"David, perhaps you're right," Anna finally said. "Maybe we should have discussed this with her privately, but I think a discussion with you would also have been appropriate. Relations between an unmarried man and woman are different in our time from yours. If you're going to stay here with us, and if you want to spend time with Mary, there are certain things you may and may not do."

There was silence for a moment. Finally David said, "Okay."

"The most important rule is that you mustn't do anything that would cause the people of this town to lose respect for Mary or question her virtue in any way. Unfortunately, the truth is immaterial—what people think and say is. Physical signs of affection can lead people to talk, so you should confine yourself to giving her your arm when you're walking. Being alone in certain places can also lead people to talk.

"As far as everyone in this town is concerned, the two of you are an item now, not simply because you were out to dinner alone, but also because you spent the latter part of the evening sitting in the cemetery, alone."

"How do you know we sat in the cemetery, if you didn't ask Mary?"

"Aha," Anna said, pointing a finger at him. "You see, you don't understand how information travels around here. Did you also know that no other man will call on her until after you're long gone? Any man who might have wanted to court her won't now, until he thinks you're out of the picture."

David was stunned into silence for a moment, then managed a firm nod and to softly say, "That's fine with me," looking toward Mary, "but I guess I'm not the one with the most to lose."

"It's fine with me, too," Mary said boldly.

David looked back at her parents. "Something tells me that it's not fine with you."

"Well, apparently the two of you have made your choice," Anna snapped. "There's nothing more to discuss." She stood, picked up her dishes, and carried them to the kitchen.

The doctor looked down at his plate and took a deep breath. "You're never to pass through that beam," he said coldly to Mary. "Never, under any circumstances!"

David hadn't imagined that this fear had preyed upon them. How could he have missed that? It wasn't just social propriety that frightened them: It was the possibility that she would go into the future with him and never return. They had good reason not to trust her to stay in Noblesville.

"I won't if you don't want me to," Mary answered unconvincingly.

The scowl did not leave the doctor's face, as if he had settled for less than he wanted. He got up and left the room without another word.

David rested his elbows on the table and his face in his hands. He felt Mary touch his arm.

"Don't be angry with them! Don't you see, they're afraid," she whispered.

"Yeah, well, so am I."

"Me too."

Before the sun rose the next morning, Harry was at the door. Clara was in labor. Dr. Harrison grabbed his medical bag, and Anna and Mary dressed quickly and followed him to Harry's house. Nella arrived at her usual time to make breakfast and a hot pot of coffee, which David carried over to the other house.

Mary was in the kitchen heating water on the stove, while Anna and Dr. Harrison were upstairs tending to Clara. Before long it was just David and Harry sitting downstairs, waiting for something to happen. Fred stopped by, then went on downtown to put a note on Harry's office door and open up the auditor's office.

Harry sat in an oak rocker, staring at the wall. David picked through yesterday's *Indianapolis Sun*.

"Do you know what we might be doing now if it wasn't for you?" Harry asked with a grave expression.

"What do you mean?" David responded, confused.

"If you hadn't stepped through that beam, if you hadn't found us by accident, if you hadn't been able to find that drug—do you know what we might be doing now, right here in this room?"

"No." David waited for a compliment.

"Having a funeral," Harry said bluntly. "There would be a coffin in the front parlor—maybe two—one for the baby. Clara dead, the baby dead, my life destroyed. I owe you so much, and it doesn't seem to affect you at all. You act as if it was trivial. But that drug transformed my life."

"I was just glad I could do something."

"If it's a boy, Clara and I have thought that we would name him David as a way of saying thank you."

David was speechless for a minute. Then he said, "Thank you! But as flattered as I am by that, you really ought to name him after your father. All I did was go and get a drug from a friend. It may seem miraculous to you, but it was really very easy. On the other hand, your father has worked so hard to take care of Clara. He did that for her and especially for you. It was his concern that prompted me to find the drug in the first place."

Harry couldn't tell David why he recoiled from naming the baby Albert. For years, some hidden resentment had blinded him to his father's care and kindness. But now, with the lives of his wife and their child in the doctor's keeping, that ice within melted.

Harry had rejected much in his father's world—medicine, the Knights of Pythias, the Republican Party—and he knew full well the pain that caused Dr. Harrison. Now he felt guilty for the disrespect he had shown his father. During these past months his father had concentrated on Clara as he'd never done for any other patient before, sending for the latest books on lung diseases, attending a medical conference on respiratory illness in Chicago. And as she got worse, despite his best efforts, he had grieved as furiously as Harry had.

Harry decided at that moment that if the child were a boy he would persuade Clara to name it Albert Robert, after his father.

CHAPTER EIGHT

The whole community was our family. It was just a feeling we all had, about each other. I'm not sure I have the words to express it. It's just that we all cared for each other. We were close to each other. We had this feeling of togetherness. We all felt it.
Elsie Perry Pane in *All We Had Was Each Other,*
Don Wallis, 1998.

Much to the surprise and delight of the grandparents, the baby boy was named Albert. He was healthy, and so was Clara. Harry strutted down Conner Street the next morning on his way to the office with a silly grin on his face, passing out cigars to every man he met.

The three Harrison women and their neighbors fussed over the infant, the baby that none of them believed would be born alive, thriving in the arms his mother, whom no one had thought would live to see the Fourth of July.

David and Mary were the town's big subject of gossip. More than one man who'd received the cold shoulder from her over the years commented on "the taming of the shrew." People didn't know what to make of it, but they were aware that Mary had grown apart from the town, and her choosing a man from far away fit somehow.

The Thursday after their date, the family's dinner was interrupted by Ben Craig. Through the front screen door, Ben could see them eating.

He walked in uninvited and went straight to the dining room. David and the Harrisons were taken aback, because he'd obviously been drinking.

"Mister Henry!" he said. "Your presence is immediately required in the rooms of the Bachelors' Club."

"It's customary to knock, Ben," Dr. Harrison chuckled.

"We don't meet till eight, anyway," David said.

"Sorry to disturb your dinner, Mrs. Harrison, but this is an emergency."

Ben took David's plate from him and started for the kitchen. David, his mouth still full, fork in his hand, stared after him, bemused.

"You've been drinking, haven't you," Mary put in, smiling.

Ben stopped in the door to the kitchen. "Shtrictly sheremonial, I asshure you."

Ben dropped the plate into the sink. "Let's go," he called as he headed for the door. David followed him.

When they came through the door of the Bachelors' Club, most of the other members were lounging about. Two empty whiskey bottles sat on a sideboard. The men, several garbed in their tattered robes, stood up as David entered.

"Vice Grand Chief Henry!" Robert Wainwright said loudly, a tumbler in his hand. "It has come to our attention that in the past week you have been seen in the presence of a young lady: one Miss Mary Harrison. How do you plead?"

It seemed like a joke, but David wasn't sure. "Well, yes, I was with her."

"Just as we thought!" Ben Craig said.

"You have already been tried in absentia and found guilty of article—" Robert stopped and looked back at the handwritten rules tacked to the wall. "Article 2 of the Bachelors' Club charter. Well done!" he said, raising his glass. The other members raised their glasses and shouted, "Hear, hear!"

Someone called, "He must be punished!"

"Off with his head!" John Davies shouted.

"As Exalted Grand Chief," Robert went on, "I hereby condemn you to buy a box of the finest Havanas for the membership. This tribunal stands adjourned." Robert slammed his tumbler on the table, and the group exploded in laughter.

"Hurry up, David," Robert ordered him. "We're ready to play cards." David went down the street for the cigars, delighted and relieved.

There was a daily routine in the Harrison house. Before going to bed, Anna would leave a note on the front porch for the dairyman. He would come before dawn and leave fresh milk, eggs, cheese, or butter in the stout wooden crate near the front door. Nella arrived at about 6 in the rickety old wagon her husband drove, pulled by a mule. He then headed off to the Strawboards factory to work an eleven-hour shift making paper and paper board. Nella emptied the dairy box, let herself in, and prepared breakfast.

By 7:45 Fred and his father were walking down to the courthouse to open the auditor's office. During the morning Nella checked the ice in the icebox; if the block had melted too much, she left a card on the front windowsill. The card simply said "Ice." This signaled the iceman to stop and bring in a new block. When the ice wagon came down the street on hot days, children ran behind to pick up broken chunks to suck on or rub on their necks and foreheads.

Nella spent her day cleaning house, doing laundry and hanging it on the line. She cooked lunch and dinner. Mary and Anna helped out with all these jobs, but Nella did the bulk of the heavy work.

Some days the men came home for lunch, and other days they ate downtown. Anna and Mary shopped nearly every other day, stopping at Craycraft's Dry Goods, bringing home the next day's necessities from Bart's and Wild's grocery or the meat market, and perhaps taking a look at a hat or a length of cloth. They carried only the lightest parcels home; the rest were delivered.

Each evening they all sat down to dinner together. While they ate, Nella's husband picked her up; Mary and Anna cleaned up the dishes. While the women were in the kitchen, the men had a smoke in the shed, or sat in the back parlor or on the front porch reading and talking to one another or greeting neighbors and passersby. Neighbors passed from one front porch to another, intending just to talk for a moment but staying for an hour or more.

As corny as it seemed to David at first, often these informal, impromptu porch gatherings would drift into a sing-along. *God, how these people love to sing,* he thought to himself. It usually started during a lull in conversation. One person, often a lady, it seemed, would begin alone without bothering to say, "Hey let's sing a song." She'd sing just a few words, "Camptown ladies sing this song," and before she got to "Do da, do da," the whole porch was singing along. When that song was over, someone else would start another. After just a few of these kinds of evenings, the corniness wore off, and David found he liked it.

He thought about these same porches in his own time, and the people who lived behind the front doors. If he and his neighbors ever got together and by some miracle decided to sing together, would they even know the same songs?

As July began, Anna and Mary went downtown and selected the final touches for their new house: fireplace mantles and ceramic tiles to surround them, gaslight fixtures, bathroom fixtures, and everything else the house would need. David, of course, was fascinated.

He went with them to the hardware store, where they picked through boxes of cast iron and brass escutcheons and knobs, hinges, strike plates, mortise and rim locks. He toured the unfinished house and watched men lay in the gas and water lines. Behind them came the plasterers, tacking down the laths and troweling on the creamy plaster. In what would be the front parlor, milled oak woodwork sat waiting for the plastering to be done. In another room, the oak newel posts and balustrade for the stairway were tucked away with the interior doors.

David spent as many days as he could hanging out at the house, rolling up his sleeves and trying his hand at laying brick or hanging windows with the building crew. They thought he was nuts: a rich boy who wanted to play at building a house. Still he persevered, ignoring their jokes and pretending not to see them roll their eyes when he approached the site. He climbed the ladder and watched for an hour or more as the crew laid the gray slate roof. He begged the foreman to let him lay a row but was sent on his way.

He eventually won them over by never refusing to help carry a heavy load or to get his hands dirty, and by displaying a reasonable degree of knowledge and respect for what they were doing.

He spent time on Conner Street, too, watching the construction of the Presbyterian Church and Will Craig's house next to it. Masons were busy laying fine, white mortar lines with the highest quality brick anyone had seen in Noblesville, combined with stone and specially made decorative brick.

On rainy days, Mary and David sat on the front porch taking turns reading to one another from one of the many periodicals Mary insisted on taking to keep her in touch with the "real world," as she put it. They read some glorious descriptions of the Columbian Exhibition and World's Fair currently being held in Chicago. Mary sometimes got a lap board and some stationery and wrote to friends from school; she wrote to Helen Garrison in Chicago nearly every week.

The Fourth of July in Noblesville was an all-day party. The streets were even more crowded than on Decoration Day. A spell of rain that year just before kept the farmers out of the fields and gave them an excuse to bring the family to town. They came in carriages and wagons loaded with children and picnic baskets, ready to spend the day. Noblesville's celebration was the only real show in the county.

The bicycle fad was still sweeping the country, so the day's first event was a nine-mile qualifying race. A third of the riders didn't even finish, their machines having fallen victim to the gravel and rutted dirt roads.

After sandwiches and sodas at the drugstore fountain, David and Mary moved with the crowd to the lawn of the high school for the oratory contest. The school yard was dotted with folding chairs and blankets where families picnicked beneath the shade of the trees. On a platform near the front entrance sat several young people, ready to give their speeches.

Would the channel-surfing Americans of the twenty-first century sit for several hours listening to teenagers give patriotic speeches? David knew they wouldn't. In this day, though, there was seldom a gathering where someone wasn't asked to "make a few remarks." These people seemed to have an almost boundless capacity to endure discussion and debates on politics, religion, philosophy or the arts. Their patience and respect for thought were a revelation to David. He knew that people in his own time, their minds numbed by a continual onslaught of information, would not be able to keep up.

That night there was a party at the Fortners' on Conner Street. A hundred years later the imposing pre-Civil War Greek Revival house would be gone, replaced by three small houses and a vacant lot. This house was one of the few large ones in Noblesville that was not painted in bright colors. Its older style would return to fashion in a decade or so: white clapboards with deep-green trim and shutters. The expansive front lawn was ringed by a simple black iron fence entwined with rosebushes.

The garden was like another world, half-hidden from the street behind the rosebushes and a canopy of massive old trees. The effect was heightened by the two dark-painted houses rising on either side of the yard. Interspersed here and there were flowering plum and red Chinese maples, giving color to the walks beneath the taller trees. Chinese lanterns had been strung from the corners of the house out to the corners of the yard, and dozens of iron and wicker chairs and tables that the Fortners had borrowed from their neighbors' porches were placed all around. As he crossed the brick and stone path toward the porch, dressed in clothes that seemed like a costume and with Mary on his arm, David felt—as he often did lately—like he was on the set of a period movie.

The porch was decorated with more Chinese lanterns and potted plants. Drifting out from the house was the music of a piano, cello, and violin. The musicians sat in the corner of the front parlor before two large multipaned windows, open to release the music. It swept through the house and across the yard, blending with the voices of guests.

Everyone who was anyone in Noblesville was there. More than a hundred people had been invited, and no one stayed away.

David hated parties where the men and women congregated sepa-rately. He wanted to stay with Mary. Each time a group of ladies led her away, he would eventually catch up and reclaim her attention, much to her satisfaction.

"You mustn't be so possessive, Mr. Henry," Katie Conwell teased as David approached a group of young women near the corner of the porch.

"Aren't men allowed around female talk? Or would I find it too shocking?"

"If you're a betting man, Mr. Henry, you can stay," called someone David hadn't met, a large young woman in an oversized hat.

"What are we betting on?"

"No, don't," Katie said, blushing as they all laughed.

"We're betting whether or not Fred will finally get up the nerve to ask Katie to go to the fireworks with him tonight," the girl announced, giggling loudly.

"I say he will," David told them. "What's my bet?"

"If you can arrange it, Mr. Henry, the royal treatment!" the loud girl said, mimicking an English accent. "While you repose on a couch, Mary will drop grapes in your mouth and the rest of us shall fan you with palm fronds."

The girls shrieked with laughter.

"You're on," David winked.

"I think you'll lose," she predicted, taking a gulp of iced tea.

"The fellow is head over heels in love," chirped Willsie Bush, "but he's terrified of her—hasn't the gumption to do anything about it."

"I'll be back for my grapes in a minute," David grinned. He walked away across the yard.

Another outburst of laughter followed him. "Don't be long," Mary called. "Your harem awaits!"

David walked straight to Fred and pulled him aside. "Mary and I are going to go down for the fireworks later, and Katie was wondering if the two of you could join us." Over Fred's shoulder David could see the group of women huddled close together, feigning conversation, with Katie red-faced in the middle.

"She asked to go with me?" Fred asked, eyes wide and mouth agape.

"Yes, well … she let it be known she'd like to."

"Sure!"

David returned to the ladies, smiling from ear to ear. "Pick your palms and find your grapes," he said, taking Mary's arm and leading her away.

Squeals of approval greeted his coup. "While you're doing so well, Mr. Henry," the loud one called, "see if you can find a man for me!"

Dinner was served buffet style: roast beef, mashed potatoes, fried oysters, fresh peas, homemade bread. Mr. Fortner said a prayer, and Thomas Swain proposed a toast to the host and hostess. The old folks sat at the dining room table, but most of the others found seats in the parlors, the porch, or outdoors, holding their plates in their laps and chattering. Soon the table was restocked with desserts prepared by many of the women.

In the backyard, Jim Bush and Mr. Locke led children in making ice cream. Each child took a turn cranking the handle of the oak freezer. When they were done, Jim handed out spoons, and the children struggled to jam them into the tub. "Every man for himself!" one boy yelled. Two older boys seized the dasher and licked the paddles.

As dusk approached, several men went about lighting the small candles in the Chinese lanterns, filling the yard with a soft light that played across the grass and the underside of the canopy of foliage. David and Mary sat alone on a wicker settee at the corner of the yard, surrounded by roses.

Mary reached over and took his hand. "What are you thinking about?"

"This place, these people. For all its faults and shortcomings, this is a wonderful way to live."

"Yes, it is," she said. "When I see them all like this, dressed in their best and everyone so happy, it seems so. And being here with you …"

He smiled and squeezed her hand. "You're making a conscious choice right now, you know."

"What do you mean?" she asked.

"Being with me, holding hands in public. People have been watching us all evening. It's like your mother said: It ruins your other options."

"Let them look! I really don't care. I'm happy being with you."

"Besides," David said, "it's a pretty safe and comfortable sort of rebellion."

"Is that what I'm doing, rebelling?"

"I don't know. What do you expect to come of this?" he said, looking down at their clasped hands.

"I'm not ready to worry about that now."

"You don't worry that I could be gone tomorrow and never come back?"

"I try not to think about it. Besides, something tells me you're right where you want to be."

"I am," he said leaning back in the seat. He wanted to kiss her but knew he shouldn't.

The guests had begun to move some of the lawn furniture up near the sidewalk to get a good view of the fireworks that were about to start downtown. Some left through the gate, walking the two blocks for a better look. Mary found Katie, and David found Fred. The four of them walked downtown—Mary and David confidently hand in hand, and Fred and Katie awkward and nervous, her hand formally tucked in his elbow.

Before they crossed Anderson Street, there was a pop and a trail of sparks rising in the air alongside the clock tower, bursting into a pink flower of light fifty feet above the tower's cap. From the courthouse lawn and behind them at the Fortners', they could hear applause mingled with "ooohs" and "aaahs."

The courthouse square was so crowded that onlookers spilled into the streets. Vendors selling popcorn and roasted peanuts did brisk business as the flashes of colored light bathed the square. People hung out of upper-story windows or watched from rooftops. Children who had run and played throughout the day's festivities rested in their parents' laps or lay on their backs on blankets spread on the courthouse lawn, looking up and waiting for each explosion.

The four young people went on through the milling crowd on Catherine Street, stopping from time to time to look up. As the display neared its end, Mary suggested they walk down to the fairgrounds. They made their way north, leaving the crowds behind. As they passed the front porches of North Catherine Street, people watching the fireworks and avoiding the downtown crowd called out "Good evening!" As they neared the grove at the western end of the fairgrounds, they heard the military band on the square playing the national anthem.

The two couples wandered apart on the paths that ran through the grove and along the river.

"What are women like in your time?" Mary asked, as she and David stopped in the darkness beneath a tree. "When my parents confronted us at dinner the other night, you said some things that were hard to believe."

David thought of Heather, and the kind of life she lived. "What is it you want to know?"

"Well, if I were living in your time, the daughter of a doctor, twenty-one years old … What kind of life would a girl like that live?"

"You'd probably be a senior at college, maybe at I.U. or Ball State, or Purdue. You'd be studying for a career."

"I could choose any career?"

"Anything. You could even go into the Army."

"No thanks!" She mused for a minute. "How would I live—what would my circumstances be?"

"You'd live in an apartment or a dormitory or a sorority house. You'd probably have your own car, and your life would pretty much be your own. If you wanted to meet a man for drinks or bring him home to your apartment, you could, and nobody would think anything of it."

Mary thought hard on that one, narrowing her eye to the dark

"When a girl is done with college, where would she go?"

"She'd look for a job, just like a man would."

"Even if she got married?"

"Most young women work even after they're married."

"Their husbands don't mind?"

"No."

David had a sinking feeling. Was she planning to go through the beam? Would that be her escape from the humdrum life of her Noblesville? Was that the reason she had chosen him?

"You look upset," she said.

David looked into her eyes. "You want to go through the beam, don't you?"

She cocked her head to one side for a moment, and then smiled broadly and shook her head. "No. It sounds fascinating, but no. Is that why you think I'm asking these questions?"

"I was afraid that was why."

"Don't you see," she said, moving closer. "I'm trying to understand how I measure up against the kind of women you're used to."

"Don't worry about it," he said, relieved. "There's no comparison." He put his hands around the soft silk at her slender waist and pulled her closer, kissing her passionately. They held each other, her arms around his neck.

To be so close to her and to want her so much scared him. "I don't know what I have to offer you," he murmured. "I don't know what kind of future there could be for us."

"No, don't say that," she whispered, holding him tighter. "Don't say things about the future … our future. Let's just be together now, and we'll worry about the future when it comes. Please."

He pulled back to look at her. Tears glistened on her cheeks. "You're the best thing that's ever happened to me, like an answered prayer," she choked. "Don't say anything that would make us choose now."

He hadn't lied when he said there was no comparison, because it had never occurred to him to compare. There was no imagining Mary in short shorts or a bikini, driving a convertible with the top down. She was not of his world. She would never have her own condo at the edge of the interstate, or shop for lingerie at a mall.

They sat on the trunk of a fallen tree overlooking the river. They could see the shadows of horses and wagons across the river, heading north up the Cicero Road; merrymakers returning to the villages of Cicero, Arcadia, and the Roberts Settlement. They lingered on, star-gazing. Across the valley and behind the trees on the high ridge beyond, occasional flickers of heat lightning pulsated at the horizon.

Too soon they rejoined Fred and Katie, and the foursome walked back through town, talking and laughing. Downtown was nearly empty now, but the streets in the neighborhoods were still alive with people. The pop of firecrackers broke the night from all over town.

The Fortners' party was still going, and a few people were dancing in the parlor. Thomas Swain and E.J. Pennington were standing by the front gate, cigars in hand. As the four came through the gate, Swain greeted them. "Nice night for a little spooning, hey gents?" he said. The men standing nearby laughed. "Oh, to be young again!" Pennington remarked.

Mary, Katie and Fred all got a bit embarrassed, but David just smiled.

"We just went down for the fireworks," Fred stammered, looking at Katie's father. "Lovely, weren't they?"

"The fireworks have been over for an hour," Swain teased.

"What's 'spooning'?" David whispered to Mary as they approached the front door.

"Exactly what we were doing," she whispered back.

As the party wore on, two different groups of teenage boys came by and stopped at the gate to serenade the guests—or perhaps one particular girl. When they began to sing, the party quieted and everyone gathered around. It was a common summer activity, Mary told David—serenaders wandering the town in the evening, looking for girls to impress.

To David, at first this all seemed like some trite, staged "Main Street U.S.A." event from Disney World, but it was hard not to enjoy the spontaneity and sheer innocence of the moment. Like so many things in this time, it was familiar yet foreign, the kind of stereotypical way his America liked to view itself, but one that had no real place in the twenty-first century. In the middle of a song, when he looked around at the faces smiling encouragement at these young boys in the soft glow of the Chinese lanterns, David had the faint recognition that he was losing his disdain for innocent, unsophisticated, unhip fun.

That night Mary taught David to dance the two-step and a simple waltz. It seemed odd to the others there that a young college-educated man wouldn't know how to waltz. It bolstered the image that townspeople had of him, a college man who had studied so hard he'd remained innocent in the ways of romance. He picked it up quickly, though, and they danced as long as the musicians would play.

Late that night Mary lay in bed in the darkness with the earbuds on, listening to the cell phone music app until the battery died. David was sitting on the front porch with Dr. Harrison.

"Just think," the doctor said, "on this day in 1776 they signed the Declaration of Independence."

"Well, actually," David corrected, "they voted to adopt it on the fourth but didn't start signing it until the second of August."

"Ridiculous, everybody knows that it was signed on the fourth."

"That's just a myth," David insisted.

"Who said 'History is a lie, agreed upon,'" David said. "There are lots of legends that people take as historic fact."

This was the sort of thing David did that irritated the hell out of the doctor. He decided to let the subject of history pass.

"The new house will be done in few weeks," Dr. Harrison grunted.

"It's really coming along nicely."

"We need to talk about you and what you plan to do," the doctor said. "In light of your friendship with Mary, I don't think you should continue to stay with us."

David frowned sharply.

"Don't misunderstand, it's fine with me if you stay in this time," Dr. Harrison continued, "but I have to think of what's best for Mary."

"So you're saying that when you move, I should find another place to live?"

"Not necessarily. You could stay in this house if you like. I won't sell it, but I'd rent it to you for as long as you like."

"I really appreciate that," David said, suddenly thinking of money

His still had much of the cash he'd gotten from the gold, but he wasn't sure he could afford to furnish and maintain the house for an indefinite period of time. Besides, in the future that money amounted to a $5,000 debt.

"Something else," Dr. Harrison said, staring into the darkness beyond the porch.

"Okay," David said apprehensively.

"Do you intend to bring any people from the future, or tell anyone that you found a way to travel here?"

David thought for a minute. "No," he said. "What that would mean, what it could do … well, it scares me so much that I don't think I will ever tell a soul."

"That's what I hoped you would say. It scares me, too. Still, you need to decide what you're going to do."

"There's a part of me that wants to stay here, now, and another part that's afraid to let go of my own world."

"I understand," the doctor said. "I would suggest that you proceed with extreme caution and not do anything final without us sitting down and talking it out. Whatever you eventually decide should be final, and then the beam must be destroyed."

David sat thinking hard. Dr. Harrison drew a match across a porch post and lit another cigar. In the light of the small flame, David could see the steady seriousness in the deep lines of his face. He flipped the match beyond the railing into the grass and drummed his fingers on the wicker side table.

"Are you afraid of the future?" David said at last.

Dr. Harrison considered. "I'm not afraid of tomorrow or the day after that or the day after that, but I'm afraid of the place you come from."

"I see what you mean, but I come from Noblesville, and from this house."

"No, you come from a foreign country—and it seems to me, based upon the things you've told me, that for all its strength and magnificence, it ain't got a soul or a conscience."

CHAPTER NINE

As we strike the earth with our bodies, for we are always falling,
and standing up, and falling again, though you call it dancing,
or walking, or flying, there is the sound of stone coming to rest
in quarries, the last spray of sand, as we knock on earth's sullen,
historical face.
Striking the Earth, John Woods, 1976.

After dinner, David and Mary took a walk with Fred. The oppressive humidity was as intense now as it had been in the afternoon. David's white shirt was plastered to his back with sweat. How Mary tolerated the heat in her voluminous clothing was a mystery. They decided to walk past the new house to see what the workmen had completed that day.

As they approached Catherine Street, they heard the heavy thumping of hoofbeats and urgent shouts: "Jump! Jump!"

An open carriage was speeding north out of control. One of the poles between the harness and carriage was broken, causing the vehicle to tilt and swerve crazily, and the terrified horse was bolting from its suddenly unbalanced burden. The driver was standing up, hauling on the reins. Two women faced the rear looking as if they were about to follow his order. Suddenly the younger woman leapt from the carriage. She landed on her knees and rolled to the curb at the corner of Emmous Street.

Right behind her came the other woman, but her foot caught the back of the seat. She landed hard, her face and breast smashing against the paving bricks.

David and Mary rushed to the women. Fred took off in a sprint down the middle of Catherine Street, yelling, "I'll follow the wagon!"

"Willsie," Mary said, putting her arms around the young woman, "are you all right?"

Willsie Bush looked blankly into Mary's face, dazed. She moaned. "I think I've really hurt my legs."

She caught sight of her mother and burst into tears, crying, "Mama, Mama!"

Several neighbors rushed from their houses as David gently rolled Mrs. Bush over. Blood was pouring from her nose and mouth, where her front teeth had been broken out. She was unconscious.

Dr. Booth ran out of his house and down the block. He knelt down and checked Mrs. Bush's pulse. He pulled back her eyelids and felt her neck, moving it gently from side to side. "She's alive. Let's get her into my house!"

David and Dr. Booth lifted the woman and carried her a block to the large house at the corner of Hannibal. They laid her on an examination table in the front room. Booth began cleaning the blood from her face while Mary and a neighbor woman helped Willsie to the doctor's house.

"We hit a chuckhole two blocks south of here," Willsie sobbed. "The horse pulled hard and when we came out, the carriage lunged forward and scared him. He reared up and the breech broke, then the whole rig was wobbling, and he bolted."

"It's all right, dear," Mary reassured her. "Your mother will be all right, and in a few minutes your father will set things right and come back here for you."

Pulling less weight now, the horse shot forward at breakneck speed. Fred ran full-out. He hoped the horse would get tangled in the traces and slow down enough so he could grab its bridle. But the carriage was a block ahead and pulling away, with Bush still pulling on the reins, yelling, "Whoa, whoa!" The carriage swerved wildly as it passed Wiltshire, heading toward the courthouse. Strollers gasped and leapt to the curb as the carriage streaked past.

When the horse got to Conner it made a desperate left turn. The carriage slid wide on the slick brick surface, heading toward the iron hitching rack that circled the courthouse. It slammed into the rack with a sickening crash. A wheel wedged on a support pole, stopping the carriage in one violent jerk. James Bush was sent hurtling through the air, head first into the iron fence. The horse fell headlong as the reins tore free.

Robert Wainwright and Ben Craig had just stepped out of the Corner Drug Store. They ran across the street to Bush, dodging the panic-stricken horse, which ran in a circle in the street before it jumped the sidewalk, fence and hitching rail in two awkward bounds, landing on the courthouse lawn. The frightened animal stomped gashes in the flowerbeds before it bolted out the main entrance, dashing west.

Almost instantly, people surrounded Bush's body. As Fred pushed through the crowd and knelt down to feel Bush's pulse, he heard the distant beat of hooves as the horse crossed the wooden planks of the Conner Street bridge. James Bush lay motionless on the stone sidewalk. A massive head wound poured blood onto the sidewalk.

"Let's get him off the pavement," Robert said.

He lifted Bush's torso and Fred took his feet. Blood soaked Robert's shirt and pants. The crowd parted as they carried him across the street. Inside the Corner Drug Store, two tables were pushed together, and they laid him on them. Ben took off his vest and folded it, gently slipping it under Bush's bloody head. By the time Fred thought to say, "Somebody get my dad!" Dr. Harrison had already been called.

In Dr. Booth's examination room, Mary took over assisting the doctor. David felt useless. They gingerly removed the broken teeth from Mrs. Bush's mouth. Her face was starting to swell. Dr. Booth guessed that her nose was broken and that she probably had a few broken ribs. David pulled chunks of ice from the ice box in Booth's kitchen, wrapped them in a towel, and crushed the chunks to shards with a potato masher. He held the bundle to Mrs. Bush's face as another doctor tried to reset her nose.

"Mr. Henry," Willsie called, lying on a couch as Mary wiped antiseptic on the cuts on her knees, "would you go downtown and see what's become of my father?"

David nodded and disappeared out the door. He got to Conner Street just as Dr. Harrison ran up. A large crowd was amassed around the storefront. Every new arrival would hear the dramatic story again. Someone called out, "It's the doctor, clear the way!" The crowd parted, and David walked into the drugstore behind Dr. Harrison.

Fred rushed toward his father. "Dad, his carriage went right into the rack. The horse must have gone crazy."

Dr. Harrison didn't stop to hear the details. He walked swiftly to the table. James Bush's body was surrounded by people. Those on the outer edges stood on the oak seats of barstools. Three children peered over the edge of the table at the motionless man, laid across tables where just minutes ago glass dishes of ice cream had sat. Too terrible to look—too compelling to look away.

As Dr. Harrison approached the table, people stepped back. The vest beneath Bush's head was soaked with blood, and the overflow was beginning to drip on the floor. One look told the doctor that Bush wouldn't live. His pulse was faint, and there was nothing that could be done for a skull fracture like this. Then Sheriff Rhoades came through the door and moved most of the people out.

"David, could you help me?" the doctor asked as he wiped at the head wound.

David froze when he saw the wound. *This man is going to die.* He suddenly felt nauseated.

"David, please," the doctor urged. "Find a cloth and see if we can get some of this blood cleaned up. There's really nothing we can do but make the poor fellow more comfortable in his last few moments."

"Isn't there something we can do?" Fred pleaded. "He's going to die here?"

"I can't undo what's been done, son. It's not in my power to build a skull. Only God can do that."

David's heart sank. He began cleaning the blood from the floor and table, trying not to look at Bush. Finally he looked up and saw tears in Dr. Harrison's eyes.

The doctor was holding Bush's hand and patting it. "It's almost over, old soldier," he murmured.

He stood holding the dying man's hand awhile longer, obviously trying to compose himself. He wiped tears and sweat from his face with his handkerchief. "David, see if the druggist here has got a sheet or a blanket," he asked quietly. And then, with resignation, "Somebody better call the undertaker."

David and Dr. Harrison covered Bush up to the neck with a checked table cloth.

"Does anybody know where his wife and Willsie are?"

"They're at Dr. Booth's," David said, staring down at the bloody, sunken crown of Bush's head. "They jumped from the carriage two blocks south. Willsie's hurt, but awake. Mrs. Bush is unconscious. She took a pretty bad fall from the carriage—fell on her face. Mary's back there now helping Booth."

"They're in good hands."

The room was silent except for the steady hum of the ceiling fans. Finally the two women behind the counter took their eyes off the dying man and began mechanically cleaning up the dishes and counter. The druggist pulled the window shades down, blocking the view of the curious who still lingered outside. Ben and Robert sat quietly at a corner table, holding their hats in their hands.

Sheriff Rhoades stood near the door, watching the crowd. Those in the room all knew they were waiting for James Bush to die. The silence and heat intensified now that the door was closed. Fred, near the end of his tether, walked over and hugged his father. He was a proud young man, and he'd tried hard not to cry, but now he seemed not to care. His father patted his back. "Everyone's time must come, son, it's all part of living. If you're going to be a doctor, you're going to have to get used to it."

The conversation of the crowd outside suddenly stilled. The reason was clear when the drugstore's door opened to admit an elderly man whom David knew as the owner of the furniture store on the north side of the square.

"Albert," the man rasped, nodding to the doctor. "Sheriff."

"It's almost time for you to take over," Dr. Harrison sighed.

The man said nothing, but walked up to James Bush and shook his head. "Such a shame," he muttered.

Dr. Harrison felt the pulse again and announced softly, "Just a few more minutes now."

He walked over and sat between David and Robert and whispered, "Boys, as soon as James expires, someone will have to go down to Dr. Booth's and let them know what's happened here. It would be better if you two went down and told Mary first. She's a friend of Willsie's and should be the one to tell her. If Mrs. Bush is in a bad way, she probably shouldn't be told right now. Mary'll handle it right. You two go down there and tell Mary quietly, and then let her tell Willsie, before one of those folks outside does."

David nodded.

"Albert," the undertaker called.

The doctor walked over and tried the pulse again. Bush was dead. He took a watch from his vest pocket and noted the time, then pulled the tablecloth over the face and stood silent, head bowed.

"Dear God," he began solemnly. Every one in the room bowed their heads as well. "Take the kind soul of James Bush; he's gone home to you tonight. He saw hell on earth in the war and found love and friendship among us these many years. James worked all his life to do your will on earth and make the world a better, more decent place for others. May he know peace in your realm. Amen." The others intoned "Amen" in unison.

Robert and David slipped out the back door.

Mary was looking out the window and saw them coming. She stepped out onto the porch, wiping her hands on a white apron tied around her waist. Their solemn faces scared her. She saw Robert's blood-drenched shirt as they stepped onto the sandstone sidewalk and came through the fence gate. Mary searched David's face as he stepped onto the porch, and they embraced.

"What's happened?"

"He's dead, Mary."

"How?" she exclaimed, pushing away and staring at him.

"The carriage went full speed into the hitching rail in front of the courthouse and he was thrown into the iron fence. Your dad came. He asked us to tell you so that you could tell his family."

Mary covered her mouth with her hand and shut her eyes tightly. Tears squeezed out as she sat down abruptly in the porch swing, tears flowing down her cheeks. David sat beside her and held her close. She put her head on his shoulder and cried softly, fidgeting with the little turtle necklace that hung across a button on her shirtwaist.

Robert leaned against a porch post. "You want me to do it, Mary?" he asked softly.

She shook her head. "Thank you, no. It's better if I do." She wiped her tears away with the apron and disappeared into the house.

Later, Dr. Harrison and Fred came to Booth's. Mrs. Bush, still unconscious, was laid on the padded seat of a surrey and taken home to her own bed. Mary and her mother stayed overnight with them, one sleeping in a rocking chair, the other on the couch, ready to help in the night should Willsie or her mother awaken.

Fred, Ben, Robert and David sat in the darkness of the front room of the Bachelors' Club, passing a bottle of whiskey, silently watching the moon creep across the sky above the courthouse clock tower.

While the four sat brooding, several blocks away another tragedy was born.

In a boardinghouse just south of the courthouse square, little more than seven blocks away, a woman bit a piece of cloth as spasms of pain racked her body. She clutched knotted edges of the bedsheets tightly in each fist. An hour earlier the girl in the next room had knocked on the door and asked if everything was all right. "I had a bad dream," Etta lied. "I must've called out in my sleep."

By 1:30 it was born—a large baby boy. Despite the heat, he shivered, still slick with blood. He snuggled between Etta's legs as she rested, trying to catch her breath. He let out a feeble squeak and then a strong cry. The sound urged her up and she struggled to clean herself and the child. Etta managed to cut the cord with a pocketknife. She bound up the afterbirth in the bloody sheets, tying it all in a ball. Afraid that the child's cries would wake up another boarder, she pulled clothes from the dresser, put the child in and closed the drawer. Dizzy and pale, she fell back on the bed trembling from exhaustion until the muffled cries of the baby sent her into a panic. She had to get rid of it!

Less than two hours after giving birth, Etta dressed and slipped out with the baby wrapped in a shawl. She had decided to weight it down with rocks and drop it into the river. She hadn't traveled far up the alley above the river when her unsteady legs failed her. She slipped into the privy behind Jacob Thompson's tin shop and sat down on the seat, resting her head against the wall, the child in her lap, its lips pursing, searching for her breast. The much-used outhouse gave off an oppressive stench in the heat of summer.

After waiting a half hour, hoping to muster enough strength to make it to the river, Etta gave up. She stood and unwrapped the child, quickly dropping it head-first into the privy vault. It fell with a wet thud into the rotting waste.

The baby was silent for a moment, then began to shriek pathetically. By morning it would be dead, she thought. Its body, mixed with the filth four feet down, would go unnoticed. Etta stepped out and closed the door behind her. The muffled screams of the infant could still be heard, but it was too late to do anything else. She returned to the boardinghouse and collapsed into her bed.

A short time later Isaac Eurick left his home on the west side of the river to catch the early train to Indianapolis. He crossed the covered bridge and passed down the alley behind the tin shop. As he passed by he heard what at first sounded like a cat crying in the outhouse. He pulled open the privy door, calling, "Come on out, kitty!" Then he realized it wasn't a cat. He poked his head into the privy hole, searching the blackness for the source of the noise. Again the unmistakable cry. "Impossible," he mumbled.

Isaac ran the block to the sheriff's house on the square and beat on the door until Sheriff Rhoades awoke and let him in. They returned with a lantern. All the way, Rhoades told Isaac that he was surely mistaken. "It's probably just an injured animal."

Rhoades lowered the lantern into the pit and was horrified to see a newborn struggling feebly on its back in the rotting waste.

The two men furiously yanked and kicked at the privy seat and supporting skirt, pulling away boards until the opening was big enough for Isaac. The noise roused a night watchman from a neighboring livery. Rhoades and the watchman held Isaac's legs and lowered him headfirst into the pit. He retrieved the baby, and they took him to the sheriff's wife.

At 4:30 a.m. David woke to the sound of the telephone and Dr. Harrison's disbelieving voice talking urgently in the back parlor. As he dressed, Dr. Harrison knocked. "You up, boys?"

"Yeah, I am. What is it?"

"Something else. Something terrible. You want to come?"

Downtown they passed the smashed carriage, still piled against the iron post. They crossed the courthouse lawn and came to the side door between the sheriff's residence and the limestone jail. Through the window they could see Mrs. Rhoades beneath a gaslight's glow lowering an infant into a large basin on the kitchen table. Sheriff Rhoades let them in and explained what had happened. David took a seat in the corner while Dr. Harrison worked at cleaning excrement out of the baby's nostrils, mouth, and umbilical cord.

"This child was born tonight," the doctor said.

"That's what I thought," agreed Mrs. Rhoades. "Who could do such a thing?" she said, drying the child and wrapping him in a blanket.

"There's many a desperate person in this world," Dr. Harrison sighed. "He's a strong little devil and will live, I suspect, if he doesn't get an infection from being down in that filth." He scooted his chair closer to the child, held tightly by Mrs. Rhoades, and inserted a small glass tube into one of its nostrils. The tube was connected to a cork stopper on a small bottle, and another glass tube came out of the stopper, which the Doctor put in his mouth. He sucked on the tube, pulling little wet fragments of black filth from the infant's nose and into the bottle.

"Could the baby have been born while the woman sat on the privy?" the sheriff asked.

"No," the doctor said, motioning for him to look closely at the stub of the umbilical cord. "That was cut with a knife."

Dawn was breaking, and already those with early-morning business around the square had heard about the incident. It spread through the restaurants that served breakfast. One man took the story back to the water company, another to the icehouse, one to the Strawboards; soon a person couldn't pass within half a block of downtown without someone saying, "Did you hear?"

Within an hour, a middle-aged woman, Mrs. Klepfer, approached the sheriff's back door and asked him to step outside. They talked in hushed tones. Mrs. Klepfer ran a restaurant on the west side of the square.

She told him that a woman who had been working for her the past year had gotten big around the waist of late. She left work yesterday saying she didn't feel well, and then didn't come to work this morning. "She lives at Mrs. Gunion's boardinghouse." The sheriff thanked her and stood on the porch for a moment, stroking his beard, deep in thought.

Finally he called back in through the door, "Doc, could you stay here a few minutes? I think I might need your help just a little bit longer."

David filled his coffee cup and followed Rhoades. He watched the blond, broad-shouldered sheriff stride across the intersection of Polk and Conner, his boots clicking on the brick pavement. He disappeared into the alley between the liveries.

David sat on the steps of the front porch and watched the town wake up. The world truly is full of desperate people, but David wasn't sure any more which era had more—this one or his own. What kind of desperation leads someone to kill a baby? In his time, ignorance and selfishness. In this time, most likely fear—fear of scandal, fear of being pregnant and alone.

Personally, though, these were peripheral issues. The first image that flashed through David's mind when he heard of the discarded baby was Heather. As he sat on the front steps of the sheriff's residence, his thoughts fell away to last winter. It had been several months since he last saw her.

He and Jeremy had met Heather and her friend in a craft brewery tasting room. She was a lovely, slender, sandy-blonde with a loud sense of humor and a quick wit. She liked his soft-spoken manner and intelligence and most of all was struck, when he took her home, that he didn't come in and have another drink. That confidence and patience appealed to her. He gave her a simple kiss and asked if he could call her. She said, "Sure, how about tomorrow?" He did call, and a romance grew out of that meeting.

Heather's parents divorced when she was a child. She grew up with her mother in an upper-middle-class neighborhood on Indy's north side. She was a little self-centered, as an only child can be. After graduating from I.U. she landed a sales job, perfectly suited to her personality, making nearly twice as much as David.

The night life made up of her college and high school friends was the center of her world, and David, with his good looks and mild yet left-of-center eccentricities, seemed to fit. She liked the fact that he didn't care much for the consumer-driven life that she led, intrigued that his needs were so simple.

He loved being in public with her, she was so beautiful and outgoing. They would do the Mass Avenue and Broad Ripple restaurants and bars on weekends, scooting through Indianapolis's downtown and north side in Heather's Mini Cooper with David behind the wheel. They ate Thai, Indian, and sushi and drank craft-brewed beer. Heather was as comfortable in a miniskirt and a low-cut sweater after hours as she was in a business suit during the day.

On cold winter Sunday afternoons, they would make love for hours in her condo in Castleton, an upscale complex near the malls that was nestled against the interstate. It was their Sunday routine: Make love, eat snacks, watch Netflix. David felt more comfortable making love to her than he had with anyone else before. Her fun-loving spirit suited him perfectly, and they both looked forward to this weekend ritual of release and passion.

One Friday night in late February, though, Heather didn't call, and David sat at home worrying. At nine o'clock the phone rang.

"David, I'm at the Wellington. Could you come down here?"

Her voice sounded distant and lost. Why hadn't she called earlier?

"What's wrong?" he asked.

"I just need to talk to you," she whispered.

He could tell she was starting to cry.

"Don't go anywhere, I'll be there in twenty-five minutes."

He drove like fury and walked through the rain to the bar, where he found Heather in a quiet corner booth, her long hair twisted into a braid that hung down across her chest. She wore a baggy pale-blue sweater that matched her eyes and thick beige corduroys. Her eyes were red and puffy, and she fidgeted with a glass of red wine.

A near-empty bottle sat on the table beside her cell phone. When she stood up and hugged him, he knew that something was terribly wrong. He tried to pull away to look into her face, but she held fast. Finally, she let go.

"What's wrong?" he said, sitting down opposite her in the little booth.

She stared at him unsteadily. "We're pregnant, David," she said flatly.

It was as if a bomb had dropped. It made his ears ring. He reached across the table and took her hand off the wine glass and held it tightly. She looked away and tears streamed down her face.

"I don't know what to say, except—I love you," he told her.

"I'm afraid that won't fix this," she muttered.

David was determined to be the man his father wasn't. He would be there for her in a way that his father hadn't been for his mother. Without really thinking about what it meant, he plunged right in. "I'll do whatever you want me to do," he said. "I'll stand by you. If you want to get married, I'll …"

"Get married and do what?" she interrupted sharply, "move into your little rat trap in Noblesville and live on your salary? I'll breastfeed the baby and wait for you to come home from school? Sorry, David, that's not exactly how I pictured my life."

His hurt expression stopped her cold. The chasm between their lifestyles and expectations had been easier to bridge when it didn't matter, when no one had to give up anything.

"I'm not saying we should get married," David said, feeling like he'd been slapped in the face. "I'm just saying it's an option I'm willing to consider."

"I appreciate that," she said, composing herself, "but I've got a career and a really fun life. I can't get married and have a baby now."

She ran her hands down the braid, playing with the tassel of hair and the fluffy elastic band that secured it. "I don't want to be divorced when I'm thirty, with a child to raise. Don't you see it's too early for us? Look at our parents; they were so selfish. We're so selfish—and why not, we're young and free …" her voice trailed off. "Why would we want to do the same things to our children that our parents did to us?"

David felt numb. He didn't want to get married, either, but the feeling of rejection was there anyway. "What do you think we should do?" he asked.

"I want an abortion, David."

There, she'd said it.

She filled her glass, emptying the bottle. "I've suspected for a week that I was pregnant. I went to the doctor yesterday, and they called me this morning. I've been going over this all day, and I've been sitting here for three hours trying to get up the nerve to call you."

"Why didn't you tell me earlier?"

"I don't know, I didn't want you to worry."

"Are you sure this is what you want to do?" he asked.

"I am. Most of all," she said, leaning forward in her seat, "I want you to say it's what you want me to do. I want to know that we agree on this."

"I don't like any of our choices, but it's your body, so it's your choice. If you want an abortion, I'll help you any way you need me to."

"You pay half, I'll pay half," she said deliberately.

He nodded.

"You're a good man, David Henry," she whispered urgently, burning a hole into his eyes and through the back of his head with a laser stare of appreciation. She patted his hand. "Thank you."

She asked him to stay with her that night, and he did. Though they slept like two spoons, he felt far, far away from her.

A week later they walked together across the parking lot of the clinic on Indy's ugly far east side. They sat without talking in a waiting room with chairs that lined the walls, filled mostly with frightened teenage girls. Some of them sat with their mothers, others with boyfriends who wore peach-fuzz mustaches. A nurse came through a swinging door, and Heather was called in.

While she was gone David couldn't stop thinking that the fetus, left untouched, would have become a person. Still, it wasn't completely real to him. He didn't feel that they were removing an unborn child—just a fertilized egg. No one would know what they had done, and they would go on with their lives as if nothing had happened.

Heather came out looking sleepy and walking with slow, hesitant steps. As they went across the parking lot, he gently asked, "How do you feel?"

She turned and gave him a hard look. "Like I've just been raped," she spat sarcastically. "How do you feel?"

Stunned, he mumbled, "Like the rapist."

Over the next few weeks they went through the motions of their relationship, but it felt as bleak as the hard, gray Indiana winter surrounding them. Something had died between them. David clung to the relationship, and that seemed to repel Heather. She suggested they "stop seeing each other" for a while—a euphemism for "it's over."

A few wagons crossed the intersection, and a train whistle broke the quiet morning as it came across the river a block and a half behind David, waking him from the memories he had replayed in his mind so many times. The train, belching steam and black smoke, blocked his view to the west. When the caboose cleared the intersection, he saw Rhoades standing on the corner, gripping the arm of a handcuffed young woman. As they drew closer, David saw that she was pale and walked unsteadily.

The people on the square stopped and stared as the two approached the sheriff's residence and jail. As they neared David, Rhoades asked, "Could you help me for a moment, Mr. Henry?" The women seemed not to notice David and struggled to keep up with Rhoades. David followed them to the side porch and into the vestibule that separated the brick house from the jail.

Rhoades called into the kitchen, "Dear, I'll need you and the doctor upstairs. Mr. Henry can watch the child for a moment."

When the word "child" passed his lips, Etta's head snapped toward the kitchen. She looked on, horrified as Mrs. Rhoades handed the baby to David. David was a bit horrified, too. He'd never held a baby, and he handled it as if he'd been tossed a live bomb.

"Why do we need a doctor? Where are you taking me?" the woman said to Rhoades.

"The doctor is going to examine you to see if you've recently given birth to a child, and if you have, I'm going to lock you in a jail cell and charge you with attempted murder."

CHAPTER TEN

The Falling Leaf
The falling leaf, the fading flower,
Remind us of this passing hour,
That days, or weeks, or months, or years
Will end our hopes and end our fears.

The falling leaf, the fading flower,
The scalding tear, the passing hour,
Will come to you as well as I,
For all that live will surely die.

His cold embrace, his bloodless eye
Is watching every passer-by.
At every corner of the street
He touches every one he meets.

He watches at the cradle side,
His eyes are always open wide.
The boy or girl in childish glee
Cannot escape, he always sees.

Be watchful then, be prayerful too,
For he will surely come to you.
Your body lie in silent sleep:
Some tender hands will ever keep,

A bud or flower on turf of green,
For every one to say when seen
How typical the fading flower.

The falling leaf this very hour,
Speaks silently to everyone
That walks beneath the shining sun
That you must lie and sleep beneath
The fading flower, the falling leaf.
T.F. Farmer, Noblesville, Indiana, 1893.

The scandal and tragedy of the past twenty-four hours swept across town. Etta Heylman remained in jail and her baby was taken to the county home. Etta refused to talk other than to say she was not married and it was not her baby.

In the night the undertaker took James Bush's embalmed body to the Bush home and laid it out on a cooling board, a portable folding table with a simple wood frame and a caned openwork top. Washing and dressing the body for the funeral were left to the family. By the morning after the accident, Mrs. Bush was awake and alert but in no condition to prepare her husband's body, and Willsie could certainly not to do it alone. Anna and Mary, who had spent the night caring for their friends, sent a neighbor to ask the doctor's advice.

Dr. Harrison sent Fred downtown to the furniture store to ask the undertaker to return to the Bush home, and then to open the auditor's office.

"Could you come along with me, David?" the doctor asked. "We'll need another strong back."

"Sure," David said, not knowing what he was agreeing to.

They found Mary in the Bush kitchen with an apron on, looking tired and pale. Though it was only nine o'clock, the table was already laden with food—a bowl of fruit, a ham wrapped in wax paper, and a pie, offerings from neighbors.

Dr. Harrison went upstairs to the bedchamber where Mrs. Bush lay, her chest wrapped tightly with bandages and her mouth and nose black and blue and swollen. He sat on the edge of the bed, holding her hand and consoling her.

After he had examined both women and assured them that everything would be taken care of, he took David and the Harrison women to the front parlor. Furniture had been moved aside and the rug rolled halfway up. A piece of canvas was spread on the floor beneath the cooling board. Bush's body lay on top, covered by a white linen. In racks under the wicker mesh, slabs of ice sat in metal trays, keeping the body cool.

Mary had brought a bucket of water and towels from the kitchen, and Anna and the doctor were both rolling up their sleeves.

"What are we going to do?" David stammered.

"We're going to wash and dress him," Anna told him.

David felt lightheaded and sat in a chair. Anna came closer and looked at him with concern. "What's the matter, David?"

"This is only the second time in my life I've ever been in the same room with a dead body—and I've never touched one," he said, heat rushing to his face.

Anna's eyes narrowed. "How can that be? Are you saying that families don't tend the deceased in your time?"

"I've never heard of it," he said. "I think it's illegal."

Dr. Harrison seemed not to be paying attention to any of this. "We'll need your help, David," he said. "Take a moment to compose yourself, and I'll call for you when we need you." He pulled the sheet from the body and they began.

David forced himself to look at Jim Bush. There were several small holes in his torso where the blood had been drained and embalming fluid administered. He watched the three at work. This was not a job they had chosen; yet out of duty, they did it.

People with every possible ailment or injury, sometimes near death, had been brought to the Harrisons' door over the years. Mary and Anna had witnessed births and deaths, the stitching and dressing of wounds, and even minor surgery. In fact, for most people of this time, death was not so far away. Babies died often, and consumption claimed many lives in small communities like this. Bodies were not whisked away from view by ambulances. Instead, they were tended and cared for and grieved over, and then they were buried in a cemetery close to people's homes, where those who mourned them could walk to visit the graves.

David, pale and uncertain, stood and walked to the foot of the cooling board. He looked down the length of the near-naked body. "Are you going to be all right?" Mary asked.

"Yeah."

"Let's turn him over." Dr. Harrison said, taking the body by the shoulders.

David grabbed the feet and the women maneuvered the torso. The corpse was stiff. The undertaker had fixed the hands across the chest and closed the eyes, placing pennies on them to keep them closed. He had tied a strip of cloth under the chin and around the head to keep the mouth shut. The cool touch of the flesh sent a chill up David's back and he struggled with the urge to vomit. When they laid the body face down, it emitted a rattling moan. David jumped back in horror.

"It's just air passing out of the lungs and over the vocal cords," Anna said gently to David. He thought he was hearing his heart pounding in his ears, until he realized that there was someone knocking on the door.

"Answer that, David, would you?" Anna asked. David escaped gratefully.

The undertaker came in and waited while Dr. Harrison dried his hands on a towel. He pulled line drawings from a folder—drawings of coffins. The doctor called for his wife to help with the selection.

David went back in the front parlor. Mary was trying to wash some of the dried blood from the dead man's hair. Tired and irritated, she turned and looked at David, wiping the sweat from her forehead with the back of her hand.

"What can I do to help you?" he asked with determination.

"You could do the legs while I finish this."

He rolled up his sleeves and grabbed a sponge, determined not to show his revulsion.

In a few minutes Anna came back in with a suit on a hanger: Bush's

Grand Army uniform. They rolled the body back over and slid on the pants. With a pair of kitchen shears, Anna cut the shirt and jacket up the back, since his arms were too stiff to maneuver into them otherwise. Once finished with the dressing, they waited for the undertaker's wagon to show up with the coffin.

Neighbors stopped by, walking into the house and making themselves at home in the kitchen. They wouldn't normally act so free in someone else's home, but now they lent a hand wherever they could, gathering in the kitchen for coffee and hushed conversation and setting out the gifts of food. A few ventured to the front parlor to view the body. None stayed long.

Around midmorning, a woman carrying a suitcase came up the walk—a sister of Mrs. Bush's from Anderson, summoned by a telegram from the sheriff. She immediately put on an apron and took charge of the house, thanking the Harrisons profusely.

The undertaker returned about noon with the coffin. A couple of men carried it in. Made of walnut, it had a small oval window in the lid just above the small pillow where Bush's head would rest. Unlike the caskets David had seen, it was not rectangular but narrow at the corpse's feet and wide at the elbows. David and the doctor helped the men lift the body and place it in the velvet-lined box. Mary and Anna readjusted the clothing.

"David," Anna murmured, "take Mary home, will you? She needs some rest and a hot bath."

Once they reached home, David brought the large, copper tub from the shed—a task usually reserved for Saturday—and set it in the middle of the kitchen. He helped Nella fill it, half with cold tap water and half with water they heated on the stove. Mary was given the privacy of the kitchen, shutters pulled and doors closed.

David sat in the summer kitchen for a while. He filled a tin cup hanging from the backyard hand pump and sipped the cool water. Nella came to the back door and spoke through the screen: "Some real awful things happenin' round here. These sorts of things happen up where you come from?"

"Yeah, I guess so. I've just never been so close to it all."

"You a lucky man."

"I guess so."

"Did you help lay him out?"

"Yes."

"You'll want to wash yourself off, too. Dead bodies carry diseases, you know, 'specially in the summer."

David washed in the backyard beside the hand pump, taking off his shirt and his socks, laying them on the back step and scrubbing himself above the waist and below the ankles. Mary, wearing a long dressing gown, came out into the summer kitchen and sat in a chair, combing out her wet hair. He had never seen her hair down, and she had never come outside when he was washing up. They went about their business, modestly pretending not to notice each other.

Mary stole glances from behind her fall of hair at the well-formed young man. As he finished washing and began drying his hair with a towel, she spoke: "What happens to people after they die in your time?"

He hung his towel over the clothesline. "An ambulance comes for the body. It's taken to a funeral home where I suppose they do all the things that have already been done to Mr. Bush. That's where people come to view the body and pay their respects."

"When does the family see the body?"

"After it's all dressed and in the coffin."

"It's never cared for in the home?"

"I think it's illegal to do embalming at home."

"Why were you so afraid to touch his body?"

"I'm not really sure."

Nella came out with a shirt in her hands. "I got you a clean shirt and some socks, Mr. Henry."

"Thanks," David said.

Nella turned to Mary. "You best get dressed, Miss. Your mama see you sittin' out here in a robe, she'll throw a fit."

"Yes, thank you, Nella," Mary said, ignoring the point.

Nella disappeared into the house, with a stern sidelong glance at David's bare chest and Mary's loose hair.

"You know, it's funny," David said. "I bet that by the time I was ten years old I'd seen thousands of murders and deaths on TV and in the movies, things you couldn't imagine. When I was a teenager my friends and I watched a video called 'Faces of Death.' It's a collection of films of people and animals getting killed—really. It was really awful, but mostly we laughed. It just didn't seem real. So I've seen more images of death than anybody in this town, but I'm the one who's afraid to be in the same room with a dead body, let alone touch it."

"Did you say you'd only been to one funeral in your life?"

"Yeah."

"Whose was it?"

"My grandfather's."

David sat silent for a while on the back steps, watching the bees hover above the grass and fly between dandelions and clover, thinking of his grandfather and James Bush's body and the baby he'd held this morning. He kept watching the bees; in the late-morning heat, they swarmed around the hollyhocks that lined the alley.

"I can't wait until the new house is done," Mary said. "We'll have indoor plumbing and a bathroom. No more trips to the outhouse, and no more setting up the tub in the kitchen." She stood to go into the house.

"Your father doesn't want me to go along when all of you move to the new house," David said abruptly.

"I know. What will you do?"

"Rent this one from him, I suppose. What would you like me to do?"

"I don't want you to leave Noblesville, or this time. If you can't live with us, this would be best."

"Then it's settled."

"Do you have enough money?"

"For a while," he said, "but I need to figure out how to make more."

The weather remained unbearably hot. That evening the Bush house was crowded with friends and neighbors. Flowers filled the front rooms, and the kitchen table groaned under the weight of food brought by neighbors. Mrs. Bush and Willsie sat on the couch in the front parlor beside the open coffin. Hundreds of people filed through the house throughout the evening.

How had Bush garnered such respect in his life? He was not an extraordinary man—not wealthy, not handsome or clever, and he did not wield great power in the community. He'd run the Ledger a short time, spent most of his adult life as a schoolteacher, and had contributed unremarkable newspaper columns on G.A.R. matters.

Many of those who filed by were young people who had been Bush's students. A small-town high school teacher in this era was a generalist, not a specialist, and many of those students had spent hours a day over three or four years in Bush's classroom. They were here tonight: They had not forgotten him. Robert, Will and Ben stood for some time with David, telling stories of their days in the classroom under Bush's watchful eye.

Then there were old settlers who had known Bush since he was a young farm boy. They, like his father, had cut farms out of the Hoosier forest. Fellow G.A.R. men from around the county came, paying their respects out of a common bond of war. The G.A.R. would pay the funeral expenses. Colleagues from the Ledger shared stories about working through Thursday nights to get out the weekly edition. There were friends and neighbors, fellow Republicans, Pythians and Odd Fellows.

David puzzled over this amazing display of affection for such a simple man. Maybe the time in which he lived was a time when the most valuable thing most people had was their connection to other people. The materialism that would be perhaps the single-most defining social aspect of the Industrial Age had not yet gripped the middle class of America's small towns. In one hundred years, lip service would be paid to putting other people first, but few would really live it. A century of striving for comfort and the relief from inconvenience would lead the middle class to gradually trade their sense of connection for a community structure that made it impossible for a strong sense of community to exist.

Neighbor women worked in the kitchen and planned among themselves who would help the family with meals and chores until they were in better health. Their husbands had already discussed who would come over from time to time to take care of the masculine chores—mowing the lawn, tending the vegetable garden, cleaning the gutters. Major Wainwright arranged a Civil War widow's pension. It would buy the household groceries, but little more.

The hearse stood in front of the Bush home, gleaming and glossy black. Inside the house, Dr. Harrison and nearly all of the members of the G.A.R. post were present in uniform. Several acted as pallbearers; another pronounced a eulogy. Paper fans on little wooden sticks flapped back and forth, creating the only breeze in the house. The ceremony was simple, not unlike the one for David's grandfather more than a hundred years in the future. Afterward, the procession made its way to Crownland Cemetery, where more prayers were offered. The flag-draped coffin lay beside the grave as the G.A.R. men fired their rifles in the air. Eventually they folded the flag and laid it in the widow's arms. Four strong men lowered the casket into the grave.

David was unnerved to see Jim Bush's face through the little window in the coffin top. Two black men in dirty work clothes leaned against shovels about twenty yards away.

The minister stood at the head of the grave and prayed one last time: "James has passed over the river to you, Lord, keep him well."

Willsie and her mother, both dressed in black and bending in slow painful movements, each took a handful of dirt from the fresh black mound and dropped it on the coffin. One damp handful made a dull "thud" when it hit the walnut box. The powerful symbolism of casting that handful of dirt struck David deeply. About thirty-six hours ago, Bush was alive. Now he lay, visible yet dead, six feet below grade, and his wife and daughter, numb from it all, performing the first act of burial. For most of those who knew Jim Bush well, the tears were impossible to hold back, for it meant farewell and acceptance, two things that did not come easily.

For many of the old soldiers, enough years had passed since the war that they could forget some of the blood and misery and in their old age cloak the war in sentimental colors of glory and camaraderie for stories shared at campfire meetings. Now though, the reality crept back for just a moment. All the flags and speeches, all the pomp and circumstance, and all the Sousa marches were wiped away for a moment by two fists full of dirt. In these seconds, as a humid Indiana summer day pressed down on them, these men permitted themselves a few tears.

As the mourners slowly made their way out of the gates and down Monument Street, the diggers were already at work, shoveling scoops of rich, black, Indiana soil on top of Bush's coffin.

"I'm home!" Dr. Harrison shouted, standing in the doorway with a triumphant smile on his face. The dishes had already been passed, and everyone stopped eating to look at him. He pulled a sheaf of papers from his coat pocket. "This is going to make us rich, Mother," he said to Anna, fanning the electric railway stock certificates with his thumb.

Anna harrumphed and turned back to her dinner.

"What's the matter?" the doctor asked, wounded.

"It's just so much money! All we've saved all these years!"

He sat down and reached for the mashed potatoes. "The crews began today, north of town," he announced enthusiastically. "Fifty men and two teams started grading land just beyond the old fairgrounds. They're headed for Wainwright's farm; going to build a bridge across the river there."

"I just hope you know what you're doing," Anna grumbled.

"Mother," he said, patting her hand—he always called her "Mother" when he was trying to persuade her—"Ramsey and Craig both bought stock at the same time I did. Now that they're digging, everyone wants in, so after today, they're not selling anymore. We got in just in time."

"I'm sure you're right," she sighed.

"Oh, you'll see," he grimaced.

While browsing in Craycraft's Dry Goods, David had an idea for making some money. He bought an assortment of hardware—boxes of ornate brass hinges, knobs, escutcheons, window locks, nickel-plated floor grates, and any other piece of beautifully cast metal he could find. He carried them through the beam and into his time.

A pile of newspapers lay on his front porch. He plugged in his dead cell phone, and as the Wifi and cell signals connected, the text and voice mail notifications whistled in rapid succession. The grass was overdue for mowing. He quickly changed into his modern clothes and began combing through the messages.

There was a text from Jeremy and another from his mother. A voice mail from Jane said: "Hi, David, it's Jane. Could you give me a call when you get back in town? A few of us have been working with the bank trying to get them to reconsider demolishing the old theater building. So far, no luck. We could really use your help."

Less than a hour later, David was in the driveway of an architectural salvage yard in Zionsville, his little pickup truck loaded with the antique hardware. Two barns and a shed sitting behind a simple vernacular house were stuffed full of old doors, windows, stairways and stained glass. The yard in front was strewn with porch posts, iron fencing, claw-footed tubs and old pedestal sinks. The tall, lanky owner, Tom, met David in the drive and eyed the old crates.

"Got some stuff to sell?"

"Yeah. A friend of mine bought an old building in … Kokomo. Turns out it was once a hardware store. All this stuff was in the attic. Wondered if you might be interested."

Tom dug through the crates. His eyes widened when he saw what was in them.

"This is incredible!"

They spread the trove on the tailgate. Tom's wife and a few customers marveled at the variety and the pristine condition.

"Think of all the times we've pulled this kind of hardware, caked with paint, out of dumpsters or off rickety old houses, and then spent hours stripping and repolishing it," Tom's wife said, running her fingernail along a floral pattern in a brass strike plate. "I've never seen any in such perfect condition."

A short time later, David, grinning with satisfaction, sped out onto the interstate with a check for $5,000 in his wallet. If he could continue to find buyers for these items, he could make himself rich.

The summer weeks of 1893 had their own rhythm. It started with a quiet walk to church on Sunday morning. The town was still except for the bells that echoed across the rooftops, and the slow clatter of the sedate carriages of churchgoers. As David and the Harrisons approached the

Methodist Episcopal Church, with its slate-covered steeple rising above the trees, the sound of Katie Conwell playing the pipe organ spilled out of the entrance, where the tall wooden double doors stood open. Anna and Mary wore their best, each carrying a parasol in one hand and a Bible in the other. On hot mornings the sanctuary fluttered with palm leaf fans. Parishioners sang and prayed, and afterward they chatted with friends on the sidewalk out front.

Sunday dinner was the best meal of the week. Harry and Clara would come over with baby Albert, and after dining they sat on the porch and talked and read. Mary and Clara would lay Albert on a blanket on the shady lawn and coo over him. There were frequent pot-luck suppers at the church, too.

Thanks to the Bachelors' Club, David made many friends and was often invited to play baseball at the new fairgrounds west of town or in someone's empty field. Baseball was not an entirely proper pursuit for Sunday afternoons, but "boys will be boys" was a sentiment that let young unmarried men off the hook. Mary sat in the grass with the other young women and watch them play, pretending not to notice when a dripping crate of ice and beer was pulled off the back of Robert Wainwright's wagon and the young men gathered around and passed bottles.

The women also had their own social life, apart from the men. Mary and Anna attended afternoon club meetings in the homes of other women: the Orpheus Club, the Kettledrum, the Neighborly Club. There was also the Married Ladies Social Club, the Bow Knot Club, the Shakespeare Club and the Tourist Club. The Harrison women attended one or two meetings a week; once during the summer they hosted a meeting, with an elaborate tea, in the small house on Emmous Street.

David often spent a day in Harry's office in the Joseph Building and ate lunch with him on the square. Another day, he might hang around the courthouse and the auditor's office, reading the Indianapolis Sentinel or the Indianapolis News with Fred and Dr. Harrison. When they were busy, he'd go up to the courtroom and watch a trial.

When Mary and Anna were shopping for furnishings, he'd tag along and usually end up at the new house on Catherine Street, helping to hang trim or watching the painters and carpenters work. Anna wanted to be in the house by August first, and it looked possible. David used some of the money he was making selling hardware to buy furniture to set up housekeeping when the Harrisons left him with the Emmous Street house. In several stores around town were pieces of furniture with a "Sold/Henry" tag.

One day each week David and Mary took the late-morning L.E.&W. train for the fifty-minute trip to Union Station in Indianapolis. Indianapolis had a population of perhaps a hundred thousand, but David thought it seemed like an overgrown small town. To be sure, its public buildings were bigger and more beautiful, and the houses larger and more elegant than those of any small Hoosier town. Woodruff Place was almost a complete town itself, with fountains and wide boulevards. The city's monuments were grander and its business district many times the size of that in little Noblesville, but its atmosphere was still warm and friendly.

Once Will Craig and Willsie Bush came with them, but usually they went alone. They ate lunch in a restaurant and walked about the city, toured the pink marble hallways of the State House, took in a public lecture upstairs at Tomlinson's Hall, or strolled through the farmers' market. They enjoyed strolling the small campus of Irvington University or down the tree-lined sidewalks of Meridian, where the grandest houses in the state loomed beyond iron fences and well-tended lawns. Like tourists in any time, they kept an eye out for local celebrities, and were rewarded by seeing former president Benjamin Harrison, who lived on Delaware Street, and the poet James Whitcomb Riley coming out of his house on Lockerbie.

They shopped in Charles Mayer's, and David often spent too much on Mary. When he found something that he felt would bring a profit in his time, he'd buy all the store had and have it sent to the house in Noblesville. They sometimes stayed late enough to dine and take in an outdoor band concert, not stepping off the train at the Noblesville depot until late.

Saturdays became "picnic day," and David and Mary would ride out into the countryside with Robert Wainwright, Willsie Bush, Ben Craig, Hanna Craycraft, John Davies, Will Christian, Fred and Katie, and a rotating assortment of other young folk. Their favorite spot was a thickly wooded grove on the west side of the river, just north of downtown, which could only be reached when the river was just a foot or two deep.

They drove north on Catherine, through the old fairgrounds, out of town and down the dirt lane that led to the river. They forded it beyond the Wainwright farm, churning up mud on the river bed. The horses climbed the west bank and were tethered beneath the trees.

The picnickers spread blankets and tablecloths on the ground and ate cucumber sandwiches, cake, cold fried chicken, fresh fruit, hard-boiled eggs and pickles. One Saturday in early July they picked overripe black raspberries from the thicket at the edge of the trees and sat for hours in the shade, drinking wine and eating the berries, their fingertips and lips stained reddish-purple. There were no members of the Women's Christian Temperance Union among them, and drunkenness wasn't uncommon by the end of an afternoon.

John Davies, who'd come to town that summer to take a job with the electric railway, most closely shared David's point of view. The two of them stood between two horses along the river that Saturday, eating raspberries from their purple-stained hands, laughing and telling jokes. Both were drunk.

Willsie Bush and the other women were sitting on a fallen tree, gently disapproving with a little wine-induced head fog of their own. "Ladies," Willsie smiled, "behold, we have four horses' asses nicely lined up before us."

"No single one wiser than the other," Mary put in. The girls all laughed.

"Now why must you be that way?" John asked. Well born and well educated, John often met David at the Wainwright Hotel to eat lunch and argue politics. David came to call the two of them the "cruise directors" of the picnic group—a phrase that puzzled the others, but there was little doubt that they organized the fun and usually pushed it over the edge.

"I can speak of tenderness," John went on, "the kind of tenderness that respects the wisdom of a woman's heart. So why would you say such harsh things about me and my dear friend, David?"

"You can speak of tenderness and wisdom?" Willsie asked.

"Yes, let me share a story with you."

"Please," Mary added. "I'd like to know what you think fits that bill." The ladies laughed at the challenge.

"Okay." John forced the last of the berries into his mouth with the palm of his hand, smearing deep purple juice around his lips.

"Oh, this should be good," Willsie giggled, leaning into Mary. "Lovely, ruby red lips, John."

John wiped his mouth with the back of his hand and winked at David. "My dear Grandpappy and Grandmammy in California are getting quite old, and recently they sat at breakfast on their fiftieth wedding anniversary." John stepped forward, gesturing broadly with his hands. "They live in a grand house now, so different than their modest beginnings. And lordy, even at her advanced age, my Grandmammy is a lustful woman."

"Lustful?" Willsie narrowed an eye at John.

"She is. God love 'er. She says to my Grandpappy, 'Do you recall, fifty years ago we sat around this very same table as newlyweds, having a breakfast just like this after a night of passion?' "

"Holy Moses!" Willsie exclaimed. "She told you this?"

"No," John winked, "Grandpappy told me after a couple drinks." He rocked his hand before his mouth, tipping an invisible bottle of liquor.

David chimed in, pointing at John. "I believe the man."

Mary caught a burst of laughter and a gulp of wine in her mouth with the palm of her hand, coughed, then pointed at David. "Well, at least there's one person who believes this story."

"Hold your horses, people," John went on, palms up to quiet the crowd. "Anyway, Grandmammy went on to say, 'Do you recall, we would sit around this table, waking up after a night of passion, sitting naked, enjoying our tea and oatmeal together? And my Grandpappy says, 'Yes, it was the sweetest time of my life.' And so Grandmammy says, 'Let's relive those beautiful moments.' And so then and there they took their clothes off and sat back down as they once did so often fifty years before."

Katie looked at the other girls, hoping someone would stop this ridiculous story. "I can't see this happening. He's making this up."

Mary, deadpan, raised a finger in her direction and said, "The second person here naïve enough to entertain the notion this story could be true. And then, realizing is isn't, thought she better warn us."

"Ladies, please," John held his hands up to quiet them. "I know this is hard for some Hoosiers to accept, but my lustful Grandmammy said, 'Even today, my nipples are as hot for you as they were fifty years ago.' "

The ladies were laughing uncontrollably. "Oh, my goodness," Willsie snorted.

"'Well, of course they are,' my Grandpappy replied with a wink and a smile," John continued. " 'One of them is in your coffee, and the other is in your oatmeal.'"

The entire group fell into laughter.

"Tell me about Chicago, and the World's Fair," David asked later as they waded in the river.

"You've gotta go," John said, shaking his head in wonder. "I've traveled across this country by train, and I tell ya, I've never seen anything like it."

"Mary and I are trying to figure out a way to go."

"Well, if you could get there and share it with a woman like that, now that would be something you'd remember the rest of your life. I'm telling you, there is nothing else in this entire nation like Chicago and that fair. It will go down in history."

"Mary's got a friend from Bryn Mawr living in Chicago. She's been invited to go stay and see the fair. She's devising a plan and scheming to persuade her parents."

"And you along as chaperone?" he smiled at David, reached out and squeezed his shoulder. "A damn lucky man you are."

David found conversation with John and the picnic group more challenging than with his peers in his own time. None of them had grown up passively watching television as he had. They'd spent their time reading or talking and playing parlor games. This made them clever and formidable conversationalists. The speed and complexity of their banter was at first beyond him. But as the summer wore on, he began holding his own.

He was able to keep up because he had changed. Being here in this environment had changed him mentally and physically.

The mental clutter of cell phone, TV, radio, music and random noise pollution was gone. Without constant distraction, his mind was free to work, to replay memories, fantasize, focus on the subtleties of his surroundings. He talked more to people and read more. His mind slowly came alive like a weak muscle exercised into regular motion, gaining strength and agility as the days went by. And without a ready supply of convenience foods, the fact that he walked everywhere, and because activities were more physical and less passive, he'd lost weight and regained his trim physique. It happened without him noticing. One day while sitting with the picnic group along the river, it just struck him that he had changed. His ability to concentrate for long periods of time, his memory, the speed of his wit, it was all improved, and simply by turning off the information that had bombarded him his whole life. And the clothes he'd bought upon arriving were loose, mostly because there was no TV to sit in front of, no tacos or pizza or snacks constantly available, and no car to get you easily from one place to another.

Anna would scold them if they came home from their picnic smelling of wine. "It's good that Sunday comes after Saturday, that way you sinners get a chance to ask for forgiveness while your sins are still fresh in the mind."

More than once Dr. Harrison defused the situation by whispering to David, "Wish I'd gone with you."

CHAPTER ELEVEN

Who are the Gossipers?
Ed. Ledger:
*If there is anything that looks bad, these lovely summer evenings,
it is to see a lot of women of a neighborhood gather together and
pick to pieces their unfortunate neighbor that happens not to be
of the party. It would be much better if they would look into their
own faults, or if they are church-members, converse of the good they
might and ought to do. Talk on subjects that will improve. Avoid
personalities when they tend to the injury of others. Good Advice.*
The Hamilton County Ledger, July 21, 1893.

Within a week, Etta Heylman admitted to being the mother and the
attempted murderer of the baby boy found by Isaac Eurick. Her demeanor
softened and Sheriff Rhoades sent her to the county home, allowing her
to stay with and care for the infant. The details of her admission were
splashed across the front pages of the Ledger and Democrat. People
whispered endlessly about it, speculating about the identity of the father.

In mid-July a rumor began to spread along Emmous Street that one
of its residents, Warren Beeman, had been "unduly intimate" with his
colored cleaning girl, America Dempsey.

No sooner had the story taken hold than Mrs. Beeman, unaware of the rumor, took her children to visit relatives in Crawfordsville. Taking the talk seriously and seeing Mrs. Beeman's departure as proof, Sheriff Rhoades had deputies stake out the Beeman house on the first night the wife and children were gone. On that night, nothing, but on the second night they found what they were looking for. Around 11 o'clock, Deputy Barnett spotted Beeman and America Dempsey in the house together.

Rhoades and Barnett, assisted by other deputies, surrounded the residence and demanded that Beeman open the door. He would not. A group of neighbors gathered on the sidewalk to see what was going on. After the deputies threatened to break the door down, Beeman opened it, denying that anyone was inside. Barnett handcuffed Beeman to a porch post, and the deputies scoured the house.

Beeman, barefoot and wearing only his trousers, suspenders dangling at his side, nervously called out to his neighbors, "I don't know what they're lookin' for, I haven't done anything wrong." After a week of rumor-mongering, few believed him. Twenty minutes later Barnett found America Dempsey dressed only in a corset and a slip, hidden under a pile of clothes in a bedchamber wardrobe.

Barnett and Garrison brought America, handcuffed, out on to the porch. Several onlookers gasped. Beeman hung his head. In a loud, clear voice, Deputy Barnett said, "I'm placing you both under arrest on a charge of fornication."

David and Fred stood on the sidewalk, looking down toward the Beeman house, wondering why a crowd had gathered. A neighbor came by, shocked but excited, saying, "Beeman's been arrested for fornicatin' with a nigger girl."

David watched Warren Beeman and America Dempsey being placed in a wagon. The stray light from lanterns fluttered in the trees and on the ground as the deputies moved around the vehicle. Neighbors looked on, some from front porches and parlor windows, others not ten feet away from the two, standing on the sidewalk. The wagon pulled away.

David knew them both only in passing. Beeman was a handsome man of perhaps thirty-five with a receding hairline and ruddy features. America, with flawless, deep-chocolate skin and Anglo features, was perhaps twenty years old. She was a beautiful woman.

Back on the Harrisons' porch, the doctor came out and asked what all the fuss was about. They told him and he looked down, shaking his head.

"As wrong as adultery may be," David said, "I can't believe that someone could be arrested for having an affair."

"It's against the law," Dr. Harrison said, rubbing the back of his neck, "though I don't imagine the sheriff would have gotten involved if it hadn't been a colored woman."

At the sheriff's residence, Beeman paid a $50 bond and went home. America Dempsey spent the night in jail. By morning, someone had paid the $40 bond for her and she was warned to appear before Mayor Jones's court at 9 o'clock. She did not.

Mayor Jones spent the better part of Wednesday morning impaneling a jury. At noon someone spotted America Dempsey leaving town on the L.E.&W., Southbound Panhandle. Deputy Barnett telegraphed the Indianapolis authorities, asking that they arrest her at Union Station. She was never found.

It was announced that the case would be called for trial in the courtroom after the dinner hour that evening.

"An illegitimate baby down a privy vault, and now this," Anna complained. "There are just too many new people coming into town; it's growing too fast. Almost wish they'd never discovered gas and this could have stayed a quiet little place. People'll be down there tonight to gawk and laugh. It's shameful."

Against the urging of the doctor and Anna, David went to the courthouse to watch the proceedings. Fred and Mary were forbidden

When David left the house he saw Warren Beeman, a block away, step down off his front porch, dressed in his Sunday best. All the way downtown Beeman was a block ahead of David. As he walked, the curious watched him pass by but did not say "hello" or make conversation, as they normally would. Beeman walked through his own neighborhood an intensely interesting non-person.

David found a seat on the main floor in the courtroom. By the time the trial began, the balcony nearly spilled over with people. Many were men who had cleared the saloons and pool halls. Adding to the rowdy atmosphere were a number of electric railway workers. Many were strangers to Noblesville; others had no families. They'd come for what promised to be a first-class bit of entertainment. A few young boys tried to slip in but were turned back at the door. David sat next to an attractive young woman seated on the aisle. She was perhaps his age or a little older and well dressed. They made small talk about how embarrassing and scandalous the affair was. The woman's name was Ida May Thompson, from Carmel. A purple silk hat with large feathers was pinned to her dark-brown hair. She wore a deep-purple dress and clutched a handbag in her lap.

"I'm from Canada and not real familiar with the way things are done here," David lied to her, "but someone suggested to me that if Beeman had an affair with a white woman, he would never have been arrested."

Mrs. Thompson looked at him as if he'd asked an impertinent question. "I suppose there's truth to that. If his cleaning girl had been just another little Irish immigrant, I imagine the sheriff would have let gossip pass its sentence, but amalgamation is a more serious matter to most people." She spoke in quick, choppy sentences, her tone opinionated. "It's just not right."

"Amalgamation?" David said.

"The marriage or mixing of colored and white. Amalgamation—it's a sin."

A hush passed over the crowd and gave way to whispering. David looked two stories up at the pressed-tin ceiling and then back at those in the balcony who were looking down at the aisle behind him. Beeman was walking in with his lawyers, Thomas Swain and George Hinds. They made their way to the defendant's table on the left, beyond the wooden balustrade that separated the public seating from the bench and jury box.

With the room of eyes upon him, Warren Beeman looked like a caged animal. Sweat ran down his forehead and gathered on the tip of his nose and upper lip. No matter how this turned out, his life in Noblesville was over. The only sentence that really mattered in a case like this had already been handed down: public knowledge of his transgression.

As the jury filed in there were no seats left in the courtroom and people were filling up the halls and standing in the aisles near the back. Deputy Barnett walked to the back and herded those without seats out of the room, closing the door behind them.

"Y'all rise," a voice called out, and Mayor Jones walked in, wearing a black robe, and took his seat behind the bench. The spectators sat.

The mayor cast a wary eye about the room. He was a short, chubby, balding man, over sixty years old. A bushy mustache hung over his upper lip. He peered out at the gallery through round, wire-rimmed glasses as if everyone there were guilty of something.

"I recognize that this case is very sensational," Jones said in a gruff voice, looking across the faces and up at those in the balcony, "but I expect that the public here tonight will behave themselves and act in a manner befitting the seriousness of legal matters. Also, anyone under the age of twenty-one should leave the room at this time, as the subject of this case is delicate and of an adult matter."

Several teenage boys were ushered out.

"Mr. Beeman, would you stand, please." Beeman stood, looking as if he might pass out at any minute. Jones narrowed his eyes at the defendant. "Do you understand the charges against you?"

"Yes, sir."

"What do you have to say for yourself?"

"I'm not guilty."

There was muffled laughter from the electric railway workers in the balcony.

"Disgusting people," Mrs. Thompson said under her breath, glancing up at the balcony.

"Tom, how would you like to begin?" Mayor Jones asked, looking down at some notes and adjusting his glasses. " I suspect we only have a few witnesses at best. I mean, the Dempsey girl's run off, right?"

"We'll call Mr. Beeman to the stand."

Beeman stood and approached the stand as if he were being led to the gallows. He sat, but then stood again when the bailiff approached with a Bible.

As Beeman nervously took his oath, David heard the woman in front of him whisper, "If the man had read that book a bit more, we all wouldn't be here tonight."

Thomas Swain stood up and swaggered across the floor. He was a big man, in his early forties and over six feet tall, with coal-black hair, a bushy black mustache and broad shoulders. If you were in trouble in Noblesville, it was good to have Thomas Swain on your side—the state senator for the Noblesville area, a Civil War veteran and a respected lawyer, perhaps next to Major Wainwright and Leonard Wild he was the city's favorite son. His body language, strutting around like a cannon ball, said he was in charge. David imagined Swain was a bully as a youngster.

"Mr. Beeman," Swain said gently, "where do you live?"

"East Emmous Street."

"Alone?"

"No, with my wife and three children."

"Do you love them?" Swain asked, resting an elbow on the stand and his other hand on his hip, looking out at the crowd.

"More than anything else in the world," Beeman choked, about to cry.

"It's all right, Mr. Beeman," Swain said, patting Warren's arm. "I know this misunderstanding is very upsetting, but we'll straighten things out; that's why you're here.

"Now, did America Dempsey work for you and your wife?"

"Yes."

"For how long?"

"About six months. Since our third baby was born, my wife's needed some help around the house."

"And what services did Mrs. Dempsey perform for you?"

The balcony erupted in laughter, and the mayor threatened to throw them out.

"Go ahead, Mr. Beeman," the mayor said sternly, looking about the room.

"She did cooking, cleaning, washing."

"Miss Dempsey was at your house late last night," Swain said. "Why was that?"

"Well, my wife is to be home tomorrow, and I wanted things to be in extra good shape around the house, figuring that she'd be tired from traveling with the kids and all, so I asked America to work late, scrubbin' the floors and washin' laundry."

"I'm going to ask you a serious question, Mr. Beeman. I have to ask it, you understand. Have you ever been intimate with America Dempsey?"

"Certainly not," Beeman said, weakly.

"It's a shame that she's not here with us to confirm your words," Swain said. "Why do you think young Miss Dempsey hid from the deputies last night when they entered your home?"

"Well, I've been thinking a lot about that today, and I think maybe

I know."

"Tell us, would you?"

"Well, my wife has been missing things lately—jewelry, a little money; nothing serious, but strange just the same. We were beginnin' to think maybe America had taken the things. Maybe she was guilty and thought that the cops were after her."

This didn't sound at all convincing to David. The act between Swain and Beeman had the flair of bad melodrama.

When Swain was done, prosecutor Simon Stuart stood and approached Beeman.

"Mr. Beeman, when you opened the door for the police last night, you were wearing only your trousers, and your suspenders were hanging at your knees. Why?"

Beeman squirmed in his seat. "I was changing clothes."

"To go to bed?"

"Um—no."

"You were changing clothes, but not going to bed, and it was 11 o'clock and your housekeeper was still there?"

"Yes."

"Do you always walk around the house half-dressed at 11 o'clock when your wife and children are out of town and your young colored housekeeper is still there?"

"No. I was walking through the house because I was answering the door."

"Why didn't America answer the door?"

"I don't know," Beeman mumbled.

"Your door was locked. Why?"

"Safety."

"What were you afraid of? You see, Mr. Beeman, I don't know very many people in this town who lock their doors. Besides, it was a warm evening. Having the door open would have let some air in."

"I just always lock it," Beeman insisted.

"Why didn't you open the door when the deputies asked you to?"

"I thought maybe it was some slick burglars, tricking me to get the door open."

"Burglars?" Stuart asked.

"Yes."

Stuart began to pace, the wooden floor creaking under his steps. "Deputy Barnett will be taking the stand in a few minutes, and while I could ask him this question—and probably will," he said, stopping and absentmindedly pointing in the air, "I'll ask you first: How long have you known Deputy Barnett?"

Beeman hesitated. "About four years."

"So, if I'm to understand you," Stuart said with a smile, incredulous, "when you looked out the front window and saw Barnett with a lantern up to his face, and he was saying, 'This is Deputy Barnett, open this door at once,' you thought it was a burglar?"

"I suppose so."

"Five minutes later when you finally opened the door, America was nowhere to be found. Yet the deputies found Miss Dempsey in the very bedchamber where you and your wife sleep, hidden in the wardrobe, herself half-naked beneath a pile of clothes that, clearly, someone else had placed upon her. How would you explain that?"

Beeman started to say something and then stopped himself, paused and then said meekly, " I can't."

Stuart paced the floor again, staring vacantly up at the second-story windows, and decided to let Beeman sentence himself.

"You're an upstanding citizen, aren't you, Mr. Beeman?" Stuart asked, now in a friendlier voice.

"I'd like to think so," Beeman replied.

"Faithfulness is an important virtue, isn't it?"

"Yes."

"Mr. Beeman, what would you think of a man who carried on with another woman behind his wife's back? Because, when you think about it, that man is jeopardizing the marital foundation that his family is built upon."

Beeman hesitated. "I'd think he wasn't a very good person," he mumbled.

"Wouldn't you also think that he had not just betrayed his wife, but his children, too, and the whole community, for that matter? Without even knowing it, children depend on their parents for love, safety, security; a man who betrays their mother betrays their needs by threatening the family base. And then the community—it depends on the parents to raise the children properly. If the man destroys the family foundation, then the community has to step in and help his family—and do his job for him. That's a pretty serious betrayal, don't you agree?"

"Yes, but that's not me, that's not what I did."

Stuart spoke as if to the ceiling and Beeman answered as if to the floor. David found himself strangely moved by the questioning and couldn't help seeing his own father where Beeman sat.

"What should happen to a man who has betrayed his wife, his children and his community, Mr. Beeman?"

"He should be ashamed of himself."

"At the very least," Stuart said sarcastically, turning his gaze to the defendant, "at the very least!"

By the time Simon Stuart was finished ripping Beeman's story apart and leading him through a moral lesson, it was dark outside. The gaslights in the courtroom were turned up full and the shutters were thrown wide open to let air in. A few people gathered along Catherine Street looking up at the windows, wondering what they were missing. Fred and Mary sat at Truitt's soda fountain in the Wild Opera House, waiting for David to come out.

Inside the courtroom, Swain and Hinds called no more witnesses to defend their client; there was no one to call. Simon Stuart called Deputy Barnett, who relayed the details of what he had seen through the window the previous night.

As Barnett testified, Beeman sank deeper and deeper into his chair. The other deputies testified as well, telling the same story. To David's amazement, and Beeman's as well, Thomas Swain asked no questions, leaving Beeman hanging. At some point during Stuart's cross-examination of Beeman, Swain had realized the futility of fighting. The stone-like looks of disgust on the faces of the twelve men in the jury box could not have been a comfort to Beeman.

When the sheriff finished testifying and both sides declared they had no more witnesses, the mayor adjourned until 10 o'clock the next morning.

Without saying a word to Beeman, George Hinds and Thomas Swain stood up and walked down the aisle. As they approached the row where David sat beside Mrs. Thompson, Swain's eye fixed on her with a start and his expression drastically changed from confidence to irritation. As he passed their row, Ida Mae Thompson reached out her hand and touched Swain's coat sleeve. He stopped and glared down at her.

"How awful it would be to find oneself in Mr. Beeman's position," Mrs. Thompson said softly to Swain without looking at him. "Don't you agree?"

Thomas Swain made no response, but looked over at David and nodded his head in greeting—saying, "Mr. Henry"—and walked out.

Mrs. Thompson turned to David, asking, "You're a friend of Mr. Swain's?"

"More of an acquaintance, really," David said, standing. He was upset by the testimony, but not completely sure why, and didn't really want to talk to her. "We've met socially."

"Well, it was a pleasure to meet you, Mr. Henry," she said, extending her hand. "Perhaps I'll see you in the morning."

David shook her hand and said goodbye.

He left by the Catherine Street doors and crossed the brick pavement. Fred and Mary were standing on the sidewalk in front of the Wild building. The gas lights were being turned down in the soda fountain behind them.

"What happened?" Fred asked.

"He's guilty as hell." David frowned.

"This really bothers you doesn't it, David?" Mary said, taking his arm.

"It's one issue that Beeman cheated on his wife and kids," David said as they headed for home, "but then the community compounds things by pulling him into court for it. He and his family won't be able to live here anymore, will they?"

"Not very comfortably," Mary said, sighing.

"More than just cheating on his wife, he did it with a nigger girl," Fred sneered, "and that makes it worse."

"Don't say that word." David sighed heavily, exasperated.

"What word," Fred asked, "nigger?"

"Yeah, just don't say it." David snapped. "And how is it 'worse?'"

David knew that they didn't and never would see eye to eye on this, but he was itching to have it out. He felt angry. The bigotry wasn't anything new; he'd heard it all his life growing up in a predominantly white community. He'd learned to tolerate it. With Fred, though, it was different. His attitude was instead the commonly held, socially acceptable opinion. But tonight that didn't seem to matter to David. The trial had mixed two unrelated issues together in his mind, and he was no longer certain which one he was most angry about. He wanted so much to let go at someone.

"First off," Fred said, angrily, "I've heard you use all sorts of foul language, so where do you get off tellin' me not to say 'nigger?' And furthermore, they're not like us. They're not as smart as us, they have filthy habits, they can't control their urges—"

"Shut up, Fred," David blurted.

He stopped right there on the sidewalk and swung around at Fred, who backed off, thinking David was going to hit him. "I've got the advantage over you, Fred. There's a hundred-plus years of history I've seen that you haven't. Narrow-minded bigotry, like what I hear coming out of your mouth, will continue to make life miserable for black people clear into my time. But you know what? As far as I'm concerned, any 'colored man' is as good as any white man—and that goes for you, too."

"David!" Mary broke in.

Fred glared at David. "You think you're so smart," he spat, "and so great because you've come from the future and seen what's to come and learned one hundred years of things that ain't happened yet. Well, you saved Clara's life all right, but you ain't no God or no ghost. You're just a man, same as everybody else. End of the day, you gotta look yourself in the mirror same as me. Besides that, you're a runaway, nothin' more. You hate the time you come from—you never stop sayin' how awful it is—so don't try to tell me that what you learned there is better than what I've learned here. As long as you keep goin' around cryin' about how bad the future is, don't try to tell me you learned how to think and feel the right way while you were there. Something tells me you ain't got no pills to cure the way I think, so it must not be a sickness. Maybe you're the one with a problem."

"Fred, don't," Mary said, reaching for him. He tore his arm away.

"I ain't no little kid anymore," he mumbled to her. "I don't need my big sister tellin' me what to do." He swung around and walked toward home.

"Fred, please," she called behind him, but he went on.

"David," Mary said, sighing angrily, "you can't expect him to think like you do, for God's sake."

"I'm just so sick of the narrow-mindedness, Mary," he said through clenched teeth. "I'm sick of hearing it."

They walked on in silence for a block, past the Wild Opera House and the First Christian Church. A woman was sitting on her front porch and called out a friendly "hello" to them.

"It isn't just colored and white, is it?" Mary asked gravely. "This has something to do with your parents, doesn't it?"

"It's all mixed together in my head, and for no particular reason, I suppose. It's his wife and kids I can't stop thinking about. Like it's me. It was me, once.

"You didn't think that kind of thing happened now, did you?"

"You know, I really didn't. I was always taught that people didn't do such things in this time.

"You know what?" David said, "If this thing happened on Cherry— well, Emmous Street in my time—there wouldn't be too many people who would get bent out of shape. There's a certain rightness about that. I mean, it's between Mr. Beeman and his wife and America Dempsey; it's not anybody else's business. But during the questioning tonight, I couldn't help wishing that my father had stood trial for what he did to my family. What we went through, just because he got bored with my mom and couldn't keep his pants up, it had the same effect as if one of us had gotten raped or murdered or killed in a terrible accident; it was a tragedy.

"When he was cheating on my mom, he was cheating on me, too, and my brother. But society takes no sides; we have no-fault divorce. The thing that bothers me most as I look back now is that my dad paid no price whatsoever for breaking up our family. Well, I imagine that a few people thought he was a bad person, but most people were unmoved. It didn't affect his job, he didn't lose any friends, nobody looked down on him; and they should have! There should have been some price, at least social disapproval, but there wasn't.

"This trial tonight was clearly racially motivated. But when it comes to divorce and adultery, I think maybe my society has gone too far the other way. I don't know what the answer is."

Instead of going home, they went to the cemetery and sat on the 1824 stone and talked. Mary asked David what the moral debate on infidelity was like in his time. David told her about "family values." She listened with interest.

"People in 1893 Noblesville would not completely understand such a debate," Mary said. "To us, 'value' is an economic term. The discussion of morals more appropriately belongs within the realm of 'virtues.'

"Your era's notion of values is at odds with our moral view of the world. The term 'values' implies a relativity; one person's values may not be those of another, or, your values depend on who you are and where you're from." Mary ended, folding her hands.

"It was a perfect reference point for the sexual revolution of the 1960s," David put in. "One person might believe that premarital sex is all right, while another might think it's a sin. It's a matter of competing moral values, one no greater than the other—just different."

"That's totally unacceptable," Mary said. "We speak of 'virtues' which are not relative, they're concrete. Either you have them or you don't. You can be taught them or they may be innate; either way, each is a specific thing, not something that is chosen based on personal preference. Honesty is honesty, and it is not relative to anything; either you tell the truth or you don't. Faithfulness, as well, is a singular quality; either you're faithful or you're not. It's an incredibly solid foundation upon which to base social behavior. Build your moral house on virtue, and you have built on rock; build your moral house on . . . 'values,' and you have built on sand."

"I never thought of it that way," David admitted.

"Virtues are not ever-changing like the ebbs and flows of social change," Mary went on, "they're ancient. Aristotle had his cardinal virtues—wisdom, temperance, justice and courage. And the Knights of Pythius have their cardinal principles emblazoned in frescoes on the walls of Castle Hall above the hardware store: Friendship, Charity and Benevolence."

"It's so different in my time," David said, shaking his head. "Now, in this time, virtuous behavior is championed in every corner."

Mary nodded in agreement. "Faith, hope, chastity and perseverance, combined with the cardinal virtues of Aristotle and the Pythians, are the publicly stated measures of a good person and a good society, our Christian and secular beliefs rolled into one. Therefore, regardless of how particular individuals like Warren Beeman fail to be virtuous in daily life, regardless of how they might cheat on the virtues privately, children publicly get one message about what is right and wrong from their parents, their neighbors, magazines, newspapers ... everywhere."

"That's a stark contrast to the world in which I grew up," David said. "I floated through my formative years in day-care centers while both my parents worked. The measure of what was right and wrong was a tidal wave of conflicting values."

Mary listened intently as David went on. "The only solid, unswerving expression of virtuous behavior I knew came from my grandparents. More than escaping the meltdown of my parents' marriage, being with them was the only place in my life where the boundaries of life were clearly defined. This was a world apart from popular American culture, where right and wrong is a constantly fluctuating value scale that people adjust to fit their desires.

"Still, the argument for values is more to my liking," David said. "I don't want to be told by someone else how to live my life."

"Yes," Mary agreed. "but when there are victims involved, isn't it better to measure the perpetrators not on their values, but on their virtues?"

David nodded in agreement. They sat silent for a moment.

"I broke my mother's heart during the divorce when I begged her to let me live with my grandparents," David said, looking out across the gravestones toward the river, where lightning bugs flickered in the dark. "I wanted to live in a place that had easy-to-see walls, that would hold me in and keep me safe, so I'd know I wasn't going to float away into the world, away from a place that I felt was mine."

"And your parents couldn't see this?" Mary asked.

"No," he said, his voice quavering. "I couldn't have even explained it, and they were too busy trying to find happiness in their own screwed-up lives. They thought they were putting me and Mike first—but providing food, clothing and shelter doesn't mean the job is over. They weren't there for me. I mean, they didn't keep our home together, they didn't make a place for us to belong. They were too busy being at war with one another, and then when that was over, trying to find someone new to fill the gap in their love lives. How could traveling so far away from it all bring it closer to me now than it was while it was happening?"

Mary, sensing that David was near a breaking point, stood up and walked around in front of him and sat on his lap. She pulled off his straw hat and kissed his forehead. "Where do you belong, David?" she whispered.

"I don't know," he said, struggling to hold back a tear.

She kissed him again and her eyelash brushed the warmth of a wet tear on his face. She pulled off her white glove and wiped it from his cheek.

"There's a little boy inside of you who's still very angry at his parents for a divorce that happened fifteen years ago … and at his grandfather for dying."

As David silently nodded, he tried to force his chin up and tighten his lower lip, but the tears came anyway. "If there was anything about my past I'd change, it would be those two things."

"Ah, David," Mary said softy, putting her arms around his head and pulling him against her. He wrapped his arms around her and cried freely.

"I've felt so lost for so long," he said. "It didn't really hurt; I just felt numb. But now the numbness is leaving and I'm trying so hard to make some sense of it all—and I just feel so angry."

They sat holding each other in the darkness. The Chicago and Southeastern westbound rumbled through the trees a hundred yards south, breaking the quiet, its headlamp flickering among the leaves. David pulled away and looked at Mary.

"I felt so separate from the divorce and my grandfather's death. Those are the two most important events of my life, yet I was kept so far away from them. It was like I was never allowed to make peace with them. If my father wanted to run off with another woman and destroy our family, that's his business and, according to life in my times, his legitimate right. Oh, sure, people felt sorry for us, but divorce was happening all the time. It's so much a part of life that I guess I felt it wasn't my right to be upset about it. And my grandfather's death—we didn't handle the body or sit with him when he was ill. He was hidden away and isolated in a hospital and died alone, and then his body came to us all dressed and prepackaged in the funeral home.

"You know what's funny? I was always taught that people in this time were so reserved and kept so much inside, and I suppose to a certain extent that's true, but on the other hand the most dramatic events of life are so crammed in your face here," he said, his voice trembling. "You can't be isolated. Few of the important parts of life are hidden, and there are rituals to go along with them, to make you a part of it all. Rituals in my time feel like just going through the motions, painting by numbers. Here, they have some purpose."

David wiped his eyes with the palms of his hands.

"So much like Hamlet," Mary said sympathetically, "so troubled by death and parents.

"You know what I think?" she went on gently, brushing the hair off his forehead with her fingers. "You're not a little boy anymore. No one can help you find your place but you. You can't blame them anymore. You're a grown man, and you have to take responsibility for yourself and your own happiness. You're a lovely, magnificent man, David. You'll find your way."

"And you," he said smiling at her, wanting to change the subject, "will you find your way?"

"I don't know," she said, turning away and thinking. "It was just about a month ago that we sat here and kissed for the first time. I sounded pretty sad then, I suppose, but the last few weeks being with you, I'd really forgotten that I felt so trapped here. You did that for me," she said, turning back to him. "You've made me feel like I'm not alone here. You understand and encourage me. I still want to go somewhere different and special to live my life, but I'm pretty satisfied being here right now with you, and I'll be satisfied to stay here as long as you do."

David kissed her. "Let's go somewhere special," he said, "like the World's Fair in Chicago. Could we do that?"

"I don't know yet, but I've got a plan."

"What kind of plan?"

"It's a secret," she teased.

CHAPTER TWELVE

*"If the Lord had placed the Garden of Eden on the banks of the
Wabash River,
Mankind would still be without the Original Sin."*
Morton J. Marcus

The next morning the courtroom again filled with the curious, though
with a workday in progress, fewer people turned out. David found a seat
downstairs and within a few minutes Ida Mae Thompson came in and
took a seat four rows in front of him, smiling and saying, "Hello, Mr.
Henry," as she adjusted her umbrella and pocketbook. She had placed
herself in the front row, just behind the railing and the chair where
Thomas Swain had sat last night. When Swain, Hinds and Beeman
came in and sat at the defendant's table, it was evident that Swain
was disturbed by Ida Mae's presence. She, on the other hand, seemed
pleased with herself.

It took the jury just fifteen minutes to find Beeman guilty. As the
verdict was read, Beeman's chin sunk to his chest and he sobbed softy.
Mayor Jones leaned back in his chair and looked out over his glasses.
"You got anything to say before I sentence you, Warren?"

Beeman said nothing, but simply shook his head side to side. Tears
trickled down his cheeks.

"I think that justice has been done here," Jones nodded, looking at Beeman, "but I don't take one iota of pleasure seeing it done. You've shamed yourself and your family, Warren. You sinned against God and broke a commandment and broke the vows you made to your wife."

The mayor paused and looked over the paper the foreman had given him, not really reading, just going over it in his head.

"We got standards 'round here. We have'ta have 'em. If we don't … Why, if everybody decided they were going to be ruled by their sinful desires, where would we be? Well, we'd be in a mess, and I guess you know that. Warren, you got a family to feed and care for, so we're not gonna put you away a long time, but I think you need some time to think this over and remember how much your wife and little ones need you to do the right thing. I'm gonna fine you fifty dollars and put you in jail for a week."

With that, Mayor Jones banged his gavel down and said, "We're adjourned, gentlemen."

At the Harrisons' new house, the painters were applying wine-red and deep-green paint to the porch posts and sky blue to the bead-board roof decking and chamfered rafters on the underside of the porch roof. Inside, wallpaper was being hung and a final coat of varnish applied to the wood mantles. Rim locks, mortise locks, and doorknobs were being installed and escutcheons screwed into place

They could start moving within a week. The carriage house in back, its shingle roof laid just a week earlier, was full of new furniture, temporarily stored. The construction debris had been removed from the yard, grass seed planted, and straw spread over it. Dr. Harrison had been coming down each morning and evening for a week to water it.

The day after the Beeman trial, David spent most of a morning watching the paperhangers. At noon he walked back to the courthouse to meet Fred and the doctor and walk home with them for lunch. As he passed beneath the teardrops of stained glass in the front transom windows, he could see the signs of furious gossip. In each office people huddled, talking, stopping for a moment and looking over their shoulders to see who was passing when they heard David's footsteps on the marble floor. When he put his hand on the doorknob of the auditor's office, he could see through both the glass of the outer door and that of Dr. Harrison's interior office. The doctor was sitting in his desk chair staring out the window onto the public square, drumming his fingers on the arm. When David walked into the outer office, the doctor was startled out of his reverie and turned around, motioning to him.

"What's going on?" David squinted.

"Close the door, will you?" Dr. Harrison said, looking back out the window. He sighed heavily. "Apparently, a woman from Carmel, a Mrs. Ida Mae Thompson, has been down to A.F. Ramsey's law office and hired him. Then they both showed up down the hall at the county prosecutor's office and charged Thomas Swain with bastardy."

"Bastardy? Is that the same as paternity?"

The doctor nodded.

David was dumbfounded. "You're shittin' me."

Dr. Harrison shook his head. "You do have a way with words. No, I'm not shittin' you."

"Is he guilty?"

"Of course he's not guilty; he's Thomas Swain."

"That doesn't mean he's not guilty."

"It does to me," the doctor said emphatically. "He's a G.A.R. man. He goes to our church. He's our state senator and a leader in the Republican Party."

"Well, I hope you're right."

David pulled a handkerchief out of his pocket and wiped his forehead. "They know each other," David said.

"How do you know?"

"I just happened to sit beside her at the opening of the Beeman trial. We talked briefly. She said hello to Swain, and it looked like he wasn't too happy to see her."

"She says she gave birth to a premature baby this summer," Dr. Harrison sneered. "It was stillborn and buried in a country cemetery down Carmel way."

David left and walked across the street and up the back flight of stairs to Harry's office. A little boy clutching his jaw with one hand and his mother's hand with the other passed him on the stairs. Harry, washing his hands at the sink, looked in the mirror and saw David come through the door.

"How are you today?" he asked, picking up his newspaper and sitting down in the red-cushioned examination chair. "You come from the courthouse?"

David nodded.

"Guess there must be a bit of commotion over there," Harry said with a grin, snapping the paper open and folding it back.

"Yeah, your father's pretty unhappy right now."

"Let me see if I can guess the argument," Harry chirped. "Beeman can't keep his suspenders up and he gets what he deserves; Swain does the same and he's, of course, 'wrongfully accused.' "

"You think he's guilty?"

"I'd be willing to bet he is—and you know what? He won't be found guilty. Mark my words. I don't care how much evidence there is against him, he'll be found innocent and he'll swagger out of the courtroom with a big grin on his face and wink at the pretty ladies in the gallery as he goes."

"Is it that corrupt?"

Harry thought for a minute. "You know how much a vote costs around here?"

"What do you mean?"

"I'm talking about buying votes. Do you know how much one goes for?"

David didn't respond.

"Five dollars," Harry said flatly. "You want to know how it goes?"

David waited.

"I'll tell you how it went. Swain's running for office—he's popular and will most likely win. He's been traveling all over the state for the party, giving blowhard speeches at county fairs and G.O.P. rallies. But just for a little insurance they decide to spread some money around. There's a local fellow who'd like to start a political career, so they give him the bag of money and put him in charge of bringing in the votes.

"You know, over the past five years, with the natural gas and all, there's been a lot of new people come to town to take jobs in the new factories. They don't know anything about local politics, and besides, they don't get paid much. Five dollars is pretty nice when you don't have much. So the man wanting to get into the business spreads the money around, and you get a lot of men going into the voting booth in pairs; one's got a checklist, and the other walks out with five dollars in his hand.

"Voilà: Thomas Swain's state senator, and Dr. Albert Harrison becomes auditor."

"You're telling me that your dad bought votes for Swain in return for the blessing of the local party?" David probed, disbelieving.

"Can't prove it—don't doubt it."

"That's why you don't take part in politics?"

"Best reason I can think of."

"Does Mary or Fred know this?"

"No, and I'd never tell them," he said, leaning forward and giving David a hard look, as if to say, "And you'd better not, either."

The initial hearing was quickly set for the next morning at ten o'clock. Swain was represented not only by George Hinds, the most prominent local attorney, but also by two high-priced attorneys from Indianapolis. They quickly asked for a postponement and the taking of depositions, claiming they needed time to evaluate Mrs. Thompson's charges and find witnesses and evidence to clear Swain's name. Without even consulting A.F. Ramsey, Mrs. Thompson's lawyer, Mayor Jones cracked down his gavel and said, "So granted. We'll convene again a week from today at the same time."

Over the weekend the Harrisons packed and began moving household items into the new house on Catherine Street. Using a borrowed flatbed wagon, the doctor, Fred, David, and Harry made trips back and forth, moving furniture from the parlors and dining room. Friends and neighbors pitched in so willingly that the men had to fight for something to carry. They emptied out the new stable of the temporarily stored new furniture. Anna and Mary, assisted by friends, unpacked boxes and crates, hung pictures on the walls, and stocked the kitchen's free-standing cabinets with staples and linens. Saturday night they slept for the last time in the house on Emmous Street, and on Sunday afternoon after church they moved over the bedroom furniture.

In the Emmous Street house, they left David the stove, icebox, breakfast table, a pie safe, the porch swing, a primitive ash rope bed with a feather mattress, and a simple dresser. Nella, Anna, and Mary came back to clean the empty house and get it ready for David's new furniture to be delivered Monday morning.

David walked through the nearly empty rooms, his footsteps echoing on the oak floors. He felt blue. The voices of Mary and Anna echoed down from upstairs where they were sweeping. Anna came down and found him sitting on the porch swing, looking distant and lost. She opened the screen door and looked at him.

"Feeling sad?" she asked softly.

"A little."

She came out and sat beside him on the porch. "Tomorrow your things will be moved in and it will look a lot better."

"I know—you're right."

"David, I know we haven't always seen things eye to eye, but I do like you, and I know that you've made Mary happy."

She had never spoken to him tenderly before, and it took him off guard.

"Thank you, I appreciate that," he said.

"I want you to think of our new house as your house. I want you to come for meals. Don't say no, because I won't hear of it. I want you to come and go as you please."

She was quiet again for a moment, hearing Mary come downstairs. Mary saw them sitting there, swinging gently, and smiled. Deciding not to disturb them, she went out to straighten up the summer kitchen.

"There's so much time between us," Anna said hesitantly. "Things apparently change a lot between now and your time. It shows on you and the way you act and the things you believe in. I admit, it hasn't always set well with me; I suppose that's why I've been hard on you sometimes."

She looked out on the street and waved at the Heinzmans as they passed in their carriage.

"Mary's our only daughter, and we want her to be happy. I worried at first what would happen between you two, but I don't anymore. You're a good man, David. Mary wouldn't love you if you weren't."

"Thank you," he smiled warmly. "Hearing you say that means more to me than you'll ever know."

By Monday evening David had his new possessions arranged to his liking. The furnishings were expensive by the standards of the day: three oriental rugs, one each in the front parlor, back parlor, and dining room; a couch and a variety of chairs, with occasional tables; a walnut dining table and chairs; a large oak wardrobe and dresser in one upstairs bedroom, and wicker pieces on the front porch.

When he took a break to stroll around town, he heard that more electric railway workers had been hired. E.J. Pennington was said to have sold more stock to out-of-town investors, though he claimed it wasn't true. Pennington hired Will Christian to petition the cities of Carmel and Indianapolis for rights of way. Will negotiated with farmers and dealt with the arguments between Castleton and Broad Ripple, which were contending for the placement of the rail line.

On Tuesday David walked back to the courthouse with Fred after lunch. The interior office door was closed, and there seemed to be an intense meeting going on. Through the glass in the door they could see Dr. Harrison at his desk, and beside him the county coroner, Dr. Clark. Standing around the desk or leaning against the walls were four other men: George Hinds, Thomas Swain, and his two Indianapolis lawyers. Seeing the young men in the outer office, they lowered their voices.

"What's the dream team want with your dad?" David quipped.

"The what? Oh, who knows—strategy planning, I guess." Soon the visitors filed out, sober-faced.

That night after dinner in the new house, Dr. Harrison motioned David to come into the yard with him. They talked while the doctor watered the sprouting lawn.

"David, I've got something pretty important to do tomorrow. I need Fred to watch the office. Would you come along?"

"What is it?"

"County business. I really don't want to talk about it now. But I'll need some help, and it would be best if it were someone from outside the townsfolk."

"Sure," David said, "whatever."

The next morning David and the doctor walked to the depot, took the westbound Chicago and Southeastern to Westfield, then switched to the Monon and traveled south. David was surprised that Dr. Harrison had brought his black leather medical bag and not his auditor's briefcase. From the bag, the doctor pulled a small clipboard, making notes as they passed through the thickets, fields and woods of Hamilton County.

When they stepped down onto the platform, David looked around the barren little town of Carmel and shook his head. He leaned over and whispered in Dr. Harrison's ear, "In a hundred and twenty years this town'll be bigger than Noblesville, and it'll be the wealthiest community in the state."

"Bosh!" Dr. Harrison snorted.

"Albert," said a voice behind them. The coroner, Dr. Clark, clapped Dr. Harrison on the shoulder. "I've rented us some transportation." He gestured to a worn-out buckboard with an aging horse harnessed to it.

"Where are we headed?" David asked.

"According to the man at the livery stable, we'll find what we're after if we head south and west," Dr. Clark answered.

They drove out of Carmel and into the countryside. David sat facing backward in the bed of the buckboard, his legs hanging over the tail and his feet just inches off the roadbed. Trees and overgrowth crowded the road. After about a half hour, the party arrived at a little white clapboard Friends church surrounded by a grove of trees and cornfields.

"This is it," Dr. Clark grunted.

They pulled into the church drive and David saw a small graveyard with simple white stones. "Would one of you tell me what we're here for?" he asked, irritated and a little worried, now that the cemetery was in view.

Two young men sitting on the back step of the church stood up at the sight of the buggy, grabbing shovels that leaned against the building.

Dr. Harrison turned around in his seat and told him anxiously, "We're going to exhume the body of a fetus."

David felt the blood run out of his face. Fear struck deep in him. His stomach tightened.

"What?" he blurted. "You brought me here to help dig up a body?"

"You don't have to dig it up, David," the doctor said. "I just need you to take some notes for me while we examine the ... You don't even have to look, if you don't want to."

"Why me?"

"I didn't want somebody who was going to spread it all over town. This is a delicate matter."

They pulled to a halt. David didn't want to be a part of this, but walking back didn't seem like a logical option.

The minister came out of the back door of the church and greeted them disapprovingly. "These boys say you're going to exhume a body. Do you have the proper papers?"

Dr. Clark opened his bag and handed over a document. "Signed by the mayor of Noblesville last night: He's also the judge in this case, but you'll notice that circuit court judge Riley signed it, too."

The minister narrowed his eyes and handed the document back to Clark with distaste. "Well, I suppose you men know what you're doing. I'll leave you to it. I need to go into town." He untied a saddled horse and mounted. "I think you'll find what you're looking for in the southeast corner," he said as he rode away.

They found the grave, newly marked with a small stone. The two young men began digging.

David ran his hand back though his hair, fidgeting and pacing. He didn't want to be here or do this. Was he being unreasonable? Would they think him a cowardly fool if he threw down the clipboard and walked away? His desire to please the doctor was being pushed to the limit.

Dr. Harrison explained the sketch he'd made of an infant's body. It showed the basic outline of a small body with the major bones drawn in and labeled.

"What are we doing here?" David exclaimed, shaking the paper at Dr. Harrison.

"Dr. Clark and myself are going to measure the body of this fetus to verify how far along it developed before she—"

"She? You mean Ida Mae Thompson?"

The doctor hedged for a moment, started to explain, and then stopped himself, saying simply, "Yes, her baby."

"All the secrecy—does she know we're here, doing this?"

"No," the doctor admitted. "But she doesn't have to know. We have the judge's signature."

"A Republican judge," David finished, "and a friend of Thomas Swain's."

"It's a small town; of course everybody's friends."

"This stinks," David complained.

"Look here, David, I need your help. Will you help me?"

"I will not lift the coffin out, and I won't touch the body. I won't even look at it."

"That's fine, you just sit over there with your back to us. As we measure, I'll call out to you and you write the figures down. All right?"

"Okay," David said reluctantly.

David turned and walked a few feet over to a stone and sat with his back to the doctors and the digging.

"Mr. Henry," Dr. Clark spoke up tentatively, "it's disrespectful to sit on someone's gravestone."

David turned around, glaring at the little man. "Yeah, right, like I need advice from you on how to show respect for the dead."

As the diggers progressed downward, David struggled with his growing panic. The experience with Bush's body had not taken the edge off his fear of the dead. Yet he resigned himself to being an unwilling bystander.

The doctors dug through their leather bags. Dividers, a cloth measuring tape, gloves, scissors, a scalpel, and a bar of soap were spread out in the grass on top of an old, stained tablecloth. David stared at the diagram, reading off the names of the bones, imagining their white, porous structure: the femur, the tibia, the ...

The gravediggers kept on. The soil, filled in so recently, yielded easily. Dr. Harrison glanced nervously at David from time to time, thinking he'd made a mistake in bringing him, wondering how to calm him.

"We're gettin' close, I can smell it," a digger said, scowling and wrinkling his nose. The next shovel down landed with a thud, and they worked around the edges of the small, white-painted wooden box. They wiped the dirt off the top and reached down to grab the sides and lift it up. They placed it on the ground before the doctors, who knelt beside the grave, tying handkerchiefs over their noses and mouths against the stench of death.

One of the diggers used a hammer and a flat bar to loosen the lid. David looked away.

"There you are, gentlemen," the gravedigger said. "We'll just sit over there by the church till you're done, if you don't mind."

David heard the nails creak as they were bent back and the lid opened. Within a few seconds, the stench reached him. He held his nose for a moment, to no avail. Breathing through his mouth, he imagined he could still feel the oppressive vapor being drawn into his lungs. Behind him the doctors worked quietly.

He felt an inexplicable urge to look at the fetus. Finally his morbid curiosity became too much to resist, and he glanced back over his shoulder.

Dr. Clark had lifted the small bundle out of the miniature coffin and laid it on the cloth spread on the grass. Bundled in a frilly white frock was a tiny human form, its eye and ear sockets dark and sunken, its fists little more than balls of flesh, its mouth open and drawn. Dr. Harrison cut the dress up the middle with a pair of scissors and peeled back the cloth. Decaying flesh that was stuck to the cloth fell off the bones.

That was too much for David. He fell to his knees and leaned forward on all fours, retching into the grass.

In movies, graves were opened at night during thunderstorms. David wiped his mouth with the back of his hand and looked up at the innocent blue sky. Puffballs of white clouds floated by; birds rustled in the deep-green trees. The peaceful summer sun shone down on the little country cemetery and the men doing this gruesome thing.

David got to his feet and went over to the hand pump next to the church and pumped the handle, scooping up handfuls of fresh, cold water and rinsing his mouth and face. The diggers grinned as they passed a single cheap cigar back and forth between them.

At the graveside the doctors measured with calipers and cloth tape. Dr. Harrison motioned David back over and he came, forcing himself to look off at the iron fence surrounding the cemetery, trying to keep his eyes from their work.

He made the notes as he was asked: width of the skull, length of the arm and leg bones, and an estimation of the overall length. "Eighteen inches long," Dr. Harrison called out. David wrote it down, his hand trembling.

When they were finished they wrapped the fetus in the old tablecloth and placed it back in the coffin. Dr. Clark clumsily hammered the lid back down with the crowbar, and the diggers came back to lay it to rest again.

David joined the two doctors as they scrubbed their hands with carbolic soap at the pump. He watched them coldly, feeling that he hated them both.

"If I ever have to do that again, it'll be too soon," Dr. Clark muttered. Dr. Harrison was silent, fearing he had made an enemy of David that day.

While Dr. Clark put their bags back in the buggy, Dr. Harrison walked back over to the diggers and paid them.

As they pulled out of the church lane and on to the dirt road, they met the minister on his horse, followed by a carriage bearing two women. David saw Ida Mae Thompson sitting beside the woman driving, looking angrily at the doctors.

"Go on, Albert," Dr. Clark urged under his breath. "Don't stop or say a thing."

Dr. Harrison tipped his hat to the women and snapped the reins to start the old horse down the road. The women looked over at the grave-diggers and then back at David, sitting on the back of the buckboard that was disappearing down the road. With a start, Ida Mae Thompson recognized him. She stood in the carriage, her face reddening with rage.

"Mr. Henry!" she screamed shrilly. "How could you men do this without my permission? How could you do this?"

Through the dust kicked up behind the buggy, David saw her fall back on the seat and bury her face in her hands. The minister dismounted and moved to comfort her, but she tore away from him, stood up and screamed, ripping the hat from her head and throwing it to the ground. But her shrieks, growing distant, were soon lost in the hoofbeats.

David's heart was filled with guilt. He had befriended her, if briefly, and no doubt she blamed him. His shame soon turned into fury at Dr.

Harrison. He had allowed himself to be driven forward all morning against his will, and now he had to get away and find some refuge.

As the buckboard bumped over a washboard section of the road, David eased off the tail. He stood in the middle of the road, watching the two unsuspecting doctors disappear in the dust. Not wanting them to find him if they backtracked, and not wanting to encounter Ida Mae Thompson on her return trip, he disappeared into the rows of six-foot-high corn and made for the creek that he knew flowed east, two miles from the Monon rails heading into Carmel.

He stumbled along the stream, frustrated and angry. Uncertain of direction and distance, he tried to figure out where he was in relationship to Carmel's old center. He decided he was near what he knew in the twenty-first century as the site of a granite and smoked-glass office tower at the corner of U.S. 31 and 116th Street. An eastward trek would eventually take him to Castleton. He walked on, calming with the exertion, until he reached railroad tracks.

David sat on a large rock beside the small stream, waiting for the Monon northbound to pass above—the train that Dr. Harrison and Dr. Clark would likely take if they didn't stop to look for him. They might just decide to let him stew in his own juices. He thought of walking back to Carmel and then changed his mind and headed east, finding another dirt road. He walked on down the deserted lane for some time, thinking about death and change.

David walked for more than two hours, replaying the image of the little corpse, before he realized he was walking nearly parallel to and just north of the future I-465 highway. It hadn't rained in a week and a half, and the breeze picked up dust and swirled it on the dirt road. He had walked through the intersection that would eventually be anchored by Toyota and BMW dealerships. To his right would loom the Keystone-at-the-Crossing edge city with its mini-high rises and its mall. A confusion of asphalt, multiplex theaters, on-ramps, off-ramps, and apartment complexes would sprawl in every direction. He walked on down the quiet dirt road, listening to the song of the blackbirds.

Trees shaded him as he walked. The summer sun, still high in the sky, glimmered through gaps in the deep-green canopy. From the tangled undergrowth he occasionally heard the scurries of unseen animals—squirrels, chipmunks, rabbits. From time to time the hedgerow gave way to a picket or rail fence and a farmer's house and fields. The corn in a field he passed was taller than he was—"knee-high by the Fourth of July," no doubt. A farmer and two children worked through the rows, chopping at weeds. They looked up and called "Howdy" to David.

At the end of four hours of walking, mid-afternoon, David found himself in the little crossroads town of Castleton. It, like Fishers Station and Carmel, would be so transformed over the next century that the original town was hard to discern. Castleton would become the center of the largest and most congested shopping area in Indianapolis, at the junction of I-69 and I-465. This sleepy little town, some ten miles from Indianapolis, would become a forest of tall pole signs. Fast-food restaurants, car washes, muffler shops, and liquor stores would line the strip later to be known as 82nd Street.

David found the little wood-framed L.E.&W. depot. He recognized the building as the site of a flower shop in his time, and perhaps the only structure of Castleton to survive the next century. He bought a ticket and a newspaper and sat on a bench on the platform to wait for the train.

Despite the time for thought he had given himself, he had made no real sense of the day's events. How should he have reacted? Was the exhumation right or wrong? It felt wrong, but he wasn't sure. These were desperate events: a prominent man charged with bastardy, a married woman giving birth to a child she claimed was not her husband's, a community with no patience for such transgressions. Was he overreacting to the necessary process of getting at the truth and the unpleasant things that entailed? Or was he simply overcome by his irrational fear of death? He wasn't sure. But at least now, on this train platform, he could rest.

CHAPTER THIRTEEN

Got nothing against a big town
Still hay-seed enough to say
Look who's in the big town
But my bed is in a small town
And that's good enough for me
I was born in a small town
And I can breathe in a small town
Gonna die in a small town
And that's prob'ly where they'll bury me
From the song "Small Town,"
John Mellencamp, 1985.

David sat on the front porch watching the evening descend upon the neighborhood, drinking a glass of lemonade cooled with a chuck of ice he'd broken from the cube in the icebox. His empty chair at the dinner table in the Catherine Street house would leave questions, but he didn't want to face Dr. Harrison right now and wouldn't know what to say if he did, angry that he had been included in the exhumation, embarrassed that he'd run off.

Mary walked up Hannibal and turned on Grant. When she came around the corner of Emmous, she saw him sitting there alone.

"What happened today?" she asked. "You didn't come to dinner, and father seemed concerned about you."

"What did he say?"

"He said the last time he saw you, before noon, southwest of Carmel, you looked like you'd been pulled through a knothole. He said that suddenly you were just gone. They didn't know whether you jumped or fell off the buckboard. He's really worried."

"Did he tell you what we did in Carmel this morning?"

"He just said 'business.' "

He ran his hand through his hair and grimaced. "It was business all right."

He told her everything that had happened, including his earlier meeting at the courthouse with Ida Mae Thompson. She listened, eyes wide, as he described the exhumation.

"Why you? Why the secrecy?" she stammered.

"Said he didn't want to bring along someone who'd spread talk around town."

"What do you think they learned?"

"Well—how big the fetus was. Other than that, I don't know."

She fell silent, lost in thought. "Aside from the fact that it was a gruesome thing to have to do and rather unfair to that Thompson woman, surely you don't think my father was doing something illegal?"

"I don't know."

"Please don't think that! Have faith in him. Don't let your cynicism make the necessary seem criminal."

David was unmoved.

Finally, she said cautiously, "Do you think Thomas Swain is guilty?"

"It's crossed my mind," David laughed, scratching his chin. "What do you think? Do you have the same faith in him that you have in your father?"

"I have this feeling—just a hunch, really—that he's guilty." She traced the braided wicker of her chair arm with a fingertip.

"Why?"

"Several things—nothing concrete. I've heard the old soldiers joke about Swain—a wink and a nod, you know. He's younger than the other veterans; he ran off when he was thirteen to fight in the war. Came home a cocksure teenager. Fancied himself a ladies' man."

"That's it?"

"No. It's something in the way he walks—he just struts, like an overgrown banty rooster." Her tone did not descend, as if she wasn't finished or was asking a question instead of making a statement.

"And?"

"He stares too much," she said simply. "Ever since I was a girl of sixteen or so, I noticed he stares at young women's bodies, as if his wife weren't enough, as if he's looking for something, looking right through your clothes. And he does it as if he owns you and he's sure you fancy him. I have this nagging feeling that a man who behaves with his sort of—"

"Body language?" David finished.

"Yes, body language! A man who behaves that way is on the prowl, you know, looking for a conquest, and most of all for a woman who might reciprocate."

"And maybe Ida Mae Thompson reciprocated?"

"Oh, I don't want to think about it!" she exclaimed. "It's all so ugly. I'd rather think about us than them."

They looked out into the dusk for a while in silence. Mary finally said, "I got a letter today—from Chicago."

David brightened.

"I've worked it all out, better than you could ever imagine," she said, bubbling with enthusiasm. "We can go to Chicago anytime this month. This evening, Father all of a sudden thinks it's a good idea. My parents will believe that I'm staying with my college friend, Helen Garrison, while you stay in a hotel. Now, we'll visit Helen, but she has told her parents that I'm staying with someone else."

"I'm confused," David broke in. "What will the truth be?"

Mary took a deep breath, blushing furiously. "We'll be staying together in a hotel somewhere," she said softly, "pretending to be Mr. and Mrs. Henry."

David thought this over for a moment. "Are you sure you want to do this?"

Mary nodded firmly.

"Okay," he said, his heart almost jumping out of his throat.

"Helen will be giving a party in a few weeks," Mary went on. "If we go at the right time, we'd be invited. It would be so wonderful, David!

Let's make this the most exciting time of our lives. We'll see the White City, we can go to the theater, the opera, ballet, the symphony. It's going to be electric."

David forgot how miserable he'd been that morning and was caught up in her enthusiasm. "Mary, do you know how much money I've got?"

She shook her head, the thin Mona Lisa smile on her face.

"I've made a ton of money off the stuff I've taken back with me. We can easily afford the best. Let's stay in the finest hotel in Chicago! Let's have a city day tomorrow, and I'll buy a tuxedo and you buy some magnificent dresses, and let's live as high as we've ever lived in our lives!"

She clapped her hands together and brought them to her face as if praying, giggling softly.

"And you think your parents will go along with this?" he asked, unable to believe their good fortune.

"I mentioned it to Mother this morning. She frowned a bit, but she eventually said she didn't see why not, as long as we were staying in separate places, and Father said at dinner that it was a fine idea."

They walked downtown that evening as if on a cloud. They sat and laughed with the Saturday picnic group and some of the Bachelors' Club members at Truitt's soda fountain and told their lie about what they planned for the trip.

Mary's choice had carried their romance across a threshold, and they found themselves unable to take their eyes off each other or to stop holding hands. The others at the little soda shop tables saw it, too.

Mary had begun to hope that she would spend the rest of her life with David. She wasn't sure what time it would be in, or if this man from the future was capable of giving up his own past life or taking her back to it, but she didn't care anymore.

David didn't fit the romantic fantasies she had created. Somehow he sidestepped them and surpassed them at the same time. He was someone she could not have imagined. He saw her as an equal and expected that she voice opinions on all things, and wondered at her silence when she demurred in front of men, as she had been taught to do. Like all other young women of her time she had been trained to be obedient to her family and her church. She had been taught to expect to spend a life serving her husband and his needs. Yet, without lecture or argument, David simply expected her to be her own person, to be obedient also to herself, and he reminded her that at times she must serve her own needs. The popular culture of the day defined women as weak, foolish and simple-minded. David's pat response to this was, "What a load of crap." He showed her a form of respect different from that of other men she had known, not placing her on a pedestal as some prized possession, but beside him as an equal and a partner in all things.

David had helped her to see the value in this community by describing a world where that value had been lost. She now feared the future somewhat, the future she had once dreamed of as shimmering and beautiful. But it still held an allure, and the trip to Chicago would be an undeniable event of attainment. She felt she was becoming as passionate and free as she had always wished to be, and with him the future no doubt would hold more wonderful events like the trip to Chicago. Perhaps together they could have this little town he loved so much as well as the rest of the world beyond the city limits that she longed to see and be a part of.

From the time she was a little girl, sitting at church dinners, barn dances, weddings, circuses, county fairs, and courthouse lawn events, she watched young couples together in their nervous expectation and wondered at the act of courting. She had come to see it as a sort of dance. It was a complicated dance in which each partner had rigidly planned movements. It was a dance that took place in clear view of the community, so false steps could cause great social injury. In the movements, the partners did not quite touch and were forever separate, tending their own interests. It was this courtship dance Mary had moved to in her young womanhood with the men whose attention she had either rebuked or tolerated.

She and David were having their own dance, though not the dance around forbidden sin that so characterized the Victorian steps of courting. Their dance was somewhere in between his time and hers. Neither sexual and aggressive, nor denied passion, it was a comfortable oneness that more than a few observers had commented upon. She freely took his hand in a crowd, without looking, knowing from habit were it would be, and she did so without awkward hesitation. He took her arm, straightened her hat, or put his arm around her in church with self-assurance. They touched one another in small ways like this in public and laughed together and teased one another, and they had been this way almost from the beginning, from that first night when their behavior practically declared to the town that they were a couple. They did it with such attractive ease that it did not cause scandal but was instead fascinating to onlookers. It was the casual attitude toward love and togetherness that David had brought with him from the future and the carefully tended caution that Mary had been trained to exhibit that blended into something quite different and lovely.

The couples in the picnic group wondered why their own relationships lacked the vibrant natural joy that David and Mary had, and because of it the others came to revere them as somehow superior, without quite knowing why. To be so beautiful and move together with such grace was a rare thing to see in public in those days.

It was within this warm, friendly atmosphere they sat that night, sipping lemonade phosphates and Moxie soda beside the drug store soda fountain, laughing and talking into the night. Will Christin and Willsie Bush sat across from them. Will was telling a joke, but Mary didn't hear, her mind elsewhere. She was watching them all, but not in the present moment.

The doors were propped open to let in the warm evening breeze, and voices chattered away inside, mixed from time to time with those of passersby on the sidewalk outside. The best friends she and David had were at the tables. Behind them the courthouse rose up, filling nearly the whole view through the huge plate-glass windows. Mary watched David as John Davies' comment set him laughing, and she studied his handsome face, and then self-consciously looked back at the rest of the group who, too, were laughing about something, though she had not been listening. Their warm, friendly faces, childhood friends and newcomers, sitting around a circle of tables—this was home and he was hers.

"What did you tell Mary?" Dr. Harrison asked, lighting a cigar and leaning back in his rocking chair. From the front porch of the new Catherine Street house, David saw the gaslights go dim in the Riley house, a block and a half down the street. The bell in the clock tower rang, and as always he counted the eleven chimes, even though he knew what time it was. The south face of the clock glowed in the peaceful summer darkness.

"I told her everything that happened."

The doctor stared intensely out at the vague silhouette of trees against the dark sky. He drummed his fingers on the arm of the chair, then methodically spun the cigar in his mouth and puffed on it. If not for these habitual gestures, David wouldn't have known that the doctor was irritated—he showed so little emotion. "Why did you run off?" the doctor asked.

"I didn't run off. Children run off. Adults leave, and that's what I did."

"Clark and I were worried about you—didn't know where you went."

"You could have guessed that I was more than a little put out with you."

"Well, yes, now that you mention it." The doctor blew a smoke ring. "Did you go back and speak with Ida Mae Thompson?"

"No. What would I say to her if I had?"

"Well I'm sure I don't know, but then, I wasn't aware that the two of you were acquainted."

"What's your point?" David asked, sensing accusation.

"No point. Just surprised, that's all."

"I met her at the courthouse last week. I told you that."

"Oh, you don't have to explain," Dr. Harrison said, with a faint hint of sarcasm.

"Listen," David sighed, rubbing his hands down his face. "I don't want to be on bad terms with you or make you angry. You've been very good to me and I appreciate that, but there are some things I won't do. I don't want to be around dead people, okay? Some people are afraid of heights, others are afraid of closed-in spaces. I just don't want to be around dead people.

"I don't want to be involved in Republican politics, either. Don't take it personally. I'll help you when you need me to, but you have to be honest with me about what's going on. You intentionally withheld your plans from me this morning. It wasn't fair."

A long silence followed, broken only by crickets and the sound of Mary raising the window in her bedroom above the porch.

"All right. Fair enough," the doctor finally replied, still not looking at David. David could tell from his tone that it was not "all right" or "fair enough;" it simply meant the conversation was over. He felt he'd been placed in the category of those who can't be trusted, those who are less than real men.

David stood. "Well, I guess I'll head home and hit the sack."

"Sounds like you and Mary are going to Chicago for the World's Fair," the doctor said.

"Yes, I can't wait to see it," David said, stepping off the porch and stopping halfway down the steps.

"I think you should go. Now is the perfect time. It'd do you two good to get away. Mary can visit her friend and you can explore the big city, maybe link up at the fair or go to a few fancy restaurants and dances."

"I hope it all works out that way," David said, now not really trusting Dr. Harrison to wish him well. "Well, good night, then."

"Yes," the doctor replied, simply.

As he started down the walk, he looked up and saw Mary's shadow in the upstairs window. She raised her hand and waved with her fingers. He smiled and lifted a hand in response.

When David turned the corner at Emmous Street he looked back and saw the red tip of the cigar glowing in the darkness on the front porch. He walked home weighed down by the feeling that his connection with Dr. Harrison had been irreparably damaged.

August passed slowly. In the courtroom, Thomas Swain's attorneys won another delay to prepare their case. In the streets, the people of Noblesville struggled with heat that hovered near 100 degrees for days on end. The street-sprinkling wagon was kept busy from morning to night to keep the dust down.

The electric railway moved forward. Surveyors were working south of town, mapping out the route toward Carmel. The teamsters and laborers north of town cleared trees and the lowland along the river, halfway to the Wainwright farm. E.J. Pennington had advertised for another crew; word spread outside central Indiana and unemployed laborers filtered into town. On the day designated for hiring the crew, more than a hundred men lined the sidewalk in front of the railway offices, all the way past the opera house to Conner Street. Dr. Harrison smiled with satisfaction as he passed them, heading toward the courthouse.

David and Mary spent an afternoon two days before leaving with a quiet walk around the courthouse square. Mary browsed in the New York Store, running her hand across bolts of fabric in the long racks on the north wall. David, bored, leaned against a pillar, eyes closed, and pictured how the New York Store would eventually be transformed into Bishop Title Services. The building had been hideously made over in the 1970s. He'd sat in a cushioned vinyl chair with his back to that wall, where the rows of colorful fabrics were now. He'd closed the mortgage on his house just fourteen months earlier in a tiny, sterile white conference room, decorated prominently with a painting of a broken-down barn with a Mail Pouch Tobacco sign on the side—a celebration of the past.

Mary turned around to ask how he liked the muslin she was holding up but caught the faraway sadness in his eyes. She studied his face as he looked up at the pressed-tin ceiling. The breeze from the ceiling fan brushed the hair back from his forehead. The rumble and thump of an electric railway teamster wagon drew his attention, and he watched it pass beyond the windows, the huge draft horses struggling north down Catherine Street.

Mary pushed the bolt of cloth back into its slot and crossed to him, taking his arm and leading him out of the store.

They went across to the Corner Drug Store. "Something made you sad in there," she murmured. "What was it? Has the New York Store been torn down in your time, too?"

"It might as well be. No, it's still there, but it's been ruined."

"How?"

"Let's not talk about it," David said, shaking his head as if to throw off his depression. "I feel like a crybaby who can't stop regretting changes I had nothing to do with and couldn't have stopped if I wanted to."

They ordered drinks. After the waitress left. David went on. "The things I hate to see go, the beautiful buildings, train travel, and probably most of all, the sense of community this place has—these things will remain for most of your life. You'll be dead and gone before the social structure of this and every other small town has disappeared."

Dead and gone. The phrase passed his lips before he realized it. He sensed instantly that those words had struck her deeply, though she tried not to show it. Life expectancy wasn't any big secret, but he had been careful not to suggest that he might know things about the Harrisons' personal futures. And they had just as consciously avoided asking.

Mr. Locke came through the door and stopped on his way to the soda fountain. "Well, hello there," the aging, rotund gentleman said, taking Mary's hand and patting it. Locke had done this since she was a child, showing her special attention, calling her "his girl," embarrassing her in front of her family with harmlessly romantic remarks. "I thought of you recently, Mr. Henry."

"Why's that?"

"I'm thinking of selling my house. With Edna gone and all my little babes grown and flown the coop, it's kind of big for just me. But a young fellow like you—maybe wanting to settle down," he said, winking at Mary, "maybe wanting to start a family?"

"Interesting idea," David said.

"Well, you two lovebirds think about it," he said, walking away, happy in the knowledge that he'd created an awkward moment between them.

Mary held David's arm tightly as they crossed the Logan Street covered bridge. They were forced to hug the wall as a wagon filled with barrels rumbled past them. The horses' hooves thundered on the wooden planks and shook the timber-frame structure. Birds swooped into the openings at either end, tending nests built among the trusses. Emerging into the sunlight and finding a dry grassy area, David and Mary sat at the top of the riverbank, halfway between the covered bridge and the Lake Erie & Western railroad bridge.

They sat watching the shallow, clear water. David threw a flat rock across the surface. It skipped four times and plunked in halfway across. A painted turtle slid from a warm rock and disappeared beneath the water. Mary held her parasol overhead against the relentless sun. She began to speak, but a train whistle sounded from the north, so she held her thought and waited for the powerful locomotive to cross the high trestle. The long ribbon of black smoke did not follow the curve of the track as the train turned south down Polk Street, instead floating east above the downtown buildings as if it knew a better way to go. Finally, Mary spoke.

"You've said there is a great library on the edge of town in your time."

"Yes," David said, still watching the water, waiting to see the turtle surface for air.

"What kinds of books are there about these years in Noblesville?"

"In the upstairs there's an area called the Indiana Room," David told her. "I take my students there to do research when they're writing papers about how local history was affected by national events. There's every newspaper, starting in the late 1840s, on tiny pieces of film called microfilm. You view them by placing the film in a machine that projects it on a screen. There is an index of births, obituaries, local history books, random family genealogies, census records, and a few photo albums with a haphazard collection of pictures from the 1860s till my time, and a lot more about Indiana history." David sensed where this was heading.

"Is there any information there about my family and what happens to us?" she asked hesitantly.

"What sort of information?"

"When we die, whom we marry, who gets killed in wars."

"Your father is a prominent doctor and active in the Republican Party. Fred seems to be heading the same way. You and your brothers will all no doubt have children, who will have grandchildren for you."

"David," she said urgently, grasping his arm, "please don't ever go there to find out about me! It's awful to think that someone could know my future. If I thought you knew when I'm going to die, who I'll marry, how many children I might have, or any tragedy that might befall my family, it would tear me apart! Those are things no one should know before they happen. But if I thought you knew, I'd make you tell me. And that would be a terrible burden for both of us."

"I promise I won't," David lied. The damage was already done.

David stood up and skimmed another stone. It hopped toward the spot where a black dot rose above the surface. The turtle's head submerged, leaving a round of ripples. Two dragonflies hummed above the water, conjoined in a double arc.

"What's bothering you?" Mary asked.

"Oh, I don't know," he said, sitting back down. "I guess I'm wondering how long this can go on."

"What do you mean?"

"Us, and time-traveling. I can't go back and forth indefinitely. Sooner or later I'm going to have to make a choice."

"Well, what does the choice really mean to you?" she said anxiously. "Where do you want to be? Do you really think you could go back to your time for good and change the things you don't like—I mean, change your community?"

"No, I don't," he muttered, despondent. "But I'm past the point of wanting to change anybody's mind. I just want to be happy. I want to belong somewhere."

"You do belong somewhere," she said, her voice trembling.

He turned and looked her in the eye, challenging her to voice the answer he already knew. "Where?"

"Here," she said with a lump in her throat.

"I want to stay," he said, "but I don't want to stay if I can't have you."

"Well," she prompted him gently.

"If I stayed here, would you marry me?" he asked.

"Yes, I certainly would," she replied softly. A tear ran down her face.

In the shade of her parasol, they kissed. Her tears fell freely at the release of a tension she hadn't even realized was building

"You'd turn your back on everything you've known?" she finally asked, wanting to reassure herself further.

"Yes, I would. Everything I want most in life is here."

"I love you, David," she whispered, and kissed him again.

As they walked home holding hands, they both felt as if they'd jumped a once forbidding wall. He left her at the house on Catherine Street, then returned to his house and stepped through the beam.

David dug through his pile of junk mail and paid some bills. As with each return, he plugged his phone into the charger, and it issued a string of whistle alerts for texts and voice mails. He scanned through

the voice mails and chose one from his mother.

"Hi David, it's Mom. Where are you? I'm starting to think you've skipped the country or something. Talked to Mike last night; sounds like they're doing fine. Please give me a call sometime, okay?"

Once the message app was opened, the first to appear was from Heather. "I've been thinking about you lately and wondered if we could talk."

There were texts from Jeremy Wren and his brother, and a voice mail from the principal of the high school, reminding him of the date of fall orientation. There were also random e-mails on his computer. He ignored them all.

Why would Heather text? He shook the thought away.

David dressed and got his truck out of the garage. He drove to the high school. In the parking lot, the band director stood at the top of two stories of scaffolding, shouting instructions at the band through a bullhorn, honing their formation for the football season.

The halls were empty except for a janitor buffing the floors and a UPS man wheeling cases of textbooks through the front door. David went to his classroom and flipped on the computer. He sat down and typed up his letter of resignation.

The change back and forth was becoming more difficult each time. He remembered a sweltering summer day fourteen years ago when he went to work with his grandfather. They called on clients hour after hour, going from business to business, his grandfather showing him off. But by mid-afternoon David was sick. The repeated transitions between the air-conditioned car, the blasting outdoor heat, and the overcooled buildings nauseated him. This back and forth between centuries caused an increasing depression, but it was only one way. Going to the nineteenth century brought comfort, while returning to the twenty-first was oppressive. There seemed to be an increasing hollowness about the twenty-first century.

Fewer children played on the sidewalks and in front yards. Occasionally he'd pass a day-care center and see children playing, corralled in a backyard playground. He missed the lively presence of horses, too. The general hustle and bustle of 1890s Noblesville had been replaced by a slow, steady hum of traffic. Cars crisscrossed the paved streets, on their way to McDonald's and Walmart, large grocery stores and shopping malls.

Once, when he was a child and staying with his grandparents, he stayed up late one night watching a black-and-white movie from the 1950s about a man who woke up one morning to find that everyone he knew was gone. His wife and children were gone, as were his friends. He walked through the town and saw only strangers who would not respond when he pleaded with them to explain what had happened.

David felt like that man now, but there was a twist. The ghosts of all the missing people were there. David wasn't on the outside, like the man in the movie—he was in the middle. In his mind, the people of modern-day Noblesville had ignored his pleas through their seeming indifference to what had been lost in a hundred years, an indifference demonstrated by their lack of compassion for the things that really have value in the life of a community.

At the same time, Mary, her family, and their town seemed to cry out to him from beyond the grave. If he spent too much time thinking about it, it was like living his own private horror story. This was an aspect of the summer's events he had never discussed with Mary.

He found himself thinking often of his grandfather's funeral and the body lying in the coffin in the funeral home. Too much make-up had been applied in an attempt to hide the ravages of cancer. They were trying to make him look "natural," as the old folks say when seeing a deceased person, but had failed. David felt they should have left well enough alone.

David recognized the face, but it didn't really look like Grandpa. And it was the same way with Noblesville. The only difference was that his grandfather didn't wait in a time before death to love and hug him. Mary did.

When visiting his grandmother after his grandfather's death, David sometimes forgot and expected to see his grandfather sitting in the recliner by the record player. Similarly, when in the present, he often got lost in thought and forgot circumstances, half-expecting Mary or Fred or Dr. Harrison to come around a corner or be sitting in a chair in the front parlor. In the split second when he came to his senses, the plainness and emptiness of modern life hit him hard.

From the perspective of the present, there was an even darker side to these thoughts. David was ever-conscious of the fact that Mary's long dead and decomposed body lay in a coffin in the Riverside Cemetery at the end of Cherry Street. He imagined the skeletons with rotted flesh that inhabited the late-night horror films of his childhood. That was Mary now.

As he fell deeper in love with her in the past, he stayed farther away from the cemetery in the present. He tried to avoid any street that would give him a view of the iron gates and the stones—especially the 1824 stone, where he had first kissed her. While crossing the Conner Street bridge, he would intentionally look north to avoid seeing the cemetery, now made clear after the demolition of the lumber company buildings. David was even jealous of the dead husband she lay beside.

"How fucked up is that?" he mumbled to himself. It was the first time he'd acknowledged the feeling.

As he drove around town, taking care of house payments and gas bills and hawking items his friends in the past thought were trash, he couldn't help feeling that the town was dead, too. Not really dead, more like a zombie in another old horror movie—functionally alive, but without a soul. The world the Victorians had known was dead and gone.

He imagined their ghosts everywhere on the sterile streets of Noblesville. In his house their voices echoed off the ugly paneling and peeling metal cabinets. Their footsteps tapped on the faded linoleum, and their eyes peeked around the cheap hollow-core doors. Even David's own restoration seemed somehow unworthy of them, and the presence of their ghosts shamed him.

CHAPTER FOURTEEN

In the still of the night
As I gaze from my window
At the moon in its flight,
My thoughts all stray to you.
In the still of the night
While the world is in slumber,
Oh, the times without number
Darling, when I say to you,
"Do you love me as I love you?"
Are you my life-to-be, my dream come true?"
Or will this dream of mine
Fade out of sight
Like the moon,
Growing dim
On the rim
Of the hill
In the chill,
Still
Of the night?
From the song "In the Still of the Night,"
Cole Porter, 1929.

David and Mary boarded the early-morning train. Fred helped unload their grips and trunks from the carriage and then drove Butch off toward home, waving as he went. Between the tracks and Mulberry Street, new rails and ties sat in mountainous piles—the raw material of the electric rail line.

The train pulled away from the depot, lurching down Vine Street and across the bridge over White River. Looking down, David couldn't see any tracks, only the shallow water below, as if the train were floating in the air. In Westfield they switched to the Monon Line.

The train passed through Sheridan, Terhune, Kirkland, and Cyclone, then made stops at Frankfort, Rossville, and Delphi. Nearly all of the passengers were headed for the fair. The women sported their best summer dresses, and some of the men wore fashionably pale suits and straw hats. A newsagent in a small compartment near the steps hawked papers, and nearly every man bought one and immediately became absorbed in it. The children tore up and down the aisles, spending the nervous energy the adults had to contain: They were all small-town people, heading off to the biggest city in the Midwest.

The late-summer sun warmed the cars. Flies and mosquitoes circled, lighting on noses and bald spots. You could gauge passenger irritation by how rapidly the paper and palm-leaf fans were flapping. An occasional man loosened his stiff collar to fan his neck. A mother fanned her sleeping baby while she gazed absently out the window, across fields and woodlots, and at the church steeples that appeared sometimes above the trees.

David and Mary went to the dining car and watched the small towns and countryside from a table covered with white linen and a vase with a single red rose. Through Monticello and Monon, David sipped beer while Mary drank tea. They snacked on soda bread, tearing off pieces as they went, half-noticing the blur of corn, flax and bean fields that rushed by the window, slowly giving way to the Hoosier industrial towns clustered at the lower end of Lake Michigan.

After five hours they reached the southwestern shore of the lake. In this corner of Indiana and in the southern outskirts of Chicago, starting with Gary and Hammond, the visual assault of industrial America struck. The fields and forests gave way to factories and tenements. By the time the train reached the southern entrance to Chicago, the single pair of tracks was lost in a jumble of parallel tracks, all running north-south. Alongside the tracks were piles of coal and slag, the input and output of the steel mills and factories that lined this superhighway of steel. From the train window they could see sparks, flames, and glowing metal within the open arches of the foundries. Hazy gray smoke hovered near the ground, and the air stank of burning coal.

Shabby apartment buildings for immigrant workers were crammed next to factory buildings that belched thick, black smoke from tall stacks. The dark, narrow spaces between the tenements were laced with hundreds of clotheslines, like the home of a huge spider that used its web to trap laundry. David had read enough to guess at the horrible living conditions that existed there.

The interstate highways and freeways—the boa constrictors that squeeze and devour modern American cities—had not yet been born. Instead, the surface streets were jammed with electric rail cars, cable cars, horses, wagons, pedestrians, and a tangled mass of railroad tracks. As the train approached the Dearborn Street Station, there unfolded around it the results of the great boom that had created Chicago and was still transforming it.

The station was a sea of travelers from all over the country, come to see the Columbian Exhibition. Under the huge canopy of the platform roof, with its lattice of iron trusses, vendors, barkers, and pimps hawked their wares: souvenir books, maps, cheap meals, hotel rooms, or companionship for the night. The confusion created by the swarms of people on the unusually short platforms and the blast of train whistles was exciting—but terrifying for those unaccustomed to the city.

David pulled Mary along, unnerved by the commotion. Despite his twenty-first century sophistication, he felt he'd been plucked down in an exotic foreign country. He tugged at her hand, urging her forward as he shouldered his way through the press of jostling bodies, past the stone pillars and beneath ornate brick arches. They emerged on to Polk Street at the base of a nine-story clock tower. A ruddy-faced Irish porter pushed their luggage on a handcart ahead of them.

He called back, "I'll load ye up in a lovely rockaway. Take ye right to the Palmer!"

Along the curb, fine rockaway carriages waited for those who could afford them, parked in a row in the only quiet space in the street. Their drivers were seated at the front and top, separate from the passenger space. Once loaded, they shot out onto Dearborn and headed north, dodging the electric trains that rattled down both sides of the street. Tall buildings rose above: the fourteen-story Pontiac Building, the Caxton and Monon. When they passed under the new elevated trains at Van Buren, the tall buildings grew denser and the street became the floor of a chasm, with buildings rising ten or more stories on both sides. They passed by the imposing Monadnock Building and the Great Northern Hotel.

Mary snuggled up to David, squeezed his hand, and smiled brilliantly at him. She poked her head out the window, putting a hand on her hat to hold it in place. "It's so beautiful!" she exclaimed.

David gazed out on a panorama of American architecture. Arched windows, keystones, bracketed cornices, striped canvas awnings, pillars, stone, brick, bright colors—a brash young empire's take on ancient styles. Many no sooner built than discarded in favor of new ones.

The carriage turned east on Adams. The entire north side of the block, east to State Street, was taken up by the Fair Store. The sidewalks were packed with people. A barefoot boy sold matches and flypaper; women dressed in Parisian fashions or simple shirtwaists and muslin skirts window-shopped. A scissor-sharpener, with his rig and stone strapped to his back, shuffled around the corner; men in ragged clothes or expensive suits jaywalked briskly. The cab driver reined his horse jerkily, trying to make the left turn on State, yelling at drivers who cut him off.

They pulled along the curb at the Palmer House and turned right onto Monroe, stopping in front of the canopy that extended to the street. A bellboy ran up and opened Mary's door, helped her down, and motioned to another to grab the luggage. David didn't want to look like the tourist he was, but he couldn't stop himself from craning his neck to gaze at the facade of the ornate, stone-faced building. This time it was Mary who grabbed his hand and urged him on through the sidewalk crowd.

Inside the opulence of the Palmer's main lobby, the commotion of the city faded to a comfortable hum. David's mouth dropped open as he surveyed the huge room. Gargantuan crystal chandeliers hung overhead;

velvet-cushioned chairs and settees were arranged in scattered groups among lush, potted palms.

"Sir, your reservation?" a polite voice called out from behind the desk.

"Yes, Mr. and Mrs. David Henry of Noblesville, Indiana," David said, suddenly awakened.

To live in Noblesville in the summer of 1893 and not know about the Columbian Exhibition and World's Fair in Chicago would be like eating Christmas dinner in 1941 without knowing the Japanese had bombed Pearl Harbor three weeks earlier. Everybody knew about the World's Fair, everybody dreamed of going; no single event in American history, before or since, attracted so many visitors.

In late winter, drawings of the exhibition's grand buildings began appearing on the front page of the Hamilton County Ledger—Machinery Hall, the Administration Building and the Electricity Building, looking like Texas-sized Grecian or Roman temples laid out before the sparkling waters of Lake Michigan. When summer began, the Monon Railway and the Lake Erie and Western had a fare war to lure Hoosiers to Chicago. By late August, hundreds of Noblesville folk had gone to the fair, along with millions of others from hundreds of American towns.

Mothers took the children for a week, or whole families went. Farmers left the fields for a day or two and went up together, a few men off to the city to see the sights, drink whiskey away from the wife, and play cards all night in a cheap hotel. Judge Riley and his wife had gone in June and come back with a tale of being caught in a storm on a Lake Michigan steamer as they approached the White City, the name given to the central buildings of the fair.

Early in the summer, Harper's New Monthly had devoted seventeen pages to "A Dream City;" Cosmopolitan printed fifteen laudatory pages on the subject. The White City, they announced, was a demonstration of what American cities should be in the future—shining monuments to the grandeur of the United States, the undeniable empire of the century to come. The accompanying drawings were almost too magnificent to believe in the scale and number of lovely buildings.

David and Mary boarded a steamer that left the dock at Van Buren Street late in the afternoon and moved out onto the lake for the twenty-five minute voyage to the fair. Judge Riley had assured them that this was the best way to get to the fair, avoiding the "cattle cars" that moved on land. They stood on the oak-planked deck, leaning against the rail and watching the shoreline glide by.

On the southwestern horizon they could see a few towers and an arch. Soon they could make out the outlines of roofs and stately buildings lining the lakefront. The towers loomed taller; an arching object, just visible above the other buildings, was moving, rotating on an unseen axis.

"It must be huge," David marveled.

"What?" Mary asked.

"The Ferris wheel. Have you ever seen one that big?"

"I've never seen one before—and neither has anyone else, until this summer. Harper's says it's the first such thing ever built."

During most of the trip their eyes had been drawn to a series of steamers coming and going from a point well out in the lake—too far out to make sense as a docking point. As their steamer made for that spot, they could see others being moored or cast off from a pier that extended more than a half mile out from shore. The pier was crowded with people who were moving but didn't seem to be walking.

"What is that, David?" Mary said, astonished.

He squinted for a better look. The steamer swung around, pointing west, coming alongside the pier. "It's a moving sidewalk!" he exclaimed.

The entrance from the pier had been planned for maximum effect. They stepped on to the wooden slats of the moving sidewalk, which pulled them forward at a measured speed—fast enough to be worth using, slow enough to build suspense as the grand colonnade and peristyle came into focus. Through the peristyle's arch and the openings in the colonnade, glimpses of glorious buildings appeared. Many of the people on the moving sidewalk had begun to surge forward, anxious to get past that central arch.

Mary flipped through the guidebook she'd bought at the hotel and found their position just as they stepped off the sidewalk. They passed under the peristyle and entered the Court of Honor.

Straight ahead of them was a glistening basin more than a hundred yards long, with elaborate fountains playing at its far corners. Just to their left, rising five stories out of the sheet of water, was the gilded statue of Republic, her face reminiscent of the Statue of Liberty, her arm reaching up to the sky, her gaze directed toward a beautiful domed building at the other end of the basin—the Administration Building. On their right, a mammoth single structure, the Manufacturers' Building, extended nearly the length of a football field west down the Court, ending at a wide boulevard that headed north. Rich in Corinthian detail, its facade was a series of bays graced with arched windows between corner and central pavilion entrances. Its roof, a striking deep sea green, was ringed with flags and statues.

On the left side, another imposing piece of architecture, shining white in the Roman style, flanked the basin on the south. Its exterior had sets of three bays with columns and arched windows, and its central pavilion was capped with a dome. Statuary dotted its roof—angels, eagles, beasts. More statues lined the walkways on both sides of the water. Gondolas slid gently across the basin, some disappearing out of view under bridges to the north and south at the far end. The scale was staggering.

Other towers and rooftops sprang up all around. The distant Ferris wheel was on the move again. Uniformed police and fair workers darted among the well-behaved, well-dressed crowds. David was so taken with the view that he didn't notice Mary had stepped away from him—she, too, was lost to the world.

She turned back to see where he was, and they stood apart for a moment, grinning at each other. She had never looked so beautiful or so happy. Her dress was so white, her hair glistening black, her waist so slender, her breasts so full, her smile so bright—and all of it for him! She called out joyously, "We've made it, we're here!" David stood expressionless, watching her and the grand buildings in the background. He wondered who he was, how he'd gotten here. For a moment his past future seemed a million years away, like a storybook about someone else. This was real, not the empty life he'd lived in a time to come.

Mary clasped his hands. "When I die, I hope I go somewhere like this!"

At the far end of the basin, past the massive Columbian Fountain with its statues of leaping horses and sailing ships, they entered the cavernous arch of the Electricity Building and paused at the base of the

Ben Franklin statue. Walking down the long eastern aisle, they passed all the new electrical inventions—motors, dynamos and light bulbs. To Mary, they were wonders. The companies that made them, like General Electric and Westinghouse, were not yet household names. At the Bell Telephone display, phones were hooked up to phonographs and opera houses and concert halls in the East—a first. They saw new inventions by Nikola Tesla and watched motion pictures in Edison's Kinetoscope.

For the next two hours they walked the central grounds of the fair. They wandered north along the canal between the Manufacturers' and Electricity buildings and around the lagoon; they stopped in the Government, Fisheries, Women's, Horticulture and Transportation buildings. They reached the southern tip of the lagoon near seven o'clock. Wanting dinner, they consulted the map and then crossed the bridge onto the wooded island, ending up in the Cafe de Marine near the Fisheries building.

Dining on a balcony overlooking the wooded island, they watched gondolas move about on the water and said very little. In fact, they hadn't talked much since arriving. There was a wondrous unreality about their surroundings ever since they had stepped from the train. Both felt in a daze, as if they were slightly drunk or still foggy from waking. From where they sat they could see even more grand buildings to the east and north—the national and state buildings—and to the west the noise and commotion of the Midway Plaisance stretched out, the mammoth Ferris wheel churning in its center.

Darkness was falling as they finished dinner and eased back in their chairs. Slowly, electric lights blossomed all around them, lighting the White City, the buildings around the lagoon where they sat, and the Midway Plaisance spotlights cast their beams into the sky, where they swung back and forth. David was the only visitor who didn't gasp at the sight. Nowhere else in the world of 1893 was a city so illuminated with electric lights.

As the steamer left the dock, Mary stood at the railing and watched the dark, star-speckled sky above Lake Michigan.

"What are you looking at, Mona Lisa?"

She smiled. "I think I found Hercules. Tell me if I'm right."

"What's your starting point?"

"I see Sarin," she pointed with her arm outstretched, "then move down and left to the legs and up and down from Sarin makes the arms."

"That's it," he said, slipping his hands around her waist.

"Out here on the water, they look so close that you could reach out and touch them—as close as the lights of the city."

With glasses of champagne from the bottle in the cooler, David and Mary sat on the couch in their sumptuous suite and made awkward small talk. Their usual ease together was replaced by nervous anticipation.

"You poor women—the shoes you're forced to wear!" David said.

"After a day of traveling like this, they do make your feet hurt," Mary said, bending down to brush the day's dust off the glossy leather.

"Hold it right there," David told her. He disappeared into the bathroom, returning a moment later with a basin of water and a washcloth. He took off his coat, loosened his collar and took off his own shoes before sitting down at the other end of the couch, laying a towel across his lap.

"Give me your feet!"

"Why?" Mary asked, with a nervous smile.

"You're in for a real treat," David urged her, gesturing for her to swing her feet up into his lap. She did so reluctantly, brushing her skirt flat.

David began working the laces loose and looked up, catching the uncertainty in her eyes. "Relax," he reassured her. "Lean back, drink your champagne, and relax."

He loosened the laces and slipped her shoes off, then, without hesitating, gently reached under her skirt as far as her knees and pulled off her stockings. She stiffened with a start, then forced herself to relax. A man had never touched her legs before.

What he did next startled her beyond imagining: He washed her feet. She'd never seen a man do such a feminine task, and for the sole purpose of comforting a woman. David washed with gentleness. The coolness of the water took away the heat that had burned deep into her feet, bound in the unforgiving leather of expensive shoes made more for display than comfort.

David dried her feet with the towel in his lap. She started to swing them back to the floor, but he held them in place. "Oh, no," he said. "I'm just getting to the good part."

After refilling their glasses, he leaned back and put his own feet up on the low marble-topped coffee table, almost facing her now. Slowly he began massaging her feet, forcing his thumbs firmly into the ball beneath the toes and working his way down the arch. Mary closed her eyes and sighed with pleasure.

He worked back, pressing his thumbs in the flesh at the base of her toes, moving them in small circles. For the first time Mary realized that the nerves in her feet were connected to other parts of her body, as her loins and buttocks began to tingle in unison with her soles. She lay her head back on the arm of the couch.

As the champagne worked on her head and David worked on her feet, she felt that somewhere in the middle, she was melting. Melting with her were the guilt and shame she had been trained to associate with sex—melting away into irrelevance. Those feelings belonged to another world, a small town in central Indiana where she had somehow found him. She was in the future now, and he had taken her there. She had seen it tonight in the White City and was feeling it now through his hands. It was freedom and comfort, release from the binding conformity of her upbringing. It had been there all along, needing only to be massaged into life.

From time to time David rubbed the palm of his hand back and forth on the arch of her foot. The heat from the friction seemed to run up her legs and spread into her body, meeting the warmth of the champagne. David ran his hands beyond her ankles and up her calves, kneading the backs of her legs with his fingertips. The warmth washed deeper into her, and she felt as if she were drifting in a warm, peaceful ocean, far from the dry, landlocked world of her Hoosier upbringing.

Almost as if startled out of a mist, she realized that he had stopped. She lifted her head and opened her eyes. He was sitting watching her, sipping from his glass, smiling his soft, warm smile. She reached out and took his hand and pulled him toward her. He stood and raised her from the couch, sliding his hands around her waist and pulling her against him. She wrapped her arms around his neck and they kissed deeply. Her nervous anticipation gave way to a sigh of release and she held him close against her, running her hands along his neck and hair and feeling the warmth of his whiskers against her cheek.

She unfastened her dress and it fell to the floor. He unlaced her tightly strung corset. As always, loosening the corset at the end of the day let her take her first deep breath since morning. She took that breath now with her mouth on his. He caressed away the reddened impressions of the corset from her back and breasts. They stood naked, wrapped in each other's arms, kissing, feeling the warmth of their bodies together. They fell onto the bed and made love.

The rich surroundings and the distance from home heightened the otherworldliness of the experience for Mary. She was again floating in the warm ocean of her dream, and he was swimming with her, inside her, indistinguishable from her. She clung to him, and in their unison he felt an inexpressible love for her, a commitment to her unlike anything he'd ever imagined, more certain and unshakable than any desire he'd ever had.

Later, they lay embraced and talked into the night.

"What kind of life will our children have?" Mary mused. "You've talked a lot about the turn of the next century, but what happens in the next forty or fifty years? What will our lives and their lives be like?"

"If we live in Noblesville, things will stay pretty much the same for the next twenty years or so. That'll be the time the automobile really takes hold—and radios."

"Why are those two things so important?"

"The liveries and the blacksmiths will be gone. Before we die, there won't be any horses on the streets, just cars. They'll cause rail travel to begin to fade. The interurban electric railway will come and go in our lifetime. And radio? People will go out for entertainment and socialize less because of it.

"Industry and factories will change things a lot. The glass factories and Strawboards works will be dominated more and more by machines, until the machines are more important than the men working. A worker's whole day—almost every move he makes—will be dictated by the needs of the machine he operates.

"A great depression in the 1930s will make life hard all over the country. Our sons will be about the right age to fight in World War I, and our grandchildren will be about the right age to fight in World War II, and our great-grandchildren get the Vietnam War."

"It makes me so afraid," she whispered.

"Don't be. I think we can negotiate our way through and make a good life for ourselves if we're careful. We could jump ahead to my time, but for what? If we could see the future beyond that, it might be worse than the one before us now."

David fell asleep and Mary lay awake, watching him, troubled by the things he'd said. She got up, tossed on her dressing gown, and stood by the open window, watching the dark, empty street below. A warm lake breeze blew in the open window and through the thin gown. She closed her eyes and for a moment relived the sensation of him moving powerfully inside of her, the feel of his warm, strong body against hers.

She hadn't known exactly what to expect, but somehow it was perfect, it was exactly what she wanted it to be. Just like loving him. But there was a point where the mutuality between them ended.

It's not that important, she thought.

Every sign she had seen, from the White City to David himself, pointed to a shining and glorious future—a future completely at odds with David's jaundiced descriptions of the twenty-first century. She could not reconcile the two visions. In David's, people seemed to take leave of their senses in a dark, violent, isolated world; Jews were herded into ovens to die; animals were cast aside for machinery; wars were spaced by generation; family and community faded and people increasingly lived lonely lives, fearful of what lurked outside their doors. On the other hand, there was the view that spread before her, just to the south.

She squinted, looking for stray light far to the south, searching for evidence of the White City over the rooftops. Today at the fair she had seen a telegraph machine that transferred handwriting (David had mumbled "fax"). She saw a machine that made moving pictures. There was an electric machine that would toast bread, electric ovens, electric motors that ran no louder than a whisper. Beneath the electric lights, smartly dressed, happy people walked or rode in boats and elevated trains. How could the future not be a magnificent place? Didn't David say that people fly in the air, go to the moon, talk on telephones to the other side of the world, eradicate diseases? Could David be so wrong?

He'd become so contemptuous of his own time that he seldom talked about it anymore, and then only when she prodded him. She remembered his description two months ago of something called a "computer." He explained it with a touch of pride, as if to say, "Look what my generation has done." He had been proud, too, of the medicine that cured Clara. That pride was gone now; it had been replaced by his passion for her hometown and the people in it.

She had read Edward Bellamy's "Looking Backward," a book about a man from her time who awakens near the year 2000. Everything the man sees is wonderful and perfect. The inequities of capitalism are corrected, the ugliness of cities beautified, the propriety of manners, dignity, and social justice strengthened. That's what she'd thought of when she walked beneath the peristyle and saw the White City for the first time. It was just like Bellamy's Boston of the late twenty-first century.

When she described the book to him, David explained how Bellamy's vision was in error. Technology evolves faster than Bellamy imagined, and while great strides are made toward improved social justice, a general decline in basic human decency scars any improvement. Crime is rampant, and the socialism that the book envisioned as the salvation of society turns out to be a deeply flawed concept.

Another warm breeze softly broke into her thoughts, returning her to the present. She felt her bare breast through the silk dressing gown. Here she was, practically naked, in a hotel with her lover, two hundred miles from Noblesville. It felt farther away than that. How strange that she felt no guilt or remorse, no thoughts of sin—only the feeling of rightness, and wanting him.

Mary looked down at the small turtle pendant still hanging from the silver chain around her neck. She opened the shell and watched the compass needle waver back and forth, finally settling on north.

She flipped it over and read the tiny inscription, as she'd done hundreds of times since her grandmother had given it to her: "So you won't lose your way."

CHAPTER FIFTEEN

O such a land it is—fabulous beyond
the miracles of strangest fact ...
James Whitcomb Riley

Heather drove north up Allisonville Road, something she hadn't done since things had ended with David. Why hadn't he returned her texts? She'd left a voice message, too, confident that he still loved her. Men always wanted her back. So why didn't he call?

Heather's confidence was slipping. Ever since the abortion, ever since she had frozen him out and sabotaged the relationship, she'd thought perhaps it had been a mistake to let him go. In June, when her company was bought out and downsized, leaving her without a job, her confidence had slipped even further.

David was different from other men. She could depend on him; his spirit was rock-solid. But when she ran into Jeremy the night before and found out that David quit his job—gone AWOL, as Jeremy had put it—she wondered whether his life was falling apart, too. *Is he lonely? Does he feel lost, too, like I do?*

She pulled up at the curb in front of his house and wondered at the tall grass, the weeds growing between the sidewalk bricks, the ladder abandoned against the gable. David was usually so meticulous about keeping things tended. She climbed the steps and looked down into an open paint can: Below four inches of rainwater was a skin of paint. The rim of the can was rusted.

Heather pulled open the screen door and twisted the bell. No answer. She walked around the house, peeking in windows. Through the garage window she saw his truck. *Strange. His truck is here, so he's around.*

Heather went back to her car to write David a note. Then she remembered that she still had the house key he'd given her.

If the outside of the house had troubled her, what she found inside puzzled her even more. The dining room table was piled with junk mail, months of it. On the floor nearby were at least fifty newspapers in a heap, still folded and bound in small plastic bags.

She peered out through the front window, then turned back and saw the glowing lights on the modem and Airport.

She went into the former apartment at the back of the house. There on the table sat the still unrepaired leaded-glass window from the stair landing, and all about were boxes, stacks of boxes filled with antique bottles and tins—boxes and boxes of them everywhere. She wondered whether David had begun to live like a hermit.

On his dresser upstairs she found a curious photograph that stopped her heart. It was a tintype of David and a beautiful brunette, both wearing clothes from a past era. It looked like a costume photo of the kind that people have taken at theme parks—but this was real tin. Furthermore, the very suit he was wearing in the photo lay across the bed before her.

She pushed the suit aside and lay down on the familiar bed, burying her face in the pillow. She could smell the familiar mixture of the soap and shampoo he used. Slowly, she began to cry. She rolled over and lay on her back and wept, staring at the ceiling, wondering what he was up to and who the woman in the photo was. Finally, missing him now more than ever, Heather left, locking the front door behind her.

David and Mary spent their first morning at the hotel in bed, making love and talking. Mary's misgivings of the night before came back to her as they ate a room service breakfast, and she wondered again at the stark contrast between David's version of the future and the one portended by the glorious World's Fair.

Last night she had wished to see the future; she wanted him to take her there, to ride in an automobile, to fly in an airplane. But the very notion of her stepping through the beam had taken on a taboo as strong as the sexual pleasure they had just enjoyed.

David scanned the guidebook, bubbling with ideas for what they might do with the day ahead. She watched him talk, not really listening, wondering what questions she could ask to bridge the gap between what she saw and hoped about the future, and what he told her about it.

She thought about all the junk he'd been accumulating in the Emmous Street house. He'd begun saving coffee tins, cigar tins and boxes, beer bottles, medicine bottles, advertising items of any sort. Why would he save trash? He said that he could sell them, that they were "collectibles." How could trash be valuable in a world where people traveled to the moon and flew in the air?

Two hours later, though, they stood on the balcony of the Fisheries Building at the World's Fair, and Mary forgot all her worries. Being there, with him, it was easy to fall into the dream and let cares fall away.

On their third day in Chicago, they had lunch in the beautiful Palmer House dining room, and Mary gave David some instructions on the finer points of etiquette. They were to visit Helen Garrison that afternoon, and David was afraid he'd make a mistake. A well-to-do family's home wouldn't offer beers around a pool and a barbecue—pretty much the limit of his social experience.

"This will be much different from Noblesville," Mary said. "People there all know one another, and they can be informal. Confine your conversation to positive topics at all times; criticize nothing. There's no telling whose toes you might step on.

"If there are any men about, watch them and do what they do. Always stand when a lady enters the room, and don't sit until all ladies have done so. You're terrible at such things. It doesn't bother me, but it will reflect badly on us both if you make a faux pas. You're supposedly from Canada, so you can play dumb if you don't understand what's being discussed; they'll even find it charming, providing you're gracious. Don't criticize the wealthy, or America, or any patriotic notion. Most important, listen closely when I whisper, and look where I look when I touch your sleeve."

The ride south out Michigan Avenue was splendid. Past the commercial zone, grand houses lined the streets, finer and more elaborate than the best in Noblesville. Some were made of high-quality brick, others of sandstone, limestone, or granite. Above tile and slate roofs rose ornate ceramic chimney pots and imposing towers. This was not even the most exclusive neighborhood in Chicago, but it was still better than what ninety-five percent of the city's population would ever know. These houses had been built by the city's new rich, the merchant princes.

Helen Garrison, a slight, blond woman with a bright, childlike face, greeted them at the door. A young Irish maid appeared and took David's hat. They walked into the front parlor, and Helen called out for her mother to come and meet the guests.

That afternoon was excruciatingly boring for David. The women drank tea and talked endlessly about topics of little interest to him. A few short months ago, the preservationist in him would have killed to be there, but he was already jaded. He was troubled to think that this was the life Mary wanted.

Helen rattled on about the lavish parties she had attended and a trip abroad she planned to take with her mother. Her description of her life was idyllic, and Mary hung on every word. Helen offered a critique of the summer social round and forecast the quality of the fall opera season. She mentioned the races, the balls, the fine restaurants, the new Art Institute—but she also spent much of her conversation on complaints about the inconveniences of her life, chief among them an inability to find the perfect clothes.

Late in the afternoon David and Mary left, promising to return for a party later in the week and also to spend a day at the Columbian Exhibition with Helen and a friend.

In the days that followed, Mary and David had the time of their lives.

They spent many days on the grounds of the fair, hiking through the miles of exhibits, eating in the restaurants and beer houses, taking gondola and electric launch rides around the extensive waterways, and relaxing in the dreamlike White City.

David's money-making schemes got a boost. In the Women's Building, he bought a small bag of commemorative Isabella quarter-dollar coins and later, a bag of commemorative Columbian Exposition half dollars—fifty of each.

Most intriguing to David was the Midway Plaisance. It extended in a strip west of the central body of the fair, its center defined by the huge Ferris wheel, with its bus-sized cars gliding 250 feet in the air for a breathtaking view of the grounds, Lake Michigan, and the city. The name "Midway" would be applied to rides and amusements at fairs all over America in the future. It was the prototype for Coney Island and Disney World. Even little Broad Ripple, just south of Noblesville, would, at the turn of the century, build a small midway amusement park and name it the White City.

Mary, in a new Paris-styled evening gown, and David, in the tuxedo made for him in Indianapolis, attended the opera and symphony. They dined in Chicago's best restaurants and often hired the hotel's rockaway for rides around the city. The money David had made bringing "trash" through the beam allowed them to taste the life of Chicago's elite.

This was the life that Helen had, and Mary loved it. She and David could have it, too, she thought. The prospect of one day moving to Chicago and enjoying this extravagant life made Mary giddy. Her speculation about passing through the beam was erased by the Palmer House service, the theater, and the expensive clothes—far removed from the dusty streets of Noblesville and its farmers in their manure-caked boots.

On the night of Helen's party, Mary donned her sumptuous gown and David his tuxedo. The Palmer House rockaway bore them out to the Garrisons' suburban mansion. As they drew up in the circular drive, they could hear music coming from the house. They joined a crowd of other magnificently dressed guests, making their way up a marble staircase to the third-floor ballroom. Waiters passed by with silver trays laden with crystal glasses of champagne. David and Mary walked down a hallway lined on the left with several sitting rooms. On the right, column-framed archways opened onto the dance floor. A small orchestra played at one end. The hallway and ballroom were laden with flowers, draped in garlands from the columns and arranged in massive bouquets on tables, and with flowering plants in glossy jardinieres. Helen and her "gentleman friend," John Howard, stood in the receiving line along with Helen's parents and two brothers. Excitement filled the air.

"That's not fair," Helen said, kissing Mary's cheek and admiring her dress. "The guests aren't supposed to be prettier than the hostess."

"Oh, you look wonderful," Mary beamed.

"Stay close to me tonight," Helen whispered in Mary's ear. "We're making a special announcement tonight, and I want to drink a toast with you two."

They did stay close. David and Mary fit in well, the handsome Canadian and the beautiful, unaffected young lady from Indiana. Their station alongside Helen and John certified their status to the other guests. They danced almost continually, with each other and with new acquaintances. They talked with interesting and powerful people—wealthy and educated, eccentrics, artists, businessmen, scholars, politicians.

This night felt like the culmination of everything Mary had dreamed of. She wasn't in Noblesville, nor was she a student, carefully watched over by teachers and matrons. Tonight she was a free adult in a world of culture and beauty. David, and the unexpected loveliness of the physical love, were the centerpiece, the core around which this glittering world spun. After one dance, she pulled David into an alcove and kissed him deeply. "Thank you for making me so happy," she murmured. "You and this are all I've ever wanted."

At eleven o'clock, Helen's father stood up in front of the orchestra on their dais and tapped a champagne glass with a spoon. The room quieted.

"I want to thank you all for coming tonight," he boomed. His wife joined him, and waiters passed among the guests with fresh glasses. People came out of the sitting rooms and gathered in the archways and on the dance floor.

"A party is, in truth, not about music or champagne, but about friends," Mr. Garrison began, "and it pleases us more than we can say that you have joined us tonight." He inclined his head to acknowledge the applause. "Tonight, Mrs. Garrison and I have a special announcement, one that gives us great joy. We would like to announce the engagement of our daughter Helen to a wonderful young man you all know, John Howard." Again the crowd applauded.

"Oh, how wonderful!" Mary exclaimed. She and Helen embraced, and John shook hands all around.

"Come up here, you two," Mr. Garrison called to his daughter and her fiancé. When they joined him, he raised his glass. "I want to propose a toast: To the most wonderful daughter a parent could wish for, and to another son: May your life be filled with joy and pleasure, may you know the happiness together that your mother and I have known. To John and Helen and their future happiness!" Every glass was lifted to the young couple—but Mary thought Helen's smile looked forced.

A few minutes later, Mary followed Helen to a small powder room and found her there alone, crying.

"Helen, what's the matter?" Helen silently held out her arms, and Mary sat beside her, holding her close. Helen wept on.

Mary was bewildered. "I don't understand! This should be such a happy moment. What could possibly be wrong?"

"I don't know," Helen sobbed. "I thought I wanted to get married, but hearing it said out loud, all those people looking at me ... I have everything a person could want, but somehow it doesn't seem right. I've felt this way for a long time."

Mary, speechless, held her as she cried.

"Is this what we wanted?" Helen said, finally catching her breath. "Is this what we dreamed of when we were at school?"

"Yes!" Mary responded, emphatic and incredulous.

"I was so much happier there, away from all this. Maybe this is what you wanted. I think now I must have just played along with your fantasies of a grand life because I had something you wanted and it made me feel privileged. But now, I feel so empty and alone!"

Mrs. Garrison suddenly came in. "So this is where you girls are hiding!" Then she saw the tears on Helen's cheeks. "My dear, what's wrong?"

"I don't know," Helen said, trying to compose herself. "I just suddenly felt very sad."

"It's your nerves. Too much stimulation."

"That's not it!" Helen said sharply.

"Then what is it?" Mrs. Garrison shot back, irritated at her daughter's tone.

"I don't know why I feel this way, I just do!"

"My God, Helen!" her mother said. "Why, any girl in Chicago would give her right arm to be in your position tonight, and you sit here sulking." She went back to the door. "Your father and I have given you the best of everything, but it's never enough to make you happy. Dear God, Helen, get hold of yourself!"

With that, she walked out.

"She's right, I know. I'm being foolish," Helen said quickly, wiping her tears. "All those guests are out there—I must go back to them."

In her about-face, Helen fussed with her hair, forcing sad thoughts from her mind. Mary's heart continued to sink. How could someone who had everything she herself dreamed of be so unhappy? They left the room together, having traded moods: Helen putting on a bravely happy face, and Mary crushed.

Mary endured her second restless night since coming to Chicago. She put on David's headphones and listened to music, watching the night activity in the streets: dray wagons carrying goods to stores, beer trucks, milk and bakery wagons, icemen, readying Chicago for another day. Those five minutes with Helen had destroyed the joy of the trip for her. She stood in the darkness, trying to make sense of it all.

What did Helen really think of her? Why had she played confidante for three years and filled Mary's head with the grandeur of big-city society life? Did Helen think of her just as a naive girl from Indiana? Helen was clever, and if she could be unhappy in her surroundings, it spoiled the dream.

Had the party guests seen her as a country bumpkin—a Hoosier? She sat down on the bed, sniffling. David woke and tried to console her. She undressed to her chemise and crawled between the sheets. David lay down beside her and held her close.

The next day David, Mary, Helen, and John stood beneath the dome of the Administration Building, looking out beyond the imposing Columbian Fountain, across the central basin to the peristyle. Through the colonnade, Lake Michigan glistened in the late-afternoon sun. Steamers dotted the horizon, moving toward or away from the city, their smoke plumes rising up and trailing behind them.

John and Mary stood together near the bandstand talking, watching the musicians set up. Helen took David's arm and led him toward the edge of the basin. They stood at the railing, surveying the magnificent, classically inspired Court of Honor, the white buildings reflected in the water. The elevated trains that carried people around the fair passed smoothly behind the Machinery Building.

"It's wonderful, isn't it?" Helen remarked to David.

"Yes—hard to believe it's all here in Chicago."

"This is a bit of a lesson and a promise, isn't it?"

"I'm not sure I know what you mean."

"A lesson in what our cities could be in the future, if we just cared enough to make it so," she said wistfully. "They don't have to be dark and ugly, filled with telegraph lines and soot-covered buildings. Men are coming to their senses! Someday all our cities will be this lovely, don't you think?"

"I wish I could agree with you," David replied. "But something tells me money will dictate that they evolve differently. They may even get worse instead of better."

"Oh, I think you're wrong," she said, smiling out across the water. A gondola laden with a happy family passed beneath the bridge from the south canal and moved into the great basin. "I think the men who planned this miracle have others in mind for Chicago and other cities as well. So much has already happened; the Art Institute, the ..."

She went on, but David was puzzling over something. He had been nagged by the familiarity of the Agriculture Building, and finally he realized how he knew it. When he was seventeen, he'd come to Chicago with his science class to visit the Museum of Science and Industry. That was its building, before him now. As he envisioned that day as a teenager, it dawned on him that all the other buildings would be destroyed before his time. The basin gave way to a parking lot, and a road covered the peristyle. As so many times this summer, he was filled with a deep, angry sadness.

"David, David!" Mary's voice was insistently calling, waking him from his thoughts.

Standing beside her, smiling and waving, were the Wises, fellow members of the Noblesville Methodist Episcopal Church. They looked the part of country folk visiting the big city: Mr. Wise's suit was twenty years old, and his wife wore a calico dress, a dead giveaway of a country woman. David walked over and heard all the past week's news from Noblesville. The electric railway was moving forward, and the Swain trial had been postponed again.

As John asked the older couple how they liked the big city, Helen eyed them with condescension. Both David and Mary felt suddenly self-conscious about their fine clothes. They looked at their hometown friends and felt like snobs. The Wises' nasal Hoosier twang, something Mary had trained away at Bryn Mawr, suddenly sounded backward.

Once the Wises had moved on, Helen said, "What quaint people." There was an air of superiority in her tone.

That careless comment cut Mary to the quick. She said defensively, "They're very nice people."

"Oh, I'm sure they are," Helen said.

They walked north. Helen broke the uneasy silence. "David and I were just talking about what the White City promises for the future. Much of this architecture is European, and when you think about it, it's really at odds with what we've been doing here in America. Chicagoans keep building upward, yet this is more horizontal, more linear."

"Something else the Europeans do," Helen said, "is to give different types of people their own space. There are places in London and Paris reserved just for refined people. We don't have that here. Just look around—there are people of every different class here, mingling together. While it seems very democratic, I don't really think it's what makes most people happy."

"I can't believe you feel that way!" Mary said, perceiving a criticism of the Wises. The world she thought she wanted was starting to look so ugly now. Mary gave David's arm a firm squeeze. "Helen, John, thank you ever so much for coming along with us today but we really must be getting back. Have you forgotten, David, we have tickets to the theater?"

After a quick goodbye, David and Mary walked on and turned west down the Midway Plaisance. "How could she look down on them?" Mary said. "She claims to hate her life but then exhibits the ugliest face of it."

"She may hate her life, but it's what she is," David said.

They had been here so many times that the street performers no longer fascinated them. The mammoth Ferris wheel no longer inspired. The *danse du ventre*—the belly dance touted on a huge poster—didn't scandalize them as it did newcomers to the Midway. This day they walked past Old Vienna, the Chinese Village, the Brazilian Music Hall, and the Bedouin Encampment, then strolled out the west gates and into the streets lined with unofficial attractions that had sprung up around the fair during the summer.

Just outside the gates on 59th Street, they came upon a carousel filled with children. As the brightly painted wooden horses spun around, the sound of the steam engine driving it mixed with the breathy sputter of a calliope, filling the air with noise and excitement. They stood for a moment watching the children spin 'round and 'round. When the carousel stopped, a mischievous look crossed Mary's face. She grabbed David's hand. "Come on, let's go for a ride!"

As the carousel turned, David watched the joy on her face and thought of how different she looked from the reserved woman he'd picnicked with at Crownland Cemetery on Decoration Day. She seemed suddenly intent on not being sad, not letting her disappointment win out.

Mary had been sitting sidesaddle but suddenly stood up on one stirrup. Holding the pole with one hand, she reached out with the other, trying to grab the brass ring. The crowd laughed at this beautiful, playful young woman, who ignored convention for the sake of a rather unlady-like bit of fun.

She reached out, clutching at the ring. David, fearing that she might fall and get caught beneath the turning deck, stood and grabbed her wrist just beyond the pole she was holding.

Mary let go of the pole, knowing he held her. She strained farther to reach the ring. The crowd exploded with laughter at David's look of alarm. He wanted to pull her back but was off-balance and could do little more than hold her in place.

When they passed the ring again, Mary grabbed it and shouted "Aha!" She leaned back and sat on her horse. The crowd cheered. Suddenly noticing them, Mary held up the ring like a trophy, embarrassed but laughing.

"I keep thinking about all the technology at the fair," David said the next morning. They sat wrapped in their dressing gowns before a room service table laden with eggs, bacon, bread, fruit and juice, talking and reading the newspaper.

"Some pretty amazing things."

He picked at an eggshell and began peeling it away, chip by chip. "There's a computer network at Noblesville High School. All the teachers' computers are connected, like telephones are connected by wires. Using a keyboard, like on a typewriter, I log in grades, attendance, and discipline reports, and save tests and lesson plans. I can print out copies, send the grades to the office for processing with the press of a button. The records are always available—no filing cabinet, no paper pushing."

"Sounds wonderfully convenient."

"Yeah, it is," he responded, spooning out the gelatinous egg white. "When I was a kid in school, they just wrote all that stuff down on a piece of paper. That worked. Why wasn't it enough?"

"But efficiency is good, isn't it?" she interrupted.

"Well, I guess. But are our lives really any better—are we any happier? I don't think so. Did we really need a $150,000 system that required hours of training for lots of people to do a job we once did naturally and easily on paper? And when the system breaks down, we go back to the pen and paper—which suddenly seems like a huge inconvenience.

"The funny thing is," David continued, "I imagined that the grading and attendance network would make my job easier and give me more time to be a better teacher, but it didn't, really. It seems like the faster we're able to do our work, the faster we have to work. Things don't get more relaxed or more thorough, they get more manic—and the more complicated the system, the less people really understand it or feel they have control over it. Without control, they feel isolated.

"What's worse: Before we adapt to the new technology, there's another new technology coming along to take its place as the end of all our problems. They just keep coming. We never ask ourselves whether they feed our souls or really make our lives happier or easier—or if they're practical, for that matter. What's more, we don't ask ourselves what kind of secondary unintended changes they'll bring.

"Think about all the things we've seen in the Electricity and Manufacturers' buildings. People walk by, thinking it's all just so wonderful. Sure, those people endure a lot of drudgery, and those machines promise to lighten the load—and maybe they will—and maybe that's okay. But how light a load is light enough? What's progress, anyway?"

"Progress is moving forward," she said. "It's improving life."

"Define 'improve life.' "

"Well, now you're being silly," she complained, shaking her head.

"Well, think about it: When people in my time lie on their deathbed, do they think about production levels, returns on investment, and how rich their lives were thanks to technology? No! They think about the same things people think about now: the people they love and the relationships they had throughout their lives, the experiences that defined them as people. That's what's important. But when new technologies come along, do we ask how they'll affect the people we love and our relationships with them? No! We think about profits and leisure time. We don't think about the implications that are going to destroy our way of life.

"So how much progress is enough?" David asked. "How much can you have before you destroy human nature as Noblesville knows it in 1893? They say 'Times change, but people don't,' but I don't think that's true. We've changed as people, and the change isn't all that good."

Mary watched David spread the egg yolk on his bread. She finally spoke. "You could add that these inventions will save labor and make certain tasks useless—but those lost tasks have meaning to people's lives."

David brightened, feeling that for once his point of view had been understood. "Yeah," he encouraged her.

"Those tasks, that drudgery, sometimes helps people define themselves and gives them value in their family and in their community. So what you're really asking is, how many meaningful tasks can you take away before life ceases to have meaning beyond … amusing oneself."

David's mouth was full, but he nodded vigorously. She'd never before taken his side on such issues, let alone fleshed out his unorganized thoughts about his own time.

"Looking back through the history of technology," David said, "over and over new technologies are introduced with the same message: 'These labor-saving devices will give you more leisure time so you can grow as a person—find yourself.' Ironically, it's been the continual embracing of technology that's led people to lose themselves. They found personal definition in the things they did before."

"I can see why people leap at these technologies," Mary said, gesturing widely. "They see what they have to gain, but haven't a clue as to what they stand to lose. If a man is a glass-blower, he's a craftsman, but if a machine can do the same job, what is he? A laborer, I suppose."

David grabbed a pencil. On the back of the World's Fair brochure he drew a pyramid. "A psychologist named Maslow had something to say about this," he told her.

Across the pyramid David drew four lines, dividing it horizontally into five sections. In the broad bottom space he wrote "physical needs," proceeding upward with "safety needs," "belonging," "self-esteem," and finally "self-actualization." Mary leaned forward on her elbow, chin in hand.

"This theory is called the hierarchy of needs," David explained. "Down at the bottom here you have the simplest needs, like hunger and thirst. When people satisfy those basic human needs they naturally start to concern themselves with the needs in the next level, creating a safe environment for the maintenance of the needs already attained. Once safe, a person starts looking for love and belonging. Then he moves up to the search for self-esteem. According to the theory, once all those needs are attained, the person reaches the top and naturally starts looking for ways to grow, to realize his talents and seek real inner happiness."

"Helen is near the top," Mary said, "and she's so unhappy."

"Exactly my point."

"Her concerns seem so petty and frivolous, it made me feel guilty for having some of the same ones." She tapped the top of the pyramid. "You can't find self-actualization at the top, you only find it while living the lower levels. It's right there, all you have to do is learn to appreciate it."

She had voiced David's feelings, which he had never formulated so clearly. Mary leaned back in her chair, crossing her arms in satisfaction. David watched her, loving her brilliance.

She added, "The catch is that self-actualization isn't a destination—it's found while living through the lower levels. Right?"

David smiled at her.

"That's what you've been trying so hard to say to me all summer, isn't it?" she said softly.

"To some degree, yes, but I didn't really know it. I was so bothered by the contrasts between my world and this one, but I didn't understand what was bothering me until you laid it out like that.

"And I've seen you wanting these things," he said, gesturing at the lavish suite and on toward the city beyond the window. "But the things I've wanted most in life—and that you already had—are in Noblesville. It's not perfect, I know, but perfect is where you start to lose yourself. What's best is imperfect.

"You see, I come from an America where people's desperate attempts at 'self-actualization' tend to lead to divorce—the disease of my time. They surround themselves with gadgets and shallow comforts. They shove their kids into day care all day so that both parents can earn the money for all this silly nothingness. While they clutch at it all, some stranger is raising their kids for them. But most of them never achieve that self-actualization, and they wonder why their marriages fail and their children go out of control.

"That's the environment I was raised in," David said, "and I hate it. I don't need the brass ring. I just want to sit on the carousel horse, listen to the music, and enjoy the ride."

Mary squeezed his hand. "We don't need all this, do we?" She looked around the room at his tuxedo laid across the chair and out the window at the city. "We don't need all these things we've seen and done since we got here—the opulent living, the servants … and most of the technology at the fair."

"Oh, they're fine," he conceded, "but not as a total way of life. Happiness in living is found in people and a community, not in material wealth. The buildings at the fair aren't made of brick and stone, haven't you noticed? They're just wooden shells covered with plaster that's painted white. We came here from a place where the buildings are real, and it's not a dream city. It's a real community, and that's good enough for me."

On the day of their departure, David and Mary threw away their Monon Line tickets and decided instead to return home by way of the heart of Indiana on the L.E.&W. This required that they take a steamer to Michigan City. By early afternoon they had made their connection, and the train was passing through La Porte and Walkerton, Rochester and Peru.

"It will seem odd to be separated again," Mary murmured, laying her head on David's shoulder. The train rushed south, cutting through the flat, northern Indiana landscape. "Not being with you at night, not able to come and go together as we please, living in different houses—will feel so strange."

"Getting married would solve it all."

She squeezed his hand. "When should we do that?"

"We could get off the train at any town along the way."

"Oh, not that way! Let's plan it ahead of time and invite all our friends. We'll get married in my parents' house. You really ought to talk to my father—as a courtesy."

"I'm not very popular with your dad right now. How do you think he'll react to a marriage proposal?"

"He'll soften up, you'll see. He just likes to rule the roost. Harry has taken the same position as you about politics, and I think it just galls Dad. He needs time to get over it. Let's wait until the Swain trial has blown over. After all, the notion of our getting married shouldn't come as any great shock to him."

"Where do you want to live?"

She knew he'd be a little shocked by her response. "I think we'd be very happy in Mr. Locke's house."

Throughout the late afternoon, the cars grew emptier with each stop as fair-weary travelers got off. As the train moved through the woods on the high ridge north of Noblesville, David and Mary could see a crew of laborers working along the river behind Major Wainwright's farm, grading the land, preparing to build a bridge for the electric railway. The clock tower didn't come into view over the trees until they were nearly in the town, and the locomotive crossed the White River, pulling them back home.

CHAPTER SIXTEEN

The wages of sin are the hardest debts on earth to pay, and they are always
collected at inconvenient times and unexpected places.
A Girl of the Limberlost, Gene Stratton-Porter, 1909.

Being in this courtroom again on a hot day felt like a continuation of the Warren Beeman trial. He was gone now, his house on Emmous Street empty. His wife and children never returned from Crawfordsville—the shame was too great.

David and Mary found seats downstairs. No amount of lecturing from Anna could keep Mary away. A few minutes later Will Christian came in and sat beside them. "Gonna be a big show," he said, taking off his straw hat.

The presence of Thomas Swain and Ida Mae Thompson sitting on opposite sides heightened the similarities for David. He tried not to make eye contact with her. The memory of the last time their eyes met on the dirt road outside Carmel was still fresh in his mind, and the thought of it shot a dagger of guilt through him. But their eyes eventually did meet, and she betrayed the steely hatred she felt for him, thinking him to be one of the enemies in all of this, one of Swain's men who dug up her baby's grave.

The Beeman trial had felt like a circus. Maybe it was the electric railway workers in the balcony, or just that Beeman was a regular guy who had been caught almost literally with his pants down. Because of Swain's position in the community, the stakes were higher now. There was enormous tension in the room. All were waiting for something of great importance to happen.

As people were milling in, the bailiff strode across the floor toward his post and accidentally dropped the Bible. The abrupt thump jolted nearly everyone in the room. A few laughed nervously at their own jittery nerves. Thomas Swain, playing the part of defendant for the first time in his life, stared down at the Bible with flared nostrils, finding no humor in the moment.

Out of respect, most people in the courtroom tried not to stare at the local hero. Some—Democrats, mostly—hoped he was guilty; others were sure he wasn't and expected to see his lawyers make a fool of this whore, Mrs. Thompson.

The plaintiff's and defendant's tables flanked the judge's bench in front of the gallery. Swain's impressive team of lawyers, three from the capital and the other his own law partner, surrounded him at their long oak table beyond the balustrade. They considerably outweighed Ida Mae Thompson and her lawyer, A.F. Ramsey, in both tonnage and distinction; they were likely to do more than tip the scales of justice. David knew Ramsey by reputation: meek, learned, but sometimes bumbling, a Democrat pitted today against the big guns of the state Republican Party. He couldn't help feeling that Ramsey had the same chance as a snowball in hell.

Mayor Jones strode in and climbed the steps to the bench. Despite his portly frame, he was quick and nimble. He scowled and arranged papers before him, looking wearily at Mrs. Thompson and Ramsey, and then at Swain and his legal entourage. Jones rested his elbows on the bench and took a deep breath, choosing his words.

"With all due respect, Thomas, would you please stand?" Swain did so. "You know why we're here, don't you, Tom?"

"Yes."

"This lady over here has said some mighty unpleasant things about you. Law is your line of work, so I reckon you understand what these charges are all about?"

"I understand the charges," Swain said with an equal mixture of confidence and controlled rage. "They're false, but I understand them."

"Thanks. You can sit," Jones nodded abruptly. He turned his glance to Ida Mae. "You sure you want to go through with this, ma'am?"

"She does," Ramsey spoke for her.

Jones looked down, frustrated in the hope that he wouldn't have to preside over this nasty event. The barely noticeable movement of his bushy mustache was the only evidence that he was biting at the skin on the back of his lip—or chewing tobacco.

He addressed Swain's table. "I suppose you men must know that what we usually do on these Tuesday and Thursday mornings is swat the hands of boys who steal apples or send the local drunk to jail for a week for making a spectacle of himself on the square. Oh, occasionally we get a horse thief, but my point is this: I don't need none of you telling me how to do my job. All we want to do here is get to the facts. If you want to make more of a name for yourself, do me a favor and do it somewhere else at somebody else's expense

"I spend most of my time worrying about volunteer firemen, the waterworks, and graveling roads," the mayor continued. "You're all learned men, and I expect you think you know how things ought to be. But you also know enough about state law to know that I can do pretty much whatever I want in this court. You're welcome here, so long as you don't overdo it. The presence of so many lawyers is kind of overdoing it as it is. Now, Mr. Ramsey, you ready to start?" Jones leaned back in his chair.

Mrs. Thompson was the first to take the stand. As she swore to tell the truth, the men in the courtroom admired her curvaceous figure and pale, classical features.

After establishing that she was thirty years old and married but estranged from her husband, Ramsey continued. "Mrs. Thompson, how long have you known Mr. Thomas Swain?"

"'Bout three years." Her voice was clear and defiant. She looked quickly in sharp glances about the court room while adjusting herself in the chair.

"And where did you meet?"

"At a political rally at Thomlinson Hall in Indianapolis in 1890. I went there with my estranged husband. We talked at length and quickly became friends."

"I know this is a difficult question," the gray-haired lawyer said quietly, tapping a pencil in the palm of his hand, "but did you have an intimate affair with Mr. Swain?"

"Yes," she said bluntly.

David expected the room to erupt in gasps and whispers, but there was silence as the gallery hung on her words.

Ramsey said, "I'm sure you know that such an admission shocks people, and they wonder why a married woman like yourself would enter into such a relationship."

"My marriage to Mr. Thompson has not been a happy one. Mr. Thompson was and is fond of liquor, and uses it liberally."

"Many men drink, Mrs. Thompson, but most of their wives don't take up with another man."

She took a deep breath. "When he drank," she said resolutely, "he frequently hit me. On one occasion he broke my nose."

"That must have been terrible," Ramsey said with warm sympathy.

"It was!" she said, starting to lose her composure. "He beat me brutally for any reason, and usually for no reason. I lived in terror." She could not suppress her tears. Ramsey handed her his handkerchief. Ramsey waited for her to compose herself and went on.

"Did he beat you because of your relationship with Mr. Swain?"

"No, he never knew about that. If he had, I suppose he'd have killed me."

"I come back to my previous point. Why the affair with Mr. Swain?"

Her eyes searched the room. The defiant woman who had taunted Swain at the Beeman trial was gone. In her place was a wounded, weak soul. "I don't know." Her voice trembled. "I guess I was lonely and afraid, and Thomas said I should have a man who appreciated me and would protect me.

"At our first meeting he spoke to me very freely. He saw a bruise beneath my eye and asked how it happened, and I was indiscreet. I admitted that my husband struck me often. I wanted so much to tell someone; I was so alone in my misery.

"A week later he sent a note from his office at the legislature and invited me to lunch—to talk about my problem, he said, and what he might do to help. I guess that's how it all started. He was so kind and understanding. He said his own marriage was unhappy and that we could comfort one another."

David watched Swain's back, looking for a reaction. The senator sat with his legs crossed and tapped the table nervously with his knuckles. The whole town would know what she said, and it was driving him mad. His thick neck, bulging above his tight collar, turned an angry red.

"So you began meeting often?" Ramsey went on.

"Yes. When my husband was out of town I would take the train to Shelbyville or Anderson, or even Crown Point, to meet Thomas for a day or a night. He was always traveling to make speeches for one candidate or another."

"How long did this go on?"

"Two years, I guess."

"During this time, did Mr. Swain make any promises to you?"

"Yes. He said he wanted to leave his wife and get out of politics. He said we could go out West, get married and start all over."

"Did you believe him?"

"Yes," she admitted, showing embarrassment for the first time. "So I left my husband and went to my sister's in Carmel and asked my husband for a divorce. It wasn't long after I left him that Thomas suddenly became too busy to see me. Oh, he answered my letters from time to time. But once when I went to talk to him at the State House, he got very angry and struck me across the face with his hand and said I should never come there to see him."

Ramsey spent almost an hour questioning her about the events of the period when Swain cast her aside. She recalled how he had abused her, just as her husband once had. They had spent a few more nights together, but any pretense of romance was gone. She acceded to his demands; without Swain, she would have no way to support herself.

Finally, Ramsey reached the central issue. "You claim that Mr. Swain fathered your child. When did that happen?"

"Last October," Ida Mae said, looking down. "I went to meet him in Martinsville on the eleventh of October. We hadn't seen each other in a fortnight. Tom spoke at a rally that evening and I went back and waited at the hotel. Later, I got a note written by Mr. Carter saying that Thomas couldn't see me. The next morning we were on the same train going back to Union Station. When we got there, he suggested that we check into a hotel for the afternoon. So we did. We went to a hotel right by the station." She fell silent.

"So that's when the child was conceived? How do you know?"

She raised her eyes and glared at him. "A woman knows."

"When you later discovered you were with child, how did Mr. Swain react?"

"He said it was my problem and if I called on him again he would make trouble for me."

"So you left it at that?"

"No," Ida Mae said, looking down and then across the faces in the court room, like a child admitting to a crime. "I got very angry. I guess that for the first time I really understood what I was to him—an amusement—an amusement that had ceased to be amusing."

"You were angry. So what did you do then?"

"They won't understand," she objected.

"Look, ma'am," Mayor Jones said, "you're the only reason we're here. Either you tell your story, or let's all go home."

She nodded once and began hesitantly. "A week before the election, with the encouragement of my sister and her husband, I sent Mr. Swain a letter and told him that if he didn't give me some money, I'd tell his opponent everything."

"What did he do?" Ramsey asked quickly.

"He sent the money right away."

"Is that the only time you asked for money?"

Again, she hesitated. "No, three more times. Again in January and then in April. Both times he sent about one hundred dollars. In June, the baby came a month early, stillborn. I asked him once more for money, but he never responded." She searched for a conclusion. "And here we are."

"Is there any chance that the child belonged to someone else?"

"I have been intimate with just two men in my life: my husband and Mr. Swain," she said calmly but emphatically. "It was Thomas's child."

"That's just fine," Ramsey said, patting her hand. "I know it's not easy being asked such questions." He walked back to his table and shuffled through some papers. "No more questions, your honor."

"Judge—that is, Mr. Beckley," Jones grunted, "I'm told you'll be running things for this side of the aisle?"

"Thank you, your honor," the lean, middle-aged member of Swain's legal team said. He stood and swept the hair back off his forehead and walked slowly toward Ida Mae. She recoiled slightly from his advance.

"Mrs. Thompson," he began, smiling insincerely. "I'd like to know more about your husband. How is he employed?"

"He's a wholesale merchant."

"Doesn't he own Thompson Enterprises, one of the most honest and well-respected businesses in Indianapolis?"

"That's his company."

"What civic organizations does he belong to?"

"Well," Ida Mae answered innocently, "the G.A.R. and …"

"He served in the War between the States?" Beckley interrupted, feigning surprise.

"Yes. He got wounded in the leg—walks with a limp."

"So, he was wounded in the service of his country. I take it you married young?"

"Well, yes, there is a bit of an age difference between us."

"Was his business successful when you married him?"

"Yes," Ida Mae said, remembering a happier time. "His business was doing ever so well, he had lots of money and …" She suddenly realized where this was heading.

"You were young," Beckley broke in, "and you married an older man, a war hero—a man who had offered his life for his country and came home wounded and built a successful business that employs many good people." There was accusation in his voice.

"You make it sound like a crime," Ida Mae stuttered.

"You have impeached his character so. I just wanted to understand what kind of man you vowed to honor and obey."

"I assure you," Ida Mae shook with anger, "the public Mr. Thompson that people know is not a saint in private!"

"I want to ask you another question: With how many different men have you been unfaithful to your husband?"

"Only one," she insisted through clenched teeth, "and that is your client."

"You have been unfaithful to your husband, is that right?"

"Yes, I've said as much."

"So we can take that as fact in this court and your admission is proof that you cheated on your husband?"

"Yes," she admitted, near tears.

"Mr. Swain says he's never been unfaithful to Mrs. Swain and there's no hard proof, no evidence to the contrary."

"There's my word!"

"Your word," Beckley repeated, incredulous. "The word of a woman who would publicly slander her husband, a wounded Civil War hero and respected businessman. The word of a woman who admits to being unfaithful to that war hero—the child you bore is proof enough of your infidelity. You also admit to extorting money. Why should anyone believe you?"

"Because it's true!" she cried. "And I had proof."

"Oh, did you really?" Beckley said sarcastically. "And what was that?"

"A picture and a letter and some other things. They were in my handbag. Last month I went to my husband's house in Indianapolis to get some of my things, and the bag disappeared while I was there."

Beckley shook his head and smirked. "Of course."

Ida Mae didn't reply.

"How many months did you say you were along when your baby was born?"

"Eight."

"Where was it buried?"

"In the Friends Cemetery, just west of Carmel."

"And one last thing: If you sued for divorce a year ago, why is it that you're still married, especially after what you've done?"

"My husband has money and friends, just like Thomas, and his friends have managed to get him a number of postponements, just like you have done for Thomas. All of you men are Republicans, just like Thomas."

"Are you a Democrat, ma'am?"

"I ain't a Democrat or a Republican. I ain't nothin'."

"Well," Beckley's smile widened, "I'll let that be the last word."

He strode back to his seat. Mayor Jones wiped his forehead with his handkerchief, glad to have made it through the morning without having to render any legal opinions. "Mrs. Thompson, you may step down," he grumbled. "Gentlemen, we'll pick things back up on Thursday morning."

Thursday morning, David and Mary passed by the auditor's office on the way to the courtroom and saw Dr. Harrison sitting behind the desk in the inner office. They stopped in and saw the exhumation notes spread out on the desk.

"Are you going to testify?" Mary asked.

"Yes, I've got to tell what we found there."

With a tap on the glass, Beckley entered the outer office.

"Good morning," he said. "Dr. Harrison, could I speak with you for a moment?"

"Well, we'll be going," David said.

"No, that's not necessary, stay put," Beckley said. "This'll just take a minute."

Dr. Harrison stepped into the outer office, and the two men huddled close together and talked. David walked around the desk and looked down at the drawing of an infant, the very one he had held in his hands during the exhumation. At all of the major bones, his handwriting marked the measurements. "Overall length was eighteen inches," he said to himself.

Ramsey's first witness of the morning was Ida Mae Thompson's sister, who confirmed everything Ida Mae had said on Tuesday. Beckley, however, pulled her testimony apart with a few simple questions verifying that she had no first-hand information about the affair.

When Ramsey rested his case, Beckley called a string of damaging witnesses, starting with Swain, who gave his own take on Mrs. Thompson. "We met much as she said we did, though I certainly didn't flirt with her. She quite brazenly accused her husband of beating her.

"As you can imagine, I was shocked at her forwardness. I politely offered her my sympathy and excused myself. She contacted me, perhaps a week later, and asked me to lunch with her. Out of curiosity, I went, but I took along my colleague in the senate, Mr. Carter. Again she complained of her problems and asked if I could help. Naturally, I felt sorry for her. I suggested she contact a friend or relative, or perhaps speak with her minister."

"Was that the last time you saw her?"

"No, we met up many times at political functions attended by her husband. Each time she made a particular point of seeking me out. It made me uneasy, but I didn't want to offend her."

"Did you ever give her any money?"

"Yes. Late last fall."

"Why?"

"She came to my office not long before the election and asked me to help her. She said she'd left her husband and was in the family way, and that he wouldn't give her any money. I suggested it would be more appropriate for her to seek help from a relative, or a local aid society. Well, she became completely unreasonable and flew into a rage and left. Later that day I got a letter from her in which she stated that if I didn't give her money, she'd tell all the papers that her baby was mine and that we'd been carrying on for a long time."

With a look of deep concern, Beckley asked, "What did you do then, Mr. Swain?"

"Well, I consulted with my colleagues, and they suggested that I go ahead and pay her to protect my reputation. So I did."

"But didn't you realize it would just make you look guilty?"

Anguish filled Swain's face and his voice became passionate. "I worked hard to get where I am. When I got home from the war I was still a kid and didn't have a dime to my name. I became a schoolteacher, then a lawyer, and started a couple of businesses. Nobody handed me anything—I worked hard for it all. I ran for the Senate because I thought I could do some good. I've got a wonderful wife and children. I was afraid her lies could ruin it all. When you're in politics, you always have enemies. So I paid. It burned me up inside, but I paid. Why, it was the only thing I could do!"

"But it didn't satisfy her, did it?" Beckley led.

"No it didn't. She wanted more. Two more times I gave her money. I kept thinking how my children would be shamed by her lies. Then when she asked the last time, that was all I could take and I said no. I decided I'd fight her if I had to, as I'm doing now. What she said in this room two days ago is a lie. I won't knuckle under anymore to an extortionist. I'm standing by my good name and setting the record straight. I've had no part in her troubles and that baby she had, God rest its soul, is not my child. Whose it is, I can't imagine."

Ramsey cross-examined Swain, digging at every inconsistency in his story, every point where it differed from Ida Mae's. Swain didn't give an inch. At this point it was still his word against hers, but Ramsey had no more witnesses.

Beckley called his witnesses in succession. Swain's colleague, Senator Carter, said he had accompanied Swain on the trip to Martinsville the previous October. "I was with Tom the whole time. We shared a room, and I never saw that woman."

"Was she on the train back to Indianapolis?"

"Not that I saw, and I sat right beside Senator Swain. Her story about checking into a hotel isn't true, either. Me and Tom waited maybe an hour in the station and took the first train to South Bend."

Ramsey took his turn at cross-examination. "Mr. Carter, is Thomas Swain a powerful figure in state government?"

"Tom's ideas are powerful and people look up to him, if that's what you mean."

"Then he's an important figure in Indiana Republican circles?"

"Yes."

"How long have the two of you been traveling the state giving speeches?"

"About four years."

"Would you say that Thomas Swain has given more speeches around the state in the past four years than the governor?"

"Yes," Carter said proudly, "he's been a real workhorse. He can whip up a crowd like nobody I've ever seen."

"So," Ramsey went on, "when thousands of people from across the state think of the Republican Party, they think of Mr. Swain?"

"Probably. He's pretty important to us."

"Too important to let him be convicted of bastardy, right?"

"Objection!" Beckley shouted. "This has nothing to do with the case."

"I knew one of you fellows was gonna start this stuff," Jones complained. "Look, Mr. Carter is a grown man and he can take care of himself. Go ahead, Mr. Ramsey."

"People think of you two as a team, don't they? Would it hurt you politically if Mr. Swain were found guilty of bastardy?"

Carter replied grudgingly, "Yes. Guilt by association, I imagine."

"Thank you, that's all," Ramsey said.

Beckley stood up, "Mayor Jones, I just have one more witness. The defense calls Dr. Albert R. Harrison."

Dr. Harrison confidently strode up and took the oath.

"Dr. Harrison," Beckley began, "you and the county coroner, Dr. Clark, exhumed the body of Mrs. Thompson's deceased infant about a month ago, is that correct?"

"Yes."

"She has claimed that the baby was born dead on June eighth of this year. Did the condition of the body bear that out?"

"Yes, the rate of decomposition seemed to agree."

"So the birth took place in early June?"

"Yes."

"Mrs. Thompson also contends that the infant was conceived on the day of October 12th. Did your autopsy on the fetus give you any idea as to the accuracy of that claim?"

"It would be impossible for the fetus to have been conceived in October."

"Why?"

"Its bone development was not far enough along. The fetus we exhumed was no more than six months along. So it would have to have been conceived about December."

"Could you give the nonmedical people in the jury an example?"

"Well, the overall length was thirteen inches. A fetus at eight months would be approximately eighteen inches long."

David gripped the back of the bench in front of him. A rush of horror passed through him, and he searched his memory, running the diagram numbers by again: an overall length of 18 inches. Oh, my God, he's lying—this was all fixed. His startled eyes met Dr. Harrison's, and a look of comprehension passed between them. David looked over his shoulder at Harry, who was sitting in the back row. Their eyes also met and Harry read the meaning in David's face. His father was lying.

Ida Mae Thompson shook her head furiously and cried, "You're lying, you've got to be lying!"

Mayor Jones raised his hand for calm: "Now, let's simmer down here. Go on, Dr. Harrison."

"Again, please, so that we all understand," Beckley said. "The fetus was six months from conception, not eight months."

"Six months at the most," Dr. Harrison said, glancing over the room but avoiding David's eyes.

"And Dr. Clark agrees with that assessment?"

"We agreed," the doctor said simply.

"She's lost now," Will Christian whispered to David.

"The defense rests," Beckley said with finality. Dr. Harrison walked out of the courtroom hurriedly.

Mary turned to speak to David and saw that the blood had drained from his face. "What's wrong?" she whispered, gripping his arm. "Do you feel ill?"

How could he tell her? How could he say her father had lied?

"No, I'm fine," he mumbled. He sat, half-listening as Ramsey gave his final arguments to the jury. Suddenly he got up with a start. "I've got to talk to your father. I'll be back in a minute."

He was stepping into the aisle before Mary could say anything. She turned around and watched, puzzled as he disappeared beyond the doors.

David ran, jumping two steps at a time, rushing to the auditor's office, ignoring several familiar faces outside the courtroom doors who asked how the trial was going. When he got to the landing off the second floor, through the window David saw Dr. Harrison walking quickly south, down Catherine Street, a block away, a bundle of papers under his arm.

"What's going on around here?" Fred asked as David came through the door of the auditor's office. "Dad came in here a couple minutes ago, gathered up some papers and left in a flash."

"Where was he going?" David asked, out of breath.

"Said he had something to do, that's all."

David went into the inner office and scanned the desk. The notepad, with its drawings and measurements, was gone.

What to do? If he went back up to the courtroom and made a scene, he'd be thrown out. How could he charge Dr. Harrison with perjury?

But how could he say nothing?

David walked back upstairs and waited in the hallway with the crowds of people who couldn't get in. David's seat had been taken inside, and no one else was being allowed in. He fidgeted and stewed for an hour as the final arguments were completed. Will Christian came out for a smoke, and they sat and waited together.

When the case went to the jury and the doors were opened, no one left their seat. Everyone sat still, wanting to wait for the verdict, certain that their seats would be taken if they left for even a moment. The hall crowd gathered around and looked in at the gallery. David peered through and Mary looked back at them with searching, wondering eyes. "Do you want my seat?" she mouthed. He shook his head and sat back down in the hall. In less than fifteen minutes, the jury filed back in and the doors were closed.

A moment later, a man with his ear to the door yelled down the hall: "He's innocent." The doors were flung open and the audience slowly filled the aisles. Swain's team could be seen smiling and shaking hands. Ida Mae Thompson sat, her face against the table, crying. A.F. Ramsey looked straight ahead, blankly. As the crowd streamed out into the hall, Mary found David and Will and began filling them in on what had happened.

"When they said 'innocent,' she let out this awful, mourning sob. It was just terrible," Mary groaned.

Swain's team came through the doors and proceeded down the staircase, pushing through the thick crowd, back-patting all around. As David, Mary and Will were heading for the stairs, a pale and haggard Ida Mae Thompson came out, Ramsey leading her by the arm.

She wanted to lash out at someone, and David was the only enemy she saw. She tore away from Ramsey and pushed past several people, quickly moving toward David.

"You bastards!" she screamed, slapping David in the face with all the force she could muster. David fell back, and she came at him again. The crowd gasped in shock. "You bastards, you bastards, you lying bastards!" she shrieked, swinging again. He grabbed her wrist and she struck out wildly with the other hand. The crowd backed away.

Will grabbed her and held her arms behind her back. She crumpled to the cold marble floor, sobbing. Ramsey knelt down and put his arm around her. David stood a yard or two away, wiping at a small trickle of blood from the corner of his mouth.

"I'm awful sorry, Mr. Henry," Ramsey said, looking up at David.

"She's gone crazy!" someone in the crowd yelled.

Mary, horrified, dabbed at the blood on David's face with a handkerchief as Ramsey led Ida Mae down the stairs. "David was at the exhumation of her child," Mary told the questioning bystanders. "The poor woman apparently blames him."

"Poor woman, my eye," a voice responded.

The crowd began to disperse. Will picked up David's hat and handed it to Mary. Friends and acquaintances patted David on the back gently, saying, "Don't let it get you down, David, she's off her rocker." But David knew she wasn't crazy.

He and Mary sat down on a bench in the hallway. "I'm so sorry, dear," she said. "And to think, you didn't want to do it at all—and she blames you. It's so unfair."

David said, "I want to go talk to Ramsey."

"Why, what good would that do?"

"I just want to."

In the sparsely furnished, dingy office above the Citizen's National Bank, Ramsey's clerk told David and Mary to sit and wait. Behind a door with a frosted-glass panel they could hear muffled but intense conversation. They sat waiting for twenty minutes.

With a metallic squeak, the transom window above Ramsey's office door opened. "Jimmy," Ramsey called from within. A boy of about ten who had been sweeping up set down his broom and went in. He came out a moment later with an envelope and ran down the stairs. Within five minutes, the wooden stairs resounded to the thunder of heavy steps, and Thomas Swain and his team of lawyers came in, looking furious. They disappeared behind the door.

Ramsey could be heard making some sort of presentation, but the words were indistinguishable. Then an indignant male voice cursed loudly from within: "Jesus Christ almighty!"

Swain roared, "Ramsey, you'll never work in this town again. I'll crush you."

"You've been sayin' that to me for years, Tom, and I'm still here, still payin' my bills, still in business—now sit down and shut up!"

Mary and David sat waiting for another half hour, overhearing enough to make it clear that negotiations of some sort were taking place. Finally, Swain, Beckley, and their colleagues emerged and departed, looking dazed.

A few minutes later, Ida Mae Thompson appeared from behind the frosted-glass door, glared at David, and left. Ramsey appeared at his office door. "Margaret, you can go home now," he said to his secretary. Surprised to see David and Mary, he asked, "What can I do for you two?"

"Could I talk to you for a minute?"

Ramsey nodded and David got up. Mary stood as well.

"Could you wait here, please?" David whispered.

"What's going on? Why can't you tell me?"

"Please, just trust me."

She sat back down angrily.

David took a chair in front of Ramsey's desk and watched the old lawyer wipe his spectacles with a cloth. He looked pale, frail. His hands were shaking as he placed the spectacles back on his face.

"Oh, what a day!" Ramsey sighed. "What is this about? Your face all right, Mr. Henry?"

"Dr. Harrison lied," David said simply.

Ramsey stared at him for a moment. "How do you know?"

"I was at the exhumation. I took down the numbers they called out as they measured. The fetus was apparently eight months old. He lied about the size."

"Were you in on it all?" Ramsey asked with resignation.

"No, I didn't know until this morning when the words came out of his mouth."

"Don't feel bad, Mr. Henry, there was a lot of lying going on this morning."

"They destroyed her," David exclaimed, wondering why Ramsey didn't seem to care. "Where will she live, how will she support herself?"

"Oh, she'll have to move far away, but she'll be all right."

"I don't understand."

"I'm losing my faith in mankind, Mr. Henry." Ramsey sighed heavily, leaning back in his chair. "I completely believe Mrs. Thompson now. I didn't always. And I know now that Thomas Swain and Senator Carter lied. And now you tell me that Dr. Harrison lied. Always liked Dr.

Harrison—not his politics, mind you, but the man—always liked him."

Ramsey shook his head. "Ida Mae told Beckley on Tuesday that she had evidence, but lost it. Well, that evidence was waiting here in my office when we came back a bit ago. Last week Ida Mae told her husband that if he'd give back her handbag and what was inside, she'd sign divorce papers that would relinquish any claim she had on his money. Well, he brought it today, and she signed—not in time to beat Swain, but in enough time to squeeze him.

"What she had in that bag was a letter, signed by Senator Carter and on the Martinsville Hotel letterhead, dated October 11th, 1892. It said that Tom couldn't meet her that night."

"Proof of an affair, and that Carter perjured himself today," David said.

"Yes. She also had a couple of cards that had come to her from Swain, attached to flowers. Turns out Swain's a bit of a poet—wrote some pretty sweet things to her in the early days. Anyway, we called them back in here and told them they could buy the things for a pretty sum—enough to support her and set her up in another town somewhere. Otherwise she'd sell them to the Indianapolis Sentinel.

"It's a hard way to go, Mr. Henry. Seems that's the way my life has been. I'm always fighting for the underdog. Sometimes you have to follow your heart and do what's right. People think I like playing that part, but I don't."

David could think of nothing to say. The truth he had brought to the lawyer was worth nothing now.

"Go on home, Mr. Henry," Ramsey said, taking off his glasses again and rubbing his eyes. "People were lying before you came here, and they'll lie some more after you're gone."

David stood up and walked through the door. Mary, seeing his stunned look, followed him down the stairs in silence.

Neither spoke as they walked the two blocks to her home. David came up the steps with her, looking purposeful. No one was in the front parlors. Mary took his hand and led him to a table in the back parlor. They sat down opposite each other.

"Why won't you tell me what's going on?" Mary asked.

"It's between your father and me. Can we just drop it?"

At that, he heard the sound of Dr. Harrison clearing his throat in the next room. David went to the door and opened it. Dr. Harrison was in the side parlor, sitting in front of the fireplace, looking out the window. In the fireplace smoldered the remnants of a thin sheaf of papers.

"That you, David?" the doctor asked dully, not turning around.

Mary started to walk into the room, but David put his hand on her shoulder. "I need to have a talk with your father."

Mary's expression turned angry. "What in the devil is this all about? Why do you keep shutting me out?" She flung away and stormed down the hallway.

David went in and shut the door. Mary stopped in the kitchen, turned around and came back, intent on having it out. Through the open transom, she plainly heard David's words.

"You lied on the stand today."

"What of it?" Dr. Harrison shot back.

"You lied. You said the fetus was thirteen inches long, when we both know that isn't true."

Dr. Harrison got up and faced him. "That woman was a golddigger, and she was trying to destroy the most important politician we have around here!"

"If she's a golddigger, what's Swain?"

"The woman engaged in immoral behavior. She was unfaithful."

"So was Swain, and you lied to help cover it up. You dug up her baby, then you lied about it and made her look like a whore."

Mary's heart sank. She knocked on the door.

"Who is it?" her father snapped.

"It's me," she quavered. "I want to talk to you."

Dr. Harrison quickly stepped over to the door and flipped the latch to lock it. "Stay out of here, Mary. David and I are having a man-to-man discussion. It doesn't concern you."

At the sound of the latch clicking, Mary's anguish gave way to rage. She hiked her skirt up above her knees and kicked the door with all the strength she could muster. The brittle cast-iron latch broke, and the door swung open with a crash against the bookcase. "Why?" she cried to her father. "How could you do it? You put your hand on the Bible and promised to tell the truth."

"Mary," the doctor said, "I've never spoken to you this way, but apparently you think you're old enough to be involved, so here it is: It's an ugly world, it ain't all black and white. Sometimes you've got to step outside the rules to preserve what's right."

"Hogwash! That woman turned to Swain for comfort, and landed in the jaws of a shark! And you helped protect that shark. You and your friends prance around town in your G.A.R. uniforms, claiming to be the embodiment of all that's right—what are you but hypocrites? If Thomas Swain carried on with that woman and fathered her child, he's old enough to face the consequences. He's just as bad as she is, and I guess you're another of the same: a liar and a cheat!"

"Mary," the doctor bellowed, "don't talk that way!"

Tears welled up in her eyes. "It's true, you're a fraud. It's awful enough that she was beaten by her husband and then had to admit in public to having an affair, but to have you and your cronies make her out to be an extortionist. How can you live with yourself?"

"You listen here," Dr. Harrison said, shaking his finger in her face, his temper raging. "You're still my daughter and you won't speak to me that way.

"And you," he said, turning to David, his voice brimming with contempt, "bringing rudeness and disrespect for authority from your morally bankrupt times! I blame you for the corrupting influence you have had over her. You leave this house at once, and don't ever come back. I insist that you pass through the beam now, and never return!"

"No!" Mary cried.

David glared at him and walked from the room, his footsteps echoing down the hallway. Mary followed him out, grabbing her handbag from the hall table.

"Where do you think you're going?" Dr. Harrison roared.

Mary turned to him. "You fool." She hurried out after David.

They walked silently down Emmous Street toward David's house. As they climbed the steps, David said softly, "I'm sorry I didn't tell you as soon as I realized what was happening. It's just that I know how much you love him, and I didn't know how to tell you that he lied."

Mary began to cry again. She walked into the house and stood for a moment staring at the beam. It glistened like a million lightning bugs swirling in the night. David wrapped his arms around her and held her tightly as she wept on his shoulder.

"What are we going to do?" he asked, mouth to her ear. "You can't stay here."

Mary pulled back and gazed into his eyes, then looked back at the beam. "I don't want to stay here," she whispered, gripping his wrists and pulling him toward the sparkling lights. He resisted for a moment, but she tugged again, pulling him into the twenty-first century.

CHAPTER SEVENTEEN

I thought instead of my paternal grandfather, who had been the first licensed architect in Indiana. He designed some dream houses for Hoosier Millionaires. They were mortuaries and guitar schools and cellar holes and parking lots now. I thought of my mother, who drove me around Indianapolis one time during the Great Depression, to impress me with how rich and powerful my maternal grandfather had been. She showed me where his brewery had been, where some of his dream houses had been. Every one of the monuments was a cellar hole.
Breakfast of Champions, Kurt Vonnegut, 1973.

Mary looked about the room. David's antique furniture deceived her momentarily into thinking that this time would not be very different. But on the marble-topped table stood two devices with blinking lights. One was slender and black; the other was gleaming white. They were tethered together with wires. Mary stepped closer, examining them carefully.

"This is it, isn't it?" she said. "The things that turn on the beam?"

David said nothing, wrestling with the urge to pull her back through the beam. But something told him they couldn't go back.

"How do you turn them off?" she asked urgently. "Or should I just move one of those bottles on the windowsill?" She stepped toward the window and David grabbed her arm.

"Don't! I'm afraid we'd never get them back in the right place again, and then we'd never be able to get back!"

His words laid bare the choice before them. She had essentially left town and run off with David, unmarried.

Finally David breathed a heavy sigh of resignation. He let go of her arm and pulled the power cord from the back of the modem. Mary watched as the beam instantly changed to a red glow. For a fleeting moment she thought she heard the distant sound of her mother's voice, but she dismissed the notion.

A whoosh on the street outside caught her attention, and she pulled back the curtain just in time to see a minivan disappear down the smoothly paved street. The houses looked foreign to her; only two or three were recognizable.

David watched her examine the street. Her eyes, still red and swollen from weeping, peered out now with a curious intensity. In her lace-trimmed blue hat and matching floor-length dress, she looked utterly out of place.

"It's not called Emmous Street anymore, you said?" she asked, sniffling into a handkerchief.

"No. It's called Cherry Street."

"Why Cherry Street?"

"I have no idea."

"May I look around the house?" she asked.

"I don't think you'll like what you find. These front two rooms are the only ones I've redone."

"That's all right," she said bravely. Maneuvering around him, she walked into what she expected would be the back parlor. "I'm sure it's all very nice." She stopped and peered down at the metal shell of his laptop computer, a small light at its front, brightening and dimming.

As she passed through the rooms of the house, she experienced just the reverse of what David had when he entered her time. Looking up the stairs at the blank piece of plywood in the landing window opening, she asked, "What became of the little stained-glass window?"

"It's in my workroom on the table saw. I haven't gotten around to repairing it yet." Mary found that the back parlor was now a dining room, the dining room was a kitchen and bathroom, and the former kitchen held a clutter of tools and a big table saw. The back room where David and Fred had slept most of the summer was still the remains of the ill-kept efficiency apartment it had become in the intervening hundred and twenty years. The transoms had been covered over with plaster, and the walls sheathed in dark-brown wood-grained paneling.

Mary stopped in the doorway and looked at the holes in the walls and the graffiti-scarred paneling. "Why was this house allowed to be treated this way?"

"Just one of many," he replied. "You'll find this kind of … abuse, common in old houses throughout town."

They had to set about the business of finding appropriate clothes for Mary. David stood back and examined her for a moment.

"We'll get you something. But there's no way I can take you to a store dressed like that."

He drove to the strip mall and went into Kohl's. He looked for the longest dress they had—something Mary wouldn't feel naked in. He bought three different sizes, just to make sure.

Mary spent the evening trying on the dresses. Her own shoes looked rather stylish with them. On his suggestion, she took down her hair and braided it as she had when a small girl. In his dresser drawer he found an elastic hairband that Heather had left behind and used it to finish off the braid.

Mary frowned at herself in the mirror. "You look perfect," David reassured her.

She felt naked. The cloth was too thin, the undergarments too few. He said they'd have to go to a mall tonight and buy more clothes for her. He suggested—to her dismay—that she shave her legs; he tried to explain modern bras. She hardly heard him, distracted by this foreign image of herself. She didn't like the way it felt. Was she even in her own skin? She considered stepping back through the beam, working things out with her father somehow. But now the sun was behind the trees, and the beam would not materialize. According to David, its duration was shrinking by a few minutes each day.

He was watching her in silence. "What?" she asked.

"Oh, I'm just not used to seeing you this way. You look right—I mean, you'll fit in just fine, but I like the old Mary better."

Those who live in America at the opening of the twenty-first century don't really appreciate how visually loud the urban landscape has become. As David's little truck sped down Highway 37 and I-69, the rapidly changing landscape assaulted Mary's senses. The speed of the cars, the harsh billboards and signs, cell phone towers, the blunt ugliness of strip malls, the blank metal walls of pole buildings, and the miles and miles of asphalt and concrete—there was little human in the view before her. Was this what people here liked, or did they even care? She stopped asking "what" and "why" and tried to take it all in.

The mall was even more disconcerting. To be sure, the shopping areas she knew were busy with people, horses, and signs. But the modern mall and the sales strategies within are the pinnacle of consumer exploitation; the science of attracting attention and tempting the passerby honed to a sharp point. A relentless myriad of spinning placards, flashing lights, powerful food aromas, glaring signs, multicolored window displays, and blaring music battered Mary's senses. Modern Americans have trained themselves to selectively block out much of it, the same way they block out television commercials. But Mary's more innocent visual perspective was defenseless and overwhelmed by it all.

David and a rather puzzled clerk chose Mary's clothes for her as she stood before mirrors in dressing rooms, befuddled by the things she found herself wearing. She stared at the people they passed as they walked beneath the mall's flag-draped atrium, stood before store windows examining mysterious goods, tried desperately to comprehend her surroundings. David had had literature, old photos, and antique stores to prepare him for the past; Mary had no comparable guides. David's long explanations of the future didn't begin to suggest the nearly total obliteration of her world. Noblesville was at the same time foreign and vaguely familiar, like an old friend maimed in an accident.

In the days that Mary spent learning about the twenty-first century, Dr. Harrison tried to deal with the fallout of his own actions.

Though he did not know it, Anna had been standing at the top of the stairs during the argument that took place after Swain's acquittal. She started downstairs as she heard Mary and her husband yelling, but stopped when the meaning became clear. Feeling suddenly weak, she half-sat, half-collapsed on the top step. When the screen door slammed behind Mary, she was still searching her mind, sorting the statements each had made, putting the pieces together. All that mattered to her was that Albert had lied in court and Mary was leaving. She replayed the sequence of statements in her mind. The air of contempt and finality in Mary's voice when she'd cried "You fool!" frightened her mother.

The doctor started upstairs. The look on his wife's face stopped him in his tracks. Guilt, then irritation crossed his face. He cleared his throat, but Anna spoke first.

"Where are they going?" she asked, distraught.

"To have a good cry, I suspect."

Anna shook her head in despair. "I don't think so."

"They're making a mountain out of a molehill," he said.

"The beam," she murmured. Then, urgently, "They've gone to the beam!"

Anna hurried down the stairs and out the front door, still hatless, apron tied around her waist. "Quickly, Albert, we must stop them!" He did not follow.

As Anna passed Harry's house, Clara called from the front porch. "Anna, is everything all right?"

"Clara, did Mary and David pass this way?"

"Yes, just a minute ago, and Mary looked very upset." Clara read fear in Anna's face. "What's wrong?"

"Nothing," Anna said unconvincingly, and hurried on.

She called through the door of David's house. No answer. Through the screen door she could see the beam. The right-hand door between the parlors was wide open, though David had always kept it closed to conceal the beam from visitors.

Anna went in and stood before the beam. There was no doubt in her mind: They'd stepped through. She was afraid to take that step herself.

She shouted into the sparkling light, "Mary! Please, come back!" Suddenly the beam disappeared. She gasped, then stepped forward, waving her hands in front of her, feeling for the beam in midair. It was gone! Her daughter was gone—run away to a place where she could never be found.

Anna stumbled home in grief. Dr. Harrison met her at the door. "Where did they go?"

She glared at him and began to cry with fury. "She's gone! She went to David's time! And it's all your fault!" She stormed upstairs, sobbing, and slammed the bedroom door behind her.

Terror struck deep in the doctor's heart. His self-righteous defiance about lying in the courtroom drained away. His beloved daughter had fled.

Days of silence and unbearable tension lay before the doctor and his wife. He lied to friends and neighbors, saying that Mary had returned to Chicago for a while, and that David had gone home to Canada; he wasn't certain how long they'd be gone.

On the third day after they left, Dr. Harrison went to see Harry. As he climbed the back staircase of the Joseph Building, he asked himself why he was going to his older son. *I lost him, too, a long time ago.* But he went on anyway, desperate to talk to someone who knew the secret of David, someone who could help him decide what to do.

"Oh, just you," Harry muttered as his father came through the door. "Any sign of them?"

"So you know where they are?" Dr. Harrison said hopefully.

"No," Harry said flatly. "Not exactly, but I'm not dumb enough to believe that nonsense you've been telling people around town. I knew by the look on David's face when you were on the stand that something was wrong. Then Clara sees them going to David's house, and Mary's crying. Suddenly, they're gone. Something you said that day set David off. What was it?"

Dr. Harrison stood with his hat in his hand, fidgeting with the brim. "I lied about the infant's size to protect Swain. David knew it. Mary found out. We argued, and they're gone."

"Figured as much. Was it worth it?" Harry asked, turning to the window with his hands in his pockets, his back to his father.

"What do you mean?"

"Doing the dirty work for your cronies—was it worth losing Mary?"

"No," he answered simply. "I don't know what to do," he said finally, in a tone more pathetic than Harry had ever heard from his father.

"Is the beam gone?" Harry asked.

"Yes."

"What you better do is pray it comes back."

"Then what?" the doctor asked.

Harry, incredulous, turned to look at his father. "Are you really that far astray? Have you been cheatin' on virtue so long that you wouldn't know how to do the right thing if that beam reappeared?

"Try a little humility! Tell them you're sorry, for Christ's sake! Tell Mary you love her and you don't want her to leave. Tell her that's more important than your petty little political career."

Harry stepped closer. "You know, that's the most ridiculous thing about all this. It's not as if you were the governor; you're just a two-bit auditor in a one-horse town. You're not a big-time crooked politician; you're a two-bit crooked politician."

Dr. Harrison's gaze hardened. "Do you hate me so much?"

"I don't hate you! I'm just disappointed. I used to watch you save people's lives. You were a good doctor, a good father. Wasn't that enough?

"Do you want to know when I stopped respecting you? It was in 1887, when you were helping spread money around, buying votes. Is that what you raised me to believe in? You always said that you and the old soldiers fought for America. Well, America's not the flag, or the Republican Party. America's right out there," he said, gesturing at the courthouse square. "Did you fight so that little towns could be filled with crooked politicians?"

"I just wanted to be somebody that people looked up to," the doctor protested.

"You were. I looked up to you, and Mary did, too."

Dr. Harrison was not a man who knew how to say "I'm sorry." He got up and hesitated for a moment, turning the hat in his hand. Harry searched him for some sign of remorse.

Just as the doctor turned to walk out, their eyes met. In the look of bewildered fear Harry saw in his father's eyes, there was an unspoken plea of forgiveness. Harry stood with his hands still in his pockets as the door closed and his father's shadow disappeared beyond the frosted glass.

During the daylight hours for days afterward, Dr. Harrison sat in David's back parlor, watching for the beam to reappear.

David and Mary tried to settle into their exile. David went about the task of trying to make the house more comfortable for her, tidying up the things he'd let go over the summer. Mary tried to do what she had been trained to do all her life—keep house and cook—but it was not easy. She was repulsed and depressed by the town around them. If she wanted to be useful and independent, she couldn't walk to the market or most other stores. David had to drive her everywhere, and once at a supermarket or strip mall, she found the choices unfamiliar, overwhelming, and confusing. No one stopped by, and there was no daily routine of socializing. They were isolated. But it was only within their isolation, together in the house, that things felt right.

Most nights, in the bedroom that had once been her parents', they made love and then lay in each other's arms talking. They had made no decisions about how to proceed in life. By the end of the second week, they were both feeling the pressure to find a direction.

"What are we going to do with ourselves?" Mary whispered late one night, cuddled against him in bed.

"I'm going to spend the rest of my life with you."

Mary pulled David's body against hers, ran her hand across his back, and kissed him passionately. "You're such a good man. I'm so glad we found each other."

Her voice trailed off, the sentence incomplete.

"But what?" he asked.

"But what are we going to do with ourselves, our situation?"

"I really don't know."

"People must think we've run off together to another town." Her voice was quavering, and she was on the verge of tears. "Think of all the talk my family must be enduring. If we returned, we could never live in Noblesville. And I look at you and I see how unhappy you are here. Our lives back there are ruined, and we're trapped."

"You're unhappy here, too."

She looked into his eyes and nodded. Tears welled up and ran down her cheeks. She buried her face in his neck and cried.

She lay awake in David's arms, staring at the ceiling while he slept. She thought back to the night in Chicago when they had made love for the first time. She had stood at the window, the view of the White City still fresh in her mind, wondering about David's description of the future. She'd doubted him, but he had been so right.

She got out of bed and pulled on one of his sweaters and a pair of sweatpants and went downstairs. She found her way to the front porch and sat in the darkness on the swing, curling her legs underneath her. The night air was cool. The breeze rustled in the trees, scattering yellow and red leaves onto the porch.

Through a gap between the houses the courthouse tower was visible. The fourth-floor spotlights were now in place and the clock tower glowed; the faces were still dark, awaiting the reinstallation of the glass. She missed the chimes and was annoyed at her century-old habit of looking up to see the time.

On the steps, the concrete felt cold and the grass was wet on her bare feet. She stood in the front yard leaning against the ladder David had left propped against the house all summer. The stars were not as bright now as they were in 1893—too many streetlights. Though more dim, they were the same stars. She found Capella, as David had taught her, and with it constructed Auriga. In its corner, near Capella, were the stars David always called "the kids."

David had been right about the future. It felt sterile, harsh, lonely. The culture of Mary's upbringing had been replaced with nothing. But, strangely, it was an enormous amount of nothing. The entire country seemed awash in a hyperactive, media-driven sea of nothingness. The traditions and touchstones of her time had been replaced with the superficiality of transient traditions contrived by advertisers and enshrined by technology. TV newscasters droned on, twenty-four hours a day, often focusing on trivialities and famous personalities, half-hour comedies that weren't funny played constantly, radio stations played the same songs over and over again, junk mail filled the mail box each day, and advertising screamed from every form of media she'd seen, all to the point that it washed into a mass of nothingness. Each had overplayed, overused and overhyped the most sacred aspects of American culture to the point that everything was shopworn and commonplace, nothing was sacred any longer.

She returned to the porch.

Sitting there in her private posture, her hair hanging loose and wearing sweats, she looked like a twenty-first century woman. But within her heart she felt alien, a transparent ghost in an inhospitable world. In her own time she had felt that she and David were part of something greater, but here they were alone. He was so disconnected from other people; she had not even met his parents, and he only talked to them on the phone. But when she thought of her own father and the argument that had led to her passage through the beam, suddenly the past seemed ugly, too.

But Mary did not know that her father had spent many days in that parallel time, sitting just a few feet away from where she sat now, waiting for the beam to reappear. He did not intend to pursue her, but in his pocket was a letter that had taken great resolution and humility for him to write. In his time, in his bed, he, too, was wakeful.

In these two troubled worlds, Indian summer had set in. The days were as warm as a mild June afternoon, and the nights as cool as an April morning. "Perfect sleeping weather," David's grandfather used to say. The stifling humidity and the searing, hazy sun of summer were gone, and the air was clear and crisp.

In one world, shocks of wheat and corn were bound together by hand with twine for drying. The smell of burning brush and leaves filled the air, mixed with the rich, earthy aroma of vegetables and fruits being readied for canning. Apples and grapes were being picked, and fresh jelly, apple butter, and apple cider were making their annual debut on tables in Noblesville. Farmers worked eighteen-hour days and children were let out of school to help.

In the other world, the ozone alert days of summer were over for the year, and school was back in session. Most people worked in the same rhythm that marked the rest of the year, and at night they stayed home and watched TV, streamed movies, or surfed the 'Net. The only human evidence of autumn was the Friday night high school football games and the huge combines that lurched through cornfields all day and into the night. Their drivers listened to music in climate-controlled cabs, harsh halogen headlights illuminating the yellow husks as they were pulled into the machine.

Though it was hard for Mary to get over the fact that the downtown Tipton she knew had been almost completely obliterated by the turn of the twenty-first century, she liked the house David's grandmother lived in. The large brick-and-stucco Foursquare was only one generation of architecture removed from what she knew. The honesty and simplicity in the shape and building materials of this 1914 house had an earthy beauty she found missing in later architecture.

Grandmother Henry heard the truck pull into the drive alongside the house. She watched out the kitchen window as they got out. She noticed how Mary moved when she walked: upright, graceful, and confident. She saw the signs of romance as Mary touched David's arm to stop him, appearing to ask him for reassurance about how she looked. Mary warmly brushed the hair off David's forehead and he gave her a quick kiss on the lips. Grandmother Henry knew two people in love when she saw it.

Mary didn't understand why they avoided the large porch and the paneled oak front door that it sheltered. Instead they entered the back door to the kitchen.

The gray-haired woman met them at the door. She wore bright white tennis shoes and a dark-blue sweatsuit with a Southwestern pattern on the jacket. Her hair, fresh from the beauty shop, swept around the soft wrinkles along the outer edges of her green eyes. She was in good shape. As David entered, she embraced him, then grasped Mary's hands tightly and said, "Hello, my dear." Grandmother Henry held her hands, gazing into Mary's eyes. They liked each other immediately.

In the cavernous living room, with its white oak woodwork and brick fireplace flanked by Mission-style bookcases, the three chatted for an hour. The television droned on in the background.

"Can I turn that off?" David finally asked.

"Oh, yes, I'm sorry," his grandmother said. "I'm afraid it's on so much now I forget to turn it off."

"Why do you leave it on?" Mary asked.

"Oh, I don't know. I'm lonely, I guess. It's a friend, it's always there. Nobody comes to visit me much anymore," she said, giving David a quizzical look.

"I'm sorry," he said sheepishly.

"David tells me you like to watch the stars." Mary said, deciding to save him, though thinking that a man who didn't visit his grandmother didn't really deserve to be rescued from a tongue-lashing.

"Oh, my, yes, we used to dream upon stars, didn't we, David, when you were just a small boy," she laughed. "But I haven't set out and checked on the stars in years."

"Why?"

"Well, David's father isn't very good at visiting, either, but he likes to spend money on gifts—that's a Henry man's way of showing affection. A few years ago he bought me one of those little satellite dishes. There are so many stations on it, I just sit in here and watch TV and do the crossword."

"You'd think he'd have the sense to buy you a telescope," David said, with the sarcasm he reserved for his father.

There was a long, awkward silence.

"Let's go look at the stars, Grandma," David said impulsively.

She smiled mischievously. "Let's do."

They climbed the stairs and passed through the back bedroom and out the door that led onto the flat roof above the kitchen. The balcony was really just a deck, some fifteen feet square, built upon a flat roof that topped the rear addition to the original house. The main body of the house rose up another story.

An ancient maple that grew along Conde Street sheltered them, so close they could almost touch the branches. The stars hung like frozen fireflies beyond the golden leaves. Half of the sky was visible.

"Remember when you were small and we would come up here in the night and lay on our backs and I'd teach you the stars?"

David looked into her beaming eyes. He could only think of the contrast between her happiness and the lonely days she had just described.

"The very last time, I think, was the first time you visited after your grandfather died."

"We just looked up then."

"Hoping we'd find a new star, I suppose."

"Let's start at the start," Grandmother Henry said. "Find Polaris, right up there. Follow it right over to the little dipper, that's Ursa Minor. Then find the loop of stars that cradle it, they're all part of Draco."

In her voice and her tone, Mary could hear David. He had said almost the same words to her months ago while they sat on the 1824 stone in Riverside Cemetery. David lay on his back as his grandmother spoke, and Mary did the same. Grandmother Henry's voice was alive and at home, speaking of the stars.

"What people can see of nature is half sky," she said, "but they know hardly anything about it. Hardly anybody even looks up."

They lay in the darkness, staring up at the sky, following the old woman's outstretched hand. "Find Betelgeuse, that's the beginning point if you want to visualize Orion. It represents the hunter's right shoulder. Do you see it, Mary?"

"Yes, I do. David taught me to find it."

"Good for you," she said to David. "The group to the lower left represents his arm and a club. Above Betelgeuse, Meissa represents his eye, and the arched group above that, the beast he holds in his hands."

"That's what men have seen throughout time?" Mary asked.

"Greek men. Now, if you were Egyptian you would see the god Osiris."

"And if you were a Pawnee Indian," David added, "you imagined deer running through the sky."

"It makes you wonder about the nature of things," Mary said, "how it all came to be, where the stars came from and why God made them."

"Stars give life to the universe," Grandmother Henry said. "All matter, everything from the moon to the ground this house sits on, is here because of stars. And even though it takes eons longer, like us they are born, live their lives, and then die."

She went on, tracing Gemini and Leo Minor, but their journey through the sky stopped when they lost sight of part of Ursa Major, blocked by the satellite dish. Grandmother Henry fell silent.

"Where did you learn about the stars?" Mary asked softly.

"From my father. He served in the Navy. He had lots of time to sit on a boat and stare up at the sky. And I studied astronomy in college for a while, until David's grandfather … and marriage got in the way," she chuckled.

After a long silence, Grandmother Henry said, "What does the future hold for the two of you?" Mary flinched a little, struck by the awkwardness of being asked about her love life as the three of them lay side by side under the stars.

"I'm embarrassing you, I'm sorry."

"No," David said, smiling and rising up on his elbows to look over at Mary, "it's okay. Actually, we've decided to get married." It was the first time they'd told anyone.

"Oh, that's wonderful!" his grandmother enthused. "When?"

"Well, maybe at Christmastime," Mary said with a little uncertainty.

"I'm so happy for you two. You're a beautiful couple."

David lay back down and gazed up at the stars. His grandmother mused, "Well, well."

As they went back down the stairs, she said, "I have some things of your grandfather's that I want you to have."

They stood before the recliner and the cabinet, where his grandfather had always sat in the evening at "toddy time" to listen to music, a martini in his hand.

"You remember when his health started to fail," Grandmother Henry said, opening the doors to the cabinet, "and your father bought him this CD player and a bunch of these music discs? I want you to have them. He never even opened most of them. He preferred his old scratchy records; he didn't like the music as well when it was perfect. Anyway, if I want to listen to music, I always use the record player, too. Why don't you take the CDs?"

David studied the cracked black vinyl chair. "I sat here with him so many times, drinking a glass of ginger ale. I tried to be just like him."

"Take them, won't you?" she said gently. "It's something the two of you shared."

The only way to go through the twenty or more CDs was to sit in the chair. He did so unwillingly at first, but then he sank in, feeling the shape his grandfather had impressed in the old cushions.

His grandmother and Mary sat back down near the fireplace and began talking. David tore the wrapper off an Ink Spots CD. He put it in the player

"I love coffee, I love tea, I love the java jive and it loves me.'" His grandmother began singing along in a frail soprano, "Coffee and tea, and the java and me, a cup, a cup, a cup, a cup, a cup, boy."

"It seems as though you and your husband each gave David something wonderful," Mary said. Grandmother Henry smiled, reaching over to pat Mary's knee to the beat. "I love java, sweet and hot, whoops, Mr. Moto, I'm a coffee pot …"

Saying goodbye was unexpectedly difficult. David felt in his heart that he and Mary would eventually return to 1893. It hadn't really occurred to him until now that this might be the last time he'd see his grandmother

She stood in the driveway alongside the truck. "Now you take good care of my grandson," she told Mary, bending down to look in the window. "A Henry man is a high-maintenance man. They need lots of care."

"He's as easy as pie," Mary smiled.

David backed out, and they waved goodbye.

CHAPTER EIGHTEEN

"She asks only in return ... that when you look upon her your eyes shall speak devotion; that when you address her your voice shall be gentle, loving, and kind; that you shall not despise her because she cannot understand all at once your vigorous thoughts and ambitious designs; for, when misfortune and evil have defeated your greatest purpose, her love remains to console you. You look to the trees ... for strength and grandeur; do not despise the flowers because their fragrance is all they have to give. Remember ... love is all a woman has to give ... the only things which God permits us to carry beyond the grave."
Sister Carrie, Theodore Dreiser, 1900.

The next day David and Mary slept late. Over breakfast, they watched out the windows as Frank's relatives helped him move from the house two doors down. The house had finally sold; David did not know what would become of it now.

In the afternoon they walked downtown and sat on a bench in front of the ice cream store, eating frozen yogurt and watching the construction workers across the street unload the huge frosted-glass clock-face panels from a truck. The highly polished Roman numerals stood in relief from the sandblasted background as a hydraulic arm lowered the round panels to the ground. A crane stood ready to lift them up eight stories and into place.

"I want to see downtown Indianapolis," Mary said. "Can we have a city day?"

They drove along the interstate, past Castleton and toward Meridian Street. Nat King Cole's voice oozed out of the in-dash CD player. Eventually they approached the strip malls and office parks at the edge of the Keystone at the Crossing.

"Can we stop off at the side of the road?" Mary asked impassively.

He brought the truck to rest with one tire in the grass just before the overpass that spanned Keystone Avenue. Mary got out and walked up the edge of the road along the overpass guardrail. A semi screamed past, its wake sweeping her long black hair over her head and into her face. She stopped in the center, resting her elbows on the bridge's concrete sides and gazing over at the six lanes of traffic that moved underneath. To the south were glass and metal high-rises and soulless concrete parking garages ringing a new mall; to the north, a sprawl of auto dealerships, gas stations, electronics stores, all identified with tall poll signs rising up into the air. Cars flashed across the overpass, just feet away.

"Where will this all lead?" Mary asked, incredulous.

"What do you mean?" David shouted above the traffic.

"I've seen the town and the city in my time, and then there's this … place. It's for shopping, but when we get out of the truck, we're taking our lives into our hands! Look at the way people stare at us as they go by—they think we're crazy. If you don't have a car you can't use this … place. It may be the ugliest, most terrifying landscape I've seen yet."

The concussion of air from another semi sent their hair whipping. "We'd better get back in the truck," David said.

As they got in and buckled their seat belts, David noticed flashing lights pulling up behind them. A state trooper parked behind the truck. He got out of his car and walked toward them, eyeing them with suspicion. David rolled down the window.

"Is everything all right?" he asked.

"Yeah," David said.

"Why are you out here, then?" the trooper said accusingly.

"Well," David said, looking back at Mary, "my friend here is visiting from … Canada, and she wanted to walk out there and look around for a minute."

"Are you aware that it's against the law to walk along an interstate highway? I could write you a ticket. Do you know you could've been killed walking along here?" The trooper shook his head. "Look, just move along now."

They left the truck in a parking garage and set out walking. The pedestrian walkway was the visual centerpiece of the Circle Center Mall, the most recent attempt to lure shoppers out of the suburbs and back downtown. Developers had gutted the historic buildings and connected them to make them more like a mall—more modern.

They walked the route they always had in Indianapolis: down Market Street from the Circle to Delaware. Mary recognized little. Her gait was not the confident one she usually adopted in this Hoosier city she had known so well; she walked hesitantly through the chasm of shining buildings.

The empty former location of Market Square Arena sprawled like an asphalt desert. She didn't even ask why there was so much ugly empty space; she just pulled her sweater closer, looking lost and craning her neck to see the tops of buildings. At the corner of Delaware, the familiar City Market was there, but beyond it, glorious Thomlinson Hall was gone.

They walked on down Delaware Street through a drab wasteland of parking lots and ugly buildings. Occasionally Mary spotted a familiar landmark, like an old friend in a crowd of hostile strangers.

Seeing Delaware Street now with Mary, David felt a pang of guilt, as if being of this time he was somehow responsible for what had become of it. Her favorite Hoosier street was gone. Without the street signs, she wouldn't have known where she was.

They walked on north, under the elevated interstate, the traffic grinding and thumping overhead. Fast-food wrappers blew among the cast-concrete pillars. The smell of stale urine wafted by. A homeless man pushed a shopping cart.

Mary stopped to read the historic marker at the entrance of what it announced as "The Old Northside." They walked on toward President

Harrison's house. Though the roar of the interstate could still be heard, the rank bleakness softened as more familiar landmarks appeared, and their trees and lawns. Mary stood silent in front of President Harrison's restored home, holding on to the spikes of the iron fence.

A beat-up car full of teenagers lurched down the street behind them. A hip-hop tune thundered from its open windows, the bass reverberating among the historic buildings. Mary looked over her shoulder, expressionless, watching the car rattle and vibrate out of sight. She looked back to the house, then at David with weary sadness.

"I came here in 1887 when I was a teenager. Father brought Harry and Fred and me, and we stood here among hundreds of people. Harrison gave lots of campaign speeches from that front porch. I stood right here, holding the rail just like this. It was more than a hundred and twenty five years ago … but just six years ago. I was fifteen —almost sixteen years old.

"That was about the last time I saw Harry and Dad really getting on well. Harry's been distant from him since then. Could something have happened around then to make Harry lose his faith in him, too?"

"I expect so. Harry told me once that the corruption in Noblesville politics was the main reason he didn't want to get involved, and we'd been talking about your father's political career."

"I wonder why Harry never told me? But he was always the protective older brother."

She turned around and leaned back against the fence. She looked north at a blank, lifeless brick apartment building with small dark windows, and then across the street at the empty parking lot of the Knights of Columbus building.

"You know what this time looks like to me? It looks like there was a terrible war fought here, and this is what's left. It's like somebody fired a huge cannon at my world, and only Harrison's house and a few others stand up among the rubble, like Atlanta after the War between the States.

"My world is gone," she whispered softly. "It's little more than a curiosity now." She looked down, fidgeting with the silver turtle necklace, flipping open the shell and looking at the compass.

"I have a confession to make," she said with pain in her voice. "I didn't completely believe you. You tried to tell me how awful it is, and I thought you were exaggerating. But, in truth, you understated it. How could people let it all come to this—these ugly, lonely, isolated cities, this inhuman environment?"

"You're seeing the change all at once," David said, "and I know how you feel—it's like a slap in the face."

"More like a blow to the head."

"These things didn't happen all at once, they came about gradually. It happened bit by bit, in small steps; people didn't see what it was all leading to. And now that they're here, they can't remember what it was like before. A couple of generations have been born and raised not knowing anything else. Those boys in that car—they don't even know that this was once a lovely place to walk. Most of them don't know what it's like to have both parents at home and neighbors who know them and care what they do. They've grown up in a violent, disjointed world, in schools with two thousand students, in front of a TV set that trains them to want and believe irrational things. They haven't a clue what's been lost, and they wouldn't understand it if you tried to tell them.

"Do you see now why I thought it was hopeless? Do you see why I don't believe that this world will even make life livable again—why I wanted to live in your time, your community?"

Mary came to him and buried her face against his shoulder. "That's not a perfect place, either."

"I don't expect a perfect place," he said, wrapping his arms around her. "I just want something a little more human!"

"Let's go home," she said, looking up at him. "To 1893, I mean. Maybe we can mend fences with my father. Deep inside, he's a good man; he's just done some foolish things. If we tell him how much we love each other, maybe he'll understand. If he doesn't …"

When they returned home, David's cell phone chirped a voice mail notice. He hadn't even heard it ring. Maybe it didn't. He woke the screen, set it on the coffee table before Mary and pressed the speaker button. The disembodied voice of his mother spoke a distant greeting, another plea for him to call. He sat and picked through the day's mail. Mary leaned over and scrolled through the screen's contents as she had learned to scroll through song tracks. She tapped the second message. There was the wispy sound of nervous breathing: "David, it's Heather. I need to talk with you, please. I don't know what's happened to me or my life. I just feel so alone, nothing seems right. I don't want to mess up your life or try to come between you and whoever you're seeing, I just need your help. Please, won't you call me?"

The message ended. Mary sat back without expression, folding her hands in her lap. David stood, putting his hands in his pockets.

"This is the woman you mentioned to me once?" Mary asked

David nodded.

"Will you call her?"

"No."

"Why not?" she asked.

"Why?"

"She sounds very upset. Is she usually so emotional?"

"No, she's not. She's usually the one telling you why you're fucked up."

Mary closed her eyes and winced at the F-word. "Then something must really be wrong. Why won't you talk to her?"

Exasperated, David searched for words. "What's happened between us this summer has so drawn me away from my life here. If I help her, I'll feel like I'm being drawn backward in time," he smiled awkwardly at the irony, "backward in my life, to a place I have no desire to be."

"Just talk to her," Mary pleaded gently. "You're such an understanding man, I can see why she called you. It won't make me jealous. Settle what's wrong between you. If we go back through the beam, there won't be another chance."

She gazed at him intently—her way of insisting.

"All right," David said irritably.

David looked out the living room window at the gray, overcast sky, waiting for Heather, watching Mary walk down Cherry Street. Mary navigated the now strange streets of her hometown. She paused at the Locke house, surprised that so many of its architectural elements remained, sad to see them rotting away. Toward downtown she stopped at the parking lot where the opera house once stood, remembering, comparing. She stopped again before the courthouse construction area, peering through the chain-link fence at the workers. Finally, she crossed Logan Street and entered the ice cream shop.

They'd only turned on the modem and Airport in the evenings and on cloudy days to avoid triggering the beam. With the solid cloud cover today, David turned them on and checked Ebay bids for his vintage items. Soon, Heather appeared at the door.

They smiled and hugged. She studied him and his surroundings. He looked like he'd lost fifteen pounds. They shared awkward small talk.

"I don't know what to say to you," Heather began uncomfortably. "I keep thinking back about the abortion, and how it seemed to define the differences between us." She sat in a chair by the front window, caressing the bushy tuft of hair at the end of her long blond braid.

"What do you mean?"

"We were fine together as long as we were playing and having fun. When things got serious, I found myself thinking that I couldn't spend my life with you, that you couldn't make me happy. I dreamed of living in a big house on the water; you dreamed of restoring this old place.

"Now, though, since we broke up and I lost my job, the things I thought were important suddenly seem shallow. What you wanted makes sense to me now. Maybe I've been looking for the same things but just didn't know it."

"What changed?"

"You planted a seed in me," she said simply, looking away. A few tears slid down her cheeks.

"I guess I never really have had any foundation," she went on, finally looking directly at him. "When I landed that job after college, I thought I finally had it all—my own place, money, social life. And then you came along. You played along with my lifestyle, but you never bought into it. I see now what you were looking for. You wanted something permanent and solid … and a family to take the place of the one that fell apart on you. When you left my place the last time, when it was over, that's when the seed finally began to grow."

A bit bewildered by the choices, Mary eventually bought a strawberry ice cream cone with the money David had slipped into her pocket. She sat on a sidewalk bench and watched the cars stream down Logan Street. A white-haired old woman passed by and politely said "Hello." Mary smiled and replied. A moment later she saw the woman stop in front of the hardware store and stare back at her. Mary smiled again and the woman did the same, looking embarrassed at having been caught staring. She disappeared into the hardware store.

Five minutes later the woman came out. She walked cautiously up to Mary. "I apologize for staring earlier, but you look so familiar to me."

"Oh, really?" Mary said politely.

"Yes," the woman said, sitting down beside her. "You look so much like the old photographs I have of my grandmother as a young lady."

It took a moment for the implication of this to sink in, but when it did, Mary's heart launched into wild beating. She tried to calm herself.

"My grandmother was a beautiful woman in her youth, just like you. Matter of fact, she was a beautiful woman all her life."

"Thank you for the compliment," Mary said, looking at her intently. Was this the daughter of a child she hadn't even had yet—David's granddaughter, too?

"I'm Edith Cottingham," the woman said.

"Pleasure to meet you," Mary said, her voice quavering. "My name is Helen. What was your grandmother's name?"

"Mary; just plain Mary. She died when I was a teenager, just after the second World War. She had lovely bright blue eyes—just like you."

"And just like you," Mary said numbly.

"Why, thank you!"

There was an awkward silence. "Well, I really have to be going," Mary said.

"Did you drive?"

"No, I'm walking. I'm not from here. I'm staying with a friend on Cherry Street."

"Well, I'm going that way," Edith said cheerfully. "May I walk with you?"

"Certainly," Mary said reluctantly, totally unnerved at having a conversation with her own elderly granddaughter.

"Where does it come from?" Heather asked. "Why do we all feel so unfulfilled now, so incomplete?"

"1 think it's the absence of cycles and rhythms in our life," David said. "We don't have any real physical connections to the basics. I'm convinced of that now."

Heather was surprised at his response to her rhetorical question She was used to his discourses, but now he seemed more confident than ever.

"Over the summer I've gained some perspective on the order of living in our time," he explained. "People aren't tied to the earth or each other any longer—technology has freed them. Central heating and cooling have freed us from the weather. Electric lights and buildings without windows have deprived us of sunrise, high noon, and sunset.

"Free?" he whispered urgently. "Free from what? From knowing our neighbors, from a sense of being a part of something greater than our own spoiled selves. We're incomplete."

"That's a one-word description of my life," Heather said. "And the crazy thing is I've had it all: a good job, money for almost anything I wanted, a great social life, good health, couple vacations a year. And I end up feeling empty. It seems like there isn't enough of anything to really make me happy."

"Well, you're spoiled, and that's how spoiled people always feel: unfulfilled."

"Well, thank you," she laughed sarcastically.

David laughed, too, realizing he'd been too blunt. "But look at the way you listed all those good things: each one in its own separate compartment. Living like that is like eating stew one ingredient at a time—eat the carrots, the onions, the potatoes, the meat and finally the spices. It's unsatisfying, so you eat more of one or another, not realizing that you have to cook them together to enjoy them. You might even have to put in things you don't like individually to get the right taste.

"What if you lived right down the block from your friends and family? What if you worked there, too, right around where you went shopping and socializing? What if you got your exercise by walking between those activities, not by paying to walk on a treadmill inside a building? If we just lived in a logical rhythm instead of plotting everything on a calendar, we'd be happier."

"Maybe you're right," she said, shrugging. "Rhythm and flow aren't words that describe the environment I grew up in, or the one I live in."

"Don't you see?" David went on. "The divorces we both experienced as children were just one factor in our disjointed lives—lives without foundations. Every time technology splits us off from the natural world, or the social world, we drift further away."

David was assuming the fiery gaze and impassioned gestures of an evangelist. "As our lifestyle gets faster and more compartmentalized, it draws us further away from our human base. And the feeling that something is wrong grows. That's what's bothering you. But then maybe we think a bigger TV would make us happy, or a new car. So we drive to the strip mall for some recreational shopping, isolated in the car, park in the concrete desert, and shop among strangers—seeking fulfillment, buying things we want, not things we need. You know, there's a difference between 'quality of life' and 'standard of living,' but most people act as though they're the same thing."

Once, Heather might have been offended by what he said, but she was being drawn in. "You're right! I've run myself ragged earning enough for the stereo, the flat-panel TV, the granite countertops, the sports car, down payment on a condo, the satellite dish, the rowing machine, the computer, the vacation cruise—"

"And you know why?" he interrupted. "We don't base our self-image on the real people around us, like people did back in the 1890s; we base it on the unrealistic lives we see on television. Our desires are built up by the constant screams of the media—the car radio commercials, billboards, TV ads, junk mail, telemarketers, e-mail spam! All this leaves us awash in contradiction, alternately desperate for the trappings of the good life and intellectually numb from the constant bombardment of information."

"Alternately freaked out from the frenzy of people at us," Heather cut in, "and then, inevitably, lonely."

"We might find comfort and support in our community, if we hadn't traded it for privacy," David said. "No wonder so many people feel alone.

Our houses are islands lined up in a row. We have everything and nothing at the same time.

"And no matter how nice that car is or how big the house or how large the new TV," he went on, "that nagging feeling of unfulfillment is never kept at bay for long. It gnaws at us, it makes us susceptible to the diseases of our time: loneliness, depression, divorce, violence."

"The things we can't live without are killing us," Heather said. "It would be funny if it wasn't so awful."

As Mary and Edith walked up Logan Street and down 10th toward Edith's house, the older woman described to Mary what used to be here or there, what the town was like in her youth. Mary said little but walked slowly at Edith's pace, watching her mannerisms, listening to her voice. Mary cared, for the moment, more about traits passed down than buildings or culture lost. They reached Edith's house and sat down on the short concrete wall that separated the front yard from the sidewalk. Edith's house was a simple, vernacular two-story, tidy in its front yard with the remains of summer flowers.

They talked for an hour about flowers, change, and Noblesville's past.

In the kitchen, David dug through the refrigerator for two beers. Outside, a sudden break in the clouds bathed Cherry Street in sunlight. The beam flashed instantly into place.

Startled, Heather jumped up and walked around it, mesmerized by the swirling, twinkling lights, like electric dust in a sunbeam. She reached out to touch it, and her hand disappeared. She moved her hands in and out of it, chilled and marveling.

David finally found two bottles of Triton Rail Splitter at the back of the bottom shelf. He rummaged for a bottle opener in a drawer. When he entered the dining room and saw the beam, he rushed into the living room.

Heather was gone!

"Oh, shit!" He dropped the bottles and leapt through the beam.

Heather was standing in the front parlor, looking out the window at 1893 Cherry Street, bewilderment and shock on her face.

David grabbed her by the arms and forced her across the room and through the beam, back into the twenty-first century. He shoved her onto the floor and turned off the modem and Airport. Heather sat up on her elbows, trembling.

In her hand she held a framed photograph she'd picked up from a table in … that other place. She looked down at it again: a photo of David and Mary in old-fashioned clothes, sitting on the rim of a white marble fountain—just like the photograph she'd found in his bedroom when she had let herself into his house.

David saw the photo and feared what it might betray. He remembered the street vendor snapping it at the World's Fair a month ago.

"What. Just. Happened?" Heather asked.

David paced the floor, running his hand through his hair. What to say, what to do?

"What just happened?" she insisted. "What was that thing I stepped through? Where did it take me?" She was tripping over her words.

"I don't know what it is exactly," he said coldly, horrified that someone else now knew the secret of the beam. But what was the point in lying? What else was there to do but tell the truth?

He told her how it had all happened: traveling through the beam, the town in 1893, falling in love with Mary, becoming a part of the community, going to Chicago, the Swain trial, being trapped here.

She disbelieved him at first, but then she remembered how the street had looked out the window in that other room—the gravel roadbed, the storybook houses, the horse-drawn wagon coming down the street, the woman in a long dress sweeping the porch across the street. She'd seen it with her own eyes; how could she not believe it?

As he told his story, David began to add details, finding that he wanted to tell her, to tell anyone. Getting this secret off his chest filled him with the relief of confession and the pride of announcing a miracle.

Heather believed him. The condition of his house when she came last month, the photos, the magical beam of swirling lights, the place beyond—they all added up.

"You're going to marry her there?" Heather exclaimed. "You're going to go live in the past? You can't do that!"

"Why not?"

"What about your family, your friends? How can you just leave them forever?"

"Look, your ancestors did it and so did mine," he said defensively. "They hated their circumstances so much that they chucked it all and sailed for America. They left their language, their families, their cultures—"

"Yeah, David, I had fourth-grade history, too, but this is different."

"Not entirely. Think of what we were just talking about. Just like our ancestors, I want a better life. I want to fall into bed at night really tired and wake in the morning refreshed. I want to live without raspberries just long enough that they're a treat when they ripen in early summer. I want to put up with the peculiarities of my neighbors so that I can benefit from the friendship, safety, and community that knowing them brings."

He paced the floor, searching for words. "I want to be cold in the winter and hot in the summer. I want to be connected to actual life, not virtual life. I want to have my own passion, instead of getting it through the TV. When I hear music, I'd like it to come out of my own mouth, or off a stage or bandstand. I want to pay with cash. When I help someone, I want to do it with my own hands, not by mailing off a check.

"I'll take the inconvenience and the lumps that go with it. Is watching a child die of consumption in 1893 really worse than watching a child of the twenty-first century destroy himself with drugs? The argument that technology has made our lives better is shit: Gain something of value, lose something of value. Everything costs something!

"I'll take the drudgery. There's a centuries-old model for living without and making do. There are no traditions for living with it all. Especially when you don't choose the 'all' very carefully.

"Remember what you asked?" David continued. "Where does that feeling of emptiness come from? It comes from a thousand little ways we've changed life, thinking we were improving it. We've given up all the highs and lows of reality. But I can have it where I'm going. I can have a life worth living!"

Edith's voice was drowned out for a moment by a gravel-filled dump truck that roared down 10th Street, ignoring the speed limit.

"Well, I must be going," Mary said, standing up. "It was such a pleasure meeting you."

"You really fascinate me," Edith laughed nervously, standing as well and stepping up onto the walk to her front door. "Your voice, your mannerisms—they remind me so much of my grandmother."

"Quite a coincidence," Mary said.

"I don't think it's a coincidence," Edith said. "I think it comes from wanting the past so much. Sometimes perhaps when we miss something and want it badly ... well, perhaps sometimes we see what we want to see."

"Perhaps," Mary said, smiling sadly, wanting to hold the woman, her own flesh and blood, to tell her the truth, but knowing she mustn't

"I don't know what to say to you, David," Heather said softly, "but I don't want you to go."

"I have to."

She took a deep breath and examined the photo again. "And I'll never see you again?"

"No. Once I've gone this time, I won't be coming back."

A tear rolled down her cheek. "A brilliant way of committing suicide, David," she murmured. "Leaving this world of unhappiness for another place you think might be better. It's just like suicide."

"Maybe."

They hugged for a moment. "And you?" he finally said.

She pulled away and looked at him, "I'll be all right. I'm not the suicidal type. I'll make the best of this world." She let go and put her hand on the doorknob.

"Please don't tell anyone about this," David begged.

She saw the apprehension in his eyes. Knowing the secret of the beam, she now had power over his future happiness. There were few times in her life when she'd made a truly selfless choice, but the soul-searching she'd been doing, and David's fervor, drew her to promise. "I won't spoil things for you, David."

With those words she walked to her car and drove away. Her little Mini Cooper hummed away from the curb, passing Mary as she walked up Cherry Street.

CHAPTER NINETEEN

America is full of people like the Hoosiers, America is a larger Indiana; and if we knew what went wrong—and right—with Indiana we might well know what has gone wrong—and right—with the nation. Indiana is a good place to look for clues, the Hoosier wind carries many a straw.
Indiana, an Interpretation, John Bartlow Martin, 1947.

The next day was gray and windy. As David stepped off the front porch, a moving van pulled up two doors away, with a minivan right behind it. As he stood beside the truck fumbling with his keys, a young couple got out of the van and walked over.

"Hi, we're your new neighbors," the young man said, extending his hand. "I'm Sean Kramer, and this is my wife, Lori." Startled, David shook his hand and introduced himself.

"We love what you're doing with your house," Lori said. "We're old house lovers, too!"

"Really?" David replied, feeling a little guilty that he hadn't done any work on the house all summer.

"Yeah, we can't wait to pull off the siding and see what's underneath," she said.

"What made you choose this house in particular?" he asked, curious, despite being distracted and in a hurry.

"Well," Sean said, "aside from the price being right, we thought that locating next to you was smart, since you're obviously restoring your place. Maybe between us we can get something started in this neighborhood."

"Yeah, that'd be great," David said, with little of the enthusiasm he would have had for the same prospect a year ago.

He excused himself and drove off to Indianapolis to show his commemorative coins from the Columbian Exhibition to a coin dealer. When he'd checked their value online, he'd let out an uncontrollable whoop. This would be his biggest payday yet.

He was to meet the broker in the downtown NBD Bank Building. He'd told the broker that the coins were in a safety deposit box there. But as he drove down Meridian Street, they clinked in a bag on the floor behind the seat.

Mary didn't want to see downtown Indianapolis again. She stayed home, reading a book and listening to a Spotify playlist on David's laptop.

David was early for the meeting. He signed the papers for a safety deposit box and put the coins in, then went back out to the lobby to wait. As he sat flipping through the Indianapolis Star, the elevator door in front of him opened and his father stepped out, briefcase in hand. David raised the paper, not wanting to be seen. But after Arnold Henry passed, David had a change of heart and followed him down a hallway.

"Good morning, Mr. Henry," David said in a deep, mocking tone.

His father spun around. "David, what are you doing here?" He put out his hand and they shook. "Shouldn't you be at school?"

"Quit my job," David said with a smile, feeling strangely confident in his father's presence for the first time.

"Why?"

"Turns out I'm good at antique dealing. I've been making great money all summer, more than I'd make teaching school for years. Matter of fact, I'm here today to meet with a coin dealer. I came across some old coins, bought them for a song, and it turns out they're worth a ton."

"You don't say," Mr. Henry grinned, giving David a gentle punch in the shoulder. "Got a little of your old man in you—got the knack for making a quick buck."

The thought of really showing his father seized him. There were few things he wanted more than to prove that he could take care of himself, and do it well.

"You want to sit in on the deal?" David asked.

Mr. Henry examined his watch. "Sure, sounds like fun."

Twenty minutes later they were sitting at a table in a private room, with an excited broker and his consultant examining the shining quarters and half dollars, all in perfect condition. The broker, a regional dealer, had driven up from Louisville.

Mr. Henry looked at his son sitting there in blue jeans, a Black Keys T-shirt visible under his faded jacket. Here he was, sitting in a bank, doing business looking like a punk. He figured David would pick up a couple thousand bucks and go home thinking he'd beat the world.

"What's it worth to you?" David said to the broker. "I'm willing to take less than their market value if you'll take them all. According to what I've read, their retail value, total, is about $225,000."

Mr. Henry caught his breath. "Are you serious?" David loved it.

The broker said, "Well, those price guides are based on retail and auction results. I can't go anywhere near them and still cover my costs. I have to find buyers, and when these start flowing through the market the price will go down. Supply and demand."

"Well," David said, "that's easy enough to get around. Make several simultaneous deals."

"Sure," Mr. Henry said, "make your deals privately with collectors and consummate them all by digital funds transfer on the same day."

The broker looked at David condescendingly. "If you're so smart, why don't you do it?"

"I don't have the contacts. But I'll give it a try if you're not willing to pay a decent price."

"I'll give you $125,000."

"One eighty," David said.

"You've got a lot to learn about the antique coin market."

"Look," Mr. Henry said to David, thinking he'd teach his son something about the art of the deal, "if he won't meet your price, go to the next name on your list. You don't need to sit here and be insulted."

David recognized his father's love of playing deal-maker, but the bluff had nothing to back it up. He didn't have a list. According to all the coin shop dealers he'd talked to, this was the man to deal with in the Midwest. "I suppose I'll have to if he can't do any better." David turned to the dealer. "I was really hoping we could develop some relationship here and I could continue to bring such items to you, but if you can't be more reasonable—"

"What else could you get?"

"Most any 1860s to the turn-of-the-century stuff you want."

"You've got a source?"

"What I've got is my business."

"Okay, I'll give you $165,000, and in return, your word that I'm the one you come to first with any other finds."

They called in a notary public from the bank, and David and the dealer signed a bill of sale. They waited for the wire transfer of the payment to be completed, and David handed over the coins. His father was impressed. David didn't want to like it, but he did.

"Let's go eat lunch," David said. "I'll buy."

They walked over to Rock Bottom and sat in a window booth looking out at the Market Street traffic. They both ordered hamburgers and beer.

"I'm proud of you, Davey boy," his father said. "Never thought you had it in you. Jeeze, one day and you walk out six figures richer. You been making these kind of deals for a while now?"

"This was my biggest one, but, yeah, I've been doing okay."

"Have you invested any of the money?"

"No. Why? I suppose you've got a deal for me."

"I was just thinking: I have a lead on some prime land—we could develop it together."

"What kind of development?"

"Housing. I got an option on a nice piece of farmland right on the other side of 37. If we can persuade the city to extend the sewer line under the state highway, we're there."

"I would," David said, "but it would have to be a little bit different." He had no intention of going into business with his dad, but he wanted to lay out some of his own ideas.

"Like what?" his father asked cautiously.

"I'd want to build a subdivision with traditional small-town elements," David said. "First off, don't give it some stupid wood name like Maplewood; name it after something in Noblesville history. And the name only stays as long as you're still selling lots—once it's sold out you take the entry signs down and it's simply another part of Noblesville. The new streets would have to line up with the town's existing streets and have the same names. And they shouldn't curve around like spaghetti, either. Keep them straight so people can find their way around, and a little bit narrower so that the houses aren't so far apart.

"Next, no lots over a third of an acre. And they mustn't be segregated by square footage or separated from rentals. I want some little houses mixed in with the big ones and a few rental units here and there. That way you get an economic mix of people. And every street has to have sidewalks on both sides, and the setbacks between the walks and the houses should be no more than, say, twenty to twenty-five feet. Next, every house has to have a front porch. Put in alley-type back access, so that the garage is in the rear instead of the house having a big, blank face.

"If there's an old barn on this property, rehab it and make it a community center or clubhouse or whatever. If there's an old farmhouse there, restore it. Use natural materials that age gracefully, instead of plastic and metal.

"Right in the middle, set aside some land for a few small convenience stores—and those can't have a setback, they're right on the sidewalk, their parking is in the rear. Also, for that neighborhood center, put in a park and find a small church congregation planning a new building and entice them in with a free piece of land right in the middle."

"No, no," Mr. Henry said, shaking his head. "You can't do all this warm, fuzzy, new-urbanist bullshit, David." He rubbed his face, exasperated.

"Look, this is business, not socialism. We're talkin' highest and best use, all right? Just because you want all this crap doesn't mean everybody else does. Zoning and the market decide what these developments look like, not ivory-tower types. We build 'em the way we do because that's what people want."

David broke in, "But the modern design keeps people apart, it destroys any natural flow you might have. I don't want to build a subdivision, I want to build a community. How do you know people don't want what I just described if you never build it and give them a chance to see it?"

"Because of market research and the state fire marshal and the Department of Transportation, that's how I know.

"First off," Mr. Henry said, holding out his hand and grabbing his index finger, ready to count down the reasons, "why do you think houses in these developments continue to sell? They sell because that's what people want. They want a deck in the back and a big yard so they don't have to be so close to their neighbors. They like privacy. Secondly, we tried to put in a back-alley access in the Maplewood addition three years ago but the Planning Department wouldn't let us. They said that according to fire marshal codes, alleys have to be big enough for a fire truck. Also, the streets in developments all wind down to a few main access entrances because the DOT doesn't want a lot of streets intersecting with the highways because it slows traffic. Furthermore, ever since the 1950s when everyone was afraid the Russians were going to bomb us, we've had road-width standards so that emergency vehicles and tanks can get around." He noticed the irritation in David's face.

"This all may sound stupid to you, but that's how it is. I don't question it, I sell it—it makes money. That's the free enterprise system. Those who succeed don't build what they want to build and tell consumers to buy it, they build what the consumers say they want. In the end it's totally democratic. Every time you spend a dollar, you're voting for something. Consumers have voted for the kinds of subdivisions I'm building, the ones you hate."

David was at a loss, but wouldn't back down. "I just can't believe that's the only way. Don't you ever get tired of the same old shit? You developers have got to be the most boring bunch of chrome-hearted fools around. Lead the public. Isn't that what marketing is all about? Hasn't the postwar marketing crowd created markets for things the public initially expressed no desire for?"

"That's easy with hula hoops and pet rocks, but we're talking about millions of dollars of investment here."

"I know that, but in the older part of Noblesville, people are moving into the older houses and restoring them. It's a real movement. Why do you think people do that?" David asked.

"Because the houses are cheap."

"To start with, yeah, but that's not entirely true anymore. But lots of the buyers aren't like me, buying at the bottom of the market. We're seeing bigger, restored homes going for much higher prices. They're starting to pay prices that aren't that different from buying a new house in the yuppievilles you build. They do this because they want to live a different way. They want their kids to be able to walk to school or downtown. They want to know their neighbors. It's happening right in my neighborhood. They are choosing with their dollars. There's a market there, I'm sure of it. Not the majority market, not the lowest common denominator, but a good-sized niche all the same. Why not fill that niche?"

Mr. Henry dabbed a french fry in some ketchup, tore at it twice with his teeth and swallowed it in a lump, like he did all his food. Calming himself, he spoke in a measured tone. "I admire your spirit and desire, I really do. But what you're suggesting goes against every assumption we make in my business. If you've got a couple hundred thousand dollars to invest, you can be a player on a team of developers and bankers. That's why I was at the bank today, getting the money onboard for a project. But that much money only gets you on a team, it's not enough to call the shots by yourself. If you want a bank to go along, you have to do things that have proven to make money. Developments are done by teams, and right now they choose big lots, curving streets and a private identity away from the rest of town."

David swallowed his beer. "Well, I guess I don't want to be on the team then."

They ate quietly for a while, then finished up their lunch talking about Mike and Grandma Henry. They shook hands in front of the restaurant. David stared into his father's eyes for a moment, not sure what he was looking for.

"Something wrong?" Mr. Henry asked.

"No, sorry, I'm just lost in thought, I guess."

They stood a moment longer in awkward silence. Traffic streamed by on Market Street. Office-tower workers passed, returning to work from lunch. Finally, David spat out what had been sitting on the tip of his tongue for years:

"Do you ever regret leaving Mom?"

Mr. Henry had been looking away but turned halfway back. He looked at David through the corner of his eye, casually stunned and rubbing his chin as if he'd just been sucker-punched.

"Where'd that come from?"

"Simple question, nothing more." David said. "Something we've never really talked about."

"Life's too short for regret."

"That's your answer?" David said with a sneer.

Mr. Henry shook his head. "Look, I'm sorry I hurt your mom. I'm sorry I ruined your childhood. Okay?" he barked sarcastically.

"You're so out of touch with what you did, aren't you? It was about what you wanted, what it took to make you happy, and me and Mike and Mom could just go to hell, right?"

"Look," his father said, measuring his volume, shooting embarrassed glances at passersby and narrowing the distance between them. "I don't know what this is all about, but my conscience is clear. I didn't do anything wrong. Nothin' lasts forever. Your mother and I grew apart. It happens."

"So if you and Gwen grow apart and she cheats on you with another man, it's okay?"

"Of course it's not okay."

"So how can that be wrong, but cheating on Mom was all right?"

Mr. Henry put his hands up and cocked them side to side as he whined. "Okay, I'm the most worthless fucker that ever lived. I'm the reason for all your unhappiness. I wish I were dead! Happy? Is that what you wanted to hear?"

"No," David said, leaning into his father's face, almost screaming. "I want some evidence that you're a real human being. Like some fool, I was hoping for some … at least … sign of remorse."

"It was nothing," his father shot back, chopping his hand in the air. "David, it was divorce, it happens every day, things didn't work out. It was fifteen fuckin' years ago. Grow up, for Christ's sake."

David backed up but not down, incredulous. "It was nothing? I'm a product of that 'nothing' you're talkin' about. You're talkin' about the most significant event of my life … till the past year, and it was nothing?"

"What do you want from me, godammit?"

"Answer my question! Do you regret leaving Mom?"

Mr. Henry turned and started to walk away but quickly came back, shook his finger in David's face and proclaimed lamely, "I didn't leave your mom, she threw me out."

"That's your excuse? You lied to Mom, told her you were out of town on business—for the tenth time—and while she was cleaning the house and ironing your shirts and giving us kids baths and tucking us in, you were sleeping with Gwen in her little apartment, and you've got the nerve to say it's Mom's fault 'cause she threw you out?" David shook his head. "How could you be my father? How could you be Grandpa's son?"

At the reference to his father, Mr. Henry sputtered something unintelligible, then spouted, "I could never please him—or you."

"We lost our house," David fired back passionately. "We lost friends, we lost our family, you ruined it. You got bored and needed a new thrill, and you went out and got it—we were just in the way. Me and Mike were left with the woman you discarded. She slaved for us while you played with your new, young wife—on vacation on a warm beach or setting up a new home. As Mike and I went between her unhappy world and your shallow, unrealistic world, we played go-betweens for you and her. And then there was the example you set: No matter how great a commitment you make to someone, break it if it feels good to ya. You didn't know how to love us, but you knew how to buy us with expensive toys and vacations. I grew up between Mom's sadness and your superficiality. That's the example you set. That's how I grew up. That's the childhood you made for me."

Mr. Henry did not respond. At those final words he turned and started down Market Street. "I could never please any of you," he called back over his shoulder.

"Maybe if you hadn't spent so much time trying to please yourself … " David called softly, but loudly enough that his father heard. There was no response. They went their separate ways on Market Street.

David was not upset, but instead felt strangely at peace, feeling as if he'd finally had his say.

As David was driving home, Mary was still listening to music and trying halfheartedly to read. She tried to watch a TV program but gave up; she didn't understand half the jokes, and the quick movements of the camera made her a little nauseous. She turned off the TV sound and left it on the weather channel, fascinated by the continual satellite views of blue cloud patterns moving over North America.

On the screen the gauze of clouds swept toward Ohio, leaving Illinois and engulfing Indiana only long enough to span the state as it headed east. Outside the window, the clouds parted for just a moment. The beam instantly appeared, spinning and churning. It startled Mary out of her reverie.

She got up to unplug the modem. Suddenly, an envelope fell through the beam. Her heart pounding, she rushed to the machines and pulled their power cords from the wall. The beam reverted to a normal reddish glow, and then even that disappeared as the thick cloud cover swallowed up the sun break.

Mary bent down to pick up the envelope. Her name was written across its front. She recognized the handwriting as her father's. The envelope was worn around the edges and creased down the center, as if it had been carried in a pocket for some time. She sat and tore it open.

She read:

> *Mary,*
>
> *Whitman or Riley, I am not. I will say what I have to say as simply as I can.*
>
> *Let me begin by saying I am sorry.*
>
> *How hollow it sounds to say that. It's such an easy word to say—'sorry.' It's appropriate, I suppose, for a moment when you bump into someone on the street, but it's hardly enough for what I owe you. Our language should have a word that is bigger than 'sorry.'*
>
> *I have been a fool and it caused you to lose respect for me. I cheated on the very principles I taught you. In your rebuke, and Harry's, too, was a lesson for me—a reminder of all I have claimed to believe in. It hurts me more than you will ever know. My pride and ambition cost me the love of two of my children and as a result, the respect of your mother. There are no courts that deal out such rapid or appropriate justice. I know now it is a judgment I have earned.*
>
> *I write to beg your forgiveness. I do not care where you have been or what you may have done. I want you to come back—with David. I have told those who asked that you are back in Chicago for a while and that*

David is home in Canada. No one suspects otherwise.

Though I have not said it to you since you were a child, I love you. You are a wonderful woman and I am proud you are my daughter. My heart aches at your absence, as does your mother's. Please come back.

Your father, Albert

As David's truck door slammed outside, Mary clutched the letter and wept—not out of relief at the opportunity to return home so easily, but because she was a grown woman in a confusing and turbulent world. Because her father wasn't the pompous fool she'd imagined him to be. And because she knew he loved and admired her.

After reading the letter, David forgot completely about the confrontation he'd had with Arnold Henry. They prepared to return, but the clouds did not break again before evening descended.

David and Mary set aside their anxiety to spend that evening attending a meeting of the Historical Society at the old sheriff's residence on the courthouse square. Thanks to county funds, the exterior of both the limestone jail and the French Second Empire residence had been completely restored. The Historical Society had raised enough money to hire a part-time director and to restore the three large parlors and central hall. As David and Mary came through the door, Jane Harding greeted them. David introduced Mary.

"Oh, I missed you this summer!" Jane exclaimed. "I could have really used your help."

"How is it going with the bank? Have they agreed to save the old theater building?" David asked.

"No, the fools," Jane groaned. "They insist that there's asbestos in there and that it would cost too much to remove. I called the DNR and they said they'd come out and test, but the bank won't allow it. They're just lying. They don't want Noblesville Bank and Trust to have it. It could come down any day now. I'm afraid it'll be gone by Thanksgiving."

The night's presentation was on the history of rail travel in the county. David and Mary sat on metal folding chairs in the restored west parlor along with about thirty other people. The director conducted them through the establishment of the first railroad, the Monon line, the Chicago and Southeastern, the Lake Erie and Western, the days of the Nickel Plate line. Then he turned to the history of the Interurban—the electric rail line.

He displayed several architectural drawings that had been found in the Rowland Printing building. "Ted Rowland found these original drawings of his building, which was the station for the old electric railway. You can see the business facade in front here, and the train sheds in back. The building was put up in 1907 and served as the Noblesville station for only about fifteen years, after which the line went out of business."

David raised his hand. "Where was the station before that?"

"There wasn't one."

"Well, how did people buy tickets before they built this building? Where did they get on and off?"

"The rail line didn't even go in until 1907."

David and Mary exchanged puzzled glances. "But didn't the electric line go in 1893?" David asked.

"Well, there was an initial attempt to put a line through in 1893, but it was really nothing more than a swindle—a fake company put up to milk investments. The money disappeared with the men who brought the scheme to town. Actually, in 1907, the Traction Company used some of the 1893 excavations that had been left incomplete for fourteen years, but beyond that the 1893 scheme achieved little, and was never really intended to."

David and Mary heard nothing else of his presentation. "My father has everything he's got in that line," Mary whispered urgently to David. David thought of E.J. Pennington's ingratiating smile.

As they left the old sheriff's residence, they saw the newly placed clock faces of the courthouse tower lit up for the first time in months, but they marked no time. The clock gears and hands had not yet been reinstalled.

They walked home down the deserted alley between Maple and Cherry, talking urgently. Motion-sensing lights came on as they passed; their voices echoed in the darkness. Had Pennington already skipped town with all the investment money? They had to get back the next day.

CHAPTER TWENTY

Matchless October! An ideal day such as no other month can produce. Here and there a tree tinted with a gold glow—the fatal hectic flush of death. Oh the rare, rare days of October! If the month could only stand still for a time! But alas all too surely they creep silently on with fatal swiftness to the end—to the desolate November! Temperature 39-65-53
Night clear.
John Wise, from his diary, October 5, 1893, Noblesville, Indiana.

The autumn sun was low in the sky. By now the beam did not appear until 10:30 in the morning, and it was gone by 1:30 in the afternoon. What had been a ten-hour window of passage in late June had decreased to little more than three hours. The cloudy morning gave way at the last minute to a little sunshine, and David and Mary quickly stepped through the beam. Mary feared scandal if anyone saw her leaving David's house now in broad daylight, so he changed into his nineteenth-century suit and headed for the Harrison home alone.

When he let himself in the front door, Nella, cleaning in the front parlor, called out, "Well, Mr. Henry, you're back!"

He walked through to the kitchen, where he heard someone clattering pots. When Anna saw him, she cried out, raising her hands to her mouth in shock and steadying herself against the icebox. He walked to her and took her hands gently.

"Where's Mary?" she gasped.

"At my house. She'll come back after dark. That's best."

Tears of relief welled in her eyes. "Yes, of course! But what made you come back?"

"The doctor dropped a letter through the beam, asking us to."

Her look of gratified surprise betrayed that she knew nothing of the note.

"I'm sorry we hurt you," he told her. "It all happened so fast; there didn't seem to be any other way."

"No, don't explain," she whispered, bowing her head. "You're back, and that's all that matters."

"I need to know about the electric railroad," David said suddenly. "Are they still clearing land—is Pennington still in town?"

"Yes, but why do you want to know about that?"

"Never mind right now. Where's the doctor?"

"Eugene Rollins picked him up an hour ago. They drove out to Baker's Corner to deliver Mrs. Rollins' baby."

David thought for a moment. "Can I take Butch?"

"Yes, go ahead. But I want to go see Mary. I'll take Clara and the baby. If we stay awhile and then leave with Mary, no one will think a thing of it; they'll just figure they didn't see Mary go in with us."

"She'd like that."

He saddled up the horse and trotted south down Catherine Street. Four blocks beyond Pleasant Street, the roadbed ended. The right of way of the electric line was visible. Even as he dropped down into the lowland between town and the eastern curve of the L.E.&W. tracks, Butch's hooves were crunching on a raised-gravel surface. There were no tracks or ties—just a ten-foot-wide swath of crushed limestone. An explosion ahead of him split the still autumn air. He urged the horse on across the muddy patch of brush-strewn field and over the Lake Erie tracks. After crossing Stoney Creek, he entered the north end of the Randolph farm. He passed the house and barn and followed a trail around the west side of a cleared field. Ahead, he could see perhaps a hundred men working with teams of horses.

In the dense woods that split the farmland, the teams were clearing the ancient trees and filling in the low spots. John Davies strained to see who was approaching and waved. "Welcome back!" he called. John rode up to meet David.

"I was starting to think you weren't coming back," he said.

"Well, I'm back for good," David replied. "Mary and I are going to get married."

"About time!" He leaned across and shook David's hand. "Congratulations! I can't believe you two waited this long."

David grinned. A hundred yards away there was another blast, and a mammoth oak tilted slowly amid the smoke and fell.

"How are things going with the electric rail company?"

"Slowly," John replied. "I don't know what they're waiting for. If they've got so much money, we ought to have several crews this big working in various places. We need to get the elevated sections in Indianapolis started soon, but Pennington says we need to wait awhile. Guess he knows what he's doing."

"Does he?" David asked.

"What do you mean by that? Don't you trust him?"

"No, I don't."

"Well, you're not the only one who's feeling uneasy, I'll tell you that. But there's too much money in this project to turn back now. Hey, I got to get back to business!"

David turned Butch and headed back to town, passing a gravel-laden wagon near the creek. He rode all the way down Catherine Street toward the courthouse. When he passed the electric railway office, he saw E.J. Pennington standing at the window, talking with Tom Wilkinson. Both men nodded politely to him as he passed.

Evening had descended by the time Dr. Harrison came home from a difficult delivery. Mary cried and embraced her father. He held her tightly; a tear shone on his weathered face.

"I didn't think you'd ever come back," Dr. Harrison said, his voice shaking.

"This is where I belong," she said. "And besides, we've found out something you need to know."

He sat down slowly in silence, apprehensive of what secret from the future she was bringing them.

David told him, "Pennington is a fraud, and so is the electric railway. There's do doubt about it. We found out that he's going to steal the funds, and the railway won't go in until 1907."

"But the work is moving forward," the doctor said, incredulous. "They're ready to build the bridge behind Wainwright's, and they're grading land out as far as Randolph's."

"All I can figure is that he's trying to make it look real to pull in more money."

"Why, they even suspended stock sales—said they didn't want to oversell. People have been clamoring to buy more."

"Pennington probably just did that to heighten interest and bring in even more money," David said. "It's a hoax, a swindle."

The next morning, David and Dr. Harrison came through the door of the electric railway office almost as soon as the secretary unlocked it. "I want to see Mr. Pennington," Dr. Harrison demanded.

Pennington, at his desk in the next room, called out to the secretary, "Send the gentlemen in."

They walked in and Pennington stood to shake their hands. Dr. Harrison shook meekly and sat down, but David stopped in the doorway and leaned against the jamb. Pennington studied him suspiciously. "What can I do for you gentlemen?" he asked.

"I want to divest myself of my interests in your railroad," said the doctor.

"But why?"

"Family affairs require some ready cash. I'm sure you understand."

Pennington narrowed his eyes, thinking fast. Finally he said, "Well, I'm sure the value of the stock has doubled since you bought it. Surely you won't have any problem selling it to anyone here in town."

"How much do you think it's worth right this minute?" Dr. Harrison shot back.

"Ah, well, fifty dollars a share, I imagine."

"I'd like you to buy me out, then."

"All your stock?" Pennington asked, shocked. "But why me?"

"Surely if the stock has already doubled in value in such a short time, you'd be glad to buy me out. Why wouldn't you?"

Pennington's personality had impressed many people in Noblesville and beyond, and had fueled his scheme, but now his confidence was shaken. If he said no to this demand, word would spread like fire and his enterprise would fall apart. If he agreed, would the doctor remain silent? Agreeing now might buy some time.

"Well, yes, I'd guess I'd be glad to help you out," he said. "I'll have my accountant draw up the papers and we'll talk tomorrow."

"No," Doctor Harrison insisted, drumming his fingers on the arm of the his chair. "Right here, right now."

"Dr. Harrison, I'm shocked!"

"I'm sure you are, but I need my money. Is it a deal or not? I'd hate to think what would happen if I should go around town telling people that you have so little faith in your own project that you won't buy back shares you claim are so valuable."

"Now, there's no need for that," Pennington said hastily. "Give me just a moment, and I'll see what I can do." He stood and left the office.

He returned with an envelope full of cash and handed it to Dr. Harrison. The doctor counted it slowly and was satisfied. He pulled the stock certificates from his coat pocket and dropped them on the desk. "Thank you, sir," he said, and walked out.

In the auditor's office, David asked the doctor, "How should we tell the town about this so that the others can get their money back?"

"I don't know," Dr. Harrison muttered, scratching his head. "If we tell everybody that it's a fraud, they'll ask for proof. What do we say then? That you're a time traveler? They'd laugh us out of town."

"At least tell people that you sold your shares, that you didn't feel confident that the project will go through. In the meantime, we can look at what they've done so far and compare it with the promises they've made in the papers. Maybe we can spread unease about it that way."

"That may be all we can do for now."

"Pennington was saying all summer he'd have Noblesville connected to Indianapolis and Muncie by early spring, and at the rate they're going, there's no way they can get there. John told me Pennington is holding up on adding to the crews."

"Well, we better get out and start talking," the doctor said. "Let's eat lunch in different places today and plant some seeds of doubt. I'll go to the barber shop and spread it among those blabbermouths, and maybe you could go hang around the stove in one of the liveries for a while and do the same."

A few days later the newspaper carried Dr. and Mrs. Albert Harrison's announcement that David and Mary were to wed on Christmas Eve at the Harrison home. That night, the officially engaged couple sat at a table at Truitt's, talking with their circle of friends.

David wanted to warn John Davies, but he couldn't figure out how to do it. Will Christian, the young attorney, was sitting beside them, too. Because of the many petitions for rights-of-way that Will had filed, the politicians of Carmel and Indianapolis saw him as Pennington's local representative. David felt powerless to help either of them.

As the young people left at closing time, John pulled David aside and asked about the rumor that the doctor had sold his shares.

"Yes, he sold them back to Pennington. He has the feeling that the line isn't ever going to be completed. He doesn't trust Pennington, and frankly, I don't trust him, either."

"But Pennington bought the shares back, right?" John said.

"He didn't want to buy them. If you had been there, you'd have seen him squirming."

"The man hasn't given me any reason not to trust him. I think the Doc just lost out on a big payoff."

The rumors that David and the doctor started had no time to do their work. By midafternoon of that day, Pennington and Wilkinson had taken the train out of town. While David and Mary were sitting in Truitt's that night, the other principals, Pontious and Geesee, were boarding another train at the depot, fleeing Noblesville.

The comings and goings of these men were common enough not to raise suspicion. But the next morning the rail line's secretary asked around town for them; there was no one to let her into the office. Through the windows, she said, it looked like the office had been ransacked. As the usual Saturday morning shoppers converged on downtown, people added this news to the rumor that Dr. Harrison had sold out.

Word of the developers' departure and the abandoned, paper-strewn office reached the Harrison house, and Dr. Harrison went downtown to hear what he could. David rode again out Catherine Street and along the railbed into the fields and woods beyond Stoney Creek. He found John Davies sitting on his horse, surveying the teams working in the woods. When David told him that the office was dark and that the principals had left town, Davies turned pale. The two rode back together.

John opened the office with his key under the eyes of a curious crowd. They found the rooms a mess. Desk drawers hung open, and the safe was empty. Will Christian came in, and the three went to work trying to piece together what had happened. They dug through the remaining files and sent for Sheriff Rhoades.

Word quickly got to the Randolph and Wainwright farms. The workers laid down their tools and returned to town. They had been told to expect their first payday—the first in three weeks—at the end of that day. As John, Will, and David searched the office, the laborers filled Catherine Street, blocking traffic. Dr. Harrison and Judge Riley, himself a heavy investor in the scheme, went in to confer with Will and John.

Will found a file of contracts he'd known nothing about and tried to make sense of them. Each made false claims, or promised future payment for services or materials. John and David sorted through a small box of bills they had found in one of Pennington's desk drawers. There were unpaid bills for the huge stacks of rails and wooden ties that had sat for weeks in the train yard alongside Mulberry Street, creating the illusion of progress. There were bills for the office furniture, fine clothes for Pennington, and stays in central Indiana hotels. The debts totaled more than $4,500. David had traded enough gold between his time and the 1890s to know that this was a lot of money. An hour later, the five men emerged to address the crowd.

Will and John watched the workers apprehensively. They filled the street for half a block, from Wiltshire to the alley by the opera house. No one was shouting in anger, but there was menace in their hushed anticipation.

Judge Riley spoke out from the top step. "Well, it don't look good, boys. What we know is that Pennington, Wilkinson, Geesee, and Pontious have all left town. Will and John don't know where they went. The safe here is empty, and about the only thing we can find inside are bills totaling a goodly amount of money."

There were groans from the crowd. One man shouted, "When are we gonna get paid?"

"Look," the judge said, "I'm as unhappy as any of you are. I invested a lot of money in this outfit and stand to lose it all. I think we're going to have to call in the sheriff on this and let him look into things. Meantime, go home. It looks like Will and John have been left holding the bag, and they've got a lot of work to do sorting this thing out."

"I'll do everything I can," Will said, his voice shaking, "to make sure you fellows don't go without the pay you've got coming to you. We'll track the company men down and find out where the investors' money went."

The unhappy crowd dispersed. A few men cursed, and some of their wives who'd come to join them wept openly beneath the shadow of the opera house. They lived from hand to mouth, and losing the job and their paycheck was devastating. Over the next several days, the shock of the swindle, and its magnitude, settled in on Noblesville and the surrounding villages.

On Mary's birthday, David secretly asked Nella to bake a chocolate cake, and he ordered some ice cream. Nella stood watching with a hand on her hip, eyebrows raised at his foolishness, while he arranged tiny candles on top of the cake in the shape of the number twenty-two. Harry, Clara, and baby Albert were at dinner, along with Fred and Katie After dinner, David turned down the gaslights and disappeared into the kitchen. A few moments later he emerged with the cake, the candles burning brightly. He sang "Happy Birthday," alone. It hadn't occurred to him that the song hadn't been written yet. He set the cake before Mary.

"Why is it lit up?" Anna asked.

David said, "This is how we celebrate a birthday in my time. Make a wish, Mary, then blow out the candles. If you blow them out in one breath, it'll come true."

She looked in his eyes. That moment, that image of her smile in the soft glow of the candlelight, would forever stay fixed in David's mind. She looked back at the candles and began to speak.

"No," David said, "you mustn't tell anyone. Make the wish to yourself and keep it a secret, or it won't come true."

She smiled indulgently, closed her eyes for a moment, then opened them. "Very well, I made my wish."

"Well, blow them out before the cake burns down to the table," he laughed.

After the cake had been cut and served, David handed Mary a small box and a plain envelope. "This is your birthday present from me." She opened the box, knowing what it was—a diamond engagement ring and matching, interlocking gold wedding band. Everyone clapped as she slipped the engagement ring on her finger. She stood and held out her hand to everyone. The other women murmured in admiration, holding her hand to get a better look.

Mary handed the wedding band to David, saying demurely, "I think you're supposed to keep this until the day." He slipped it in his pocket. She leaned across the table and kissed him.

"Don't forget the envelope," David urged.

Mary slid her fingernail under the flap and tore it open. Inside was a postcard photograph of William Locke's house. Mary's mouth dropped open. The others could see the photo from where they sat. "Oh, my goodness!" Anna said, realizing what it meant.

"You bought it?" Mary asked.

"Not yet, we'll do that next week. Mr. Locke and I agreed on terms this morning."

Fresh from the sale of the World's Fair coins, David set about completing his final money-making enterprise. The collection of items he'd begun saving—empty coffee tins, cigar boxes, medicine bottles, milk bottles, signs and advertising items, and tools—had grown to mammoth proportions. He'd added a selection of toys and novelties, too. Nella would watch him with suspicion when he pulled tins and bottles from the trash, wash them, and slip them into his pockets to take home. He carried his finds through the beam and packed them into his garage. He'd made arrangements to sell it all at an auction at the 4-H grounds.

On a sunny, windy Wednesday, Mary and David sat in the Citizen's National Bank with William Locke, A.F. Ramsey, and the bank president, Major Wainwright, to sign the papers for the purchase of Locke's Italianate house at the corner of Anderson and Emmous. David paid in cash, signed the papers, and shook hands all around the table. Locke handed them a massive ring of keys.

David and Mary walked the two blocks over to the house, excited to inspect their future home. Locke had already moved out. The stable on the alley was empty except for a few bales of straw in the loft. "We'll need to buy a horse and a carriage of some sort," David said, feeling a bit odd having said it, as anyone born in the late twentieth century would.

They peeked into the summer kitchen, then walked around onto the front porch. On the south end was a glassed-in conservatory that Locke had built in the 1880s for his prized roses. A water-powered ceiling fan overhead cooled the space on summer days. "We could fill this area with plants, and it would be a lovely place to sit on spring and fall days," Mary said.

Beside the conservatory was the main entry. Mary pulled back the double screens, their frames bracketed with spool-and-knob woodwork. David unlocked the right-hand door. He pushed down on the brass bell handle, and a loud "bong" echoed through the empty house.

Locke had built the house well. A glorious walnut staircase flanked the left side of the central entry hall. From a huge turned newel post, the handrail and balusters rose up and curved around at the landing. An ornate brass gas fixture hung above. Besides the kitchen, the downstairs had four major rooms. To the right of the front door was a parlor with a marble and tile fireplace. A set of double doors opened up to a larger central parlor, whose corner fireplace featured an oak surround. This room had two sets of bifold doors that, when pulled back, opened nearly the entire west wall to another parlor. Here another double set of bifold doors opened up to the dining room.

Back in the 1870s, Locke had used the best hardwoods he could find—maple, walnut, and butternut—for the elaborate, built-up woodwork in these downstairs rooms and the floors underfoot. Glorious gas fixtures hung in the middle of each room, with small sconces on each wall.

"This is so magnificent!" Mary said, grabbing David's hand. "With all these doors closed, we have three cozy private parlors and a dining room, and with them open, we'll be able to entertain half the town!"

Upstairs were three bedrooms, not counting the maid's room in the back. The middle bedroom had a sitting room or nursery off its west side, and there was another sitting area at the end of the hallway overlooking the front entry. At the top of the stairs was the feature that had stimulated a great deal of discussion in town five years earlier: a bathroom with an oval pedestal sink, a big, enameled cast-iron tub, and one of the first indoor toilets in Noblesville.

In the empty master bedroom, Mary wrapped her arms around David. "I love you," she said. "This will be the perfect house for us, the perfect house for raising a family."

In the days ahead they shopped for furniture. They bought what they could locally and found other things at the Fair Store and Wasson's in downtown Indianapolis. They spent many afternoons at the new house. Wallpaper was being hung, some new plumbing installed, the entire house cleaned, and some of the exterior paint touched up. Every day, it seemed, a deliveryman came knocking on the door, bringing not only furniture but also framed prints, mirrors, and knickknacks. At Hare's, they bought a drop-front phaeton, and Robert Wainwright sold them a fine bay mare.

David had decided to shut down the beam forever in early November, after the auction of his hoard of collectibles. They would clean out the Emmous Street house and move his belongings into the new house. Mary's things would come in during the week before Christmas.

Will Christian and Deputy Barnett went to Chicago to track down the treasurer of the proposed electric railway, the Englishman, Thomas

Wilkinson. They came home two days later, empty-handed. Pennington was rumored to be in Cincinnati but was never found. The documents left in the Catherine Street office disclosed the full extent of the swindle. How far it would have gone if Pennington hadn't been scared off by Dr. Harrison's buyout was anybody's guess. The hoax, when viewed alongside the tragedies and scandals of the summer, left many Noblesville residents worried at the direction their town was taking, worried that the gas boom wasn't all good. Too many strangers were coming to town, too many people whose virtue was unknown, and in the short time they stayed to do business—unknowable.

Will and John worked tirelessly to raise money to pay the railway workers what they were owed. Dr. Harrison contributed the profit he had made reselling his shares to Pennington. They pursued Pennington and placed liens against land Wilkinson owned in Chicago. In a town that was already growing so fast that housing was scarce, churches sought shelter for the laborers who could not pay their rent. Ladies' groups cooked meals for the workers' needy families. The owners of the Strawboards and Carbon Works and other local factories and businesses agreed to offer new jobs to displaced railway workers. Locals gave them small jobs and meals. David and Mary hired the crew's carpenter to do repairs on their new home. Major Wainwright found work for several clearing fencerows and brush.

"There was a war in the early 1990s," David told Mary. "It was called the Gulf War. And not long after that there was a terrorist bombing of a federal building in Oklahoma City, and then an even more terrible attack on the World Trade Center in New York that killed lots of people. I witnessed these brief national moments of community spirit, but like most other Americans, I wasn't in Kuwait or Oklahoma City or New York. I saw it all on TV.

"At the same time Americans kept on ignoring the homeless and crime victims just outside their doors, and clung desperately to the feeling of community with people they'd never met. The real world around us wasn't as real as the one on TV. People sent money to Oklahoma or New York for the children of victims or slapped an 'I Support our Troops' bumper sticker on their cars during the war. Their disconnected, vicarious brand of sympathy was nothing compared to what people here in Noblesville are doing to help the railway workers."

The townspeople busied themselves preparing for winter. There was the last of the canning to do, windows and shutters to repair, summer kitchens to dismantle and reinstall in the house proper, saddle blankets to buy, hay and straw to lay up in the stable lofts.

In late October, the Bachelors' Club held a dinner in honor of David and Mary's engagement. H.D. Hull & Sons catered the meal, and the rooms of the club were tastefully decorated—for a change. Around the tables, faces glowed in candlelight; champagne glasses were filled; and at the end of the meal, Ben Craig stepped to the front of the room with a plaque in his hands.

"Could I have everyone's attention, please! Before we commence with the evening's home-grown entertainment and the lampooning … um … I mean honoring of David and Mary, we wanted to take a moment for solemn recognition."

Sternly, Ben declaimed, "Every organization such as this should recognize its fallen members, and tonight we want to dedicate this plaque, which is to be hung here in the rooms of the Bachelors' Club." Snickers broke out. "As time passes, it will bear the names of members who have fallen to the dreaded institution of marriage." A roar of laughter sounded.

"Please," Ben commanded, holding his hand up, "this is a serious matter. The first name on the plaque is, of course, David Henry." The audience applauded loudly.

Robert Wainwright stepped forward, and the room again quieted. "David and Mary, we know you've already picked out a house and are starting to furnish it, and we're aware of how expensive that can be. So, to help you along in setting up housekeeping, the boys have taken up a collection." He motioned to Will Christian, who pulled an envelope from his coat pocket and handed it to Robert. "How did you do, Will?"

"We really beat the bushes to get together a nice little nest egg for the future Mr. and Mrs. Henry."

"Thanks, Will!" Robert opened the envelope and pulled out a silver dollar. "One dollar!" The room erupted in hysterical laughter. "I hope you'll put this to good use," Robert said. "Don't spend it all in one place."

He handed it to Mary. "Since I'm sure you'll be wearing the pants in this blissful family, I'll just dispose with any needless pretense and give it to you straight away."

Mary took the dollar, laughing so hard that tears ran down her face. For half an hour or more, Bachelors' Club members and their lady friends sang love songs with parody lyrics; John Davies led the future Mr. and Mrs. Henry through a farcical rendition of the traditional wedding vows.

In the cheerful mingling that followed, David looked about the room. After the wedding he would come here no more. Robert Wainwright, standing near the window at the rear of the room, motioned for David to join him. Robert raised the window and they stepped through onto the iron fire escape, holding their glasses of champagne. It was a chilly evening, and they could see their breath as they shivered in their dinner jackets. They looked out across the rooftops of the houses along Anderson Street, where smoke and warm gas vapor plumed from chimney tops.

"I just wanted to offer you a special congratulations," Robert said. "I've known Mary since we were children. She's a wonderful woman and, even though I'm gonna miss you around here," he laughed, "I hope the two of you will be very happy. I'm sure you will be."

"Back last summer, I wasn't sure you'd feel that way," David said.

"Oh, in a way I was relieved, I suppose. I think the idea that we'd marry one day was entertained more by our parents than by the two of us. You just can't tell two people to fall in love because it would suit others.

"I guess what I really wanted to say," he added, "is that you're a good friend, and I'm really happy for you and for Mary, too. There's been talk around town that the two of you would go elsewhere to live. I'm glad you're staying here."

Robert shifted his champagne glass to his left hand and extended his right to David. David did the same and they shook. "Thanks," he said.

At that moment they both noticed Mary standing inside the window, smiling at them through the glass. "What are you two fools doing out there?" she called.

Once they got back inside, the remaining champagne bottles were collected, and the entire party of forty people walked to the Locke House for an impromptu tour. All the parlor doors were opened, and they talked and laughed and sang in the glow of the fireplace and chandelier gas jets, the ladies in what chairs there were and the men standing or sitting on the floor. By big-city standards this was a modest house, but for most of these young Hoosiers it was as much as any of them dreamed of. David and Mary were joyous to shelter all this friendship under the roof where they would find so much pleasure in years to come.

The now tipsy gathering played a game of tableau. The first team huddled and whispered in the dining room and then arranged themselves sloppily on the floor. Two of them inexplicably sat, each holding a single curtain rod out to the side like a wing. It wasn't until Willsie Bush turned her hat sideways on her head, put one foot on Ben Craig's back as he knelt on all fours and then put her hands on her hips, thrusting out her chest, that someone finally guessed that this was a poor attempt at mimicking Washington crossing the Delaware.

Well after midnight, as the last of their guests walked down Noblesville's familiar streets to their own homes, David and Mary turned off the gaslights but stayed behind. In the empty, darkened house, in the half-furnished bedroom that would soon be theirs, in the bed Mary had chosen, they made love for the first time in this town, in this time. It was the first time that she had slid her hands down David's bare body and felt his hands on her breasts and legs and his breath on her neck, without worrying about the phases of the moon or the consequences.

She felt married already. Ahead lay a life like this. Until very recently this was not the place she had dreamed of. Now, there was nowhere else she could imagine being. The contentment and fulfillment she sought had been there all the time, needing only David to awaken her to it, to show it to her through the freshness of his perspective. Somehow it seemed that the truth in the lessons she had learned had always been with her but had been denied. It felt like accepting the obvious and unchangeable. The thought of being here for the rest of her life, growing old in her hometown with him, was the most comforting and alluring of prospects.

In the intoxicating feeling of his body moving in unison with hers, within four walls that were theirs, the last fears she'd harbored vanished, replaced by an unshakable faith in him. Thinking of their approaching marriage and the emotional turbulence of the summer behind them, she felt for the first time like a woman instead of a girl.

"What will you do with your life?" she asked later as they lay together in the dark. "I mean, what kind of work?"

"I don't know. Since Jim Bush died, I've been thinking about the newspaper business. What would you think about me starting a paper?"

"Sounds fine, but we already have a one of both stripes here."

"How about an independent paper, one that just prints the news without taking sides. We could do it together. You could write stories, too."

"Yes," she said, laying her head on his shoulder, "we could do it together."

In the middle of the night, she slipped out the back door, crossed the darkened alley, and slipped quietly into the back door of her parents' new home, unnoticed.

Late the next morning, David passed through the beam to get ready for the auction. Soon he would return for good, destroying the beam behind him.

CHAPTER TWENTY-ONE

*Life still flows on like a stream of water. You can hold your finger
in it for a while but when you take it out there will be no hole left.
Life goes on. … We are really not too important. We find some niches
in life where we work and spend our days then we grow old, retire
and die. There are not very many people who really care or know
about us. What do we really know about those who lived fifty years
ago in our community? It is true that with few exceptions they are
now just names and dates carved on a tombstone. … It is so true
that in this stream of life we leave no hole in the stream of events.
(Yet), influence of those long gone lingers on and on. It comes from
every life and it may be evil or it may be good. In part it comes
from the things we do and say, from the example we set. … No one
can really estimate the true power or effects of his influence. Neither
can he tell for how many generations it will endure. This I know, I
have been a part of it. All that I met and all that has passed before
me. My shadow may fall where I may never be.*
Ralph Waterman, Hamilton County, Indiana,
from his notes, "I Have Done All These Things," 1978.

Most of the items for the auction were in place, spread out on tables
in a building on the 4-H fairgrounds. The auctioneer and two teenage

helpers had arrived at David's in an extended cab pick-up truck pulling a huge horse trailer—which had never held a horse—and spent two hours loading the bottles, tins, crates, toys, tools, signs, books, and tack that David had accumulated. The auctioneer was astonished at the extent of David's vast assortment of what was now called "collectibles."

David planned to add the proceeds to the substantial nest egg he had already amassed, and then he and Mary would be set for life. He could have stopped before this final deal, but couldn't. Like his father, he loved making the sale and walking away with the check.

After the auctioneer pulled away, David found a few more boxes in the basement. He brought them up one at a time and began loading them in his truck. His neighbor Jim, across the street, was mowing his lawn for the last time this year. As David snapped down the vinyl cover on the tailgate, the droning lawn mower gave a metallic "clunk," and the engine died. Simultaneously, David heard a tinkling crash from the front of his house.

The mower had hit a rock, slinging it across the street and into the stained glass panels of David's front window. The blood seemed to drain from David's body as shock struck him.

"Gee, I'm awful sorry!" Jim called, but David wasn't listening.

David ran into the house. The corner panel of stained glass and the medicine bottle that had worked magic all summer were shattered. Thin red shards lay on the floor among the broken chunks of the bottle. Desperation gripped him. "It can be fixed! It has to be fixed!" he shrieked, his voice out of control. He closed his eyes and tried to calm his racing heart. "Gotta figure out how, gotta figure out how!" he whispered.

He fell to his knees, cupping his hands over his face, trembling. What could he do to fix it?

He went to the kitchen and dug through a cabinet until he'd found two small ziplock bags. One he filled with the broken red pieces, the other with the bottle shards. His hand trembled as he picked up the pieces. "Oh, God, please don't take the beam away, please don't let this happen," he pleaded as he collected them. "I've got to get back!"

He drove to the 4-H grounds and burst into the building where the auctioneer and his helpers were setting up. They watched, thinking to themselves that he must be crazy as he picked through the boxes and inspected the tables of items, comparing a bag of broken glass to medicine bottles on the tables.

David looked terrified. He knew they were watching, and he searched through bottles, self-consciously glancing at them as they pretended not to notice his strange behavior.

He rummaged through the antique mall downtown in the old Wild Building, where Truitt's Drug Store and Tescher's Clothing had once been, looking for antique medicine bottles and deep-magenta stained glass that matched his shards.

As he waited impatiently at the cash register, with the courthouse clock tower in full view behind the plate-glass windows, he heard the bells toll for the first time since last spring.

"Seems funny to hear that again," the man behind the counter said. "They just got it hooked up this morning. Now, finally, it counts the right time." David paid for the glass he'd bought and then stood on the sidewalk for a moment, looking up at the clock face.

He drove to antique stores throughout the area, filling his front seat with bottles and stained glass. He sped furiously, running red lights and cutting in front of other drivers.

In Zionsville he went to the architectural salvage yard where he'd sold hardware earlier in the summer. He rummaged through the milk crates and dusty shelves of hundred-year-old stained-glass pieces. By the time he got home, the late-afternoon sun was beyond the trees and his chance at a test was lost for the day.

He shoved the accumulated junk mail off the dining room table and onto the floor and spread the glass out, comparing what he'd bought with the original broken pieces. The three remaining panels of red glass in the other corners of the window were his best bet, so he strung a trouble light out into the front yard and stood on the ladder, chisel in hand, removing the glazing and push points and then the glass, labeling each piece by location.

When he had done all he could without sunshine, he collapsed into a chair, staring numbly at the ceiling. He went into the bathroom and splashed his face with water, then just stared into the mirror. *What if I never get back?*

It would be at least fourteen hours before he could try the new pieces.

Anticipation mixed with fear tied his stomach knots. He was too restless to sit still.

David dug through the piles of junk mail that he'd shoved onto the floor and found the yellow legal pad that held the notes he'd made back in June, when he went to the library to look up information on pneumonia. On the second page were the names of the Harrisons, with their dates of birth, marriage, death. He stuck it under his arm and shot out the back door.

Soon he was in the Indiana Room with four boxes of microfilm on top of the machine, two from the *Ledger* and two from the *Democrat* from the 1890s. He skimmed through the summer of 1893, finding mention of himself here and there, the Beeman trial, the Swain trial, Etta Heylman and her baby, James Bush, the World's Fair. In early November he found a story about his disappearance: DAVID HENRY MISSING.

There were expressions of concern from Dr. Harrison, and the fact that David and Mary were engaged. "Sheriff Rhoades ended speculation that Mr. Henry fled the impending marriage to Miss Harrison by pointing out that all of Mr. Henry's belongings were in place in the house. There was a cup of coffee on the table, an open book in the bedroom, and his substantial financial accounts at local banks are untouched."

He went on through the weeks and found fewer and fewer notices about himself. In the week in December when he and Mary were to have married—nothing.

He continued to scan headlines and personal notices on into 1894

In a spring issue of the *Noblesville Democrat* he came across a headline that read "Auditor Harrison seals his political fate." At the state Republican convention, Dr. Harrison had pulled Hamilton County votes away from Judge Beckley, Thomas Swain's ally in court, causing him to lose renomination.

David went through the obituary file and found a card for Mary's death, still filed under "Wainwright." He went back to the microfilm viewer and found her obituary:

"Mary Wainwright died in her sleep of heart failure at the old family home on South 9th Street. She was preceded in death by her husband, Robert, and her eldest son, Robert Jr.

"She was born in Noblesville in 1871, and was the daughter of Dr. Albert R. and Anna Harrison, both deceased. She was active in community affairs throughout her adult life. Mrs. Wainwright was instrumental in bringing the library to Noblesville and worked on numerous productions at the Opera House." It went on with details of surviving children and grandchildren.

To think of her married to someone else—sharing a life with Robert instead of him—ripped at David's heart like a dull knife. He felt as if he were experiencing her death for the hundredth time. Trembling with emotion, he ran a copy of the obituary and then stared down at the legal pad, wondering why he'd come here. *What does it matter? I'll get back.* He saw the note, "Edith Cottingham, S. 10th St." Mary's granddaughter. It was the name given to him by the elderly lady he'd met here when he first came to look up the Harrisons.

He wondered about Edith Cottingham. That there was someone here in Noblesville, still alive, who'd known Mary, was somehow comforting. He circled the name and went back home.

The sun was low enough in the sky that he would have just a couple hours to test the new stained glass and bottles he'd bought. As he climbed the ladder, David thought of the day back in the spring when he'd put it here; he hadn't moved it since.

In the morning he placed one of the pieces of glass from another corner of the window and lined the medicine bottles up across the floor in the front parlor. He then spent two hours cutting the pieces of glass he'd bought to the right size.

While he worked, the auction of his collectibles began at the 4-H grounds. Collectors and dealers from across Indiana packed the building and filled the metal folding chairs set out on the concrete floor. People milled up and down the aisles between the tables, marveling at the array.

At 11:30 the sun seemed to be at the right height and David feverishly tried each medicine bottle, changing the position of each several times. Occasionally he'd get warm red tones to bathe the parlor doors—but no beam. He changed to the next piece of glass and tried each bottle again. As the minutes ticked by, the sun passed over Jim's house and on west, and with each failure David became more desperate. When he'd gone through every piece of stained glass, he went back and started over again, wondering what would happen if he rotated each piece. He did it over and over again, thinking mathematically through every possible combination. Before he'd finished, the sun crept behind a tree and he had to quit.

The auctioneer came by to show David the receipts, only to be offended when David shut the door in his face. "Look," he shouted, tapping on the window, "I made you $125,000 today, and all you can do is slam the door in my face?" He walked back to his truck, scratching his head. "I'll bring by a certified check tomorrow," he shouted at the house.

After a sleepless night David tried again, with no success, and again the next day, trying each piece of glass again and again. When the sun disappeared behind the trees on the third day, he collapsed onto the couch and fell apart. The horror of being marooned in his own time, combined with lack of sleep, took its toll. After sobbing for an hour, he fell asleep on the couch and didn't wake up until morning.

David had passed this house hundreds of times and taken little notice. Just three doors north of the Locke house on 10th Street, it was a turn-of-the-century vernacular, painted dark-chocolate brown with white trim. He knocked on the door, and a moment later a pair of bright blue eyes below a fringe of fluffy white hair peered out of the window at him. There was no mistaking those eyes, or the shape of the face he knew so well.

"Pleasure to meet you, Mr. Henry," she said when he had introduced himself.

"Please, call me David."

"And you may call me Edith."

In the entryway a staircase ran along the left wall, and a fireplace surround rested against the wall on the right, not connected to a chimney but as a decorative piece, supporting a dried-flower arrangement.

"That's a really beautiful mantle," David said, running his fingers along the vaguely familiar carvings.

"It came from the old Wild Opera House."

"How did you get your hands on it?" David asked.

"When they tore that place down it was enough to make you cry," she said. "Nobody was taking anything out, so I went over the day before with a crowbar and took it off the wall. My husband thought I was nuts. I stored it in the garage for ages and then had it refinished a few years ago. "Come on in," she smiled, leading him into the living room.

The room was filed with antiques and overstuffed chairs, bookcases lined with old books and photographs. A familiar upright piano stood in one corner, and David walked over to examine a cluster of old photographs. Mary appeared in two or three of them, one young, as he had known her, sitting on the front steps of the 9th Street house with his own cat, Sophie, on her lap, and another, a studio shot of her sitting beside Robert Wainwright—perhaps a wedding picture. His stomach tightened. In two others she was a woman in her sixties, still lovely, in the way that Edith was. There was a photo of Dr. Harrison in his G.A.R. uniform, and one of a middle-aged Fred, balding and wearing a suit, posed in profile, sitting in an oak armchair.

"These are the people you're researching," Edith said, "my great-grandfather, my great-uncle, my grandparents, my parents and brothers."

"What about Fred's children and Harry's?" David asked.

"Like my children, they're all over the place. One of Harry's sons went to California, another went to Texas and then Oregon, and Fred's grandchildren are in the Indianapolis area."

"Are you the only Harrison descendant still living in Noblesville?"

"My daughter lives in town, but that's it," she said, smiling with a hint of sadness.

"You've done a good job hanging on to your family's memories," David said, trying to hide the pain that pierced his heart as he noticed, on Edith's right hand, the engagement ring he'd bought for Mary. He looked away and focused on the photo of Mary sitting with Robert.

"She was a beautiful woman."

"Yes," David replied, lost in thought.

"I have this ring she gave me," she said, holding her hand out to David. "But you know, one memento I wish I had was the little necklace she's wearing in this picture." She tapped at the photo.

"What is it?" David asked, knowing well.

"It was a small, sterling silver turtle with a hinged shell. When you opened it up, it had a tiny compass inside."

"What happened to it?"

"I don't know. My mother told me that Grandmother Mary always wore it, that she'd worn it every day since my mother could remember. But around the end of World War I, one day she noticed that her mother wasn't wearing it. She asked where it went, and Grandmother Mary said she'd given it to a friend. My mother was crushed. It had an inscription on the bottom of some sort. My great-grandmother had given it to Grandmother Mary when she went off to college. Oh, enough about such things! Sit down, won't you?"

Edith was perhaps in her early eighties, but she was a lively looking woman dressed in sweatpants, an Indiana University sweatshirt and tennis shoes. When David had seen youthful pictures of his grandparents, he remembered being shocked at how beautiful his grandmother had been and how handsome his grandfather was. Edith had obviously been a Hollywood-style beauty sixty years ago. The wrinkles and the sagging chin could not hide the features she had inherited from her grandmother, his Mary.

She asked where he was from and he gave her a quick synopsis of his life. She brought coffee and cookies and chatted pleasantly. She asked, "Tell me what kind of research you're doing?"

David gave her the same false story he'd given when he called her on the phone earlier. He said he was trying to write an Indiana history curriculum for fourth-graders. He would choose a family and follow their lives through the settlement and growth of Indiana, with the aim of showing the students how historical events and social changes had affected them.

"Why the Harrisons?"

"I've been restoring a house that Dr. Harrison—your great-grandfather—built in 1891. As I researched his life, I thought that family looked like a good choice. His father—your great-great-grandfather—was an early settler in Indianapolis. Dr. Harrison fought in the Civil War, then was a small-town doctor and politician. His son Fred fought in the Spanish-American War, studied at Johns Hopkins, and ran a field hospital in France during World War I. One of Harry's grandsons fought in World War II. It's a great family to use as an example."

"What do you want to know that you haven't found out already?"

"The women—Anna, Mary, your mother. There's almost nothing to follow in newspapers, so little information that would tell me what they were like, how they viewed the world."

"I think it's a wonderful idea," Edith said. "What can I tell you that would help?"

"Did you know your grandmother, Mary Wainwright, well?"

"Oh, yes, she was a wonderful person," Edith smiled. "She lived in the same house with us when I was growing up. The house stood where the phone company building is, a block away on 9th Street. It was lovely old place. Her father built it in 1893. She was a grown woman then, in her early twenties, and she just lived there for a few years until she married my grandfather, Robert Wainwright. She moved out to his family's home north of town and lived there for many years until her father, the doctor, died. Then, I guess it was maybe 1912 or so, she and Grandpa Wainwright moved in with her mother, who was living in the house with Harry Harrison's widow, Clara. By the time I was a little girl, in the late 1930s, Anna Harrison, Clara Harrison, and Grandpa Wainwright had all passed away, and my family lived there with Grandmother Mary."

"She was the last of that group of Harrisons from before the turn of the century?" David asked.

"Yes, she was, but she didn't seem out of step or old-fashioned like the other kids' grandmothers. She had a kind of elegant wisdom. I always got the impression she had settled for less, living in this town with Grandpa Wainwright. She always spoke highly of Noblesville, but you could tell that she dreamed of other things. She knew about music and the arts and seemed to care a lot about architecture. She and I would go to Indianapolis and see shows. I remember once when I was a girl she took me to the old theater, the one they're tearing down on north 9th Street, and we saw Tom Mix perform on stage with his horse. I know that's not really the arts, but she humored me and took me just the same. She loved movies and took me nearly every week, whenever a new one came to town. She died in the house on 9th. Right up till the end she persisted in calling 9th Street by its old name, Catherine, and 10th Street by the name Anderson. She was like that—a bit of the old with the new."

"Tell me more about her," David urged. Like the elderly people he had talked to in college oral history projects, she was thrilled to tell what she knew of the past, excited that somebody cared.

"There was a dark side to her personality, a lot of sadness. She lost her oldest son, my uncle, in the first world war. That was a tragedy she never really got over. We'd go through old pictures sometimes, and she'd get misty-eyed when his photo turned up. She was also skeptical of technology and new things and would pick and choose very carefully what she let into her house.

"I loved jazz and big band music when I was a girl, which horrified my parents, but not Grandmother Mary. Oh, how she loved that music! We'd listen to records all the time—drove my parents nuts."

"Did you know your Uncle Fred?"

"No, he died before I was born. Grandmother said that he came home from France in 1919 weak and sick from something that they never quite figured out and then died several years later after an appendicitis operation. He and Mary were close growing up, and I think his death was especially hard for her, coming so soon after the loss of her son. Harry's wife was still around, old Aunt Clara, but I don't think they were close. Grandma Mary and Aunt Katie, Fred's wife, were good friends, though."

They talked into the late afternoon. Edith got out photo albums and they went through pictures taken during the century. David stopped at every picture with Mary in it, searching her face for some clue to her thoughts. She had grown to look like Edith today: piercing eyes and a crown of white hair, her features strong, her figure slight. But there were no more clues—just the thin smile that, as always, suggested she knew something you didn't. He heard about the lives of all of Mary's, Fred's, and Harry's children, where they went and what they did.

"What's become of your sisters?"

"Ellen is gone, and Sylvia lives in Florida. How she survives in Florida I'll never know. I like visiting there well enough, but I couldn't live there."

David had run out of history questions, and he could hardly ask if Mary had ever mentioned him. Edith said, "I find it interesting that you're so fascinated in the life and times of my grandmother."

"Well, as I said, there just isn't much documentation about the lives of women." He attempted to draw her back into her past. "You know, hearing you talk about the time when she was still alive, it sounds like that was a very special time in your life."

"It is more and more as I get older. As I sit here in my little room, watching the world go by from my window, I've come to think of my grandmother's death as a turning point. Community life is dead now. Oh, I suppose America has always been changing, but before the war we kept our sense of community. Our daily life slowly changed through the forties and fifties and sixties, and now it's pretty much gone. The social life of this community is nothing compared to what it was when I was a girl. Today, social life is ... watching TV or texting people on your phone, I suppose.

"As I look about America and the life that my husband and I made for our children and grandchildren, so much of it is wonderful, and so much of it is just plain terrible. I find myself reminiscing about those times when I was young, and wishing my generation had done so many things differently."

"What would you do differently?" David asked.

"You know what I thought of the other day? I thought about dying. I do that a lot any more," she laughed, "but really I was thinking about my birth and my grandmother's death. I was born in that house on 9th Street where the Ameritech office is now, in an upstairs bedroom; the same one my grandmother Mary died in. I was even born in the same bed she died in. That tells you how much things have changed!

"When I was growing up, a child saw the whole cycle of life right in the home. Elderly people weren't so strange; they lived with you." She talked on as the cars droned by and the clocked ticked on the wall.

"I saw babies born in our house and I saw my grandmother die there, too. You didn't have to tell me what life was about; I knew. Kids today don't."

"Oh, they're worldly enough," David broke in, "but without a basic sense of the truths of life."

"Yes," Edith agreed. "A worldly person in my day could choose his destiny. But parents today are alone guiding their children through this world. When I was a young girl, home was the whole town." David nodded in agreement as Edith talked on, critiquing how the media culture was sabotaging families.

"When I was a girl, I knew where I fit into things. I saw the people of this town go about their business, and they saw me go about mine. I knew what I could do, and what I couldn't. We didn't need so many laws, because we could see every day how we all depended on one another. There were certain things you did and didn't do. You didn't have to ask the difference between right and wrong very often; you knew.

"Kids don't have the slightest practical idea where they fit into things because everything's so mixed up." She described in detail the neighborhood schools she attended, the same ones her parents attended.

"Now children go to school out where there was a cornfield a couple years ago. Nearly every kid rides a bus to a part of town they barely know. When they go shopping or to a movie they go to the mall, where nobody knows who they are.

"And my grandchildren don't even know some of their neighbors. So when they smoke cigarettes or drink beer or raise hell, who's there to say, 'That's not the way we do things'? Strangers aren't going to tell them.

"My grandchildren couldn't walk downtown for ice cream if they wanted to. They live in the Prairie Towne subdivision, cut off from everything. If they want to go somewhere, their parents have to drive them." They talked on about social isolation for a half hour.

"Technology hasn't brought us together, it's made us too self-sufficient," Edith scowled. "We all live alone, apart from anyone or anything that might annoy us. So when we have a crisis in our lives, who do we call? Technology? It might solve some of our problems, but it's not much comfort to the soul. You know what Ogden Nash said about progress?"

"No," David said, loving her tirade.

" 'Progress was a good idea, it just went on too long.' Progress has torn us apart. With all the ways we have to communicate, people probably spend less time really talking to one another than they did when I was a girl." And for another twenty minutes, they picked apart technology.

"With progress and technology, we always see what we're getting, but never notice what we're giving up as our lives change," David agreed.

"You know, after my husband and I got married and started a family, we so often said that we wanted a life for our children that was better than the life we had. I'm not sure that was so wise. What most of us had wasn't so bad. As I look out my window I wonder where the signs are, the signs that children follow to find their way in this world."

Edith fell silent for a moment.

"Signs? I'm not sure I know what you mean," David said.

Edith chose her words slowly, gazing at her interlaced fingers. "I knew what the possibilities were for a girl like me, there were examples all around. Like a sailor at sea, we had stars to guide us. Most people in town behaved in an honorable way. They set examples for us. There were signs that told us which way to go at different times in life. The morals to stories, the behavior of adults, the lessons we learned in church—everywhere there were clear signs that most everyone agreed on."

"I see what you mean. And what are the signs today for kids? What signs are they gathering from television and YouTube? With so much conflicting information, how do kids know which way to go?"

"I sometimes think Americans are like a child who's been allowed to choose whatever he wants for dinner. A small child would choose candy. It tastes good, but it's not very nourishing. Eventually the child gets fat and his teeth rot. We're a lot like that as a nation. We choose the bright, flashy things that will make our lives fun and easy. Now look at us, we're a fat and decaying society."

"You're a wise woman," David said. "I can't disagree with a thing you've said."

"I'm a woman with a big mouth," she laughed, suddenly embarrassed. "I'm sorry you had to sit and listen to me rant and rave."

"Don't apologize. You were right on target." He could hear his own words, and Mary's, trickling down through the century. The lessons they learned that summer had, in some small measure, survived in her descendant.

"You know something else? My grandmother told me, a few days before she passed on, that she was glad to be dying. She said that a lonely, ugly time was to come. I don't know just why she was so sure about it. I suppose in hindsight it's easy to see the world changing."

David made no response. Edith looked down at her hands for a moment and then gazed out the window. Slowly, a sly smile spread across her face. "If I tell you a secret, will you promise not to tell anyone? You can't put it in your notes."

"I promise."

"When I was about fifteen years old, I had my first crush on a boy.

I didn't feel I could talk to my mother about it, but I knew I could talk to Grandmother Mary. I asked her if she ever had her heart broken, and she said yes.

"She said that in the spring of 1893, a man reached out and touched her shoulder and changed her life forever."

David's face suddenly felt hot. His heart beat wildly.

"I asked what she meant by that, and she said she meant what she said. Mysterious, huh? According to her, they spent that summer together, and it was the love of her life. Now, this shocked me, of course, because it was hard to imagine this old lady being young and in love, and to think that she loved someone else more than my grandfather. When I asked her if she loved this man more than Grandpa, she said simply that she never forgot the man and that even after she was married, she thought of him every day.

"She told me all the things they did that summer, and her face was alive with so much happiness! The man's name was the same as yours: David. When I asked her where the man was from, she said he was from the future. At first I thought she was being whimsical and meant that he was ahead of his time, but she looked me straight in the eye and said, 'He was really from the future.'

"Grandmother Mary was a bit eccentric, so I took all this with a grain of salt. I just assumed that there was something about what went on that she didn't want to tell me, so she cloaked it in make-believe. But if there was something she was afraid to say, it must have been pretty bad—or just plain weird—because she told me something as unbelievable as anything could be to me, then. You know what she said?"

"What?" David whispered. His mouth was so dry he could barely make a sound. He was no longer on the edge of his seat, he was sinking into it. The desperation he'd felt for three days was gone. In its place was a soul-wrenching sense of loss. It was over, really over. For the first time since the window had been broken, he believed that there would be no return. For the first time in his life, he wished he were dead. But he kept listening, wanting to be reassured of how Mary had loved him.

"Well," Edith continued, giddy with excitement over the secret she was about to share, "my grandmother told me that she slept with this man. Can you believe it?" she said, laughing nervously. "I couldn't. In the 1940s when she told me this, I was young enough to think that only terrible sinners did such things out of wedlock and that married women only did it to conceive children—and even then, they didn't enjoy it.

"They went to Chicago in August of 1893 and stayed in a hotel as man and wife. They went to the theater and a grand ball and the World's Fair. I asked her if the man had forced himself on her, and she said no. She said that it was very mutual and that she never regretted it for a moment.

"I asked her what happened to him and how she got her heart broken. She said that a few days before Halloween, he left and just never returned. They had planned to be married. When I asked her where he went and why he didn't come back, she simply said she thought he got lost in the future. Now, I can tell you, this sounded pretty crazy to me, but my grandmother was anything but crazy.

"Her eyes got dim when she was telling it," Edith continued, staring out the window. "When I asked her if she still thought of that man or wished she could go back and relive those days, she said, '*Love is now the stardust of yesterday, the music of the years gone by.*' Words from a song she loved."

Edith stopped, hearing a sound from David that startled her. She saw that he was crying. With his elbows on his knees and his face in his hands, he was weeping with the rare, deep sobs of a grown man.

"Why are you crying?" she asked him.

David tried to speak, but couldn't. He wiped at the tears with the back of his hands, not caring anymore for secrets. Finally he said, "I'm the man from the future."

Edith continued to stare into his face, giving him a worried smile. "What did you say?"

"I said, I'm the man from the future. I'm the David your grandmother loved."

"What?" Edith asked again, but she had heard what he said. The look of concern drained from her face, replaced with a look of fear. "What do you mean you're the man from the future? You couldn't be."

"I am. Something amazing happened in my house this summer and I was able to travel in time. I met your grandmother and we fell in love. But it's broken now—ruined."

"That's not possible," Edith whispered, her eyes opened wide and fixed squarely on David. "Why are you saying this? You're scaring me."

"It's true," David insisted.

"I think you're a sick man," she said angrily, her voice breaking, near tears, "and I'd like you to leave now!"

David reached into his backpack and pulled out an old photograph— the one of him and Mary sitting on the rim of a great fountain at the Chicago World's Fair more than a hundred years ago. He looked at it for a moment, then handed it to Edith. "Do you recognize this couple?" he asked.

Edith took the photo and studied it. She quickly turned to look at the youthful picture of her grandmother, then back at David's photo. She looked up at him and again back at the handsome, smiling couple. She dropped it in her lap and put a wrinkled hand to her mouth, bewildered.

"Hold out your hand," David said.

She did not. She seemed frozen, unable to move.

David reached into his pocket and pulled out the interlocking wedding band. He leaned down and took her right hand and slid the band onto her finger. It fit snugly around the diamond on her ring. Her eyes widened even more.

He stood and gathered his backpack. "I don't care if you believe me," he said with resignation. "I just wanted to talk to someone who knew her; I miss her so much."

He reached out and took the photo from her, placing it back in his pack. "You can keep the wedding band. They were a matching pair." She said nothing as he walked to the door. "I'm sorry I upset you," he added.

As he put his hand on the doorknob, though, Edith spoke out. "If you're the man she told me about, answer a question."

David nodded.

"This man had a pet name for her. He used to call her—"

"Mona Lisa," David said quickly.

Edith gasped. "You couldn't know that!"

"It's from that song by Nat King Cole, just like the lines from 'Stardust.' I took my cell phone with me and played those songs for her."

Edith closed her eyes as if bracing herself for another shock. "Was she here, in this time, in Noblesville last month?"

"Yes," David said, his eyes narrowing, wondering how she knew.

"Ohhh," Edith moaned, tears welling up in her eyes and trickling down her face. "I met her downtown last month," she cried. "We talked—we sat right out front on the stoop and talked."

He watched her searching eyes for a moment and then left, realizing there was nothing more to say.

CHAPTER TWENTY-TWO

Nobody cares if you're left behind,
The stardust train still leaves on time
So I stood on the platform wiping my eyes
As the faces in the windows waved goodbye
Stardust Train
Stardust Train
All on board for the stardust train
From the song "Stardust Train,"
Bill Wilson, 1975.

David turned left and headed toward downtown, passing Tescher's house, now covered in dingy asbestos siding, the ornate porch long since ripped away. Where the Fortners' house once stood he stopped and looked at the spot in the yard where he and Mary had sat in a wicker love seat on the Fourth of July over a hundred years before.

The continual drizzle soaked his clothes and shoes. A semi sped past and sprayed him with mist.

He walked on through downtown, past the rubble of the Diana Theater and the storefronts; even those that had been restored looked terribly different than they had when he and Mary had strolled by them. He came to the parking lot where the Wild Opera House once stood.

Two teenagers crossed the lot, smoking cigarettes, laughing and playfully jostling each other. One of them shouted to the other, "Fuck you!" The echo of those words bounced off the backs of the century-old buildings.

David closed his eyes and imagined Mary standing in the arched stone entrance of the opera house, smiling when she saw him come up the street. He walked on, turning left at Cherry Street.

He stood in the darkness, just a few feet from the front porch of the Locke house. It had been converted to offices. The darkened windows looked lonely and sad, and he felt an emptiness deeper than he'd ever known in his life. The house that was to be theirs was rotting from neglect, the entire kitchen wall sagging. Water ran down the siding in places, dripping from behind rotted eaves.

David looked west down Cherry, wondering why he was stalling. He would have to do it sooner or later. He began walking west again, feeling stronger now.

Three blocks down the dark street, he could see the glow of a streetlight above the entrance to Riverside Cemetery. He walked through the gate and stopped at the 1824 stone. Kneeling down, he rubbed his hands across the wet, moss-covered limestone and ran his finger along the carved dates, remembering, putting off what he knew he must do.

He stood and looked across the gravestones as the cold rain dripped off his face. He could hear the rush of the swollen river just beyond the trees. Finally, he made his way among the stones toward the one carved to resemble a cut tree trunk with ivy growing around it. He fell to his knees at the base and wrapped his arms around it, sobbing.

The drenching sheets of rain that had fallen all day coasted to a steady, soft downpour by nightfall. For Jane and her husband, it was now or never. As she picked through the pile of debris that had been the Diana Theater, the rain matted her hair to the side of her face. She had difficulty seeing through the water-splashed glasses that kept slipping down her nose.

The bank, pleading insurance restrictions, had refused to allow the demolition crew to help her find the time capsule or remove the stone inscribed "Diana Theater 1919," which was centered just below the roofline and covered by the newer stone facing. She was allowed to pick through the site only after she signed a document releasing the bank from liability if she was injured, and then only after the demolition crew had gone for the day. A crane with a wrecking ball and a backhoe sat in the middle of the debris, looking like a pair of mechanical dinosaurs waiting to devour their prey. They had reduced the building to rubble in the past two days. Jane stumbled through the broken bricks and steel beams.

They found the inscribed stone without much digging. It was in two pieces, broken rather cleanly in half. With all the strength they could muster, Jane and her husband carried the pieces one at a time and dropped them into the back of their little station wagon. It took them another hour with a crowbar and sledgehammer to reveal the small lead box that had been nestled inside two carved pieces of sandstone on the lower left corner of the building's facade. Her grandfather had put it there in the cornerstone himself, nearly ninety-five years ago. On that bright sunny day in 1919, he was a well-respected businessman bringing a new theater to town. Tonight she was considered an anti-business nuisance, picking through a demolition site in the rain.

With a mixture of excitement and grief, Jane looked back for a moment before getting in the car, the lead box under her arm. She remembered Sunday afternoon double features and free cartoons after the community Easter egg hunt on the Saturday before each Easter.

"Goddammit," she muttered to herself. "Goddammit."

By nine o'clock that night, David was on his fourth beer. He'd kept the door locked and the porch light off. Still, occasionally a child dressed as a skeleton or ghost would come to the door and ring the bell, and at least one peeked in to see him sitting on the floor, ignoring the bell. He sat cross-legged on the floor in the front parlor, drinking. He heard footsteps coming up onto the porch and the screen door opening. Someone twisted the bell. He didn't move. He didn't want to see or talk to anyone. The bell persisted. Then the visitor began pounding on the door and calling out, "David, I know you're in there! Please open the door, please!" It was Jane.

He got up and went to the door, opening it just enough to see her, but making it clear that she was not invited in. She saw his red, swollen eyes and the lines of anguish on his face.

"What do you want?" he finally asked. He could see that not all was right with her, either. She wore an expression of disbelief, confusion, and her lower lip trembled. Without another word, she held out a sealed envelope.

"I-it was in the t-time capsule," she stammered.

He took it and read, "Please deliver, unopened, to David Henry, 1242 Cherry Street." It was Mary's handwriting. The blood drained from his head and his knees went weak. He leaned against the door jamb.

"That envelope was inside an another, unmarked envelope. What's going on, David?" she asked urgently.

He didn't answer.

"How could someone in 1919 know that you would live here?"

"I can't tell you now, Jane," he said. He closed the door and collapsed on the couch.

Jane remained on the porch calling, through the door. "David! What the hell? Tell me what's going on! There's another letter here addressed in the same handwriting to Edith Cottingham. I'm afraid to take it over to her if I don't know what's going on!" A few minutes passed with no answer, and she finally went back to her car.

David sat staring at the familiar handwriting. If Mary had placed this in the time capsule in 1919, she had been forty-eight years old. She had done the only thing she could to communicate with him beyond the years.

He tore open the envelope and found another envelope within. Inside that one were several pages. From among them fell an 1893 silver dollar. He remembered the night at the Bachelors' Club when Robert had given it to them as an amiable joke. Then something else fell out: the turtle necklace. He knelt down and picked it up, feeling the worn ridges on its back. Pulling open the shell, he watched the little diamond-shaped needle quiver and then point north. He rolled it over in his palm, reading the inscription: "So you won't lose your way."

Setting down the dollar and the necklace, he opened the letter.

May 12, 1919
Dear David,

I assume that if you are reading this that it is perhaps just a few days since you last saw me. How I envy you, so close to that last moment. For me it has been twenty-six years. I am forty-eight now, half of my lifetime away from that summer. Time can play cruel tricks, as we both know.

I feel awkward and nervous writing this to you now. It is a letter I have written hundreds of times in my heart since the day you didn't return. I wrote it again the day I was married, and on the days my children were born. I wrote it on the day Harry died, and the days Father and then Mother died. I wrote it when my husband was thoughtless or cruel or petty. I wrote it the day I realized that there were more automobiles than horses on the streets of Noblesville. When the war came, I felt as though I was in a canoe without a paddle on a swift river, heading for a waterfall, and I wrote to you then. I wrote again two years later when I was notified that my older son had been killed in France, and when I embraced Fred when he came home from the war. Now, as they break ground on the theater, I'm writing it for real.

Thinking back on the days after we last parted, it's hard to convey my anguish. I checked the front parlor of your house for weeks, hoping for the beam to appear. Eventually mother convinced me to spend my days at home. Father kept the house empty, with everything as you had left it, for nearly two years. In the summer of 1895 when we removed your things, I made peace with the loss. In my heart I still loved you, but I was no longer waiting with any real hope. It was the most difficult thing I'd ever done—accepting that you were not coming back.

Much was made of your disappearance. Because we were engaged, sympathy was heaped upon me. The police suspected foul play because all your things were in order there as if you expected to get back any minute. My family said nothing of what we knew. Who would believe?

After we moved your things out, I sold the Locke house. We spoke of you seldom. I think everyone wanted me to get on with my life.

The impact you had on our lives was profound—for me, of course, and for Father, too. I realized that the night he returned from the Republican convention in 1894. We sat up late and he told me how he had played one last dirty political trick—one he thought you would approve of. He prevented a corrupt judge named Beckley—one of Swain's attorneys—from being renominated. It destroyed father's political career and sent him *back to medicine. He never regretted it. That night, for the first time, he shared with me his own grief over your loss. We cried and laughed and said the things we had never said to one another. We had another grand heart-to-heart about you the night before I married in 1897. More tears and laughter—mostly tears.*

In later years, often on Christmas Eve, Harry, Fred, Father and I would stay up late, talking around the fire. Eventually, someone would say, "I wonder what happened to David," and that overwhelming panic I felt in the early days after you disappeared would come back to me, and all of the pain and sorrow, too—not fitting for a married woman to pine for a man who disappeared twenty-six years ago.

You've haunted my life like a secret ghost.

It has never occurred to any of us that you chose not to return. We have a deep faith in you, so don't fear, I never believed that you didn't love me. I know you did, and that something beyond your control must have destroyed the beam.

Knowing what your state of mind must be, I'm searching my heart to find the words that will convey to you something that I have learned in my life, something that will help you to live with your situation as I have tried to live with mine. The things we learned together that summer have been my guide. I wonder what I can share with you to ease your pain?

You taught me many things about the future, but I know something about the future that I believe you have never accepted: I'm going to die, and so are you. My time will pass away, and so will yours, and so will all the people we love. You were given a brief, golden opportunity to escape a hundred years of death and change, but it didn't help you accept the changes. They will come nonetheless, and they are with you now, inescapably.

You taught me that having the brightest and biggest isn't always the best. You don't have to catch the brass ring, you can just enjoy the ride. So stop raging against death and change and embrace the beauty and joy that surround you. Find love and fellowship in those you have turned away from. You are a good man, and you can make a good life for yourself, as I have done. But that doesn't mean I've ever abandoned my love for you.

In the still of a summer night when a warm breeze blows through the window and across me as I lie in bed, I close my eyes and dream of the nights in Chicago when I was young and we loved each other so. When my mind is especially clear I can feel your body against mine and your breath on my neck, and recall the beauty we shared and the music that drew us together. Even now it brings bitter tears—yet I do not regret a moment that we shared—I only regret that fate prevented us from growing old together.

Though it brings me great joy to go back for a moment or two and wipe away an unhappy day and relive a love that still resides within me, I will not live in the past, nor should you.

I am dead, you must know that. And so is the time we knew together and the stage where it was played out. It was not the most wonderful stage, nor the worst. What stretches out before you is your chance. You will die, too. You will live out your life on another stage, though not the one we planned. It's not the most wonderful stage nor the worst, but it is yours; you cannot deny it any more than you can deny death.

Let go. Though I am dead, you did not have the opportunity to wash my body or drop a handful of dirt upon me, sending me back to earth. You are gone from me, too, and I haven't even a stone to leave flowers upon. We've been given no rituals to say farewell. In the end, our remembrance must take place in the heart.

Save what you can of those days, whatever mementos that are with you—a photograph or a house, a compass or a dollar. But know that those mementos only have value as tools for helping us to move on in life. Hold on to those memories, but don't let them trap you in the past. It took me several years to make that journey of acceptance—and you must make it, too.

I will love you always and wish you the same happiness I have found in this little town.

Mary

David laid the letter on the table and ran his hands over the paper, trying to feel the places where her pen had moved across it. For a moment he was beyond tears, numb. He hated the days of anguish and sulking. This was not him.

Pacing, he walked to his workroom, flipped on the lights, and looked about the room. There on the edge of the dusty table saw, where it had been all summer long, was the little leaded glass window from the stairway landing. He walked over and slid it to the center of the table. The blue and sea-green flower of glass was warped out of shape, raised in the center, the connecting soft lead having given way to a hundred years of heat and gravity.

He pressed gently on the high spot, flattening the panel back into shape.

As if possessed, David worked in a fury through the night, listening to music while he reglazed the leaded-glass panel and stripped the paint from the wood frame of the window.

ACKNOWLEDGMENTS

I sincerely thank Shari Smith and Kerry Brooks of River's Edge Media for making this publication possible. Shari has been my friend since our teen years. I've found her support and encouragement vital to my writing. If not for her, literally, this publication would not have happened. Kerry also saw something in this story worth the retelling. His passion and energy are inspiring.

Jim Wilson edited like a good therapist, asking me of troubled passages of text, "How does that make you feel?" coaxing me back to the drawing board for another try and a tighter story. From their offices overlooking the Arkansas River, the designers and marketing department at River's Edge Media did a lovely job totally redesigning this book and creating a finished product I'm truly proud of.

And finally, thanks to my many friends of modern Noblesville who helped this story along. Jan Masuik, the late Joe Roberts, and historian David Heighway each offered assistance or advice along the way that made this story better. And thank you to the descendants of Dr. Albert R. Tucker, who let me fictionalize their family's history.

FROM THE AUTHOR

This story first came to life in the early 1990s. I was in my 30s and my children were small. I had no writing credentials and no reason to believe I could write a book, but the story was in my head and needed to come out. When finally published in 2002, it was titled, "Stardust." I had no idea an author named Neil Gaiman had published a book by the same title in 1998. Hoagy Carmichael's classic love song of the jazz-era inspired my original title.

That readers of the small initial printing continue to write letters or stop me on the street to complement or ask questions about the book, is rewarding. To revisit this story again after so many years and make David Henry not a Gen X-er, but a Millenial, was a rare treat.

The places and locals in the story are/were real and are described as accurately as possible. David Henry's home was in reality my first restoration project and still stands a block from where I live today. To see photographs of the 1890s settings in the book, please visit my author page at www.kurtameyer.com.

CPSIA information can be obtained at www.ICGtesting.com
Printed in the USA
LVOW10s0309020216

473294LV00004B/225/P